LAURA'S GOLD

Mary Mills-Maclaren

All rights reserved. As long as Author is notified, extracts may be used and made available for educational purposes.

Copyright © 2013 Mary Mills-Maclaren

ISBN:- 10:   1492727938
ISBN-13: 978-149-272-7934

Other books by this Author:

The Four Elizabeths (2011)   )
Sequel...*Elizabeth's New Life (2012)*) Both published Xlibris.com
Flashes (2013) Published on Createspace.com

All books available on Amazon.Books
            Xlibris.com
            Createspace.com
            ...and as Kindle ebooks

Autographed copies can be acquired direct from Author, at no extra cost.   Email: marym224@hotmail.co.uk

Web: https://www:marym224.co.uk

DEDICATION

To all the women in my family, and all the world, who have had to rely on their personal fortitude to make their way in life.

And to George, who gave me so much support, and encouragement as the story evolved.

And to my dear old computer, that never let me down!

CONTENTS

1	LAURA
2	BALLARAT
3	SYDNEY
4	JEMIMA'S BABY
5	HARGRAVES SHOP
6	SETTLING INTO HARGRAVES
7	KATE
8	BABY JOSEPH
9	LAURA'S LIFE CHANGES
10	WEDDING, BIRTHDAY, BABY
11	TANGARRA
12	ANOTHER CHALLENGE
13	JOSEPH
14	LIFE CHANGES AGAIN
15	THE FIRE
16	PHILIP LINCOLN
17	ELUSIVE HAPPINESS

1   LAURA

The small buggy swayed gently behind Daisy, an ancient but adequate piebald pony, as it made its way back to Tolton township in Essex. Dappled sunshine flickered through the hedgerows, and vast fields beyond them were dazzling yellow with rapeseed plants..

In the warmth of a lovely English evening, in September 1876, the two women aboard jostled in silence, each sunk into her own thoughts. The wedding had been pretty; the bride had blushed, the groom was enthusiastic, and the guests had been patronising.

Twitching the reins, the older woman broke their reverie. "I can't understand why you haven't married by now, Laura. The good Lord knows you've had plenty of chances. He endowed you with the good looks of the Marchant family, and you've done nothing to take advantage of them. Whatever's the matter with you, girl?" Her voice thinned to a whine as she twitched the reins more firmly and continued, "Little did I know that when my dear brother..."

"Aunt Marchant, I do wish you wouldn't..."

"...your mother did a cruel thing to him, dying like that. And when he asked me to take you in, before he died from overwork himself, little did I know..."

Laura turned angrily on the uncomfortable boards. "Aunt Marchant, if you can't speak to me without making me feel like a festering boil on your neck, I'll thank you not to speak to me again"

Mrs Marchant reined-in Daisy with unnecessary force and the pony objected loudly. "Laura Marchant! I'll not have you speak to me like that. You've received the shelter and education under my roof that allows your poor father - God rest his soul - to rest easy in his grave. If he had even suspected that you would become such a rebellious child, and now such an aggressive young woman as you are..."

"I know..." Laura sighed, "he would have given me to an orphanage." Her aunt had repeated this tirade so often, and as the time passed, she was finding it difficult to hold her tongue.

She smoothed the skirt of the blue crepe gown that sculpted an already attractive figure, and turned her head away to look steadfastly at the road ahead, while her aunt tweaked Daisy into progress once again.

Uncle Marchant had died when she was three and from that time, Aunt Marchant never lost an opportunity to chide Laura for being the cause of the misery that had afflicted her. For the last eight years, Aunt Marchant's main purpose in life had been to coerce Laura into the 'ideal' marriage - ideal for Aunt Marchant, that is. One that would have ensured financial security and perhaps some little luxuries in her waning years.

The bride at the wedding was a daughter of Aunt Marchant's friend; a plain little thing but she had "gained more common-sense in her eighteen years than you have in twenty one, m'girl." Laura knew her spinsterhood was a frequent topic at the social afternoons her aunt hosted, and it hadn't worried her until lately.

Mrs Marchant guided Daisy into the small stable alongside their cottage in Tolton, dismounted and stumped angrily away, leaving Laura the task of taking the pony out of the shafts and removing the harness.

"I don't know, Daisy," the girl murmured, smoothing the familiar rump. "I sometimes think you are the only real friend I can claim in the whole of England. How I wish I could be like you and take no notice of... but I can't. I feel so..."

A familiar longing rose in Laura's breast as she leaned her head into the pony's neck. If she could only have the courage to do something, to get away - as far away as possible.

She turned away from Daisy and her gaze settled on the pile of old newspapers in the corner of the stable. The top one was open at the Positions Vacant columns, and an advertisement caught her eye.

Lady's Companion/Nurse.

Laura caught her breath and Daisy nuzzled into her while she picked up the paper and read more.

Required for family moving shortly to Australia. Apply in writing to Mr J Martin, c/o The Strand Gentlemen's Club, London.

Thoughts raced through Laura's mind in a whirlwind of excitement and trepidation. She had spent two years as Governess to a young girl in Tolton recently, until her charge had been sent to a finishing school in Switzerland, and she'd left the appointment with a glowing reference. Surely a Lady's Companion position wouldn't be so very different? Anyway, she had enough wits about her to cope easily and she could not deny the added chance of going to Australia, appealed to her immensely.

No doubt this Mister Martin would be paying her fare as part of her entitlement, if she qualified for the position - unless he was advertising on behalf of the family concerned. It was impossible to tell from the brief advertisement. Of course, she reasoned with herself. He would hardly be living at a Gentlemen's Club in London if he was the family referred to, would he?

She had secretly saved just forty pounds which would surely suffice until her placement and income began? She had closed the stable door when another thought stopped her. Perhaps her application would not succeed, or worse still, if there was a subsequent interview with Mister Martin, perhaps she would not satisfy the demands of the family. Were there any children? If so, how many? How old would they be? She wondered why would Mrs Martin require a Companion? Perhaps she was sickly? Laura hesitated - she did not enjoy the thought of caring for children and an invalid.

"Tush!" she scolded herself softly. "The only way to find out, is to write and apply for the job."

Did she dare? Could she make it happen? What an adventure. What an escape.

A week later, she had dared.

Aunt Marchant was full of curiosity when Mister Martin's reply arrived at their cottage on the Monday morning. She was also livid because Laura refused to divulge the contents of the letter.

She had been requested by Mister Joseph Martin to meet him at Lyons Tea House in London, and hundreds of questions raced through her mind during the train journey from Tolton. She walked from the station to Piccadilly, and on her arrival at Lyons Tea House, a waiter escorted her to Mr Martin's table.

He greeted Laura formally, with no attempt to shake her hand. Evidently in his early thirties, he was an impressive man - probably due to his careful dress, regal beard and the direct gaze from light grey eyes. But they were hard eyes, and Laura began to doubt the wisdom of her decision.

There was no inquiry as to whether she would like any refreshment, it just arrived within minutes of her being seated. Joseph Martin sat back while the waitress, perfect in the obligatory black dress and white apron, poured a minute amount from the silver teapot into each dainty china cup. Laura watched silently as the tails from the waitress's white lace cap slipped forward when she bent over.

"Now, Miss Marchant," Joseph Martin began, sitting erect. "Your application for the position has impressed me, and I feel you would be suitable."

"Thank you," said Laura, a little taken back by his bluntness. There were no preliminary questions, and after her apprehensive train journey from Tolton to London, she was somewhat relieved. Parched for the cup of tea, but waiting for him to pick up his cup first, Laura sat quietly while he outlined the situation. It was brief and to the point.

Contrary to her initial reaction to his advertisement, he revealed that he had a new wife who was young and childless, and as she was bound to become pregnant during the voyage, he'd decided on having a companion.

He lifted his cup and sipped his tea, and Laura did likewise. She studied her cup as she did so, and mentally summed up his attitude. His description of the 'young and childless' wife and him taking the decision to employ a companion grated on her, He went on to discuss her salary and mentioned (not offered) a small monthly payment. In view of him paying all their fares to Australia, Laura's stipend would remain 'small' until he was sufficiently established in Australia.

Insultingly small, Laura thought, but the prospect of a young person as her mistress and a new life in a new country intrigued her, so she just nodded dutifully.

A flutter of anticipation accompanied her back to Tolton on the train, and she tried to recall the details of the interview. All she could remember however, was a tall, black-coated gentleman with a bushy brown beard that revealed his lips only when he spoke, or when he sipped at the dainty cup that seemed ridiculously small in his hand. His steely grey eyes had branded her memory as cold and unsympathetic, which matched his revelation that his purpose for going to Australia, was to get rich.

At breakfast the following morning, Laura, dressed simply in a pastel green day-gown that complimented her coppery hair, smiled briefly at her Aunt's look of astonishment and disbelief. She gathered her courage and braced for the inevitable reaction when she repeated her words. "I have accepted the position of Lady's Companion to a Mrs Martin, and I shall be going to Australia with them shortly."

Mrs Marchant's face turned florid, almost purple as she furiously fanned herself with a napkin. "You've done what? You're going where? You can't - I forbid it!"

"I am to join them at London Docks at midday on November tenth," Laura continued defiantly. "I have booked a hotel room for the ninth, to be near the ship's berth, and we all sail the following morning." Laura took a breath. "And now I am twenty-one, Aunt Marchant, I doubt whether you have any right to 'forbid it' as you declare."

Laura shook inwardly at her temerity and concentrated on her meal, while her aunt alternately issued the familiar tirade from across the table, or left her chair and advanced to within striking distance. Once, she actually raised her hand, but the steady gaze from Laura's hazel eyes sparked a warning, and the irate woman retired, defeated.

"Ingratitude will be the end of you, my girl. You mark my words."

Laura did, wryly, not knowing they were the last words she'd ever hear her aunt utter.

Passengers boarding the *SS Mariana*, on the typically misty and crisp November morning, were at once excited, confused, and full of trepidation. Few had travelled by sea before and certainly none of them had ventured so far from Britain's comforting familiarity. The dockside was bustling with porters, passengers, luggage, crowds of well-wishers, carriages and carts, children and animals, and seemingly unshippable mounds of cargo which gradually disappeared into the bowels of the waiting vessel.

The atmosphere on deck was redolent from huge coils of oiled rope, casks of unknown contents, and the sweat of seamen trying to go about their duties amongst the milling passengers. The imposing figure of the bearded Captain Foster, who was desperately trying to organise the chaos, bellowed orders from the bridge. "Bosun, clear that trunk from the gangway. Why isn't it down below with the rest?"

The Bosun gave a sketchy acknowledgement of the order and passed it on to a nearby seaman, but didn't try to explain the offending blockage, primarily because he had no idea who's trunk it was, and much less interest. There was one hour to sailing time and the steam engines were idling gently. Soon they would be out into the comparative silence of the ocean.

Laura, who had boarded at the first opportunity, stood against the ship's rail, watching the furore below and around her, with amused interest. The flecks in her eyes were lit with expectancy, as she strained for the first glimpse of her new employers coming up the gangplank. Joseph Martin, in a confirmation letter sent to Tolton, had enclosed her ticket and informed her that he and his wife would be in Cabin 20. Her own passage was booked in a berth in steerage, and Mrs Martin would expect her to present herself at eight o'clock sharp each morning. "However three o'clock on the first afternoon of our embarkation will suffice."

Laura had instinctively bridled at the high-handed tone of his letter, and the fact that he had not seen fit to give his wife a Christian name. However, filled with excitement, she brushed aside any doubts as to the wisdom of her decision.

The two days of total silence she'd endured without so much as a farewell gesture from her aunt, were already a vague memory.

Her meagre belongings, mostly dresses and shoes, had been packed neatly into a small trunk that had already been stowed. She had dressed sensibly she thought, in a navy-blue serge travelling skirt and jacket with prim white blouse beneath. This was no occasion for large bonnets, so she'd firmly attached a small pillbox hat atop her thick hair. Clutched tightly in her gloved hand was a manageable brown carpet-bag that contained her wealth; almost thirty pounds after paying for her transport to London and overnight accommodation.

She had also invested in three pairs of bloomers at a big department store that morning, together with two white blouses. One was prim with a peter pan collar and long sleeves, the other had short sleeves and was prettily decorated with white lace around the neckline. Several dainty handkerchiefs nestled at the bottom of the bag, one of which was wrapped around a pair of silver sugar-tongs that had been engraved with her mother's initials - Lydia Marchant.

Laura was seventeen when she discovered the tongs at the back of the cutlery drawer in her aunt's sideboard. When she'd enquired, she'd been told off-handedly that they were among the few possessions passed on from her parents, "amongst other valueless items, like you, m'girl!"

"They should be mine, then," Laura had said hotly. "Even the initials are mine!"

"Rubbish," was the reply and the tongs were never referred to again.

But Laura had often secretly fondled the only link with the life that could have been, and she had no pangs of guilt when she finally removed the tongs, and wrapped them with her belongings. She smiled inwardly as she realised that some ninety years before, she could have been convicted for such behaviour, and deported to Australia anyway.

A long soulful hoot steamed from the ship's siren and into the August noon. It jolted Laura from her reverie, and her heart began to pound faster when she realised the gangplank had been raised, railings secured and an almost imperceptible drift from the wharf signalled they were under-way. She had not observed Mr. and Mrs. Martin come aboard and for a moment, panicked. Had they been delayed and missed the sailing? Could something have happened to alter their plans and they didn't advise her? What if she was on the *SS Mariana* entirely alone? Should she see someone to let her off, or should she travel to the first port and then disembark?

"Tush! Laura," she said under her breath. "Go and find Cabin 20 and make sure they're on board. If they are not, go to Australia - after all, your passage has been paid."

Chuckling inwardly at her affected heroism, Laura decided to follow instructions and wait until three o'clock before going to Cabin 20. Instead, she watched as women waved to loved ones below, then sobbed into their handkerchiefs, knowing they would probably never meet again. Children around her screamed with excitement as they flapped their arms at the diminishing dockside and some men slapped each other's shoulders or shook hands, revelling in the adventure of their migration.

Crowds behind Laura pressed her hard onto the gunwale but she felt no fear, only a small sadness that none of the crowd on the dock jetty had come to wish her well. The waving figures became too small to distinguish, and the passengers began dispersing to their appointed berths. The well-to-do knew their cabin number; steerage passengers were herded towards the steep ladders that led aft, and below decks.

"I'm not concerned with Captain Foster's orders, man! That trunk is to be placed in my cabin and remain there throughout the voyage - do you understand?"

Laura hesitated at the bottom of the first flight of steps and let others surge around her as she recognised the commanding tones coming through the open doorway of Cabin 20. She wondered what could be so important about the trunk? A crewman stepped angrily back into the corridor and muttered under breath as he brushed past Laura, presumably to report the incident to the Captain. She smiled - at least she had confirmed that her employers were aboard.

She carried on her way and found her sleeping quarters. Cramped, but adequate, there was room beside the bunk for her bag and a rail against the opposite wall for hanging things. She decided there and then she would not be spending a lot of time here, and acquainted herself with the eating area.

There, she met Mr and Mrs Drake and their son, whom Laura estimated would be in his early twenties. Geoffrey was obviously dismayed that his parents had chosen steerage accommodation and tried to console himself by striding around the decks with a superior air, that bordered on arrogance. Mr. and Mrs Drake seemed unconcerned by their son's behaviour - despite this, Laura's instinct urged her to become friends with them.

"You will join us when we eat, dear, won't you?" pleaded Mrs. Drake. "I dread to think how boring this voyage is going to be."

"Of course, and thank you Mrs. Drake," Laura chirruped. "I should be honoured to, and we do have Christmas celebrations at sea to experience."

"It won't be the same," mourned Mrs. Drake.

"Well, we may find similar interests," encouraged Laura.

"Do you play chess?" Mr Drake chimed in.

"I regret I don't," said Laura.

"Have no regrets," he replied. "I'll teach you."

"Why, thank you, Mr. Drake," Laura said.

"Call me James," he said, and they shook hands.

Having settled down and made friends already, Laura was quite pleased with herself. Hopefully her association with Mr. and Mrs. Martin would be as satisfactory.

Promptly at three in the afternoon, she tapped on the door of Cabin 20. Joseph Martin opened the door and said, "Ah! Miss Marchant. It has been a tiring day for Mrs Martin, so I recommended she take a nap. As arranged, we shall expect you at half past eight in the morning."

Laura began, "Very well, Mister Martin," but the door was closed by the end of her sentence. Again, his arrogant attitude bridled her, but she was grateful for the rest of the day to herself. It would give her the chance to familiarise herself with her new surroundings.

She slept surprisingly well that night, even though the rocking, as *SS Mariana* made her way dutifully through the Atlantic sea, was a new experience. One or two passengers were violently ill with sea-sickness, but luckily her country life with Aunt Marchant had afforded her a strong stomach.

The following morning as she left the breakfast table, Laura wished the Drakes a good day, and made her way to Cabin 20 again. Promptly at half past eight, she tapped gently on the door.

"Come!" said the familiar growl. "Mrs Martin is waiting."

Laura let herself in carefully, and nodded in a friendly way. "Good Morning Mr. Martin, Mrs Martin. And a lovely morning it is. You'd hardly believe it was November."

Mrs Martin smiled from the lower bunk, but she looked a little pale. She extended her dainty hand and their fingertips touched as she said, "Please call me Jemima. May I call you Laura?"

"Of course," Laura replied. "Have you a wish to do anything in particular this morning, Mrs...Jemima?

"Yes," came the reply. "I think I'd like to try and go for a walk along the deck." She turned to Mr Martin who was poring over a book about shopkeeping. "What do you think, dear?" She rose as she spoke, and went behind a small silk screen beside the bed, to dress.

He answered, "Hrrmmph!"

It crossed Laura's mind that even a businessman should be polite enough to say 'Good morning,' but didn't dwell on the thought. Jemima dressed quickly in a sky blue travel gown, that highlighted her fair hair and china blue eyes. She decided to carry a matching parasol to protect her face from the sun, which was already a golden orb blazing in the sky, and the temperature was rising rapidly..

Laura loved the sun, and to make the most of it, she wore a white organza blouse with leghorn sleeves, over a silver grey skirt. Mrs Martin gave her husband a perfunctory kiss, and the two young women went up on deck.

The brilliant blue sky made everything on board look good, and Jemima breathed in deeply. Two dolphins had been following the ship, and they suddenly broke through the surface, looking beautiful and extraordinary. The children who had spotted them, squealed in delight.

Laura and Jemima lunched on deck. They bonded like sisters, laughing at the same at humorous family stories, and revealing their tastes in food, music, and colour.

"My favourite of all perfumes is that of the honeysuckle." confided Jemima.

"Mine is of a newly bathed baby," said Laura.

"Well, you'll have plenty of that perfume next year," laughed Jemima. "I'm hoping to be pregnant very quickly."

Laura smiled nervously. She finished her duty around five o'clock, and back on the steerage deck, James Drake asked Laura if she had the time now, for a lesson in the game of Chess.

"Oh, yes please!" She followed her tutor to his berth, and was pleasantly surprised to meet Mrs. Sarah Drake, preparing an afternoon cup of tea.

The intricacies of Queens, Kings, Knights, Bishops and Pawns soon settled into Laura's head, and gave her much pleasure.

"This voyage won't be so bad, after all," chortled James Drake. "One thing you can't become when playing chess, is bored."

Days became weeks, and Laura looked forward to her stroll on deck with Jemima. The weather varied as time passed, and on one windy day, Jemima's parasol blew overboard.

"Never mind," Laura consoled her. "There are probably lots of shops in Australia, where you can get another."

They learned a lot about each other, and in between Christmas plans, they exchanged more family information. Jemima, it seemed, had been brought up in a family of four girls, of whom she was the youngest. Quite naturally, she had been cosseted and cared for like a fairy doll, and when Joseph Martin had approached her father for her hand, he was delighted to see his favourite daughter wed to such an imposing man.

Joseph lived on the next property and had watched Jemima grow from a delightful child to a beautiful woman. However, when Joseph announced his intention of going to Australia to make his fortune, Jemima's parents had been extremely upset and she had found herself stretched like a piece of elastic between them and her new husband.

He hadn't made it easy for her, insisting that her parents had no jurisdiction over her now that she was his wife, and refused to try and console them. Jemima was constantly torn between her love for her parents and her sense of marital duty.

Laura's life had been quite the opposite, and she often made Jemima giggle with her imitation of Aunt Marchant's whining voice and the gardener's growl. She tried not to overdo things because, although Jemima loved to hear about Daisy, and the pony's antics when Aunt Marchant reigned her in too tightly, Jemima's laughter always ended in a bout of coughing. On dull and rainy days, they sat in the first class passenger lounge and Laura read classic stories to Jemima.

Jane Austen's "Pride and Prejudice," and Laura's dramatisation of the character Lizzie, and her sisters' voices, invariably brought a smile to Jemima's face. Often the reading session would end in hysterical laughter, after Laura's interpretation of Mrs Bennet's fidgety or vexatious remarks. All too frequently however, the irritating cough that had plagued Jemima since they sailed from England, left her pale and tired, and she would rest on one of the narrow bunks in Cabin 20.

The Christmas period brought on homesickness and although the usual celebratory service, given by the ship's chaplain, gave some comfort, the holiday feeling was extremely subdued. Especially when the ship's galley crew, added salt to the Christmas pudding, instead of sugar.

The New Year of 1877 greeted the passengers with the turbulence of a frightening storm, and the *SS Mariana* fought valiantly against the elements. Seasickness again afflicted most people but in the manner of all similar upheavals, the incident passed, and boredom became the main hardship. The children combated this with mischievous escapades, and on many occasions Laura found herself assisting in a frantic search for them. She never ceased to be amazed at the nooks and cranny's they found in which to hide.

Passengers in steerage soon got used to the incessant throb of the ship's engine and grind of the rudder being redirected, and, in contrast with the elite cabin passengers, managed to break their boredom by occasionally singing or dancing.

Much of the day was engaged in promenading around the deck, especially after the ritual of a roll-call. Occasionally, Joseph Martin honoured the ladies with his presence. Laura stayed a step behind Jemima when she strolled arm in arm with Joseph, regarding her employer's imposing figure with a little curiosity.

Apart from these occasions, he spent very little time in his wife's company always seeming to have many business discussions with Captain Foster. She had asked Jemima one day, who confessed she knew nothing of her husband's affairs, but was quick to reassure her that Joseph Martin was well satisfied with his choice of a

Companion. Apart from his aloofness, he seemed to personify the ideal husband to Laura and she hoped fervently that Australia would provide a similar man for her when she was ready.

'Not quite so haughty, and a little more feeling - more like Mister Darcy,' she thought then surprised herself by thinking how much like Jane Austen's Mister Darcy, was Mister Joseph Martin. "Tush, woman, you're a hopeless romantic," she muttered, relieved to know her soft words were lost on the breeze.

They had been at sea for two months when Jemima greeted Laura one morning with an unusual light in her eyes. "Laura, I am quite sure now that I am to have a baby when we reach Australia"

Mixed feelings coursed through Laura. The initial delight such news brings, was tempered by her concern that Jemima seemed so young and frail to undergo the rigours of pregnancy. However, Jemima's joy could not be denied.

"And Mister Martin," said Laura, "he is well pleased, no doubt?"

"Not at first," Jemima confessed, her face clouding. "But when I assured him the baby wasn't due until early in September, and he realised you would be with me all the time, he kissed me and accepted the matter happily."

'How magnanimous' Laura thought wryly.

"You will be the baby's Nanny, won't you, Laura?" pleaded Jemima.

"Of course," said Laura with a little more confidence than she felt. She considered Jemima was barely out of her own childhood and wondered what lay ahead for both of them.

"Well now, Mister Martin isn't the only one with many plans and preparations to consider, which is wonderful. It will make this interminable voyage seem that much less to endure."

It was early March and *SS Mariana* was just two weeks away from her antipodean destination. Jemima's pregnancy had been difficult, with debilitating morning sickness, made worse by being at sea. That, and her persistent cough kept Laura busy, soothing the young expectant mother's trepidation, and several times an experienced lady in the special steerage cabin had given helpful advice, which had eased the situation. Laura arrived at Cabin 20 as usual and was startled to find a very pale Jemima sitting up in her bunk alone.

"Jemima, you don't look at all well. What's wrong? Have you eaten breakfast?""

"I'm afraid not, Laura. I was quite sick during the night, and..." The fragile girl broke into paroxysms of deep chesty coughs, and Laura held her hand. Not knowing quite what to do, Laura patted her on the back, to try and ease the bout

"Good Lord, Jemima." Laura's concern was rising. "Has Mister Martin sent for the ship's doctor?"

Jemima panted with the effort of coughing, her free hand laid gently on her stomach. " It is as I had feared, Laura. He has become extremely angry because the cough disturbs his sleep, and says my vomiting has made it impossible to stay in the cabin with me."

Laura was aghast."Do you mean ...?"

Jemima nodded."He's gone to ask Captain Foster for alternative accommodation, and said he will visit me daily."

"How kind of him," Laura said sharply. "And will he?"

"Oh, yes. He is not a complete ogre, Laura, and I can well understand how distressing it must be for him."

"For him!" Laura retorted scornfully, then regained her composure when she saw Jemima's pained expression. "But what if you should need assistance during the night?"

She wanted to add her fear for Jemima should she miscarry, but held her tongue, knowing the prospect would only distress the young woman more. If Jemima had already considered the threat, she said nothing but sat swaying with the ship, her eyes closed.

Laura remained quietly thoughtful and a few moments later, said, "Jemima would you like me to stay in the cabin with you? I would willingly pay my share of the extra passage, but you really should not be alone at a time like this."

Jemima's eyes widened and she stared at Laura."Oh, I could not trouble you to such a degree, and besides ..."

"Are you concerned that Jo... your husband would object?"

Slight colour stained the girl's cheeks and her hands fluttered on her stomach as Laura persisted, "I would be perfectly willing to approach him myself, if you feel ..."

"Ah, there you are!" The recognisable voice as the cabin door suddenly swung open, startled them. "How are you now, my dear?"

"Better, thank you, Joseph," Jemima said nervously. "Miss Marchant has charmingly volun ..." Jemima's nerves overtook her, and Joseph looked with impatient confusion from one woman the other

"I wondered, Mister Martin," Laura broke in, "would you be amenable to my staying in your cabin ?" She broke off, not wanting to say that Jemima had discussed their arrangements with her and yet aware that her words could not be misinterpreted. She felt uncomfortable under his gaze, and knew that Jemima was just as embarrassed.

Joseph did nothing to ease their discomfit, apart from saying, "If that would help to settle you, my dear - of course. In fact, Miss Marchant, I have found it necessary to engage on copious business discussions with Captain Foster and others, which makes it necessary for me to be quartered elsewhere." Jemima's relief was undisguised as he continued. "Perhaps it would be propitious if Miss Marchant stayed here for the rest of the voyage."

It wasn't a question, but a dictatorial statement and Laura pretended to contemplate his words. He'd made it sound as though it was his proposition, and for a moment, Laura was reactively preparing to refuse, but Jemima pressed her forearm in silent plea.

Joseph's brows lifted a fraction then he said magnanimously, "I will not expect you to pay the difference between steerage and cabin, Miss Marchant. My wife will appreciate your company." With a curt nod to Jemima, he strode out of the door.

Laura thought she had never met such a frustrating man but one look at the happiness on Jemima's pale face and she decided to ignore the man's lack of sensitivity. "It will only take me a moment to get my things from steerage - will you rest here until I return?"

"I will," said Jemima, and pressed Laura's arm again. "Thank you so much, Laura. I know I shall feel much better, and I promise not to be a burden, if I can help."

Despite Jemima's genuine promise, the remaining part of the voyage was uncomfortable for both of them. Laura insisted on exchanging bunks, to avoid the young mother having to climb around the large trunk that dominated the space between them. She ignored the pleas of wastage, and liberally sprinkled the cabin and bunks with Jemima's large bottle of Lavender water.

"It was a wedding present," Jemima wailed.

"From what I have learned," said Laura, airing her newly-acquired knowledge from the Emigrant's Guide "we'll have little need for such niceties in Australia. I am certainly not expecting a life of leisure." Laura perched on the trunk. "Of course, it may be different for you ..."

"I really don't know," said Jemima. "Joseph has not told me about his plans."

"Seems to me that most of the men are on this ship in the quest for gold. Personally I shall be happy to start a new life, maybe find a suitable husband, and rear lots of children."

Jemima's severe bout of coughing and sickness that night gave Laura cause to wonder at her aspirations. Was motherhood so attractive, in the light of this poor girl's suffering? Joseph hadn't considered it necessary to advise his wife where his new quarters were, but he did visit his wife every day, as he had promised. There was no visible concern for her condition - he acted as though childbirth was entirely the responsibility of his wife, and once, when Laura lightly asked him if he had a preference for a son, his answer was curt. "Of course."

He entered the cabin without knocking on Tuesday morning, March 28th. It was a habit that annoyed Laura intensely, as there was little or no privacy at the best of times.

"There is to be a final roll-call on deck this morning," he said. "We shall arrive in Melbourne tomorrow. I shall come back and escort you, shortly." Having delivered his salvo, he promptly disappeared.

"Thank goodness, breathed Jemima, "I can't wait to get off this ship and back into civilisation." The increasing heat as they neared their destination had taken a toll.

She was wearing the new short-sleeved blouse that Laura had bought in London, the white lace at the collar lending her an even more fragile appearance above the mound of her tummy."You are such a dear friend, Laura. This blouse is so much cooler."

"And it becomes you," smiled Laura."You shall keep it." She cut the protestations short by adding, "You shall buy me a new one when your husband finds gold."

The two had developed a close friendship by this time, and Laura felt fulfilled, knowing that Jemima's journey would have been horrendous without her company. Her friend's tentative voice reclaimed Laura's attention. "I really can't imagine how I would have survived this voyage without you, Laura. Nor indeed, how we shall survive Australia."

Laura tried to reassure her. "You will be perfectly all right, I'm sure. No doubt your husband has already made arrangements - in fact, I wouldn't be at all surprised to learn he has a lovely house, and a full complement of staff waiting."

"You could be right," said Jemima doubtfully. "But strangers, Laura, all strangers."

"Your baby will arrive to keep you company soon and very shortly, you will be surprised how well you have settled down."

Instead of comforting the girl, the prospect seemed to disturb her more and the familiar plea clouded her face. "I have never been taught to run a household Laura, let alone raise a child. When Joseph approached my father with his proposal, he had never discussed the subject of marriage with me."

"Who hadn't? Mister Martin or your father?"

"Both of them. "

"Do you think your hand would have been refused if your father had realised this?"

"Oh, goodness, no - it wasn't a proposal of marriage. It was for my father to invest in Joseph's plans for Australia."

Laura felt a little out of her depth and she knew she shouldn't pry into her employer's business, but curiosity won out. "But how ..? I beg your pardon, Jemima. This is none of my business."

"How did I become his bride, you mean?" Jemima coughed a little before continuing. "Father was hesitating over the proposal. Joseph is the son of his best friend, but my father did not become a rich man with hasty decisions. Then Joseph apparently added the comment that a man would be held in much greater esteem with an English bride at his elbow, and he would be happy to take me with him as his wife. It seems Father then agreed to grant Joseph a dowry for me, as an investment."

"Without consulting you?" said Laura amazed.

"Well, I had admired Joseph since I was a very young girl," blushed Jemima. "So the news that I was to be married to him was not altogether abhorrent to me except ..." Laura waited quietly. "Except, it all happened in such a rush and I did not relish the thought of going so far away from Mama. But Joseph seemed so full of confidence."

"Your husband should consider himself an extremely lucky man." Laura's tentative esteem for Joseph became smaller with each revelation. "I should have thought a caring husband would pay more attention to his wife's ..." She stopped, conscious that she was overstepping the bounds of her position again, and not wanting to sour their friendship.

It was a relief when Joseph opened the cabin door at that moment. "Come along, it is time." He offered his arm to Jemima and Laura was mollified.

Most passengers had become used to the ship's plunge and roll, but Jemima's balance was impaired, due to her condition, so she was always grateful for assistance. Laura followed them along the corridor and watched keenly as Jemima spoke animatedly with Joseph. His straight back and lifted chin indicated nothing, but as he stood aside to allow Laura to precede him up the gangway, he looked at her strangely. Laura noted this, but said nothing.

The roll-call completed, Captain Foster wished his passengers Good Luck in the new country, then added that all luggage would be offloaded in the reverse order to which it was loaded at London docks, so Laura acknowledged her trunk would be amongst the last to be put on land. She had on her second-best blue linen skirt with the other new long-sleeved blouse from London, but the cloistering heat of such a different climate was making her legs uncomfortable. There was an Autumn chill in the air, but the day was going to be very warm.

When she suggested they sit on deck awhile. Jemima readily agreed, and Joseph lingered long enough to address Laura briefly.

"We will not be in a position to pay you extra as a Nanny, when the baby is born, you understand? And there will be no days off. But you will be housed and fed."

Jemima's face was a mixture of concern and joy. She had suggested to him earlier, that they could use her dowry to increase Laura's salary. However, she was too nervous to contradict him. Laura felt her answer was somehow crucial to Jemima's mental welfare, but Joseph's blatant arrogance annoyed her and she blurted, "Supposing I wish to marry, Mister Martin?"

His reply was as flat as his earlier remarks. "Then you will be free to go."

Jemima was holding her breath Laura knew, and at the same time she recognised that at this stage, she had absolutely no other prospects. At least arriving with some sort of security, would be better than nothing. "Very well, Mister Martin."

"We leave for Ballarat immediately we disembark," Joseph added.

"Is that the name of our home, dear?"

"We'll see," answered Joseph enigmatically.

Laura spoke quickly."My trunk will not be put ashore until well after yours, Mister Martin. Especially as yours only has to be removed from your cabin." She thought her comment would annoy him, and fully expected him to renege on his offer of employment.

"Then Jemima can wait with you, and I shall return to the dock in an hour or so. I have an important appointment."

The two women looked at each other then at his retreating figure. Neither of them knew what to say.

2 BALLARAT

The *SS Mariana* docked at Melbourne in the early hours of the morning, amid even greater fuss and chaos than Laura remembered at London. Together with smaller luggage, the large trunk was removed from Cabin 20 with much grumbling by the seaman allotted the task. As soon as it was sitting on the wharf, Jemima and Laura disembarked and perched on it, while the me-lee continued around them. Gazing around excitedly, Jemima spotted the sign-age on a warehouse wall alongside the wharf. "Oh, look, they've spelled 'coals' the wrong way, Laura."

Laura turned to look. "I don't think that can be the coal we know, Jemima. It seems to me that Coles would be the name of the owner of that warehouse."

"Of course," chuckled Jemima. "How silly of me."

By eight o'clock the heat was almost unbearable even though it was Autumn in Australia. Despite the breeze that wafted from the water occasionally, both women had soon removed their travelling jackets. Some passengers were being met by more suitably dressed Australians, others looked about themselves, at a complete loss as to their next step.

A family who had been among the steerage passengers, clattered down the gang plank in excitement, especially the young ones. The mother who had been so helpful in the early stages of Jemima's pregnancy, kept amazing control while her husband left to arrange transport into Melbourne. She indicated swiftly to the eldest daughter and within seconds, the girl had approached.

"Excuse me, ma'am," she said to Jemima, handing over her open parasol. "But Mother says in your condition, you should be more protected and insists that you have this."

Jemima started to protest; but her girth had increased noticeably during the last week, and she sat instinctively with her hands across her stomach. But Laura said, "Thank your Mother very much, please. Mrs Martin is truly grateful for her kindness. I shall return the parasol the moment our transport arrives."

"No, please keep it," said the girl shyly. "We have others in our luggage." Waving at them, she rejoined her family, and Laura sighed.

"What a wonderful thing to be as organised as that family is. I've no doubt they will find great happiness and fortune here."

"They certainly are very kind. Oh, Laura, I can't help being a little excited," said Jemima with a nervous cough. "I'm certain Joseph has things organised for us as well."

Laura smiled at her youthful enthusiasm and accepted that she would have been as excited herself, if there had been someone to organise 'things' for her. Instead, foolishly or not, she had set foot on this strange shore with little but her willingness to work and her trust in good fortune to support her. She did not consider her acquaintance with the Martin family as a destiny-merely as a stepping stone, until a more secure future presented itself to her.

Jemima was still prattling. "Ballarat is probably a lovely house - do you think it will be anything like my parent's home in Sussex, Laura?"

"I wonder how he managed to buy a house from England?" Laura commented.

"Oh, I did overhear him tell my father about some dealings he'd had with a gentleman in London, and an Agent in Australia."

"Hasn't he told you anything about them?" queried Laura.

"Good Lord, no. I suppose I have been too sick and disinterested, or maybe he wanted to keep as many surprises for me as he could."

"I dare say," said Laura, without conviction. "I do hope he won't leave us here waiting for too long, though. It is getting hotter by the minute, and I would dearly love to have a bath, as no doubt you would. Oh look, there's my case. Wait here, Jemima. I won't be a moment."

Laura retrieved her case, having proved her ownership with a receipt for her passage, and a dockside worker carried it over just as Jemima dissolved into a bout of coughing. She had undone the top buttons of her pink silk blouse and was fanning herself with the bonnet she had worn ashore. When the bout had subsided, she said, "I wonder how often it is a hot as this?"

Laura didn't answer; she was scanning the city end of the wharf, hoping she would see Joseph Martin appear. They had been waiting for well over two hours by this time, and Jemima was beginning to appear distressed. All the passengers had disembarked and most had disappeared. Seamen stood in small groups, obviously discussing the voyage they had just completed, or the one they were about to embark upon, and what seemed to be warehouse officials, were already inspecting and dispatching the various shipments that had arrived in the hold.

Captain Foster descended the gangplank, with an overblown woman on his arm. She laughed loudly at something he'd said, and as they passed, the Captain touched his cap. "Goodbye, Mrs Martin, Miss Marchant."

As they walked away towards the city, the woman said, "Is that Joseph's Martin's wife, then? Poor little thing."

Jemima looked at Laura with question, but Laura's quick mind had connected Joseph's 'Card Games with the Captain.' She rearranged her navy skirt and said indignantly, "Why do people refer to pregnant women as 'poor little things'? I wouldn't consider myself 'poor' if I was carrying a child."

Jemima smiled wanly. "You would if you were as sick as I've been."

"No doubt," said Laura gently. "I'm sorry." A movement beyond Jemima drew her attention and she cried out with relief. "Oh, look, here comes Mister ..."

Her words faded as she observed that Joseph was sitting on a wooden seat as he guided a dilapidated dray along the waterfront, the flushed expression beneath his hat indicating that he'd not found it easy to control the two brown horses between the shafts.

Laura, politely, did not indicate her surprise but was certain from Jemima's small "Oh" that the dray was far below standard to the transport she'd expected. Used to travelling in her parents' landau, or the hackney-coaches in cities, Jemima was hardly prepared for the low wooden cart without sides, and of indefinable age, that rattled to a halt beside them.

Joseph managed to stop the skittish beasts, dismounted and handed the reins to Laura. "Hold these till I get someone to put my trunk aboard."

Climbing aboard the dray, she assumed he was referring to all of their luggage, as he made no attempt to load her much smaller case, nor even the two travelling bags containing her personal items and some clothing. Laura bit back her reply, and did as she was told.

He strode towards a group of seamen who stood leaning against the warehouse wall, smoking and drinking beer. It was obvious from the shout of laughter that he'd expected one of them to load the cart without payment. A few of them made lewd gestures, and blustering, Joseph fished inside his waistcoat pocket. He displayed a coin to the men, but none moved. With every movement impatient, he produced another coin and one of the men snatched at his hand. Joseph withdrew it sharply and the women heard his raised voice. "Only when the trunk is loaded, you ruffian!"

Again there was a hoot of laughter, but the volunteer levered himself away from the warehouse wall, and moved without undue speed towards them. They stood away from the trunk as he approached and he nodded. "Ladies."

He swung the lighter items aboard, then tested the big trunk before signalling his mate. The two men lifted it like a box of matches, and crashed it heavily into place beside them. Laura had to fight to retain control over the horses as the dray vibrated with its weight but her experience with Daisy was helpful and they responded to her low words. The men swiped their palms with a loud smacking noise, and the first one turned towards Joseph with his hand out. "Easy!"

The two coins were rammed ungraciously into his palm and he swaggered off. Joseph assisted Jemima onto the buggy-board, then took his place beside her and reclaimed the reins from Laura.

He jerked his head towards the rear of the dray, saying "Make haste, we have a long way to travel before dark."

Laura fitted herself between the trunks and luggage and stifled a retort, being more concerned with Jemima's comfort. Joseph wheeled the horses around roughly and within yards, Laura knew from the jolting that they would arrive at their mysterious destination with most uncomfortable bottoms.

Jemima coughed pitifully during the first two hours of their journey, by which time the sea, the *SS Mariana* and Melbourne's City centre was well behind them, and clouds overhead looked black, and angry. Laura's own anger simmered; Joseph Martin may well have possessed a brilliant business acumen, but he displayed very little sensitivity.

They journeyed in relative silence; now and then the women would point something out to each other, but Joseph seemed wrapped in his own thoughts, with mostly a grunt in reply to any remark Jemima addressed to him.

Some four hours later, as the horses plodded along and the dray rocked like a ship travelling through the Roaring Forties, Jemima ventured, . "Joseph, dear, could we rest awhile, please? I think I would be far more comfortable riding behind, with Laura."

Joseph's answer was to rein in the horses, and wait silently while Laura rearranged the luggage, and assisted Jemima to climb in beside her. They shared the parasol so kindly given on the dockside and Laura breathed a sigh of relief

"Thank you, dear," Jemima said to Joseph, and the journey was resumed.

They had put their jackets back on before leaving the dockside; but the air was humid and the skies heavy with coming storm. Laura removed her jacket again, and suggested Jemima do the same. She bundled the two garments together for a makeshift pillow behind Jemima's back, then placed her arm around her young friend. "Rest your head on my shoulder, Jemima. I doubt you will sleep, but it will be more comfortable. I'm sure we'll be there, soon."

'Where?' she asked herself, as Jemima closed her eyes. 'Dare I ask how far this Ballarat is?' She twisted her head to look at Joseph's back - it was straight and unapproachable. The few words they had exchanged since they became acquainted had told little of what the man was thinking. In fact she had the distinct impression that in his opinion, shared confidences were the domain of ineffectual women.

Laura watched the countryside go past with interest. Some of the trees resembled those in England, but there were other strange bushes and trees. An almost overpowering scent of eucalyptus pervaded and there was the occasional shack, which Laura thought could be a farm shed or a dwelling. One was made of tree trunks stood side by side, it seemed. One or two were cut away to create the semblance of a window, but without curtains.

The roof was no more than sheets of bark strapped together, and Laura wondered what animals were kept inside? There was an opening to represent a door, and she was startled when several children, naked as the day they entered this rough world, flung themselves into the yard, obviously stirred by the rattle of the dray wheels.

"Where'ya come from?" yelled one, waving frantically.

"Where'ya goin'" called another. He climbed upon a tree stump that stood alongside the 'house', and thrust out his grubby foot when a small sister tried to join him.

Jemima opened her eyes wide. "Oh, Laura. Those poor children. They must be orphans, or from the slums!"

A tall woman appeared and fished a cloth from her apron pocket which she proceeded to use like a fly swat, herding the children back into the dwelling. She finally raised the cloth in acknowledgement to the travellers. Laura raised her hand and smiled. Joseph made no indication that he'd noticed them at all.

They had been travelling for almost four hours by this time, and the women had filled in the time by talking quietly, or drifting into companionable silence.

"Joseph, dear," called Jemima shortly after, "I do admire you for knowing where to take us. How did you know?"

Joseph turned, and for the first time, Laura noted a glint of satisfaction in his eyes. She was startled to observe pleasure in his face and she looked away quickly, almost as though she'd inadvertently intruded on his privacy.

"Instructions from the agent," he replied.

"Is it far?" ventured Jemima.

He consulted the silver fob-watch he extracted from his waistcoat. "Another hour, according to the agent."

"Oh" Jemima answered, with little enthusiasm. She turned back to Laura and quietly said, "I am getting quite uncomfortable."

Laura cuddled her charge closer and noted that Joseph turned back to the horses and flicked at the reins to encourage their pace. The horses had steadied more over the journey, but his goading caused one of them to object loudl y. The sound ricocheted around the bush and Laura noted they seemed nowhere near civilisation, as yet. The road - hardly a road in comparison with the neat kerb and guttered thoroughfares they were accustomed to - meandered ahead of them like an aimless lizard, and its tail disappeared behind them into the unfamiliar countryside, until it felt as though the dray and horses were the only moving things on earth.

The heavy sky gave no indication of their whereabouts and Laura shook her head at the wisdom - or folly - of her decision. Thanks to the newspaper advertisement in Daisy's stable, her life was no longer an adventure. She felt, it was in downright danger.

It was close to an hour and a half before the scenery changed. The threatened storm broke, doused them all, then dried them just as quickly as it passed on and allowed the afternoon sun to shine through again. Joseph was obviously getting agitated at not reaching their destination within the given time, and for the last thirty minutes had looked again and again at his watch.

They rounded a long bend in the road, and a paddock dotted with black cattle came into view. Beyond it, another seemed to be the domain of a huge black bull, and a third was occupied by a homestead. Not a brick multi-storey mansion by any means, but certainly a step up from the shack with naked children they'd passed, some hours ago.

Jemima coughed piteously again, then saw the homestead and sparked with interest. "Is that it? Is that Ballarat, dear?"

Joseph didn't answer, but flicked the reins again. The pace increased slightly as they carried on, so did the bumping and jolting and Jemima had become desperately pale. Laura lifted the long black hair away from her damp neck, and smiled reassuring!y.

"Can't be long now, Jemima. Look, there's another dwelling over there, and another there ... see? We must be getting near civilisation."

Jemima smiled a little but she was obviously too tired to get excited. Laura hoped fervently that this ghastly journey on land would end quicker than the one they'd endured on water. It was getting late in the afternoon but the temperature hadn't reduced very much.

The dray swung around another bend in the road and the luscious green paddocks and contented cattle disappeared. Laura sucked her breath and tightened her grip on Jemima as ahead of them she could see paddocks that were bustling with men working There was all manner of equipment and shabby tents scattered around, but not a blade of grass.

A dust haze hung over the entire scene. Two rows of more substantial buildings that boasted verandas formed a street, but there was not a kerb or gutter to be seen. Unless you could refer to the ditch each side of the street as a gutter. There was water in it that ran for a yard or so then formed a pool, before it overflowed and ran again

Shabbily dressed children splashed in and out of the pool, their bodies as brown as the water they played in. Two horses tethered outside one of the larger buildings were drinking from a trough that looked just as unsavoury, and a few men lounged on the boards in front. They watched the dray approach but didn't stop drinking or talking.

Joseph reined in the tired horses and they struggled to reach the trough. "Hold still, there!" he bellowed. "Come and hold the horses, Miss Marchant."

Laura seethed, but extracted herself from Jemima who was obviously too weak and weary to cough properly. She demounted and her skirt caught on a splinter, which caused the drinkers to hoot and holler. She pulled her skirt roughly from the splinter, and glared at Joseph as he tossed the reins down to her. She moved forward, and smoothed the brown flanks, then held the tossing heads.

"Got a way with her, cobber," yelled one man to Joseph. "Picked a goodun there, y'did."

Laura glared at the men as Joseph ignored them, and went inside the building. She pointed to the back of the dray. "Mrs Martin is quite ill. One of you should fetch her some water."

"Oh, should we now, Miss High 'n Mighty?" The older man sniggered. "She'd rather a slug of whiskey to stand 'er up, I bet!"

Jemima coughed again, the dusty atmosphere obviously doing nothing to aid her breathing. A tired-looking woman with her hair drawn back and her long black skirt stirring more dust, walked towards them. She looked at Jemima, then at Laura.

"That's my place over there." She indicated the building across the way. "Shall I take her for a drink? She looks worn out, poor little thing."

Laura's relief showed. "Thank you so much, ma'm. I'll inform Mister Martin when he comes back. He shouldn't be long. Just one moment... " She took the horses a few paces to the trough and tethered them there as they drank noisily. Remounting the dray, she assisted Jemima to her feet, and the woman lifted her arms to steady the young mother as she got down.

Jemima's legs almost gave way under her, but with support she managed to cross the street and enter the building. Although stuffy, it was a good deal cooler than outside, and the woman dragged forward wooden chairs for them both, before dipping water from a barrel in the corner of the room. She poured it into enamel mugs and handed her visitors one each.

"Me name's Bel Carter," she began. "Well, Isabel really, but none of these ignorant sods around here can be bothered to say me full name. Where've you come from, then?"

Laura and Jemima drank gratefully. "This is Mrs Jemima Martin, and I'm Laura Marchant. We arrived from England this morning on the *SS Mariana*".

"Well, I'll be damned," said their new acquaintance, smoothing calloused hands over her wispy hair, as though Queen Victoria herself had graced her humble shack. "Well, what you doing in Ballarat, then?"

Jemima roused feebly. "Ballarat? This is Ballarat?"

"'S'right," chuckled Bel Carter. "The most God-forsaken part of the country you could've come to."

"But ..." Jemima appealed to Laura. "I thought ..."

"That was Mister Martin I saw going into the Land Agent's office, I suppose?" Bel continued. "Looked a bit of a gentleman. What's he here for? Mining? Or is he an Assayer?"

Bel may as well have been talking in Chinese, because both the English women were too weary to understand, or ask questions. Laura answered politely, "Yes, that was Mister Martin."

"Mister Joseph Martin " Jemima added dutifully.

"You sisters?" Bel asked.

Laura took another sip of the welcome drink, then raised a smile. "No, I'm Mrs. Martin's companion nurse."

Bel's eyebrows rose as she said, "Ooh! Posh."

Not sure how to take Bel's remark, Laura continued casually, "Mining? This is a mining area?"

Bel Carter cackled loudly. "Strewth ... don't tell me you don't recognise gold-fields when y'see 'em? The place is full of miners, no-hopers, and them that's making a quick quid out of those who's trying to find the big one."

"Big one?" asked Jemima innocently.

"Yeah," said Bel. "The floater, the big slug ... the pay dirt!" She emphasised her last words when she saw the women's blank faces. "If the work don't kill you, then the fever will. My old man scrounged the dirt until it turned his head. Then he thought he'd struck lucky, the Assayer said it was worth nothing, and the bastard went out back and shot himself."

"Oh, Mrs Carter!" exclaimed a horrified Jemima. "You poor thing."

"Poor thing nothin'," Bel chortled. "I was fed up with him drinking and bashing me to get his own back, so I was glad to see the back of him. Lucky I got me own ways of keeping alive."

"It can't be easy," Laura offered. "How do you manage it?"
"I cooks. Up at the miner's camp, don't I? It's hard work, the buggers are always whining, but I gets fed meself, that way. Now, would you like another drink?"

"No, no thank you Mrs Carter," said Jemima hastily.

"Bel - call me Bel. Don't you go giving me no airs, Missus Martin. Them sods wouldn't let me live it down."

Laura spotted a movement from the building opposite. "I think I will let Mister Martin know where we are. Thank you for your kindness, Mrs ... Bel. You will be all right, Jemima?"

"Course she will," Bel chimed in. "You leave the little girl with me. I'll look after her. In fact, how would you like to lie down awhile, Missus?"

"Oh I couldn't trouble you ..."

"Yes, y'could. Come on. It's not Buckin'am Palis, but it's not the wooden floor, neither." She eyed the luggage Laura had carried over.. "Now which is your bag?"

Laura left as Jemima was taken under Bel's wing, and crossed the street to where Joseph stood talking angrily with evidently the Land Agent.

"Excuse me, Mr. Martin. Jemima is ..."

"One moment, Miss Marchant," frowned Joseph, and continued his conversation. His voice was thick with anger. "So you're telling me that this claim I purchased in London is worthless?"

"Worked out nearly two years ago," the Agent said. "The bastard left town owing everybody for food, tools, and beer. I heard that he had gone back to London. Probably made more money there selling false claims, I'd say."

Joseph's face was florid under his bushy beard and his eyes had a hard glitter that again Laura wished she hadn't observed. She knew that Jemima's innocent dreams of a mansion in a park must already be as dusty as the real Ballarat. And the fact that this overbearing man apparently paid no heed to his wife's needs, angered her immensely - far beyond the ladylike decorum she'd had bred into her.

"Mister Martin!" Her voice was so steely, both men halted their conversation. "Your wife has suffered enough. She is in no condition to continue any further, and I suggest you seek lodgings for us all, before the evening closes in."

Her temerity startled her, and nerves knotted her stomach as Joseph's expression darkened. "Where is my wife?"

"Across the street, being cared for by a Good Samaritan!"

A small crowd had gathered by now, including the men who were drinking on the verandah. "Watch her, mate, them copper-nobs can be worse than alley cats."

Laura spun to retaliate, when another said, "Good Samaritan? Bel Carter? You're round the twist, lady."

"Where, Miss Marchant?" pounded Joseph above the laughter. Laura turned on her heel and walked across the road, fury lifting her chin. Joseph brushed the laughing men aside as he followed her, and they arrived at Bel Carter's door together. The formidable lady, who had watched the fracas across the road, was already barring their way with arms folded. "She's sleeping."

With a soft tone that startled Laura, Joseph said, "I'll thank you to clear the way, woman."

The ploy worked, because Bel gave way, pleading, "Ah, let her rest, Mister Martin. She's a poorly little thing, and her with …"

"I am well aware of her condition," said Joseph firmly. He fished a few coins from his pocket. "I will send for her in the morning."

He made her sound like a shirt he was having repaired rather than his wife, but his actions were unexpected and Laura began to wonder if there wasn't another Joseph hidden behind his imperious façade? She wasn't to know, however, as Joseph strode back across the street, with no indication as to what Laura should do. Her baggage and clean clothing were still on the dray, so she chose to follow him.

"There's Bert Figg's rooming house at the end of this street," the Land Agent informed Joseph. "Not very posh or comfortable, but it's a roof."

Joseph made no offer, but Laura didn't give him any choice. She hopped up quickly besides the trunks at the back of the dray and ignored the louts who kept calling at her as they drew away. A cloud of dust signalled their progress, but Laura was able to distinguish some of the signs on the street-side buildings. There was a blacksmith, the Assayer's office, Cobb & Co Coach depot, a bread shop and the ubiquitous pub. In fact, there were three pubs before they reached their destination.

"Bert Figg's Rooms" was a small narrow building and had another sign that read, "Horses and buggys around back." After rescuing the smaller bags containing their toiletries and tethering the rig at the back as instructed, Joseph and Laura went to investigate Bert Figg's Rooms.

A double bed, sir?" inquired the obsequious owner, who wore his brown side-whiskers each side of his mouth, like theatre curtains.

"Miss Marchant will take her own room," said Joseph primly. He scribbled his signature on an old pad which served as the Guest Register.

"That will be sixpence, if you please, sir." Figg's slid the pad along to Laura. "And sixpence for the lady. That includes a meal which I'll bring you at seven, t'night."

Joseph slapped a shilling onto the wooden bench in front of Figgs, and said, "Miss Marchant, I plan to leave early in the morning. I trust you will not keep me waiting."

Laura's room was hardly bigger than a cupboard with a bed squeezed against one wall and an ancient table against the other. By now, she was so exhausted, both physically and mentally, that she would have been glad to sleep on a bench in the garden. There was no mention of joining her employer for the meal, so Laura resigned herself to eating alone in her room. She gasped at the slice of lamb and mound of potatoes and peas that arrived, but tucked into the repast. 'Like a road-worker,' she grinned to herself.

Half an hour later, Laura stretched back on the narrow cot and thought of their first endless day in Australia. Joseph's boorishness had not seemed quite so pronounced while they were aboard *SS Mariana*, mainly because she had little contact with him. Admittedly, the occasional incident had irked her, but Jemima's welfare and comfort had become so much of her day that she had easily quelled her annoyance.

Today however, in continuous proximity with this brusque man, she found it difficult to excuse his behaviour. She decided she would stay with the Martins until the child reached one year, then leave. For where and what Destiny she was suddenly too tired to ponder.

3   SYDNEY

The travellers were too weary to notice their uncomfortable beds and surroundings that night and woke next morning, disoriented. Installed in Bel Carter's own bed while her hostess had spent the night quite happily wrapped in a blanket on a kitchen chair, Jemima was roused by the clattering of pans. She gave a chesty cough then mumbled, "Laura?" She came through the fog of an exhausted sleep and lay on her back looking around at the tiny room with its canvas lined walls, a rug on the floor made from twisted scraps of material, a chipped and painted chair that was now draped with her skirt and blouse, and a small window which looked as though it had never been cleaned.

The scene outside was indistinct, but in her imagination, the beautiful countryside she had woken to all her life in Sussex was there, and it painted a picture of happiness and well-being. Already the sun had lit the brown-striped bed cover she lay under, and as reality cleared her mind, her baby fluttered and she put a hand on her stomach.

Then events of the past six months came crowding back, bringing a frown to her alabaster face. When Papa had announced Joseph's proposal, Mama had dedicated a whole half morning to revealing the duties of a married woman. At first she had been horrified when Mama lectured that it was God's will and that He would always help her tolerate 'things'. Joseph's demands on their wedding night were not excessive, and Jemima accepted her new life.

They had spent less than twenty-four hours in Australia, and she realised that Mama had done nothing to prepare her for the rigours she'd already endured. Mama probably would never have been able to anticipate them. Her earlier eagerness that Ballarat was to be their magnificent new home in the country, brought stinging tears to Jemima's eyes. They rolled silently across her pale temples and onto the striped pillow-ticking beneath her head.

Her chest grew heavy with sadness, then she recalled Joseph's direction that he should not be kept waiting when he arrived to collect her, so she hurriedly threw the bed cover aside. She splashed her face in the bowl of water provided, and dressed hastily in the now crumpled pink blouse and suit, Bel had insisted she remove the night before.

"You'll not be able to breathe in them things. Give that baby a bit of relief, at least."

The bedroom led into the low-ceilinged room where she and Laura had been entertained the afternoon before, and the kitchen was nothing more than a lean-to. Quickly gathering her senses, Jemima called, "Bel?"

The ample woman appeared, wiping floury hands on her apron and smiling expansively. "Well, now, little filly. Feeling better this morning? You'll be ready for a bite, no doubt. I've a nice rabbit broth and dumplings ready for you - that'll put stuffing under y'shirt!"

"Oh, no thank you, Bel. I couldn't. Not at this hour in the morning. I'm sure it would make me ill. May I have just a little tea, please?"

"You won't survive long if you don't eat, m'girl," said Bel, her smile fading. "I'll tell that husband of yours that he's got to look out for you a bit more. Slip of a thing like you - and being as you are ... when's y'time, then?"

"The beginning of September," Jemima replied softly, holding her belly protectively. "I really am looking forward to holding my baby."

"Ah yeah," said Bel wryly. "You'll be like all us Mothers - spend the first year coaxing the little blighters to walk and talk, and the rest of y'life telling them to shurrup and siddown!"

The concern on Jemima's face made Bel laugh raucously, and she disappeared into the kitchen to set a cup of tea. Jemima followed her hesitantly and gazed around at the whitewashed walls, huge fireplace set into the back wall and black iron kettle. Already steaming over the fire, it was swinging from a metal arm that Bel swivelled forward, then poured the boiling water into an equally large enamel teapot. Jemima asked, "May I help?"

"Yep," said Bel. "Go and get two mugs off the shelf for us. Won't be a minute."

Jemima did as she was asked, and looked with curiosity at the one faded sepia photograph that graced the wall just by the front door. A younger Bel sat in the ornate studio chair with a child of about three on her knee. A boy or girl Jemima couldn't decide, and turned to ask as her host entered the room, bearing the teapot and a plate of bread and cheese "Bel, you have a. child?"

"Did have," she nodded, slamming the heavy pot by the cups on the wooden table. "Poor little mite - couldn't fight the fever. Knew she had something wrong from the beginning - even let one of them Chinese miners have her, but no good."

It seemed to Jemima that every moment she spent in this wild area was full of mystery. The vision of a Chinese man 'taking' Bel's little girl caused her eyes to round with alarm. "Do you mean you let him steal her? Bel, what on earth ...?"

The generous no-nonsense woman clicked her teeth in sympathy. "Where did they bring you up, m'girl? I can see you won't have an easy time in Australia - you don't seem to know nuthin!"

"I'm sorry ..." Jemima began.

"Sorry nuthin'," said Bel, "you got nuthin' t 'be sorry for. Just a crying shame I reckon that they allow such innocents into this God-f'saken country. Why, I bet you've never even seen a snake, let alone have one slide up y'kitchen window!"

Jemima nearly fainted with the thought, and after setting her quickly into a chair it was Bel's turn to say sorry. "Please," Jemima breathed deeply, "you mustn't apologise to me either. I really must try and be stronger - my husband will not appreciate any 'fits of the vapours' as my Mother used to call them. Please, what did you mean about the Chinese man?"

Bel pushed one of the cups of tea she'd poured towards Jemima and lowered her voice. "I don't tell everyone mind. He's dead now, but at the time he could've been strung up for what he did. He said he would take my little Nora somewhere for three weeks and if she could be cured he'd do it. I was desperate. My old sod was drunk most of the time and there was no way we could afford to take her to one of them city hospitals in Melbourne."

They both sipped gratefully at the brew then Jemima used her handkerchief delicately to smother the cough that attacked her. "Excuse me, Bel," she gasped, "please go on."

"You seen a doctor with that cough of yours?" Bel queried "Sounds more'n a bit set in to my liking. How long you had it?"

"I've always had a bit of a cough," Jemima said. "It seemed to get worse on the boat." Bel tutted. "Maybe it is something to do with the baby?" Jemima added.

"Doubt it," answered Bel pragmatically. "Seems I'll 'ave to have words with that husband of yours, when he gets here."

"Oh, please don't," Jemima pleaded, and to change the subject quickly she continued, "You haven't told me about your daughter - and the Chinese man."

Bel shrugged. "Not much to tell. Three weeks she was with him. A lot better when he brought her back I'll admit. But she died in the end."

"But what did he do?" insisted Jemima

"Dunno. She was too young to tell me, and he said what I didn't know I couldn't get in trouble for."

"But what made you let him take her?" asked Jemima, curious beyond courtesy by now.

"He had a name for curing people here in Ballarat, but no one would talk about it. Just that he cured people of all sorts of ills."

"How mysterious." Jemima coughed again.

"Pity he isn't still here," nodded Bel. "He could fix that for you, I'll lay odds. Funny thing, though, when he died." Jemima waited. "Them Chinks always send the belongings back to China when one of 'em dies. When they stripped his tent, all they found was a tin box with all sorts of Chinese signs on it."

Jemima sipped her tea again, but her mind was full of curiosity as she succumbed to the hint of mystery and magic. Much as she had been as a very young child, listening to nursery tales of Rumpelstiltskin or Jack and the Beanstalk. In awe, she asked, "What was in it?"

"Nothin,'" came the flat reply, "except a load of long spikes. Like skinny needles they was."

"Jemima, are you prepared?" Interest in Bel's tale had made Jemima lose track of time, and she jumped at the timbre of Joseph's voice as he appeared in the doorway.

"Yes, of course, dear, I'll get my bag," she fluttered, then turned to Bel. "Thank you so much for your kindness, Mrs Car ... Bel. I will never forget you. Perhaps I could write to you when we are settled in our home?"

"Me? Get a letter here in Ballarat? Strewth, they wouldn't stop talking about it until the next shaft caved in." Bel was obviously pleased at the prospect and although Jemima didn't quite understand her reply, she shook her hand and kissed her cheek. Bel looked startled. "Go on with you, I'll fetch y'bag."

Jemima and Bel followed Joseph out of the shack into the sunshine that had already raised the temperature to more than an English Summer afternoon. Laura had the parasol open waiting for Jemima to climb aboard and smiled at her young Mistress. "Good morning, Jemima. Did you sleep well?"

"Like the babe she is," put in Bel loudly, swinging the bag aboard. She quickly rolled the blanket she'd used while sleeping on the chair. "Here, put this under your backsides."

She waved aside protestations, then addressed Joseph, who had gained his seat behind the horses, and was jostling the reins in his hands. "I 'ope you're not thinking of travelling too far, Mister Martin. 'Specially on a day like this." She indicated the overhead sun. "That wife of yours is not a strong bull, y'know."

The comparison made Laura and Jemima chuckle softly, but Joseph glared down at this Australian woman, who dared to give him orders. "I'm perfectly capable of making decision for the good of us all, Mrs ...er ..." His thick bushy beard and piercing eyes did nothing to intimidate Bel.

"Carter," she said pompously, and again the women chuckled, recognising the clash of personalities.

"Good morning to you, Mrs Carter," Joseph emphasised with an air of dismissal, and flicked the reins.

"Look after her, Miss Marchant," Bel waved as they moved away, and as the cart went back along the route they'd used to enter Ballarat, she called, "And look for a Chink, when you get there!"

Joseph gave no indication that he had heard Bel's parting words, but question was written all over Laura's face as she turned to Jemima. "What does that mean?"

Jemima patted her knee. "I shall tell you the story later." She swivelled to address Joseph's stiffened back. "Where are we going now, dear?"

"Sydney." Joseph answered, as though the colony's famous birthplace was but a few miles along the road.

Laura was very glad to see colour back in Jemima's cheeks and she breathed in the freshness of the early morning The sky was cloudless and Laura couldn't remember having seen it so densely blue. Jemima was refreshed and excited as she clapped her hands. "Oh, Laura, I've often heard my father speak of Sydney. It must be an exciting place, so many people visit there. And I believe they even have opera there - oh, won't it be exciting to visit the opera again, Laura?"

"I couldn't say," answered Laura "To my knowledge my aunt never went to see any operatic company that ventured into Tolton, and I certainly didn't."

"You shall come with us, one evening. I'm sure you would agree, Joseph?"

There was no answer. His wife's youthful prattle rarely interested him, especially when his mind was focussed on the immense challenge he saw ahead, to emulate many of his forerunners in Australia and 'get rich quick'. His shoulders jostled as he settled himself to driving the horses wondering if he had been entirely wise to marry Jemima. Practicality prevailed and he thought of her Father's generous dowry that had enabled him to get this far as well as afford a companion to occupy his wife. He overheard Laura point out one of the strange bushes they were passing and brushed aside the thought that the companion was more like the type of woman he should have used in his endeavours, although he thought her sometimes a little too presumptuous.

Either way, he was confident that Jemima's father could look forward to a handsome reward for his financial participation, especially when all Joseph's plans came to fruition.

Ballarat had been a setback and he ground his teeth remembering the substantial amount he had paid the London Agent for a so-called established gold claim. However, the Ballarat Land Agent had given him the address of someone in Sydney who could give him good advice, and possibly lead him to more lucrative fields. They should be easily located - the address was safely tucked away in his belongings.

"You will, Laura, won't you?" Jemima was persisting. "Besides, the Opera will be only one of the many delights we can share. There's bound to be a theatre, and museums ..."

Laura hesitated, unwilling to stem the freshness of an early morning enthusiasm but she had to remember her duties. "My place would be to care for your baby, Jemima, but you can tell me all about it when you return home." Whether she'd replied that way to pre-empt any retort from Joseph, she wasn't sure, only that she had no intention of being indebted to the arrogant man.

The boredom of their journey descended much more quickly than it had on the previous day. Laura didn't know if Joseph had breakfasted, assumed that Jemima would have with the generosity of Bel Carter, and was comfortable from the toast and tea that Fred Biggs had brought to her room. The heat was soporific, and she shaded Jemima's pale skin with the parasol as the young mother dozed against her shoulder.

She'd also read of Sydney in Tolton Daily News, and remembered articles by returning visitors that described the City glamorously. It had an impressive Town Hall apparently, with columned façade and clock tower, and a grand railway station. Laura sighed gently for fear of disturbing Jemima. Thoughts of riding on a train, the comfort of brocade upholstery, protective windows against the steam and wind; the convivial company, all made her yearn for the civilised decorum of her native land

Joseph Martin's insistence on the most uncomfortable method of travel puzzled her; he was evidently a man of some means and could well have afforded something more suitable, especial!y taking into regard his wife's condition. His meticulous attention to the safety of the trunk that commanded the largest amount of space in the dray vaguely interested, and yet annoyed Laura. Jemima obviously did not regard it as her prerogative to question her husband too much, and Laura would not have considered questioning the man who presently guided their Destiny.

A few hours later, when they had travelled endless miles of uninterrupted bush and rural landscape, and many more miles of seemingly unused land, they approached a place called Canberra. Just outside, there was an inn, and Joseph guided the dray into an area of stunted and dry growth, that served as a courtyard.. The long, low-roofed stone building was set on its own, on the side of the road, like an oasis in a mindless landscape.

He dismounted, tethered the horses, and said to Jemima, "We will rest and have a meal here. You may join us if you wish, Miss Marchant."

Laura gratefully accepted.

The two women wrinkled their noses at the mixed aromas of farm dung, dust, ale and sweaty bodies that pervaded the dim interior, but the publican, grateful for the patronage of a higher-class of person, made sure they had no complaints about their food. The plateful of cold mutton, fresh vegetables and home-made bread was eaten by Joseph with a glass of ale, but Laura and Jemima were amply fed with the vegetables and bread, and cooled with a glass of lemonade.

"I must ask you to pay for your own food, Miss Marchant," said Joseph unexpectedly as they prepared to leave. Laura looked at him keenly, ensuring this wasn't a flash of humour, and Jemima stifled her gasp. There was no humour and Laura stared at his back, as he crossed the room to pay the landlord his share of the meal and drinks.

"Laura, I can't think ..." Jemima began with embarrassment.

"Pay no heed," Laura replied tightly. "I have some money." She fumbled in her bag and withdrew a precious pound before following Joseph, and handed it to the curious landlord.

"Jist a minit, Miss," the landlord muttered. "I'll go out back and git y'change."

Laura stood stiffly at Joseph's side and looked straight ahead, not trusting herself to speak or she would regret releasing the sharp words that were fluttering on her tongue.

He half turned to her and said quietly, "I had planned that we settle at Ballarat, Miss Marchant. This further move to Sydney is an unexpected financial burden, so your forbearance is appreciated."

Laura was inclined to ask if she would have to pay for her own accommodation in Sydney, and what would have happened if she'd had no money of her own? Instead, she bit her lip, remembering she had told him at their first interview that she'd a small amount to take with her. She nodded imperceptibly and put out her hand to receive the change the landlord brought. As she placed that safely in the bottom of her bag, she wondered what had occurred to make Joseph change his plans?

She recalled that his manner had been tense while talking on the Ballarat Agent's verandah and being rather surprised that he did not retaliate when she sharply drew his attention to Jemima's whereabouts at Bel Carter's. But there was no time for conjecture, he had already led Jemima back to the dray, and she had no wish to antagonise him by tarrying.

Their stay in Canberra passed quickly, and it hardly meant anything to the two girls now, when he described some of the political events there. Politics was the last thought on their minds, so a good night's sleep meant freshness for the morning.

It took another grinding day and another uncomfortable night, before the outskirts of Sydney City drew jagged designs on the horizon, during which Joseph had only asked that Laura pay for her meals. There was much to advertise the approach of the colony's oldest settlement; ramshackle houses interspersed with substantial buildings that signified the wealth of their owners.

Rows of buildings proclaimed their purpose with boldly painted advertising boards above the awnings. Bob Clark, Butcher of fine meat, resided alongside Miss Hannah's High Class Millinery, with windows full of feather and tulle creations, that looked proud to be standing beside The Bank of New South Wales.

The travellers passed through areas with strangely familiar names; Sydenham, Newtown and Surrey Hills until they found themselves at the western end of George Street, with its imposing buildings, scurrying people, and grandiose business houses. Few people paused to scrutinise the dray and its cargo, and Joseph urged his team of horses along while he looked for a particular address. He found it quite close to the Harbour.

"Miss Marchant," he ordered as he prepared to alight. Laura obediently clambered from her perch on the large trunk and made her way alongside the horses to hold the reins. She left Jemima reclining on Bel's blanket underneath the parasol which had proved invaluable during their long and tiresome journey.

While Joseph disappeared up the stone steps and through an imposing glass door, Laura gazed around with great interest. She and Jemima had succumbed to the incessant heat by rolling up their sleeves, and leaving blouses unbuttoned in the most unladylike fashion.

Jemima's bulk made the temperature an excruciating experience for her, and several times she had dissolved into quiet tears on Laura's shoulder."I feel as though I've failed Joseph already," she said. "Ah, Laura, I wish I could go home to Mama and Papa."

She seemed already to have forgotten that her parents virtually used her as a pawn in their quest for the riches Joseph had convinced them would overflow into their coffers. Laura could do nothing but soothe Jemima with the prospect that matters would surely improve rapidly, as soon as they settled - she was convincing, because she dearly wished it for herself, too.

Next door to the building into which Joseph had disappeared was an equally sombre multi-storey edifice, identified as a Sailor's Home. At that moment, two men came through the swing doors, evidently the worse for a generous ration of liquor, and looked at Laura with unmistakeable grins on their stubbled faces. They absorbed her dusty and provocative figure beneath her opened blouse, and the sunburned nose and cheeks that did nothing to lessen her attractiveness.

"Well, look what they've got waiting for two honest sailors," quipped one. "This is a generous country, all right."

"Yeah," said the other as he approached the dray to slip his arm around her waist. "What's y'name, ducky?"

"Go away," said Laura impatiently, twisting from his grasp.

Jemima raised to her elbow and called nervously, "Laura?"

"It's all right, Jemima," said Laura. "Stay where you are."

"Ay ... 'Laura' is it?" The drunker of the two men tried to grab her again. "Well, come on Laura - 'ave a a bit o' heart. Give us a kiss."

Several people had passed by. None seemed inclined to concern themselves with what was going on, and Laura felt a terrible panic invade her. Retaining her hold on the reins she ducked under the horses' heads, yelling, "Go away, you drunken tramps!"

"Oy, she called us 'tramps'," said the first sailor indignantly.

"No sheila calls me a tramp." He passed roughly in front of the horses and they skittered, bowling him over as they scuffled forward impatiently.

"Whoa!" called Laura, terrified they should bolt and of the consequences to Jemima. Her raised voice, Jemima's accompanying scream and the loud voices of the men finally drew attention and within moments, a policeman was thrusting his way through the now gathering crowd. "What's going on here, then?"

Everyone began talking at once. Laura stood her ground, doing her best to subdue the brown beasts, and Jemima dissolved into terrified tears. There was general chaos until Joseph appeared at the top of the steps. "What is the trouble, Officer?"

His voice boomed through the me-lee, and Laura quaked even more at the anger it revealed. His eyes glinted as they assessed the situation and he strode down the steps and through the gathering like *HMS Victory* sailing into Portsmouth Harbour. His demeanour quickly dispersed the crowd, including the two unsavoury sailors who'd begun the fracas, and the policeman drew himself up to try and match Joseph's imposing figure.

"There's no harm done, sir," he said as though he had been the sole instrument in diverting the skirmish. "I trust you and your ladies will continue without further mishap, wherever you are continuing to." His last words faltered when Joseph made no reply, but grasped the reins from Laura's shaking hand.

"Get on board," Joseph ordered. "My wife needs you." His anger because his party had been accosted, simmered as he boarded the dray. "Are you in the habit of encouraging such attention, Miss Marchant? Button your blouse!"

The tension between them crackled, and Laura was still shaking as she took her place beside Jemima to hold the trembling girl tightly. She wanted to protest her innocence and castigate Joseph for his lack of sensitivity, but held her tongue. The boards creaked as he settled behind the glossy black tails that swished and almost tangled in agitation, lifted the leather straps and twitched the horses into forward strain.

They had travelled just two side streets, when the dray was again drawn to a halt outside Mrs Daley's Select Boarding Rooms. The relief on the two women's faces as they clambered down was evident; neither asked questions, merely following instructions until the horses and dray were cared for.

They found themselves sharing the largest of Mrs Daley's guest rooms. It consisted of a double bed, and a somewhat dilapidated chaise, whose green velvet tapestry covering had long since faded in the harsh sunshine that streamed through the window. Musty wine coloured Hessian curtains and carpet of equally worn and faded patterns just softened the noise of creaking floorboards. Beneath antiquated rose wallpaper and an old Victorian print in a weary gilt frame, stood a table that supported a crazed china wash bowl and jug. Several wash cloths and three green towels with a small cake of soap were stacked alongside the wash bowl.

A small polished dining table and four high-backed chairs occupied a corner near the door and, standing on a worn Battenburg lace doily in the centre of the table, was a grotesque ornament depicting a Greek goddess feeding bunches of metal grapes to equally unrealistic panthers.

Jemima sank gratefully onto the damask bed cover, her face as white as the pillows she lay against, and closed her eyes. Laura paid no attention to Joseph who stood looking out of the window and down to the dray tethered in the yard. She poured a little water from the jug and dipped a towel before applying it to Jemima's forehead. Only Jemima was concerned when he turned on his heel and walked out of the room. "Joseph..."

"He'll be back shortly," interposed Laura without knowing why she said this. "Now you rest. I'll draw the curtains for a while."

While the exhausted girl did so, Laura crossed to the window and reaching for the curtains, she observed Joseph in the yard below, driving the dray away and out of sight. For a moment her thoughts spun ... was he leaving them here? He held no responsibility for her she knew, but surely he wouldn't abandon his wife? Why was the man being so mysterious about their destination and purpose? But she said nothing to Jemima and quietly drew the drapes.

A mid-afternoon torpor overtook her, and she lay gently by the now sleeping Jemima, allowing the events of the past two or three days to merge into a haze of relaxation.

They both roused some hours later, disoriented but thankful to see they had been disturbed by Joseph's return. He sat heavily on the chaise-longue and removed his leather boots; they no longer had the shine of a gentleman of means, his hat was covered in dust and having refused to travel without wearing his jacket, his shirt had become sweaty and crumpled. But he had obviously visited a barber during his absence because his hair was clean, his beard well groomed and both were neatly trimmed. "I have deposited our trunk in a warehouse," he said without preamble. "It will be conveyed to Hargraves when I send for it."

"Hargraves?" said Jemima weakly. "What ... or where is Hargraves?"

Laura exchanged places with him when he moved over to sit on the bed, and for once she saw a softer side of the man who'd done little to gain her respect. He patted his wife's hand. "You know of course, my dear, that we are presently in Sydney. Hargraves is some three hundred and fifty miles West of here. We shall travel by train to Bathurst, then acquire another dray to take us the extra journey to Mudgee and on to Hargraves."

Laura didn't know whether to be excited at the prospect of a train journey or sceptical at the sound of their destination. Within seconds, more questions flashed through her mind. How far from this place called Bathurst were they to travel? And more importantly, thinking of her dwindling finances, how much was it going to cost her?

"Of course, dear," said Jemima softly. Then, after a moment's thought asked, "But, why Hargraves?"

"Because," said Joseph grandly, "there's been gold there."

"Gold?" cut in Laura. "You mean it is a gold-mining town? The same as Ballarat?"

"Was Miss Marchant," Joseph answered, warming to the apparent interest. "There is very little gold there, now. The largest deposits are being mined further South of Hargraves, at Hill End."

"But, I don't understand, dear," said Jemima, "what is the point of ...?"

"Because the miners are slowly moving out of Hargraves, and selling their land at very low prices. I have already purchased a shop, and two acres just outside the village, on the understanding that occasional spots of gold can still be found, and another half acre that runs down to Louisa Creek where much of the earlier gold was found."

This was the most information Laura had heard Joseph impart in all their time on the voyage or since. She was stunned - no more so than poor Jemima. "But Joseph ... what about somewhere to live. Do we have a home?"

Laura's thoughts flew back to tales that Bel Carter had told them during their stay in Ballarat and she shuddered to think how Jemima would withstand the travails of building one of the shacks they had seen on the way into the gold mining town, let alone living in one. Her heart plummeted when she thought how the hitherto protected Jemima had been thrust into this environment. For herself, she considered herself well prepared for all sorts of eventualities, but

Jemima ... And in a condition that was concerning Laura more each day. The cough would not abate, the baby was obviously not going to be a tiny mite like its mother, and Joseph seemed to have little, if any, consideration for his wife's predicament.

Her growing anxiety finally prompted her to speak her mind to Joseph, and now seemed as likely an opportunity as she could expect. Especially as he seemed softer and more approachable this evening. Laura took a deep breath.

"Mister Martin." Her nerves jangled slightly when he turned his piercing gaze on her, but she gained courage because there was no rancour. "Mister Martin ... I feel I should point out ...er, draw your attention to the fact that Jemima is not well. Not well at all, and that her pregnancy is tasking her a great deal. Would it not be better if we stayed in Sydney until the baby is born, and then follow you to Hargraves?"

There was a small silence broken only by Jemima's small gasp when the suggestion was made. Laura knew the new wife would be torn between loyalty for her husband and her weakening condition. Nevertheless, enthusiasm lightened her features, especially when Laura, in view of Joseph's silence, pursued the idea. "Jemima needs to build her strength during the next few weeks - I'm certain you realise the effort that is involved in childbirth."

The challenge in her words had gained momentum and she was determined not to leave the suggestion unresolved. "I will happily stay with her in Sydney and accompany her to Hargraves after the event. Besides ..." she added cunningly, "you would probably achieve your goals much quicker, unhampered by ..." - she was going to say "us women", - but changed her mind quickly and finished "...by extra responsibilities."

Joseph stiffened. "I never shirk my responsibilities, Miss Marchant. However, your words have some merit in the light of other information I have."

"And what is that, dear?" queried Jemima, gaining courage behind Laura's bravado.

Joseph lifted his legs onto the bed beside Jemima, and Laura felt most uncomfortable, as though she were an interloper in a married couple's privacy. "Hargraves has no supply store, the nearest being in Mudgee, which is a township some twenty-five miles away. I intend we should open the shop to supply the remaining population and the odd fossikers who still live in hope of finding traces of gold there."

He turned to his wife, effectively shutting Laura out of their conversation, which made her discomfit worse. "We shall operate our store on the system that, should a miner have purchased his equipment and supplies from us, and then wish to leave the village, we will buy back the goods (at a much decreased price, of course). That way we will profit several times from the same equipment, and in my estimation, make a good deal more than the poor souls who have succumbed to the gold fever. At the same time, I shall continue to acquire any land they wish to sell, which judging by arrangements I have already embarked upon, would be another source of guaranteed investment."

His wife's eyes were round, innocent, and bewildered. "But who will run this store you propose?"

Joseph's manner hardened imperceptibly. "It will not be the high-priced department store you are familiar with in London, Jemima. I am quite sure you will be able to cope."

"Me! But, I've never sold a thing in my life. I've never handled money. And the baby ... oh, Joseph, I know I shall be a bitter disappointment to you." She swivelled her gaze across the room, seeking moral support. "Laura ...."

"Miss Marchant will be there to care for the child," Joseph continued tetchily. "Good heavens, you have some sort of intelligence, don't you, Jemima? I haven't married a complete imbecile, I trust."

Tears sprang to Jemima's eyes, and Laura's reserve was broken. "I will most certainly assist, Mister Martin ... at the outset, anyway. However, I trust you will remember your agreement to release me if I should wish to marry, for instance?" She bristled with challenge, quite prepared for a barrage of scathing remarks in Aunt Marchant's style, about any man who would be willing to take on an evidently rebellious woman of her age.

The day's events, Joseph's declared intentions and Laura's challenge was too much for Jemima and she dissolved into tears. Laura sprang to her feet, expecting Joseph to explode with exasperation, but again he caught her off guard. He leaned over and completely ignoring her outburst, gathered Jemima in his arms. "Hush, dear. All will be well - trust me. Now it is getting late. I have asked Mrs Daley to bring up a meal for us shortly. We will enjoy that, then retire. We have an early start in the morning."

Laura simmered in confusion. It had been easy to despise the tyrannical and insensitive man; his newly-revealed propensity to opportunism gave him another face. and yet his will had dominated the conversation Her own tenacity refused to let the matter go unresolved.

"You have not mentioned my proposal, Mister Martin. Will you leave us here in Sydney until the child is born?" She trembled inwardly at her temerity, but her chin was firm and Joseph stared into unwavering eyes before he replied.

"Recalling events earlier today, Miss Marchant, I hardly think it would be appropriate to do that. However, your suggestion does have merit. We will all travel to Bathurst, and I will arrange lodgings for you and my wife there until such time as I have made suitable arrangements in Hargraves. Will that satisfy you?"

Laura knew that if she challenged him further, even that condescension would be withdrawn; she struggled with her impulse to clear the air, then capitulated and nodded. A knock at the door prevented her agreeing verbally, and she rose to let in Mrs. Daley's housemaid.

The woman went to the table and dumped the Greek ornament unceremoniously on the floor. She then replaced the icon with a glass shrouded candle.'Remind Mrs Daley that the cost of one meal and breakfast is to be charged to Miss Marchant's account," said Joseph with authority, causing Laura to bang the cutlery noisily as she laid it out.

"Yes, sir," said the woman,and quickly left the room.

Jemima's tears had abated with the prospect of the Hargraves store being pushed into the background, at least until after the birth, and she blew her nose. Despite her own misgivings however, her conscience about another financial burden placed on Laura having to pay for her meal prompted her to murmur, "Dear, could we not ...?"

"Miss Marchant is well aware of the arrangement, Jemima. I have already explained and she has agreed. So let's hear no more and enjoy our meal."

Agreed nothing, thought Laura angrily. Just foolish enough not to disagree. The tension eased while they ate and afterwards, Joseph left the room with the excuse that he would return the dinner tray to the kitchen.

Jemima smiled benignly. "He is giving us time to prepare for bed, Laura. You see? He's not altogether insensitive."

Sensing that Jemima was aware of her estimation of Joseph, Laura blushed and out loud, acknowledged he could not be a complete chauvinist. "Let us hurry before he returns, then," she said, and poured water from the ceramic jug into the bowl for them to wash before retiring. Having completed their ablutions, the two women donned their nightdresses and folded down the damask cover.

"He has not mentioned the sleeping arrangements," Laura observed.

"Well, of course not," laughed Jemima, happier now that the air was clearer and something definite was planned. "He will doubtless sleep on the chaise. We will share our blankets so that he is covered."

They were removing one of the two heavy blankets from the double bed, when Joseph returned. "Ah, almost ready, I see. You will be most comfortable on the chaise, Miss Marchant, I've no doubt. And after such a full and eventful day, sleep will not evade you for long."

His tone brooked no argument, and when the dining table candle was doused and they settled into bed, a thick silence lay over the room's occupants. Laura twisted herself more comfortably on the unyielding couch, and snuggled deeper into the blanket. Events of the past few days paraded through her sleepless mind. Was she the same person who had discarded a comparatively ordered life for one of uncertainty, aggravation, and frustration? Was it meant to be like this, or had she unwittingly let her soft heart be invaded by the plight of a young girl who had no place in this heathen country? How on earth had she allowed herself to be tangled up with such unpredictability?

Her thoughts were disturbed by the rustle of bedclothes and a murmur from Jemima. "Is something troubling you, Joseph?"

"Nothing, my dear," came the low reply. "I have just realised that I need to see someone in town. I will be back well before morning. Go to sleep."

Laura held her breath, then let it go slowly, feigning sleep. Both she and Jemima knew that Joseph's 'need' was the drive all men seemed to be afflicted with and most women either tolerated or tried to ignore. Few women, in Laura's limited knowledge, apart from those who lived by serving the needs of men, looked forward to such an intimate encounter. Was it possible to love so deeply that the "disgusting, messy habits of men," as Aunt Marchant had referred to them, could become beautiful?

She listened as Joseph dressed himself and left the room and her disrespect for him rankled as Jemima tried to stifle her tears into the pillow. She didn't let her young mistress know she was awake, aware that it would only deepen the embarrassment for both of them; furthermore, Laura knew she had no right to intervene.

Having returned around four in the morning, Joseph appeared to have resumed his non-communicative cloak at breakfast, and once the bacon and eggs had been eaten, they left the boarding rooms to hire a horse-drawn cab to take them to the railway station. While Joseph paid the cab driver and bought the necessary railway tickets, Jemima and Laura observed the elaborate sandstone façade and ornate decoration inside the cavernous building. They marvelled at the various stalls selling newspapers, sweets, and flowers that looked somehow different to the dainty roses, blue delphiniums or yellow daffodils they were used to. These flowers were bigger, highly coloured and had names like 'proteas' and 'callus lilies'.

Hundreds of people scurried like mice, leaving and entering different doorways and gateways, as though their destinations were a mystery to them. No more so than ours, thought Laura wryly. The railway line connecting Sydney to Bathurst had not long been put into operation and although the rail carriages were nowhere near the British standard when the trio boarded, they were a vast improvement on the comfort of the old dray in which they had travelled so far.

Their luggage, minus the large trunk, was loaded into a special compartment behind the steaming engine that fretted and snorted like an iron rhinoceros trying to escape. However, no animal could have hauled such a weight of train carriages across the mountain ranges they were to travel before they reached their destination .

With a whistled scream, and a screech of iron wheels, the six o'clock train for Bathurst laboured into motion. Jemima grew quite excited as Sydney's grime and bustle gave way to rural scenes similar, in many ways, to those she'd known all her life. As the grim vistas gave way to dense trees and bushes, more olive green than the jewel green of England's forests, a brilliant sun again shone from an azure, cloudless sky. The noisy train began its climb through the area they learned from other passengers in their carriage, was known as the Blue Mountains.

Apparently, the colour and density of eucalyptus trees on the mountains, seen through morning mists from Sydney, created a blue haze and the original pioneers in 1788 had created the name. As it invaded the peacefulness of their territory, strange animals leapt away from the steaming monster.

"Kangaroos?" asked Jemima in awe. Laura nodded. "Oh, Laura, isn't it a huge country? I declare I have never been able to observe so many miles at once. The horizon, at times, seems a mirage."

The greenery gave way to hilly, then flat country as the train approached Bathurst's railway station, Both women grew nervous whenever the terrain changed and the train whistle screamed through steep ravines as it hurtled downhill. Joseph was engrossed in the newspapers he had purchased at Sydney station and looked up only once, when the women commented on the kangaroos. Once over the mountains, the vastness of the Western Slopes again took their breath away, but the effects of a prolonged drought seared their eyes. Years without substantial rain had left corn stubble and yellow grass, scores of unidentifiable bushes and trees were yellow, as though they had never borne green fronds. Patches of scorched countryside left evidence of bush fires that were explained to them by another traveller in their carriage, and neither Laura nor Jemima could begin to imagine the horrors of such disastrous events.

Joseph said little, but read the several copies of Sydney newspapers for information or opportunity that could offer him a chance of wealth. He read that the penal settlement at Port Arthur was to be finally closed in September, after seventy four years of operation. Luckily, Jemima had no idea that Joseph was wondering about the real estate that might become available in Tasmania. Was it worth a visit? He would write a letter of enquiry to his Melbourne Agents, as soon as he could.

The journey took four and a half tiring, dusty hours, and having removed their jackets, both women were sitting with blouse sleeves rolled and throat buttons undone by the time the train steamed into Bathurst. The dust had brought frequent spasms of coughing to Jemima and Laura suggested that whilst they were in

Bathurst, they should visit a local doctor to see if there was a cure. Joseph seemed disinterested, but did not disagree.

If the women had expected another Sydney or Melbourne development, they were greatly disappointed, Once they all started looking for a suitable lodging house, it became obvious that Bathurst and its inhabitants did not believe in setting up a welcoming party for visitors. Its resources were badly stretched.

Council members were not so interested in the welfare of its citizens as in point-scoring, and politics of men who each paid more heed to wealth and material possessions than municipal progress. Shops in the main street advertised goods at "Sydney prices" then blatantly charged almost double, using freight costs as their excuse. Professional people such as solicitors, lawyers, doctors, even real estate agents, claimed that the tyranny of distance made it imperative to charge higher fees than their colleagues in the cities. And business participants in general, followed suit.

"Good Lord, woman," expostulated Joseph when quoted a weekly rate for board and lodging at a hotel in the main street. "People can't afford that!"

"Oh yeah?" came the laconic reply. "That's all you know. They knows they have to, and they pays up. You'll not find a better rate elsewhere in Bathurst."

Joseph refused to believe the hotel owner, and having left Laura's small trunk and some of their luggage at the station, they traipsed from place to place getting the same information. Until one kindly gentleman, taking in Jemima's condition, agreed that she and Laura could stay in the one room for a few shillings less than others had quoted.

Old Billy King, as he was known to the locals, had been a widower for more years than he cared to remember, and his own daughters had left Bathurst to live in Melbourne. He missed them sadly, having brought them up single handed, and he saw a salve for his aching heart in Laura and Jemima. He showed them to their room which was upstairs in the two-storey building, one block back from the main street.

The edifice had originally been painted white, but age had prevented Billy King from continuing the annual task, and scorching sun after heavy winter dews had deteriorated the wrought iron decorations that bordered the verandahs. But inside, the atmosphere was homely, thanks to the efforts of Mrs Wilkes, who came weekly to clean the house, as if it were her own.

"I'll get a bloke to bring your luggage from the station," Billy volunteered. "We'll soon have you comfortable."

Joseph set about buying himself a dray and horse, which, early the following morning, would take him on the final part of the journey to Mudgee, thence to Hargraves.

"I have arranged to stay at a local hotel in Mudgee for the night," Joseph announced.

Jemima looked disappointed, but only asked, "How long before you return?"

"Cannot say," was the terse reply.

When the luggage arrived at Billy King's house, Laura busied herself storing their belongings in drawers and cupboards. She had her own thoughts about Joseph choosing to stay at the hotel in Mudgee. She brushed it aside, preferring to enjoy the fact that she and Jemima would be able to sleep comfortably for a while.

Their room upstairs was equipped with two single beds, each with a side-table and pretty lamp and offered the most acceptable accommodation they'd experienced since landing in Australia. Joseph did not notice such things, and continued, "I shall join you here for breakfast before I leave."

"Will it be long before you return, dear?" Jemima asked tentatively again as they sat at the table the following morning, enjoying Billy King's version of "a good hearty meal."

"I doubt I will have things ready much before the child is born," Joseph replied flatly. "Miss Marchant will take care of you and if you really need to contact me, do so by sending a message through to Mudgee post office."

'Miss Marchant' sat to one side of the room, wondering if Joseph Martin was expecting her to pay for her meals as long as they stayed in Bathurst. March, and already her financial reserves were below twenty pounds. She dreaded the thought of how quickly they would disappear between now and August. When unpacking the evening before, she'd discovered the precious sugar-tongs lying forgotten at the bottom of her small bag, and the thought that she should perhaps try to pawn them had crossed her mind. She'd dismissed the notion almost immediately, but the more she pondered, the more she thought it totally unfair that Joseph should not pay for her meals, as well as lodgings.

After all, she had not quibbled at the meagre salary he'd offered for her services, but that was long before they arrived. She and Jemima had been under the impression that they were to be installed in a decent home in Melbourne, not trailed around such an unforgiving country, having to lodge here, there, and everywhere

Her ire boiled over. At the risk of upsetting Jemima, she could not let Joseph abscond to chase his particular rainbows, without at least some attempt on her own behalf. The knotted nerves in her stomach made her feel sick.

"Mister Martin," she began, drawing a deep breath. "I may as well reveal to you now, that I have no more resources to pay for my meals. I know you explained the situation when we left Ballarat, but you did not mention the length of time I would have to pay for my own food. I have not come to Australia with a fortune, and I repeat my finances have been depleted sadly. Unless you are willing to at least pay for my meals while we are here at Bathurst, and until we move to Hargraves with you, I shall be forced to find employment elsewhere. Better paid employment," she emphasised.

"Oh, Laura, no," came Jemima's pitiful wail. "Joseph, we can't lose Laura now. I fear for my life if I am left alone. Please, Joseph ..."

A soft knock on the door prevented any answer from the astounded Joseph, who blurted, "Come in." Billy King entered and glanced nervously at Laura, having overheard her outburst. "Yes, Mister King? What is it?"

"Sorry to barge in, Mister Martin," said Billy, "but there's a bloke outside who's just driven up with an 'orse 'n cart for you."

"Very well," Joseph barked. He reached inside his pocket and brought out a £50 note. "You may take this, Mister King, to cover the lodging costs we are incurring. I will send you more next month from Mudgee, as there is no post office at Hargraves. You will see to it that these ladies are housed and fed adequately until such time as I send for them."

"And what about a midwife, if she's needed?" asked Billy unexpectedly. "Will you agree to pay for her should I have to engage a local nurse?"

Joseph bristled at the old man's affront, and Laura turned away, afraid that her involuntary smile should betray her. Joseph's grunted reply could have been taken either way - then he turned to Jemima and kissed her cheek lightly. "I will see that you want for nothing," he said gruffly. Without acknowledging Laura, he turned on his heel and headed for the front door.

"Joseph!" Jemima cried. He halted and turned to look at her without compassion, and Jemima's nerve buckled. "I will not let you down, dear."

Laura noticed that before he went through the door, he turned again and looked directly to her, and she thought she observed almost a flicker of amusement. As though he approved of her ability to stand up for herself, and there could be no doubt in his mind that he was leaving his family in capable hands.

They all walked out to the street, and the women watched as he paid the man who'd provided the cart, and proceeded to get aboard. Without a backward glance, he headed North towards and through Bathurst's main street.

They watched him drive away from Old Billy King's Guest House, his back stiff and uncompromising, and Laura put her arm around his wife. He had made no formal agreement to her request, almost as though he did not want to be accused later of committing himself, and yet their unspoken bargain had evidently been sealed. She shook her head mystified, and gently led Jemima back towards their room.

"I'll bring you a nice cup of tea," said Billy. "You English ladies like a nice cup of tea, don't you?" Both women smiled, and so began the final wait until the birth of Jemima and Joseph's child.

4   JEMIMA'S BABY

The only contact from Joseph in the ensuing months, was the transfer of moneys between the Mudgee and Bathurst post office - one was addressed to Billy King, the other to Jemima. Laura seethed because Joseph obviously didn't trust his wife to give an amount to Billy from the one transfer, but the slight didn't occur to Jemima, so Laura didn't raise the point. Bathurst proved to be a developing town, but the heritage of English reserve, and not being permanent residents, made it difficult for the two women.

When they ventured into the shops, so many items like materials, clothing, even medications were vastly different, and the accents of shop assistants didn't help. Australians spoke with a lingo that had evolved over seventy-five years of emigration, forced or voluntary. Within the trickle that had quickly become a steady stream of people, the different dialects from countries such as Cornish burr, the Yorkshire twang, and Gaelic intonations was already blending and writhing with Cantonese, and other accents from countries like Germany and Holland. The dedicated English diction spoken by Laura and Jemima stood out, and branded them immediately as 'new chums'. However, they were women alone in a 'man's land' and they were grateful for Billy King's paternal interest.

Jemima had implicit faith in her husband's ability and spoke of him in glowing terms whenever the subject arose. Laura nodded agreement when necessary but found it difficult to discuss him. At night, when Jemima's even breath of sleep allowed her to relax and think of other things than her Mistress's welfare, she found herself conjecturing on his lifestyle at the moment. Where was he living? What was he doing? Who was he associating with? Did he ever think of his wife and their coming child? Did he ever think of her? The question jolted her - why should she care if he did? He stalked and paraded through her thoughts some nights, and she always awoke with a strange mixture of anger and pleasure which she brushed aside as dreams - or nightmares.

They spent the month of June chatting with Billy King, reading, sewing, or planning for the coming event. When Laura pointed out that baby clothes and requirements would evidently not be available in Hargraves, and as they had no idea of Mudgee's ability to provide, they agreed to prepare for the baby now.

Billy King's concern for their comfort, made what could have been a lonely time much more tolerable, and his increasing interest in the coming baby pleased both of them.

It was the second week of July, and they were sewing baby's clothing in the shade of an orange tree in his back garden, when he brought them a welcome cup of tea.

"Getting a mite cool our here these days, ladies," he observed. "I'd put another blanket across Mrs Martin's knees if I were you, Miss Marchant. Winter in Bathurst can get very bitter with very little warning, and she can't risk a cold on top of everything else."

"Yes, I will," said Laura, smiling at his benevolence.

"There's plenty 'o extra blankets in the chest in your room." He'd placed the prettily laid tray on the garden table between them and poured from the rose-painted teapot. "I 'ope Mister Martin doesn't send for you before the mite is born," he observed, handing Jemima her cup. "You're much better off having the baby in Bathurst. Lot more help available, y'see ..."

"That is a kind thought, Mister King," answered Laura, savouring the familiar brew as it slipped down her throat "I must admit I agree with you."

With Joseph's prolonged absence, the young wife's romantic image of her husband had brought about an adoration he did not deserve in Laura's estimation, and the longer they remained in Bathurst, the better she like it. The time had settled them into a restful and slow routine, and Laura had no wish for it to be disturbed.

"The beginning of September is still five weeks away," observed Jemima, "I'm certain Joseph will come for us long before then."

Laura exchanged a meaningful glance with Billy, then bent to sew white lace onto the tiny gown she was making. She had donated one of the two petticoats she had in her trunk, thereby conserving their finances for items like lace, sewing cotton and buttons. If nothing else, Baby Martin was going to be well dressed.

Jemima's cough had eased after they visited the town doctor that Billy recommended, and a rather unpleasant-tasting medicine had been prescribed. The extra rest her mentors insisted upon had also helped, but the problem never really cleared away. She had more colour, but as July wore on, some days and nights became bitterly cold and in desperation Laura would keep the fire in the grate in their room burning all night.

"I declare I shall never get used to this topsy-turvy weather, Laura," Jemima said during the second week in August, after recalling the balminess of an English July temperature. "It seems so strange that right now, Mama and Papa will be visiting Bournemouth and enjoying the summer sunshine. I wish I was with them."

Laura murmured soothing phrases as she adjusted the blankets around her charge, and reflected how quickly her own maternal instincts had made it important that Jemima should be free of worry. She thought quickly, to change the subject. "We will talk to Mister King in the morning, about having a cradle made for the baby. He is sure to recommend a good carpenter in Bathurst."

The suggestion placated Jemima, and she closed her eyes happily. Laura doused the candle and went to bed herself, thankful for the dark. She stared out at the star-strewn sky awhile, then allowed herself to fall asleep.

It was almost three in the morning when a small cry from across the room roused Laura. She lay still in the dark, trying to determine if she had misheard, when another sound from Jemima made her swing back her bedclothes and fumble for matches to light the lamp. "Jemima? Is there something wrong?"

"Oh, Laura," said Jemima in a strained voice, "I feel so ill, and my back ..."

'Oh, my Lord,' Laura thought, as the candlelight illuminated the pale and perspiring face. 'Not yet, it isn't time. Please, not yet.' A protracted moan from Jemima confirmed her fear. "I'll get Mister King to send for help."

Jemima clutched at Laura's nightgown. "Oh, please don't leave me, Laura. I'm so frightened. What is happening?"

"It's all right," Laura soothed with deceptive calm. "All will be well. I think your baby has decided it has waited long enough to be born."

"But ...," - a fit of coughing followed another wave of discomfort and Jemima's eyes were dark and wide with fear as she struggled to speak. "It is only the beginning of August yet ... it can't be the baby ... it's something else surely?"

Laura tried to calm the panic that rose in Jemima's voice and in her own breast by setting down the lamp, gently releasing Jemima's clutch on her gown, and tucking her in. "Now try to relax. If it isn't the baby, we will handle it. The doctor will be able to tell us when he comes."

She wished she felt as confident as she sounded, and made her way to rouse Billy King. His sleep-fuddled mind snapped to attention and within minutes he was dressed and on his way to fetch the doctor.

"I'll call on the midwife while I'm at it," he mused, hurrying into a main street that was devoid of traffic and bustle at this early hour. He shrugged into his overcoat and pushed his fists deep into its pockets, wishing he could remember to keep a pair of gloves handy when Winter came around. He glanced up to the stars that glittered like sequins through a block of black ice and muttered, "It'll snow before morning, more'n likely."

He hurried towards the doctor's house, thinking of the cry he'd heard as Laura let herself back into their room, and recalled his wife's travail when she gave birth to his two girls. "Poor little mite, she's no more than a baby herself."

By six that morning, the doctor had confirmed Jemima's labour and was about to leave the midwife, Miss Hills, in charge. While Laura applied wet cloths to Jemima's forehead, he muttered to Miss Hills, "The baby is large, and she's such a frail little thing, but I can see no complications. Send Billy King for me if any problem develops."

"Very well, Doctor," Miss Hills replied. She had helped hundreds of mothers in Bathurst and the outlying districts, so she was no stranger to the routine. While she rolled her sleeves and set to the task of birthing yet another scrap of humanity, however, she did wonder at the frailty of English migrant mothers.

Jemima's labour was prolonged and painful and tears ran down Laura's face as for long hours, she watched her tortured body twist and arch in agony, with pitiful cries escalating to screams that filled the room. She held Jemima's hands, and winced at the surprising force that built up with each wave of pain that engulfed the girl, as she fought to expel her baby.

"Not yet, not yet, Mrs Martin," admonished Miss Hills. "Try not to push the baby out yet."

"I can't help it," screamed Jemima and gripped Laura's hands tighter. "Oh, Laura - there's something wrong, isn't there?"

"Of course not," reassured Laura, but Miss Hills' expression struck a doubt into her heart that she hid from Jemima. "It will soon be over, and you'll be holding your little baby. Be brave, my dear, be brave ..."

Jemima didn't hear Laura as another wave of indescribable sensation jagged around her back and down her abdomen forcing her to screw her eyes shut until small lights dashed around the inside of her eyelids. She clenched her teeth and held her breath until the effort forced an almost inhuman, guttural groan from her throat that rose in intensity; the spasm eased for a brief moment and Jemima panted, as if drawing another deep breath was beyond her strength.

The pendulum clock on the wall between their beds swung with monotonous regularity marking the minutes and hours as late afternoon approached, and no-one observed the sky darken and become heavy with snow-clouds.

Billy King knocked politely several times during the day inquiring if he could do anything, and seemed relieved when Laura asked if he would bring more wood to stoke up the fire. The clock had already chimed four when snow began to fall silently, in complete contrast to the bustling activity and human endeavour filling the room. Soft white contours lay over the trees and bushes in the garden, and the seats where Jemima and Laura had sat so often, became pristine sculptures.

Another contraction contorted Jemima's face, and tears mingled with beads of perspiration when she eventually fell back against the damp pillow. "I can't do it, Laura," she sobbed. "I just can't do it any more." The girl's body paid no heed to her mind, however, and began to force again. The bedsheets were saturated with her blood and Miss Hills alternately mopped and prodded, trying to ease the baby's large skull through the opening until, with a scream from Jemima that transcended all the others, the taut flesh around the birth canal split apart. Still the infant did not progress, and Miss Hills raised her voice to Billy King, whom she knew was hovering the other side of the door.

"Go and fetch the Doctor, Billy."

Her call was a knife into Laura's brain, and when Jemima lost consciousness, she wept openly. She padded Jemima's white face with a cloth, not knowing if she preferred the girl to remain oblivious to her plight or regain her senses to endure more pain.

"Rouse her," ordered Miss Hills, "she must push now or the baby will die."

"Jemima," called Laura with trepidation. "Jemima, can you hear me? Please, dear, please ... you must try ..."

But it was another spasm building that roused the poor girl and she clamped into a breathless, soundless effort with such strain that Laura was terrified her heart would explode. The child's head suddenly broke free of Jemima's birth-canal and Miss Hills worked desperately to extract the little body that had taken on a curiously blue tinge. Jemima and Joseph had a son; Miss Hills immediately grasped the child by its ankles and inverted it while she slapped at the soft buttocks. The baby boy shuddered, gave a gurgled cry, and reverted to a more natural colour while the umbilical cord was quickly tied and cut.

"Here," she commanded, handing the tiny scrap to Laura. "Clean his mouth out and wrap him while I see to the afterbirth."

Laura looked away from Jemima who appeared to have slipped back into unconsciousness and held out her hands. She had never touched anything so frail and new before and concern for his mother made Laura obey Miss Hills quickly. Mucus slicked the child's hair to his skull, blood spots smeared his little face and the unbelievably small limbs jerked spasmodically as he cried, until she wrapped him in a clean cloth.

A great wonder at the miracle of creation flooded though Laura, until she looked back again to Jemima. The wonder was replaced with fear. Jemima's eyes remained closed; her tear-stained face remained still while the blood-sac attached to the remaining umbilical cord slid effortlessly into the bowl Miss Hills held in readiness. Her breath had reduced to shallow almost imperceptible pants, and it seemed endless minutes until her eyelids fluttered apart.

With great relief, Laura leaned over with the baby and said "You have a son, Jemima." But there was no response, almost as though the curtain of pain had refused to clear, and Jemima's eyes stared blankly into hers. "Jemima ..."

Miss Hills finished cleaning Jemima and gently removed the stained sheets. With practised efficiency, she eased a clean one beneath the young mother then covered her, just as the doctor stepped through the door.

She wiped Jemima's quivering lips then stood aside to allow the doctor to make his examination, answering his curt questions briefly. "Too big," she muttered. "The girl was too weak"

As if viewing the scene from a distance, Laura automatically rocked the baby, while her stricken eyes never left Jemima's face. The child was quiet as if he knew of the grave danger for his mother, and Laura cuddled him reassuringly. She couldn't understand much of what the doctor and midwife were discussing, and a million questions tumbled through her mind. She had dressed hastily when Jemima first went into labour and with her free hand she now tweaked at the collar of her blouse and smoothed her skirt, as if she were trying to bring some sort of order to the situation.

Joseph Martin must be notified - she would ask Mister King to send a telegram to Mudgee Post Office. She wanted to cross back to Jemima, hold her hand, tell her all was well. She willingly handed the baby over to Miss Hills who, at that moment, finished her conversation with the doctor and bustled over to relieve her of the child so that she could wash him. Laura knelt by Jemima and cupped her cold hand, lifting it to her lips. The warmth roused Jemima and she weakly turned to the only true friend she'd had since leaving the sheltered life of England. Laura could not stop her tears from welling, but she fought not to give way. Jemima's voice was barely audible "Laura ..."

"I'm here," Laura reassured her. "Rest now, and all will be well."

"My baby ..."

"A fine boy, " Laura answered quickly. "The midwife is washing him, then she'll bring him to you for you to hold." She glanced over her shoulder to see the baby laid on the table and the doctor holding his stethoscope to the tiny chest. "He is being cared for," she said, turning back to Jemima. "I shall ask Mister King to notify Joseph. I'm sure he will come straight here." Laura tried to make her confidence ring true, but she had no need; Jemima smiled wanly and closed her eyes again, her hair matted and damp on the pillow.

She reminded Laura of the porcelain doll she'd owned as a little girl, which she'd named Emily. She'd been sent out to the garden to play by Aunt Marchant, but defiantly wandered into the adjoining meadow and accidentally dropped her doll into the nearby stream. Weeds caught in Emily's hair as she'd fished her from the cold water and Laura, upset at the indignity to her only friend, but wary of the tongue-lashing she would get from Aunt Marchant, laid the doll on the warm grass to dry her little pink dress quickly.

Emily's blue glass eyes had closed as she'd laid her back and she'd plucked the weed away and spread the hair in the effort to bring things back to normal. Laura had eventually returned to the house and received several smacks to her bottom for having mud at the edge of her own dress, but the biggest tragedy was that Emily's hair never regained its original gloss and Aunt Marchant had made her toss the doll into the garden rubbish when the cloth body mildewed.

Laura now smoothed Jemima's fair hair as it clung to the pillow and the young mother opened her eyes. "Remember he is to be named Joseph, Laura," she whispered urgently.

"Of course," said Laura. They had often discussed naming the child while sewing in the garden or wandering through the Bathurst shops. A frown creased Jemima's brow and she tried to cough but had little strength to draw a deep breath first.

"Doctor," said Laura softly over her shoulder.

He crossed quickly to the bedside and bent over. "Try to rest awhile now, Mrs Martin." He laid his palm across her forehead and addressed Laura. "She is a little feverish. Try to make her sleep, Miss Marchant. I will go and fetch some medicine that should reduce her temperature and make her more comfortable. Miss Hills will stay for a short time to keep an eye on things."

"Thank you, Doctor," said Laura fervently. "I... Mister Martin will be most grateful."

"As long as he pays the bill," said the doctor pragmatically. I'll be back later this evening."

Laura glanced at the clock and saw with a start that it was now six o'clock in the evening. Poor Jemima had fought for more than fifteen hours to birth her baby, and it was too late for Billy King to send a telegram today - it would have to be done first thing in the morning when the telegraph office opened.

How long would it take to reach Mudgee? she pondered. How long would it be before Joseph actually received it? How long before he returned? Surely he would leave immediately and come to his wife's bedside? True they hadn't been married long enough for a depth to evolve in their relationship 'but long enough for him to put the girl through the most tortuous year of her life', Laura thought ruefully. Her contempt of Joseph Martin was continually being fed by such events and yet she could not help but sympathise with the man who had set himself such high ideals and aspirations.

But courtesy, morals, love - was there love? she pondered - dictated that he should return to his wife's bedside immediately. Jemima shuddered slightly and whimpered, and Laura's heightened fears amazed her by releasing a genuine desire for Joseph's presence. 'Dear God, this can't be happening, please let her hold on. Please help me to hold on.'

By eight o'clock that evening, Miss Hills was preparing to leave after giving Laura a string of instructions about caring for Jemima and the baby, and ensuring that Billy would be on hand should an emergency arise. Jemima seemed a little more at ease although her breathing was shallow, but she gave Laura the impression that only the frail body and translucent face was there. Her personality, her soul, had deserted her.

Laura thanked the buxom midwife most sincerely for such a long day's work, adding, "You must be exhausted Miss Hills. You really haven't rested for a moment since the early hours of this morning."

"Go on with you!" said Miss Hills, a little embarrassed. Most women she dealt with were toughened country mothers, who merely accepted the fact that she was an integral part of a birth - not an individual with thoughts and emotions of her own. "I'm quite used to this and unlike yourself, could keep going through another birth if I get called tonight. I suggest you take the chance to sleep now - Mrs Martin looks comfortable enough, and that baby will give a lusty yell when he decides it's time he was fed."

"Oh my Lord, " exclaimed Laura. "I hadn't thought...how am I going ...? Jemima is too weak."

Miss Hills smiled at Laura's confusion as she swung her cape around her ample shoulders and secured the button at her throat. "No need to panic, Miss Marchant. I'll call in again tomorrow morning and we'll get things going. This isn't the first time a baby has been left without a mother to rely on, y'know." She patted Laura's arm. "Now, you go and get some rest."

Laura saw her to the front door and exclaimed, "Oh look, it's been snowing. Isn't it beautiful?"

"Depends on whether you have to trudge through it or not," Miss Hills answered ironically. "As far as I'm concerned, snow belongs on them English Christmas cards, and nowhere else. Good evening, Miss Marchant."

The air was extremely cold and Laura closed the door quickly before leaning her forehead against its comforting timber. She felt like sinking to her knees as she allowed a wave of exhaustion to flood through her. She wanted to laugh because the long awaited and dramatic event was over, cry because of Jemima's pitiful condition, and be angry that she should have had to endure such an episode without the moral support of Jemima's husband.

Billy King's soft voice behind startled her. "I'll get you a nice cup of tea, Miss Marchant. Been a bit of a day, hasn't it?"

"Thank you so much, Mister King, that would be very welcome."

While they shared tea and toast in Billy's small kitchen at the back of the house, she arranged for him to send the telegram to Joseph Martin first thing in the morning, and insisted that she should wash the soiled sheets from Jemima's bed.

"Won't hear of it," the old man said vehemently. "Mrs Wilson is paid to handle the laundry, and seeing as how she is nine times a mother herself, I can't see any fuss about it. She's a good woman, that."

"You are a very good man, ... and friend," Laura replied tiredly. "I'll make certain Mister Martin appreciates your kindness, too." She wasn't sure how she was going to achieve that promise, but right now, she knew Miss Hills was right, and she should get some sleep. "I must go and check on our patient now, Mister King, so I'll bid you a very good night."

For three days and nights, Jemima hovered between a weak consciousness and sleep. Any strength she gathered seemed to dissipate when her shallow breathing dissolved into a cough. There had been no word from Joseph and any sympathetic thoughts Laura had for him, gradually dissolved into pure contempt. During the long watchful hours at Jemima's side on the fourth night, she composed her speech to him when - and if - he arrived. She would no longer be overwhelmed by the man, no longer reticent for Jemima's sake, she would speak her mind, even though that would lead to her dismissal.

She passed her hand wearily across her eyes, admitting she could not bear the thought of leaving Jemima and her son to a man who's only real concern was ambition. Nevertheless, she would have her say - at least it would clear the air once and for all. Wouldn't it? Her vacillating thoughts tired her, and with logs crackling an accompaniment from the fireplace, she drifted into a fragile sleep.

It was close to three-thirty in the morning when Jemima stirred and Laura snapped awake. "Jemima? What is it?"

"Nothing," whispered the girl then looked at Laura with her eyes large and liquid. "My baby ... Joseph ..?."

"Your son," broke in Laura, "is going to need a mother who is strong and well, so don't tire yourself too much. He is feeding well, thanks to Miss Hills who has brought goat's milk for him from a nearby farm, and his father will be here very shortly."

Laura made it sound as though Joseph had been in contact and hoped fervently that Jemima wouldn't pursue the matter.

Jemima gave another wavering sigh. "He doesn't cry very much ..."

For a brief moment, Laura wasn't sure if she referred to her son or her husband, then turned aside to hide an involuntary smile at the ludicrous picture of the senior Joseph Martin in tears. But the smile quickly dissolved when Jemima's frail body started to convulse, with coughs that tried hard to escape but remained tortured beneath her ribs in spasms. Flooded with alarm, Laura tried to sit her up a little and stroked the clammy face as if willing her own life stream into the girl's ebbing strength. Unable to control the sobs that rose from her own throat, Laura clutched the young mother to her breast and rocked her like a child, murmuring into the long dark hair, "Jemima. Oh, dear, sweet, Jemima. Oh, dear God, don't take her."

The sonorous ticking of the clock seemed to be measuring Jemima's last seconds; a deep sigh and sudden stillness confirmed Laura's worst fears and she knew it was an empty body she laid back against the pillow. Still holding the girl's hand, Laura's head sank to the counterpane and she emptied her heart against Jemima until the tears no longer flowed and her own body vibrated from soundless sobs.

As if sensing the tragedy, little Joseph woke and started to cry. For a brief moment, Laura refused to raise her head. It was as though she wanted to punish the remaining members of the Martin family for contributing to Jemima's death. A deep shuddering anger rose in her breast, until common-sense prevailed, and she reluctantly released Jemima's hand. She hesitated, but could not bring herself to cover the girl's face with the sheet.

Exhausted with sorrow, she got to her feet and lifted the fretful baby from the cradle. She paced slowly around the small room, lightly massaging between Joseph's eyes and making soothing, sibilant sounds until he quietened and went back to sleep. Her forefinger stilled against the downy cheek and she gazed at the innocent face until her sobs threatened to return and disturb him again. She laid him down gently and rearranged the soft blanket Mrs Dawes had knitted for him, then crept into the hallway and tapped on Billy King's door. There was no reply so she tapped a little louder. "Mr King?"

A scurried movement inside and a muffled "Just a minute" preceded his dishevelled appearance. The question in his face, was answered by Laura's sudden inability to talk - she merely shook her head and Billy understood. They both went back to the bedroom and almost as if she had hoped it was a bad dream, Laura clasped her mouth and gave a little cry when she looked again at Jemima's face.

"I'll go and get the doctor," said Billy hoarsely.

Laura rubbed her puffy and aching eyes, with first instincts telling her there was little the doctor could do for Jemima now. Practicality then told her the doctor would have to confirm and record Jemima's death.

"First light, I'll get another message off to Mister Martin," Billy continued dully. "You'd best take the baby downstairs into my room, Miss Marchant, and make yourself a cup of tea while I'm gone."

Like a clockwork doll, Laura did as Billy King suggested. She sat in front of the rekindled fire, warmed her hands around the cup and stared into the lively flames, before the tea brought stability to her thoughts.

She glanced at the cradle nearby and wondered what Joseph Senior would decide for the infant's future. He was hardly the sort of man to bring him up alone; dear God, don't say he would place the child into an institution? He could marry again, with more attention to convenience than love, as he had last time, He could employ a Nanny .... She sipped her tea again nervously - what if he asked her to remain as the baby's Nanny? The prospect stunned Laura into blankness again and she escaped into the pictures leaping among the flames. The top surfaces of the logs were already turning to embers, and the play of heat sent black shapes dancing amongst the orange.

The Tolton wedding, the tolerant Daisy, even Aunt Marchant's face appeared in the glowing logs until the increasing heat stung her wet cheeks, and she came back to reality. She poked angrily at the logs sending a cartwheel of sparks up the chimney then, on her back, she felt the bitter cold that had crept beneath the door. She took a blanket from Billy's settee and wrapped herself in it. Three quarters of an hour later, Billy arrived back with the doctor, and the formalities began.

By noon, with Jemima's body having been removed by the local funeral director, and another message was well on its way to Joseph, Laura sat back upstairs in their room, feeding the baby from Miss Hills' supply of goat's milk. Satisfied, and warmly oblivious to the dramatic turn his little life had taken, little Joseph was settled back into the cradle and Laura rinsed his bottle from the water jug on the table. She moved to the window and gazed into the garden that she hadn't seen for an eternity, it seemed. "The snow has melted away and it's quite bright," she murmured to herself. "Oh, Jemima, if you hadn't left us, Mister King would have been helping me in a short while, to take you into the garden for an hour. I'm sure that would have benefited you greatly."

The door burst open and Billy King just managed to get out, "It's Mister Martin!" when Joseph strode in.

"Good afternoon, Miss Marchant," he said, with suspicious brightness, Laura thought. "I have a son, I'm told. I came as soon as I had the message yesterday. I'd been in Sydney for a few days."

Billy King retreated, thoroughly confused. No more confused than Laura, as the imposing figure purposefully crossed to the cradle. "But Mister Martin ..."

Still bent over, Joseph said, "Jemima? She is well. ..?"

He straightened, remembering she should be behind him on the bed, and his brow beetled when he looked over and saw it was empty and neatly made. Tears filled Laura's eyes as she realised that he had not received this morning's message but had ridden overnight to get here. Her empathy was hard-pressed however, when Joseph looked at her full of question and accusation. "Miss..."

"I'm so terribly sorry, Mister Martin," Laura began jerkily, "but Jemima died in the early hours of this morning." She wanted to scream at him that he should have been at Jemima's side, not gadding about the country in some quixotic quest to satisfy his ambitious craving. He should not have made his poor wife endure such hardship as a pregnancy, at such a tender age. He had no right to make use of a young woman as he had - as a mere chattel, an acquisition, a form of income. The words burned in Laura's throat, but with a deep quivering sigh she succumbed to the shock registering on Joseph's face.

"Good God," he said quietly, and slumped to a chair by the table.

"I'm so very sorry," Laura repeated sadly. "She fought many hours to give birth to your son and was pitifully weak afterwards. However, the doctor said it was the ravages of psthitis that she finally succumbed to."

"Psthitis?" Joseph asked, his brow furrowed

Laura nodded. "You remember her consistent cough and difficulty with her breathing?" She heard the scornful note that crept into her comment without intention, and tried to disguise it with another question. "May I offer you a cup of tea?"

Joseph appeared not register her sarcasm and merely nodded wearily, while passing his hand over his forehead and smoothing his beard. Laura could not stay in the same room with him, and was grateful to go to Billy.

"I'll make the tea, Miss, don't you worry," said Billy, after Laura had explained Joseph's sudden appearance. He'd never had a very high opinion of Mister Martin, nevertheless, he was a man and had just received a dreadful shock. "I'll bring it in for you when it's ready."

Laura did not relish the thought of rejoining the man who had earned her contempt, but maternal instincts made her open the door to their room quietly and look in. Her hand flew to her mouth as she saw that Joseph was trying to blow his nose softly, not to disturb his son. He shook his shoulders as she entered slowly and murmured, "Mister King will bring the tea to us."

Joseph's voice was deep when he replied, "Thank you."

There was a small silence, then they spoke simultaneously. "My wife ..." "Jemima ..." -he inclined his head to allow Laura to speak. "Jemima's body has been removed by the funeral director, to his parlour in Bathurst I was to attend first thing in the morning to arrange her funeral, but as you are now here ..."

"I shall see to things, of course, Miss Marchant." He rose and crossed back to the cradle to draw the cover away from his son's face. "He has very fair hair, like his mother."

Encouraged by his attitude, Laura moved to the cradle and started when Joseph's hand brushed hers as she adjusted the blanket around the tiny form. The contact burned like fire, and Laura felt an annoying surge in her cheeks. The last few days had jangled her nerves enough and this morning's tragedy had left her shattered, unsure, and she knew she was thinking irrationally. Why be surprised that the sudden physical contact with the man all her irrationality centred upon, spun her into an even deeper confusion? Pull yourself together, girl, Aunt Marchant would have said. For once, she agreed with her.

Joseph appeared not to notice her inner tussle and to cover herself, she stuttered, "Jemima said he should be called Joseph."

Joseph Martin nodded, and the tension eased as Billy King knocked softly and brought in a carefully laid tea-tray. "Missus Martin used to like drinking from my best teacups" he muttered, setting it on the table. "Just give me a call if you want the pot refilled, Miss."

He studiously ignored Joseph and left the room. Laura bustled slightly as she poured the hot liquid and forced herself to ask lightly, "Sugar and milk, Mister Martin?"

Again he nodded, then looked at her squarely. "We must discuss the future, Miss Marchant."

Laura gave a small gulp. He wasn't going to waste any time obviously. Why, poor Jemima wasn't rested in her grave yet, and already he was moving on in life. How could he be so unfeeling?

And yet, not a moment ago she thought she saw a softness that maybe even Jemima had not known. He had begun to talk but Laura wasn't listening; instead she was watching his face. Was it a little paler than she remembered? Had those piercing eyes softened a little since they shared a pot of tea for the first time, at the Lyons Tea Rooms in London? She watched again as his lips moved, then parted to sip from one of Billy's dainty cups. Suddenly, what he had said registered with her and she jumped a little when he repeated his question.

"Well, Miss Marchant. What is it to be? If you cannot agree to remain as a Nanny to my son, I fear I shall be forced to find someone else. Or deposit him in an institution!"

His bluntness shocked her into reality; she straightened her back and spoke with a scathing bitterness. "I doubt even a man like you would do that to a newborn son, Mister Martin."

"What choice does a man have?" he shouted angrily

"What choice does little Joseph have?" she retorted just as loudly, her fingers itching to slap the arrogant man's face. Ridiculously, she told herself his beard would only soften the blow. Torn between her nonsensical thoughts and her dismay at the turn of conversation, Laura rose abruptly and crossed again to the window overlooking the garden. The thought of being in Joseph's employ a moment longer, urged her to resign on the spot and take her own chances in the new country. She would advertise her skills in Bathurst's weekly newspaper and had no doubts that any well-to-do family would jump at the chance of employing an English Governess.

Billy King, Miss Hills, already a number of people would probably give her a reference, and together with the one she had brought from England, her prospects were bound to be excellent. Then her mind tracked over the last few months and the heartbreaking commitment she had made to Jemima ...

"I am waiting for your answer, Miss Marchant," Joseph said tightly.

Laura turned slowly to look at him with little emotion and no sparkle in her eyes. "Perhaps I may have considered your proposal, Mister Martin, but only as a request, not a demand." She steeled herself for the angry outburst and the palpable tension weighed like a cold stone in her breast. "I will, of course, remain to assist you with the funeral."

She turned back to the window, wishing he would leave without further argument. What thoughts were going through his mind she dreaded to think, and that their relationship, albeit a tenuous one, had ended with such a futile altercation saddened her, if only for Jemima and the baby's sake. But she refused to regard him as anything but an insufferable employer and one she did not have to tolerate.

He remained motionless at the table staring at the strong woman, then passed his broad hand over his forehead before mumbling with difficulty, "Please."

Laura stiffened then turned to see if she had misheard the man. He stood and cleared his throat before continuing uneasily, "I told you once before that I fully understand my responsibilities, and now my son is one of them. Regardless of any impression you may have of me, Miss Marchant, I have not been oblivious to your capabilities and I doubt I could find another Nanny I would trust with my son's care. So, would you please reconsider?"

Laura was baffled. One minute this man seemed worthy of every modicum of scorn she could muster, now he stood before her ...grovelling? Oh no, his stiff-backed demeanour confirmed he was not grovelling. His head was raised now with a directness that could never be mistaken for grovelling. She knew what her reply must be.

"Because I loved Jemima," she said with an oblique accusation, "I will stay with your son for his first year. Further than that, I will not commit myself."

"Thank you," he said quietly.

Two days later, Laura stood outside the Funeral Parlour nursing the baby, and watched as his father and Billy King headed the cortège for his mother. The coffin looked unbelievably small behind the glass windows of the black curtained hearse; it was drawn by two black stallions and Joseph had paid the extra charge for long black feathers to be set at their noble heads. Miss Hills the midwife, had attended the small service held in the Funeral Parlour, and she patted Laura's arm as the sombre procession disappeared along Bathurst's main street.

"I'll walk back with you, Miss Marchant," she said. "Burying's is no place for us women. You can visit her grave later."

The following day, having told Laura that he had purchased premises at Hargraves and would return in a month for her and his son, Joseph left again for Mudgee. In a way, she was pleased that

Joseph hadn't expected her to travel with him immediately, but her sadness for Jemima was mixed with doubts that seemed so real that night. Would he return? Could she believe in his moral fibre? She lay for endless hours imagining just what dilemma would engulf her if he never returned, and she was left to care for the baby alone. The thought twisted her heart and several times she chided herself for having weakened to Joseph's plea.

A little less than a month later, the weather began to lose its cold bite and was pleasant enough to sit outside every midday for an hour. "Goodness, it's the first of October already," she said to Billy, who was carefully tucking a rug over her knees, after settling her into a wicker lounge chair under the big orange tree. "When does it start hotting up again, Mister King?"

"In a few weeks," answered the old man, "you'll be wondering how you could have stood blankets around you. There's not much ceremony between seasons, especially in the likes of Bathurst. One minute it is snowing, the next minute even a cotton singlet is too much to bear."

"Oh, dear," Laura said nervously. "I hope I shall soon get used to it."

"You'll have no choice," Billy laughed. "You can always jump in the river- that's what most of the kids do."

"Let's hope there's a river to bathe in," Laura smiled, remembering the sparkling river-pool that delighted the children each summer near the outskirts of Tolton. "Is there a river at Hargraves, Mister King?"

"I'm told there is," said Billy. "But it's for the gold - you might not feel like a dip in it with all the mud them fossikers stir up."

Again Laura wondered at the future she had let herself in for. Meanwhile, Joseph Junior had gained a strong hold on life, and Laura who had become surprisingly efficient at bathing and caring for him, delighted in his progress. The soft-hearted midwife was no longer needed, but during her visits she'd taught Laura simple knitting stitches, and a growing supply of baby jackets and dresses had begun to gather in the bottom drawer of the chest in their room. She put her knitting aside, and left her chair to tuck a blanket closer around the baby and move the cot into the weak sunshine.

A movement at the door leading back into the house lifted her head ready to greet Billy King, but her smile froze when she saw the unannounced visitor was Joseph Martin. He stood uncertainly, slapping the gloves he held into his palm.

"Good afternoon, Mister Martin," Laura began coldly. Suddenly, all the words and castigations she had planned over the past four or five weeks refused to coordinate in her mind. She had not allowed for such an unexpected appearance of the man who was the butt of her anger. She turned abruptly, and lifted Joseph Junior into her arms to show him to his father, determined that he should acknowledge the son Jemima had borne so bravely for him. He gave an aloof nod and said, "I trust you are prepared to leave? We start for home first thing in the morning."

For an instant, Laura was confused. Home? Back to England? Why? What had occurred to make him take such a decision?

"No need to look so blankly, Miss Marchant," Joseph reproved. "Did you think I would not return for you both? The premises in Hargraves I purchased are now ready for us to move into."

Laura blushed at his directness and hid her embarrassment by placing the baby back into his cot with meticulous care.

"I will stay at the hotel in Bathurst for tonight," Joseph continued, and collect you in the morning early." Laura struggled to remain placid but her anger flushed her cheeks and sparked her eyes. The man had the gall to stand there ordering her around and she had no doubt why he was to spend the night at the Hotel again. "Please be fully prepared as we have a long drive to Mudgee where we shall stay overnight. And I have many other things to attend to once we reach Hargraves."

"Mister King ..." Laura began, determined to get a word in.

"...will be paid," interrupted Joseph. "I have everything in hand. Is there anything else?" His question was dismissive. After a small delay to gather her thoughts Laura opened her mouth but again, too late. "Very well, I shall expect you to be ready when I come for you in the morning. Good afternoon, Miss Marchant."

5   HARGRAVES SHOP

He disappeared through the door as quickly as he'd come, leaving Laura with a frown and tightened lips. What have you let yourself in for she asked herself, then the baby whimpered. She turned to placate him and muttered, "and all because of you." He snuffled the air and rubbed his downy head against the pillow before drifting off again, and Laura had that sinking feeling that nobody really cared what she thought or how she felt. "Tush," she said out loud, "you'll drown in self-pity if you don't look out."

"You all right, Miss Marchant?" Billy King had come into the garden as Laura spoke.

"Yes," she said quickly looking to the now cloudy sky. "I think it's time we took the little fellow inside before it rains." Billy carried the cradle inside, and she went on, "Thank you, Mister King. It seems we are to leave for Hargraves in the morning. I suggest that if Mister Martin is in your debt for any amount, you should prepare an account for him and present it before ... There must be outstanding accounts for the doctor and Miss Hills?"

"Don't you worry about all that, Miss Marchant," he replied sadly, putting the cradle down, "that's men's business. I'm real sorry to be losing both you and the baby, though. I trust whenever you come into to Bathurst, you will come and have a cup of tea with old Billy King."

Laura assured him she would. She spent the next hour or two packing their belongings and making suitable preparations recognising that the baby would require a supply of milk for the journey. She had no way of knowing if they were to stop on the way to Mudgee, or indeed, how long the journey would take. During the evening she shared the last dinner she would enjoy cooked in Billy King's kitchen, and discussed the future.

"It's heartbreaking to realise that Jemima won't have the pleasure of using all her new things," said Laura. "While we were on the ship, she used to love describing to me all the wedding gifts she had packed into the large trunk they brought - I think I will feel guilty having to use them myself." Billy King clucked sympathetically. "Apparently there's new crockery and cutlery her parents gave them, and lovely new linen given by another relative."

Billy patted her hand. "Now don't you go feeling guilty, Miss Marchant. Missus Martin would have been very happy for you to use them, I'm sure - she had a lovely nature, that young woman. You just cheer up now, and think of the pleasure you'll get unwrapping them all. It will be like Christmas for you, opening all those packages." Laura nodded, but her heart was heavy and she didn't rest easy all night.

At sunrise, the birds were already twittering comment at the cloudless sky and drifts of mist on the surrounding hillsides, as though Dawn had caught her skirts on the treetops when she fled the night. Watching from the front window, Laura saw Joseph appear at the end of the street and took a deep breath. Another episode in The Great Adventure, she thought a little sceptically, but turned to put on her travelling jacket.

Joseph was driving a buggy that had a roof of brown leather stretched between wooden corner poles; the wide seat behind the buck-board was high backed and padded and a large shelf projected from the rear as though it had been especially attached. It was by far the most luxurious transport they'd experienced since arriving in Australia. The buggy was drawn by a strong black horse; and when Joseph stopped, Laura held the reins, and murmured admiringly while she stroked the horse's glossy hide.

She waited until the men had loaded the baggage and cot and then handed the reins to Joseph. Before she climbed into the seat beside him, however, she kissed Billy King's cheek. No words were said, but the moistness in his eyes spoke volumes. She waved back to him until the cart turned the corner into Bathurst's main street, then checked again that the baby was secure. They had travelled several hundreds of yards to the end of the main road, when Joseph drew the horse to a halt outside the hotel where he'd stayed the previous night. As though by arrangement, the Publican's wife appeared and handed him his travel bag. Laura detected the familiarity when with a cheeky grin she said, "See you next time you're in town, Mister Martin. Have a good trip."

By two in the afternoon, they approached Winton - a settlement that was too big to be called a village and too small to be a town. There were some shops along the main road, interspersed with the now familiar bark huts huddled together. There was a motley of children, some almost naked, and all without shoes, scampering and chasing each other along the street and groups of men stopped talking for the briefest of moments to take in the new arrivals. Then they returned to their pipes and bottles of something Laura guessed, was more potent than lemonade.

The huts had women who wore the outback uniform of a black dress and a white apron, and they stood, or leaned with their arms folded. All had tired hair that was drawn into the semblance of a bun and pinned to the back or the top of their heads. The arrival of the strangers hardly raised an eyebrow - in these days of itinerant workers and gold-seekers, new faces were part of daily life.

The settlement also boasted three pubs, with most of their customers grouped on the verandahs outside, and another establishment that sold an assortment of sweets and tobacco. It also served as a tea shop, and Laura gave a sigh of relief when Joseph reined the horse outside it. Nevertheless, she hesitated while he dismounted.

"Well, come along," he said sharply, then turned to stride into the teashop. She grabbed a bottle of milk and lifted the tiny Joseph into her arms before descending. When we get there, she brooded, we are going to get a few things straight, Mister Martin - you mark my words. My duty I will do, as I've promised, - toddle behind you like a naughty child, I will not.

They set off again within the hour after a refreshing cup of tea and a buttered scone. Joseph commented that they should arrived in Mudgee around nine in the evening. Late afternoon closed around them and although the temperature dropped, it was somehow magical with the spectacular sunset in front of them. Laura broke the silence by saying, "It gets darker so much earlier here than at home."

"Hrmmph," was the reply.

Unfamiliar trees passed them like shadowy sentinels, a small lamp on the front of the dray casting minimal light for the horse to pick its way along the indefinite track. Then the terrain became firmer and more defined as they approached Mudgee. They arrived at a quarter past nine - although not bitter, the coolness of the evening had caused Laura to spread an extra blanket over the baby and one over her own knees. A green woollen shawl she'd completed recently, kept her shoulders warm.

The houses on Mudgee's outskirts looked much the same as those outside Melbourne, perhaps more spread-eagled, but the standard of building was not what they could refer to as "high class." Discernible in the dim light of the street gas-lamps, gardens appeared to be well advanced and some were already displaying colourful borders of Summer flowers. The closer they came to the centre of town, the wider the streets spread, with many shop fronts and awnings below buildings that proudly displayed their date of origin, giving the clear impression of stability.

This area was more developed and had a street of shops, with three pubs, one of which, The Greyhound, proved to have some accommodation, so they stayed there overnight. Joseph spent the evening drinking ale with the locals, while Laura was very happy to feed and comfort the baby up in her room, before falling asleep.

Next morning, over breakfast, she learned that Joseph had already driven to the large department store in Mudgee, where he purchased some fresh supplies. The trunk which had been held in storage for him at Sydney, then Mudgee, was now tied onto the prepared platform at the rear of the dray. Shop assistants in Mudgee had loaded the supplies he'd purchased.

When they prepared to leave for Hargraves, which was some forty-two miles further west, Laura noted various household items: a box of pans and a large kettle, a pair of shop scales, a blue-flowered china basin and jug, a white enamelled chamberpot, and several closed boxes. Two ledgers protruded from a brown paper bag which, from its shape, contained other items of stationery, and Joseph had lifted another smaller brown paper bundle, tied with string.

"I'm told that material will be suitable as curtains," he'd said briefly as he jammed the bundle between boxes. He mounted the driver's seat, flicked the reins, and said, "As I was saying Miss Marchant, there will be plenty to do."

As they proceeded through Mudgee, she turned aside to observe the assortment of people that were already moving along the walkways beneath the awnings, or dodging transport that varied between farm wagons, bicycles, even perambulators that crossed the main street. The vitality of civic activity around her, brought a spark of interest to her eyes and she ventured a comment to Joseph. "I hope this is a foretaste of Hargraves, Mister Martin." she said naively.

"Hargraves is much smaller," said Joseph.. "However, as it's just a few miles away, I'm sure arrangements can be made for someone to look after the shop and the baby for an afternoon, and we can go into town at times."

Laura said nothing, but glared ahead. Look after the shop indeed - there had been no mention of that ...of anything, she thought despairingly. Again she determined that having seen that the baby was well established - say in six months from now, she would leave the Martin household and make a life for herself in this big country. Perhaps she could get employment as a Governess for one of Mudgee's more wealthier families or maybe even travel back to Sydney somehow, and try her luck there. She smiled wryly to herself. Already her financial 'backing' had dwindled to ten pounds, and the only wealth she could lay claim to was the pair of silver sugar tongs that lay snugly in the bottom of her carpet-bag. Hardly a dowry to attract anyone, she grimaced.

The dray lurched onwards under cloudless and intensely blue skies, through another few hours of bush track. Laura was convinced that she had never seen, nor imagined, a countryside with the vastness of Australia. She could not stop herself from casting her mind back to the neat fields and green hedgerows intersected by narrow lanes, where she was raised. The road, if you could call it that, was tortuous at times and she often nursed the baby, fearing that it was being tossed around in its crib too much.

She spotted more kangaroos and wallabies, and breathed in the pervading smell of eucalyptus from all the gum trees. It seemed ludicrous to compare the wild life to the soft-tailed rabbits and cheeky squirrels that scampered just as freely through English woods and forests. Here, the huge animals stood and stared towards the disturbance as the wheels ground across the clay and gravel, their reluctance to run, or leap away, a complete contrast to the timidity of more familiar country animals.

'Such strange creatures,' Laura thought, then roused herself. 'No stranger than your present circumstances, my girl.'

An adventure? Was it adventure that made her defy Aunt Marchant? Why had she really come to Australia? To find a husband and happiness, perhaps? Surely not only to escape the stifling life she led?

Thinking about the bundle Joseph had put on board, Laura remembered Jemima mentioning some curtaining had also been packed into the large trunk. But she made no comment. At least he was putting a home together for them. No doubt she could use it for bed covers or something.

A few miles outside Mudgee's perimeter, there was sparse evidence of habitation. The wide streets had quickly given way to a dirt track, and their carriage wound through scrub, tortured its way up hillsides and slid down the other side with hazardous abandon, aided obviously by the weight of the goods strapped on board.

The hills grew larger, and at one time the track clung to the side of a small mountain with an horrendous drop below them, with no chance for their lives had the horse lost its footing or the buggy wheels strayed. She clung to little Joseph as though he were an anchor and felt impelled to ask his father, "Are you sure we haven't taken the wrong road?"

Joseph dared not take his eyes from the track and replied gruffly. "Of course not." However, even his brow cleared as they rounded another bend and the track opened out into a wider course between two hillsides that led gently down into a short valley. At the end of the valley, undulating spaces spread each side. They were dotted with old gold mining evidence. Grassed over mullock heaps, rusting equipment cast aside, odd sapling poles that had once supported tattered canvas to create a dwelling for the hopeful and hopeless. There was movement of one or two fossikers, who refused to believe the gold was almost petered out, and a few mangy dogs littered the Hargraves main street.

They trundled down another small hill before rattling across a narrow wooden bridge that had no side rails, and grated loudly at the weighty load on its back. Clear, laughing water skittered over the pebbles below and a small hand-painted sign at the opposite end indicated that they had just crossed Louisa Creek. On their right, was a long low building, with several small windows, two green painted doors, and a bright red tin roof. It had a wooden sign outside that identified it as Hargraves Arms, Licence to Sell Liquor given to David ...in 1860. The publican's surname had flaked away.

Laura hoped Mister David had made his fortune in the past seventeen years, because the village of Hargraves, with no more than a dozen buildings visible, was hardly bustling with activity. Joseph reined in the big black horse outside one of those buildings, some fifty yards further along what appeared to be the main street. It was a single-storey whitewashed establishment, and obviously from one large window each side of the splintered door, was 'the shop'

Laura couldn't guess when it had last been used as such. A painted roof was well weathered from blistering summer sun and bitter winter snows; the windows were boarded up with ant-ridden timber, and spider webs on the wooden handrail that bordered the worn stone steps into the building, were silent testimony to a long period of disuse.

Joseph alighted and handed the reins to Laura, who had also climbed down from the buggy, and he ignored the look of mortification on her face. He mounted the steps and brushed impatiently at the webs as he pushed the timber that was the door. It gave way with a protesting creak and Laura gave an involuntary shiver as she tethered the horse. Undeterred, and without a backward glance, he went inside. Laura could hear his footsteps echoing on the boards within.

She looked around at the rest of the seemingly deserted village. Two or three houses bordered the road which curved towards the other end of the street, and a white wooden building on the right identified itself as a church with the ubiquitous cross at its peak. Alongside the church, a nondescript building sprang to life as several children peered hesitatingly through its open door, and giggled shyly.

"That's enough!" a strident but kindly voice cried from inside. "Back to your seats."

"At least there's a school," Laura muttered with forced lightness. "All is not lost."

A house, somewhat grander than the others, stood proudly astride two blocks on the property opposite 'the shop'. It had two storeys, the upper floor displaying two chalet-type windows, and the larger of the lower windows was a bay, complete with small panes of glass. It reminded Laura of Elizabethan manors back home. It had a semi-circle of leaded glass above its large front door, and Laura shook her head in wonderment. Such opulence in an apparently dead village.

Joseph reappeared, coat-less, from their building. "Start unloading, Miss Marchant. Leave the big trunk. I will get a man to move that." He reached into one of the boxes, retrieved a large claw hammer, and began to remove the rotted boarding from the windows.

"We must get the baby out of the sun as soon as possible," Laura said. She then lifted the cradle from the buggy, and looked across to the now perspiring Joseph, who tore planks away with abandon. "Mister Martin. Are there beds inside?"

Joseph hardly stopped in his efforts. Breathing heavily he replied, "They are to be delivered from Mudgee this afternoon, together with other furniture items."

"Isn't there a chair?" expostulated Laura, her anger sparking the flecks in her eyes. "Mister Martin, I really must protest ..."

What Joseph might have answered was interrupted by a figure appearing at the door of the grand house opposite. Far from the Elizabethan gentleman Laura expected, the small man was wizened, his frame hanging thinly inside a checked cotton shirt and his feet disappearing into boots that looked three sizes too large. "G'day. You the new people, then? Would the lady like to bring her baby over here? It's getting too hot for young'uns like that."

"Well, thank you, Mister ... " Laura ignored Joseph, and spoke loudly to the baby as she started to cross the street. "Come on, little one, we have a Sir Galahad." She hoped Joseph heard her above his hammering, but he didn't pause in his efforts.

The man opened the gate for her to pass through and followed her into the welcoming cool of the foyer. Inside the house was an unexpected comfort in both the surroundings and the welcome. "Dave Lee's the name," the small man began."In here, Mrs ...?"

"Miss Marchant," said Laura wearily. "I am the baby's Nanny. You are very kind, Mister Lee."

"Is that the little'uns father?" Dave Lee jerked his head towards the other side of the road.

"Yes. Can I put the cradle in the corner here?" She crossed to the hearth, and made sure the baby was comfortable. "He's Mister Joseph Martin, and this is his son."

"Come to Hargraves to live," Dave replied, stating the obvious. "Damned if I know what the attraction is - the old village has been lifeless lately. What's he got in mind? Not going to open the old shop again, is he?"

Laura knew better than to discuss her employer's business, but Dave's interest was genuinely friendly and she warmed to the old man. "He's a man with a lot of ideas and ambition," she said, trying not to sound sardonic. To veer the conversation away, she asked, "Was it your name I spotted, as licensee of the Hargraves Arms?"

Dave nodded. "Been very little doing for over a year now, since the miners moved on to better and more gold at Hill End."

"Hill End?" asked Laura.

"Carry on down the road for another twenty-odd miles, and you gets to it. I wouldn't, though. Hell of a road - more like a wallaby track!"

Laura decided it must be practically impassible if it was to be considered worse than the track they had travelled to get here from Mudgee, but brought her thoughts back as Dave Lee continued.

"The ol' pub? -well, I just opens the doors for an hour every evening now, and afternoons of a weekend, for the passers-by. Lot of them travel from Mudgee through 'ere, to spend a bit of time fossiking f'the yellow stuff at Hill End. It's got a lot of other attractions, too .... if y'know what I means." He winked broadly, then asked "Will you have a cup of tea? Or a glass of beer, perhaps?"

A little surprised at being offered a man's drink, Laura refused politely, saying "I'll leave the baby in your kind care, Mister Lee, if you don't mind. I should help Mister Martin get us settled."

Dave Lee looked startled, then pleased as he answered, "O'course, Miss, er... what's y'name?"

"Miss Marchant," Laura repeated.

"No - I mean your real name, y'first name?"

It was Laura's turn to look startled, and she hesitated before answering, "Laura." She hadn't expected 'outsiders' to use her Christian name.

Dave spotted her confusion and said, "You ain't Australian, are you?"

Laura shook her head. "We arrived early last year, from Britain."

"Oh, I wondered," said Dave. "We nearly always use first names in this country. Off you go then, I'll keep my eye on the young'un here."

With great relief, Laura made her way back across the road, and hauled two of the smaller bags from the dray before going into 'the shop'. Her eyes tried to adjust to the gloominess, and her nostrils flared at the mustiness that hung in the air like a London fog. Joseph removed the last board from outside the windows and strong sunlight poured in, revealing a large room, devoid of everything except two scarred and splintered counters, set at right angles to each other.

She caught her breath at the dinginess, and dust rose from her feet as she took a step forward. Spider-webs wafted from the exposed ceiling beams, in the fresh air she brought in with her. Sounds came from a doorway in the wall behind one of the counters, so she went around it and entered a back room.

It was half the width of the shop, and the stone surround of the fireplace was chipped and blackened. The wooden floorboards were heavily worn and stained, and the room had a tiny window, set high into the back wall. Underneath the window was another latched door, which Laura assumed would lead to the back yard.

Another door on the left, and sounds of Joseph moving about, indicated another room. Laura dropped the bags and investigated. This room was smaller, and another window dimly illuminated the small and ash-filled fireplace. The stale air was full of dust motes.

Joseph was not in there, but a door on the other side of the room, led to an amazingly light area. When she investigated, it proved to be a washhouse, that had only wall and a roof. A cement tub with the smallest brass tap she had ever seen, was set into the wall and a bucket stood alongside.

Further back into the garden was a shed, with a door which was suddenly flung open and Joseph appeared, fumbling with his crotch. "Good heavens, Mister Martin, what ...? "

"Good God, woman, a man might expect some privacy when ..."

Laura gave a little cry of realisation, turned on her heel and ran back into the front room of the shop, before putting her hands to her flaming cheeks and chiding herself. "You foolish woman, take control of yourself."

Her mind flitted like a Chinese firecracker as she worked out the accommodation. They would have to live in the large room behind the shop area but there was only one other room for a bedroom. Somebody would have to sleep in the laundry and she was doubtful it would be Joseph. She began to get depressed, but stoically set to unloading the dray with whatever she could manage. She stacked the boxes of supplies and equipment into the main room; set the luggage into the bedroom then decided that before she could go and get the baby, she should at least attempt to clean the place up.

Joseph removed the harness from the horse and balanced the shafts of the buggy on the handrail outside the shop, tying them securely so that the heavy chest remaining aboard did not slide off. He then produced a saddle from beneath the driving seat and declared he would ride the horse to acquaint himself with the area, and try to find some assistance with the big chest.

Laura was thankful to see the back of him and crossed the road. Having borrowed a large pail and scrubbing brush from Dave, she accepted the bar of soap he offered and set to cleaning the shop. She slapped the webs from the walls with an old cloth, hoping the builders of those webs were too startled by her activity to hang around. She almost wrenched her wrist trying to turn on the laundry tap that had jammed solidly.

She carried water from Dave's house, cursed the splinters that jagged into her soft hands when she scrubbed the counters and floorboards, and cleaned out the blackened fireplace. A great pile of soot descended from the chimney that had evidently not been used for many years, but perseverance saw her clean it, then start a fire in the grate and make sure it was burning well. Her work was done, and she returned to Dave Lee's house, just as the baby began to wake.

"Strewth, Laura, you look a sight." Dave could not suppress a grin at the sight of his new neighbour. Hair wispy and blackened, face smudged, and wearing a blouse and skirt that would require at least a week's soak before it could be washed and worn again. "I have a proper bathroom," he added proudly. "Go and fetch clean clothes, and you'll soon be back to normal."

Gratefully, Laura did as he suggested, and by the time Joseph returned at five-thirty, they were sitting on Dave's porch, sipping a cup of tea. The temperature began to plummet to the country evening chill, rarely experienced nearer the coast.

"Over here, Mr Martin!" Dave called to Joseph, who was hitching the horse. "Come and have a hot cup of tea before you do any more." Joseph looked as if he was going to refuse, but had second thoughts and crossed the road.

"Mister Martin, this is Dave Lee," Laura jumped in. "He has been so kind and helpful to me, this afternoon. He is the owner of the Hotel we saw advertised, by the bridge over Louisa Creek."

Joseph extended his hand, obviously pleased to meet a man who's influence could be extremely useful in the village. "Pleased to meet you, Mr. Lee".

"Dave," came the reply. "I'll call you Joseph."

Laura looked quickly at her employer, but he didn't seem put out by the informality.

Dave rose to his feet. "I'll get you that cup of tea, then we can have a chat." He added, "Extra good girl you got here. She's spent all the afternoon cleaning up the old place over there. You should have seen her fifteen minutes ago!" He retreated, chuckling.

Laura felt a little embarrassed, but she was glad that her industry was brought to the notice of Joseph. "Looks much better now," she said mildly, although she waited for a snapped reply.

"Thank you, Miss Marchant," he said evenly. He looked down at her red hands, and said, "You weren't employed as a housemaid, Miss Marchant, but I do appreciate your efforts."

Taken aback by his approach, Laura was about to answer, when Dave came back in with a mug of steaming tea for Joseph. "There y'go, mate. Anything I can do over there?"

Joseph shook his head then drew a sharp breath, because the tea was so hot. "Well, as a matter of fact, Dave, you might be able to give me a hand with things. There's a wagon due from Mudgee with some furniture for us, any minute now."

"You're on, mate," answered Dave, just as a wagon drove down the main street and pulled up at the shop.

"You come, too, Miss Marchant. Bring my son with you."

Laura gathered up the baby and followed the men.

Two strong brown mares hauled the wagon, and two strong Brown brothers drove it. One brother gave a sketchy salute as Laura approached, but he was obviously acknowledging Dave. "G'day, Dave. New neighbours at last, eh?"

Without thinking Joseph said, "Know each other, do you?"

"We all knows ol' Davey," smiled the taller brother. "We all owes him money!"

For an hour or so commotion reigned as, with Joseph in command, the Brown brothers, and Dave, humped, shifted, moved and re-moved the heavy trunk and various furniture items were put into place. The shop gradually took on a semblance of habitation and Laura was happy enough to nurse the baby in the first chair that became available, on the verandah. She was surprised at first by the Australian earthy jokes and jibes, but very happy with the friendliness shown to the two 'new chums'

Not once did Joseph comment on the comparative cleanliness of the building he'd left, but by this time, Laura was too tired to care.

When all was done, Dave declared that such a momentous occasion required that the Hargraves Arms be opened this evening, for two hours. The suggestion was heartily applauded by the Brown brothers,, and seeking to further his knowledge of the area, Joseph agreed to join them. Talking noisily, they all walked along the street to the pub, leaving behind a strange quiet that Laura found almost comforting.

It occurred to her that Joseph had been hesitant to introduce her as his son's Nanny, knowing full well that she was to be cook, housekeeper, shop assistant. She looked about her and took stock of the small and, as yet, un-homely premises. Poor Jemima would have finally broken at this, even if she'd survived the journey from Bathurst to Hargraves. It was a far cry from the romantic idea she'd left England with, of a fine husband and a comfortable home.

Laura knew she did not have the energy to discuss arrangements with Joseph tonight, and as nothing had been said, she bathed and fed the baby, settled him into his cradle, and carried it into the bedroom, which was now dimly lit by an oil lamp. The trunk had been placed at the end of the new double bed. A smaller single bed had been placed in a corner behind one of the shop counters which Laura realised had been destined for her, but she presumed Joseph would use it now, rather than sleep with the baby.

Wearily, she undressed and tumbled under the one blanket that had been thrown over the mattress for the night. Just before she went to sleep, she decided that next day, she would remove the new linen from the trunk, and make the bed properly.

She did not hear Joseph come back to the shop much later.

Dave Lee's 'two hour opening' had been stretched without compunction, knowing there was little chance of the law interfering in such a distant village. Neither did Laura wake when he lit the oil lamp, and stood looking down at her sleeping form. He was trying to clear his ale-fuddled mind, and decide if there should be a woman in his bed. This was not his diminutive wife ... it couldn't be. Fate had already wiped her from his life. This woman had to be Miss Marchant ... but a Miss Marchant he had not seen before.

He'd been aware of her ... oh, how he'd been aware of her, as a spirited woman nearer his own age, one who would enable him to proceed with his ambitious plans without, the encumbrance of his child. But he'd never before seen her in repose like this, her brown hair tousled and loose against the pillow, her breathing deep and even, like the babe in the cradle beside the bed.

Like any red-blooded man, he'd noticed her attractiveness at their first meeting that afternoon, in Lyons Tea Shop. But this was the first time he'd ever really let himself notice how her eyelashes lay gently against her smooth cheeks when she slept; how fine a brow she had and her lips no longer drawn tightly, as they were most times when he had occasion to speak with her. Mellowed by liquor, he stood for a long time regarding her, before his natural masculine desire, and his deep disappointment that Jemima had not survived the change in their lifestyle, made him put his head in his hands and sit on the bottom of the bed.

His weight creaked the wooden frame and Laura stirred; she woke drowsily, saw the large silhouette at the end of the bed and snapped into a sitting position. "Wha ... who ... Mister Martin! What do you think you are doing?" Her voice was sharp with anxiety that turned to indignation.

Also startled, Joseph began, "It's all right, Miss Marchant. I didn't think ..."

"Think I'd mind you jumping into bed with me" Laura was livid "You're disgusting - your wife is not cold in her grave yet, and already you are more interested in your own pleasures." She made to get out of bed then realised her gown was on the chair beyond him and clasped the bedclothes against her pounding throat.

Joseph rose angrily to his feet and towered over her like a black mountain. "I was about to say that I didn't think to find you sleeping in here, Miss Marchant. I had planned that my wife should share this room with me and you would use the bed provided in the shop."

"You had planned ... you had planned," said Laura scathingly. "Since the day I first made your acquaintance there has been nothing but talk of 'your plans'. No consideration for others to fit into 'your plans', no thought that others around you might have their own wishes ... no concern that the dear girl you bought from greedy parents, travelled with the dream that 'your plans' included a comfortable home and lifestyle for her."

By this time, Joseph had stalked furiously back into the shop, and Laura leapt out of bed to quickly put on her gown. But it did not still her tongue. All the anger she had quelled over the months was released with her fright, and phrases she had rehearsed so often at Bathurst in her moments of solitude, sprang from her throat easily. "I constantly flinched when you gave out your orders. Orders that would have been much more acceptable as requests. But more so, I cringed at the way you expected Jemima to follow you like a pet dog, never letting her share 'your plans' as a wife has every right to …"

Any more words she wanted to throw at him were choked by an uncontrollable sob. Her throat felt sore and her head throbbed, like she'd received a hard blow against her temple. She fought to regain her control, and was aided by a sudden cry from the cradle. She returned to the bedroom and picked up the baby, knowing full well he was hungry, but rocked and patted his back with an urgency that showed her ire was not spent. "Yes, you can cry, little man. Cry for the mother you should have had, cry for the father that didn't even have the decency to stand by her when she needed him."

She was trembling pitifully as she reached for the bottle she had prepared earlier and stood on the table by the bed The baby gulped greedily as soon as he sensed the milk near his searching mouth, and only then, did Laura become aware of the terrible tension emanating from the other room. But she did not care; she had overstepped the bounds of her position, she had been frightened out of her wits by having been woken in such a manner, and if Mister Joseph Martin wished to order her out of his life, he could jolly well do so.

"Miss Marchant," his voice boomed. "Would you please come out here?"

"I am feeding your son," she replied defiantly, expecting immediate dismissal. She looked down at the life she had nurtured for almost six weeks now, and her heart tore at the thought of leaving him - to what? To some strange woman that his father would employ? And how long would she last? How long could any woman tolerate such an insufferable man? Would there be a succession of 'Nanny's'? Would his father ...?

Little Joseph had gone back to sleep, and Laura laid him gently in his cot. She looked up as Joseph Senior re-entered the bedroom, and, not wanting to waken the baby again, Laura brushed past him out into the shop. She turned to see he had followed her, expecting to meet a glare from the man who had, in less than a year, given rise to such a plethora of emotion within her. He stood by the fireplace with his ramrod back to her, his hands clasped behind in a white-knuckled grip. His head was held high at first, then it tilted forward and in a low voice, he said,. "I had no idea that was the impression I gave you, Miss Marchant."

No idea? ... did he have no conscience? Did he lack so much feeling that nothing could breach the ice barrier he had for a heart? Laura opened her mouth to continue her tirade, but was stunned into silence when he said quietly, "I am sorry."

"I beg your pardon?" she quavered.

He turned to face her and Laura's stomach lurched when she saw his haunted expression. His eyes were bright, but he shut them tightly and frowned, before murmuring, "I said ... I am sorry."

"I think, Mister Martin," Laura replied, trying to regain calm, "it is your poor wife's memory you should be saying that to, not to me." He opened his eyes and a confused weariness crossed his face. He looked so downcast that Laura's decorum returned and she felt obliged to follow in the tradition of her English breeding. "Shall I make us a cup of tea, Mister Martin?"

He nodded, and feeling quite strange, Laura lit an oil lamp and placed it on a counter. She drew her gown closer, as the chill of almost two o'clock in the morning enveloped her. She bent to rekindle the fire and was startled when she realised Joseph had moved over to her.

"Here, I'll do that," he said gruffly. "You prepare the tea."

An eeriness stretched through their tension, like a dark animal waiting to leap into their presence at the slightest provocation. Laura kept sidling a glance at Joseph - watchful, apprehensive, but without a shred of contrition for her outburst. She set out the enamel mugs Joseph had acquired at Mudgee and prepared the pot, before sitting at the table to wait for the hot water.

Joseph balanced the iron kettle on the already glowing logs, removed his coat, and took a chair opposite her.

"I think for the sake of my son, we should work for a more amicable situation, Miss Marchant. I see now that your stinging words were not entirely uncalled for. Although I wish it hadn't been necessary to speak them."

Laura found herself off-guard again and opened her mouth to reply, but Joseph held up his hand. "I will not be called Joseph, in view of the confusion that will arise as my son grows. However, as a fresh beginning, I will, in future, call you Laura."

Laura gaped, her mind frantically trying to read his. Was this some sort of mental game he was playing? Was he trying to mollify her in order to attack her vulnerability? His request was on his terms as usual - but what if she refused to be called Laura unless she could use his Christian name as well? Did it matter all that much to her?

Steam poured silently from the kettle-spout and for a moment, Laura was so engrossed in trying to fathom Joseph, it was impossible to look away from him. Then she stood hurriedly, and rescued the boiling water, as it started to splash onto the fire. She poured it into the pot, her hand trembling and tried to find words to answer his latest 'order'.

Hearing Joseph speak her name had combined an unexpected pleasure with her amazement, and again her self-control was dislodged. 'Tush,' she thought, 'take a hold of yourself, Laura.' She passed one mug across the table to him, and found he was staring at her keenly. "I think I deserve the courtesy of a reply," he said.

Laura cleared her throat as she sat down and nodded. "Very well, Mister Martin, if those are your wishes." Then she added softly, "...and for little Joseph's sake."

They sipped at the warming brew in silence, then Joseph said, "You may sleep in my bed, Laura." Horror screamed through her already over-wound nerves, and she almost dropped her cup but he continued, "I shall occupy the small bed in the shop just for tonight. I'll be leaving early in the morning. By the time I return I've no doubt you will have the household organised, and you will be able to open the doors of the shop shortly afterwards. I have put in an order for gold-mining pans and shovels for my stock - they should be here tomorrow."

He did not refer to her outburst again, and Laura could not make up her mind whether it had made things easier. Too weary to ask questions, Laura finished her tea and moved towards the bedroom.

"Good night, Mister Martin."

"Good night...Laura."

6 SETTLING IN TO HARGRAVES

Joseph left for Bathurst the following morning, and two weeks passed before Laura heard from him again. In this time, she'd found a spot on the wall opposite the shop window to display her treasured picture of an English countryside, made pretty curtains from the material he'd purchased at Mudgee, and become firm friends with Dave Lee. She'd made the acquaintance of Clem White, the schoolteacher, and several other villagers who seemed pleased that the little shop was to reopen shortly.

The baby had settled to a routine that often allowed her time to ponder her position, and she became increasingly aware that she wished Joseph wouldn't travel so often. Dave had loaned her a rocking chair which she sat in, outside the shop most afternoons, crooning to the baby and revelling in the comparative peace of the isolated village. She had already determined to asked Joseph if the contents of the large trunk could be finally unpacked, and looked forward to setting out the new linen, cutlery and crockery. She even felt guilty about the feelings of being a new bride this gave her, but soon lost them when she heard other village women describe the hardships they'd endured in earlier gold rush days.

Dray wheels crunching across the creek bridge and towards the shop made her open her eyes, and she couldn't contain her rush of expectation and pleasure when she saw it was being driven by Joseph. She got to her feet and held the horse while he dismounted, courtesy demanding that she murmur, "Good afternoon, Mister Martin."

"Laura" he nodded briefly, and said no more until all was secured, and they were inside the shop. He rescued several boxes from the dray and set them on the waiting counters then surveyed his haul triumphantly. "Well, this is the beginning. You can use that counter for the daily necessities, and this one here for the fossicker's supplies. I'll place the heavier items, then we shall sit down over a meal and work out our trading prices."

There was no word about the improvements she'd made, including the new curtains and bedspread. She'd used the material he'd bought at Mudgee, and the trunk stood unopened at the end of the bed in the bedroom.

Laura felt the old chagrin returning and felt impelled to ask, "Would you like to know about your son?"

"We can talk as we work," he replied. "Best to use whatever daylight we can."

"I'll bring him inside, then," she said huffily. "The nights are extremely chilly here in Hargraves, I've found, even though it's summer."

She received a grunted reply as he tore open the first box and proceeded to set out shallow metal pans, pick heads and handles, coils of rope, oil lanterns, oilskins, some on the counter, others hanging from large nails in the wall he'd prepared, when they first got there. Following suit, Laura found several bales of cotton material, sewing supplies including buttons and threads, a small white cardboard box containing a selection of fine embroidery colours, and three pairs of scissors.

Next she unpacked a selection of men, women's and children's undergarments, some ladies' and gents' handkerchiefs made of fine lawn, cooking bowls, spoons and ladles - even a large copper kettle. Yet another box revealed exercise books, pencils, and blackboard chalks. The final carton contained tinned foods. Laura blurted, "How on earth will we sell all these items, Mister Martin? And to whom?"

"I have considered the prospects thoroughly," he answered, looking around at the display, "and have reason to believe these are the kind of supplies an isolated village like Hargraves needs. Especially during high temperatures, when travel to the nearest town for a length of rope or a needle, is impractical."

Laura couldn't argue his logic, having learned from Dave and Clem about the many isolated properties in the area. "Now, if you would be good enough to make us some dinner, we will set up the cash box and books afterwards, to make sure you fully understand them."

Laura glanced around the shop doubtfully, then carried the sleeping baby into the main living area where she laid him down, and peeled some potatoes ready to boil. Joseph remained for some time, adjusting, rearranging things to his satisfaction, before he joined her. He stooped to regard his sleeping son, then said, "I shall wash before eating."

The conversation was desultory during their meal, until Laura broached the question of the large trunk at the end of the big bed. "Those are my belongings," Joseph said sharply. "In time I shall provide my son with a grand home like Dave Lee's, and he will never find himself short of good books or fine instruments to use. I even had the forethought to bring a telescope and microscope with me, doubting that Australia could provide such instruments when I needed them."

"But..." Laura stuttered, "Jemima said ... the household linen and other wedding presents ..." She stopped, unsure if she had earned the right to question him in this manner.

"Decisions had to be made," Joseph said evenly. "Such items, I could be sure of obtaining here. Besides, I was certain such fripperies would be grossly out of place in our new life."

Visions of unwrapping the treasures that Jemima had believed were with them, washing fine white linen sheets and pillowcases carefully for their first use, or displaying the bone china tea-service with its Royal Albert design, crumbled before her eyes. Her heart ached realising the tremendous disappointment the poor young mother would have endured, had she known the truth.

She stared at Joseph busily finishing his meal, then lined up her knife and fork on her plate, and pushed it aside. She did not know whether to feel sorry for her own predicament, sad for Jemima's memory, or confused at Joseph's almost naive belief in his ambitions and ideas.

He set aside his plate and looked across the table, and with a catch in her throat, Laura recognised behind the bushy beard and clear direct eyes, a man with intrinsic faith in his own abilities. Then to add to her confusion, he smiled at her, and she found herself blushing. She pushed hastily away from the table and gathered the plates, before busying herself with the teapot.

"I know," he announced suddenly. "I shall show you."

A startled Laura watched him go into the bedroom, and retrieve a key from his pocket. He released the trunk's padlocks, lifted the lid and, almost lovingly, removed several wrapped packages, until he reached into the bottom. From there, he extracted a long cylindrical container, followed by a black metal tripod.

"Come. Come and see," he said excitedly, heading through the small laundry door, out into the back yard, where he quickly assembled the telescope and aimed it towards the sky. Full of curiosity, Laura followed him and looked up. There was no moon, but filling the black void with a silver and white sweep of myriad stars, the Milky Way hung above them like a fairy curtain.

Joseph was already training and adjusting the telescope onto the sight, and when he was satisfied, urged Laura to peer through the eyepiece. She gasped at what she saw; she had never seen the familiar spectacle in such brilliance, even from the countryside around Tolton. "It's heavenly, " she breathed.

"Of course," said Joseph proudly, as though he himself had placed it there. "This telescope will be an important part of education for my son - hardly compares with matching cups and saucers and fancy linen, wouldn't you agree?"

Laura looked back at him as though she were meeting him for the first time, and nodded silently. They stood enjoying the spectacle for some minutes, before Laura shivered, and begged to be excused as it was time to feed the baby. She left Joseph in the yard squinting along the barrel of magic that focussed on the stars, and drew her shawl closer as she went inside. Her employer was an enigma.

Before they retired that evening, Joseph listed their stock, and drew up the prices, while Laura marked each item carefully. Finally they equipped the metal cash box with coinage to the value of ten pounds, as an initial float for The Hargraves Store. He tutored Laura in the meticulous care of sales transactions and records, then startled her by announcing that he had an appointment with a land agent in Mudgee early next morning, and that he would likely return at the end of the week.

She lay in bed watching a small square of The Milky Way through the high window and couldn't decide if she despised, respected, or admired her employer. Little Joseph snuffled in the cot beside her, and she knew she loved his son.

Feeling extremely ill at ease, Laura opened the shop door the next morning, just an hour after Joseph left the village. She stood behind the counter, smoothed her apron, and tweaked her hair into place, and considered herself ready. After a while, with no visitors, she relaxed and decided to knit more of the baby's tiny socks. No sooner had she settled, than the door bell jangled. She got quickly to her feet and went into the shop for her first customer.

"Just thought I'd have a sticky-beak," Dave Lee quipped, gazing around at the stock. "Got a lot of courage, that bloke."

Laura thought it was she who was going to need the courage - how did one go about selling goods? She'd never been behind a counter before. "Good morning, Mister... I mean - can I get you ..? " Dave moved to inspect a coil of rope and Laura held her breath until he replaced it on the counter.

"Oh, I haven't come to buy anything," he smiled, recognising her apprehension. "Just nosey."

Laura gave a huge sigh of relief. "Thank goodness. Oh, Davey, I'm so nervous."

"No need to be," he answered. "You won't see a rush in these parts any more, not for gold, not for anything. But it's handy to know what you've got."

Dave was right. By the end of the first week, Laura had checked and rechecked the sale of one sewing needle in Joseph's record book, and found that far from being hassled and stressed, she was already bored with the restrictions placed on her, by having to be in attendance all day.

Previously she had been able to take a short walk around the village and down to the creek with baby Joseph during the warmest part of the day; now she was too wary to do more than sit in the rocking chair on the verandah and wait for a customer. She had drawn a sign that announced The Hargraves Store opening hours, which left Saturday afternoons and Sunday free. She dabbed a flour and water paste onto its corners before, attaching it to the window.

Not that it made an impression - the sale of the sewing needle had occurred at nine one evening, when Mrs Brighton, housekeeper for Clem White, had knocked on the shop door. "Broke me last one sewing his shirt," she'd pleaded, "and he's got to wear it tomorrow."

Laura had carefully entered; "One sewing needle. ld".

Dave Lee had volunteered to bring more supplies or anything that Laura and the baby needed, back from his regular Friday trip into Mudgee. Laura had decided to use Saturday afternoons, after closing the store, as her baking day. Young Joseph was a placid baby and when not sleeping, he lay contentedly in his cradle, occasionally cooing or discovering his tiny world of fingers and clothing.

    The village children, free from the tyranny of daily lessons, were at their favourite game of splashing in the creek, or chasing a ball around back paddocks, while their mothers baked or sewed. And their fathers slept on verandah chairs - the fathers that weren't out at Hill End that is, convinced this would be the weekend of the big discovery. A few more active men scrambled around Hargraves' deserted paddocks or sifted water from the creek languidly, and talked endlessly about the time the big nugget had been found by an old Aborigine employee on Doctor Kerr's property several years before. Apparently, the stock-man had been sitting on it every day, down by the creek, to eat his lunch..

    "Don' know why 'im fuss," the stock-man had said. "It only lump of yella rock."

    Laura watched one or two children run past the shop as she secured the front door one warm Saturday afternoon in November, and remembered the disappointment on their faces when they'd discovered The Hargraves Store didn't stock sweets. "Why don't I try to make some toffee?" she murmured to herself. "I've plenty of sugar."

    Pleased with her new enterprise, she headed for the kitchen table and soon the saucepan of boiling sugar and water had her cheeks flushed with achievement. She was so engrossed in her efforts that she was not aware of the disturbance as six horses and their riders clattered across the Louisa Creek bridge and pulled up outside the Hargraves Arms.

    Dave had swung the doors open wide to admit the small amount of breeze that drifted through the village, and his two customers, the Brown brothers, eyed the newcomers over their glasses. The unshaven and shabbily dressed men dismounted and their boots clumped on the wooden floorboards. With much ribaldry, they entered the pub and their leader swaggered to the bar, demanding drinks. Dave Lee obliged, happy to have any extra patronage.

    "Passing through, mates?" he asked, filling the sixth glass with beer. "Heading for Hill End, I'll bet."

    "Yeah," said the leader, "but we're 'aving some fun on the way."

Dave's instincts flashed a warning, but he turned his attention to one of the brothers who ordered another drink. "When d'you reckon you can take something off your slate?" he asked the taller one, but grinned, knowing it would be a long time before these boys would have any spare cash. Cattle prices at the slaughter-sales had dropped badly and didn't look like recovering until the drought ended.'

The older Brown brother scooped the glasses off the bar and passed one to his junior. "As soon as ..."

"Yeah, I know," smiled Dave. "Soon as y'cows come home."

"Hey, did y'hear that lads?" shouted the leader of the noisy group. "He gives the beer away in 'ere. We shoulda come here before."

"No such luck," parried Dave. "These boys are local, whereas you ..."

He didn't finish his sentence because the man had leaned over the bar and grabbed him by his shirt, twisting it as he dragged Dave nearer to his face. The Brown brothers banged down their glasses and rose to assist Dave, but were quickly challenged by other members of the gang, two to a man. The sixth man, a puny runt who usually provided all the fun for the ugly men, stood by and giggled like a schoolgirl.

Without letting go of Dave, the burly leader raised the entry portion of the bar and dragged him even closer. "Don't like strangers, eh? You outback blokes think you're better'n us, eh?"

"Don't be bloody stupid ..." Dave managed.

"Oh, 'stupid' 'n all, are we?" The hammy fist drew back and slammed into Dave's face.

The enraged Brown brothers threw all caution to the wind and waded into their opponents, while their leader continued to taunt and thump Dave about the head and body. Their idiot colleague pranced out of the way of flying fists and shouted encouragement, as though this was the greatest thing that could have brightened his afternoon. The fight rattled out into the street and having beaten Dave senseless, the big man turned to wade in with his compatriots.

Laura had set out the toffee attractively on a tin tray, and was placing it in the shop window with a ticket that read; 'Home made toffee. ld piece.' She looked out in horror at the fracas, not recognising the brothers at first. Then she screamed softly, as a blood-spattered Dave staggered to the door of the pub. Her fear suddenly vanished, and was replaced with an anger that would have terrified Aunt Marchant, if she'd witnessed it.

Laura looked wildly around the shop, and chose a miner's pick as her weapon, then unlocked the door and ran towards the fighting men.

"No, Laura ..." said Davey weakly, but there was too much noise and confusion for his words to reach her.

"Stop that, stop that, do you hear me?" She brandished the pick over her head like an executioner's axe, and the unexpected sound of an English woman's voice cut through the combatants' brains. The scuffling men separated breathing heavily, the two brothers bloodied and dazed looked at Laura in amazement.

"Well, I'll be damned," leered the big man. "It's a bloody sheila. And a pretty one, too ..." He lurched forward but stopped when Laura waved the pick at him.

He grinned. "Y'know what's we does with Pommy Cats?"

Terror put a voice back in Dave's throat. "Run, Laura. F'christ sake, run!"

The tremendous odds against her quivered her resolve and she spun on her heel, back to the shop. She had slammed the door behind her by the time the ugly brute reached the steps, but her fumbling fingers couldn't operate the lock. His weight pounded against the frail door like a ton of rock, and Laura screamed as his bulk filled the frame. The baby woke and began to cry which confused her attacker for a moment, but he ignored it and advanced on Laura, who had by now, retreated behind one of the counters, still brandishing the pick.

"Get out of here, or you'll wake my husband," she shouted. The man glanced towards the back room. "And he's got a gun," Laura added.

"Oh, has 'e, then." The tones were heavily sarcastic. "An' what's his name, then?"

Laura quaked, her fear increased by little Joseph's cries. "Joseph. Joseph Martin." She backed away and felt the wall trapping her.

"Joseph. ay, Jo ...seph!" the man taunted. "Are you in there, Joseph?"

Laura swung the pick high when he moved around the counter and she whimpered as it crashed through her print of England, showering her with shards of glass. With bravery born of terror, she tried to calculate his next move. 'Dear God, Joseph,' screamed through her mind. 'I wish you were in there.'

Two others of the gang appeared in the doorway, having left their mates to continue the fight with the Brown brothers, and Laura's knees buckled.

"She says Joseph's in there," the leader jeered, "with a gun." The other men hesitated. "But he's not, is he, darling? I got you all to myself."

"Leave some for us," said one man with an ugly laugh.

Laura's eyes flew to the man's crotch as he undid the buttons and released his reddened flesh. He took a step forward and she threw the pick at him with a force that he easily ducked, but which took one of the others by surprise when it hit his head, dropping him like a stone.

His mate, still very drunk, looked down in disgust, and booted him in the ribs. "Downed by a sheila, y'fart." He spotted the toffee in the window-tray, grabbed a handful and took off.

Meantime, Laura was screaming and struggling with her attacker, who had grabbed her and forced her to the floor at the doorway to the main room. She clawed at his face, but he grabbed both her hands in one hammy fist and forced her arms above her head, while the other tore at her skirt. and pulled at her petticoat and bloomers. Her screams became intense and the rough floorboards felt like iron as his weight bore down on her.

His sweat, beery breath, and the pain of his entry, made her vomit into his slavering mouth and she would have fainted, had it not been for the continuing and pitiful cries of the baby. The brute had thrust himself twice into her, when his head was jerked back. His mouth gaped open to release a terrible yowl as a pair of scissors was jabbed into his throat.

She trembled and sobbed uncontrollably, aware only that his ugliness was hauled away from her and there was a confusion of voices, as though she had been transported to bedlam. She could not control her sobbing and her head felt as though it was going to split open. A girl raised her to a sitting position gently, and wrapped a blanket around her bruised body. Laura could not stop sobbing, and buried her hot face into the blanket.

"Leave her to me, Uncle Davey, " she heard the girl say. "You blokes had better get this sod out of here and make sure the others don't get away. Dad's sent somebody back to Mudgee to get the police."

"Keep still, Dave," she heard a man say. "You've got a nasty lip, there."

"Never mind about me, Norm," Dave mumbled awkwardly. "See to Laura."

"Stubborn ol' ..." The man he'd called Norm turned away and as he bent over her, Laura was aware of a faintly antiseptic smell. Her self-control slowly returned and when she opened her eyes, she saw the man Norm, greatly resembled Dave. His hand, when he felt her brow, was cool not callused like Dave's and she instinctively tried to draw away from him. . "Try and relax," he murmured.

Laura nodded, but another cry from the bedroom tensed her. "Oh ...the baby …"

"It's all right," soothed the girl beside her. "I'll see to him."

Laura studied her rippled ash-blond hair and pert face, then relaxed when she went on, "I'm Kate Lee. Norman is my father, and he's a doctor."

"And my twin brother," added Davey. "Good thing they came to visit me this afternoon. Now, come on, Laura, you're coming over to my place for a while."

A great tiredness suddenly overcame Laura, and she covered her face with her hands. Doctor Norman Lee lifted her gently to her feet, adjusted the blanket around her shoulders, and propelled her towards the shop door. Laura looked back anxiously, but Kate was there crooning to the comforted baby, so she allowed herself to be led outside.

A group of villagers had gathered, and the women yelled abuse at her attacker.

"Hang the bugger!"

"No, that's too good for him. Split him in half!"

The men carried the attacker's dead body away. The scissors had severed his jugular vein and he'd quickly bled to death.

Once inside Davey's house, Laura was put to bed and told not to concern herself about the baby, as Kate would care for him.

7 KATE

Dave had allowed his brother to tend his wounds, and he was persuaded to lie on his sofa. Laura had been put in Dave's bedroom upstairs to rest, and Norm drew the curtains. "Just call out, if you need me, Laura " he said.

Laura nodded weakly, gradually becoming conscious of the bruising she had sustained, and she turned her head into the pillow, letting tears of anguish and relief flow. She was still shaking uncontrollably at the raw memory of her ordeal, and she felt so vulnerable and helpless.

A black abyss of panic took over – what was this horrifying life she'd let herself in for? Less than a year ago, she was an English virgin, looking forward to freedom, a happy life and family. This hot and frightening country would have been beyond her belief, if she'd known what was going to happen.

Even Aunt Marchant's taunting seemed easier to condone, even though her comment would have been, "Serves you right, m'girl. From High and Mighty, into Hell!" Laura could not stop her sobbing. Then the tablets that the doctor had administered started to take effect, and she slowly drifted into a semi-conscious state that relaxed her body, but did not stop her mind racing.

What foolishness to intervene, she scolded herself. What rashness to think fighting men would heed her. How Joseph would berate her for thoughtlessly leaving the shop and baby... Joseph! Oh, Joseph ... why hadn't you been there? We needed you ... your presence, your strength, your willpower ... oh, Joseph, I needed you so much.

Her despair brought further sobs, but her brain succumbed fully to the medication, and she fell asleep.

Kate peeped into the room a little later, and her face contorted at the sight of Laura's flushed and tear-stained face. Her fists clenched in anger at the vulnerability of her sex, and she closed the door softly.

It was several hours later and dark, when Laura roused with a small, startled cry. For long moments, she could not take in her surroundings. Then the afternoon's trauma returned, and she wept again, but quietly. After a gentle tap on the door, the doctor's young daughter came into tbe room. "Laura? Are you feeling better?"

Laura nodded and took a deep breath. "Th ...thank you, yes. Kate, isn't it?" She sat up quickly, and her eyes widened. "My baby ...?"

Her baby? Yes, of course he is now, she thought fiercely. He's every bit mine, part of my life, part of my world ... part of the man I love.

The realisation took only seconds to register in her mind, and she felt a surge of new strength that put her feet on the floor. She started searching for her shoes, then became aware of her torn clothes.

"He's fine," said Kate, handing her the shoes she'd put beneath the bed. "A bonza kid. He's been bathed, fed and changed, and is now entertaining Dad and Uncle Davey."

Laura's relief was obvious, and Kate noted her hesitation. She went to a cupboard and withdrew a skirt and blouse. "Here, put these on. They belonged to my aunty when she was alive and Uncle Davey refused to let them go."

Laura smiled for the first time, and said, "You call him Uncle Davey?."

"Have done, ever since I was a kid."

Laura's eyes suddenly clouded. "What happened, Kate?"

The girl's eyes rounded. "Y'mean, you don't remember?"

"Of course," said Laura petulantly. "But who rescued me, and how ...?"

"Me and Dad rode into the village just as some men were tackling the gang. Apparently the kids down at the Creek had heard the row, run to fetch their Dads, and Uncle Davey was staggering towards your shop by that time. He saw us coming, waved us ahead and Dad rushed in to find ... well, you know."

Laura dressed as she listened, and reached for the small blanket that had been around her shoulders. She wrapped herself in it and rose to her feet, smoothing her skirt and hair as if trying to brush away the memory.

"I saw Dad yank that bugger's head back as Uncle Davey and some others came in behind me, and someone grabbed a pair of scissors off the counter and stuck them into the bastard's throat."

Shock blanched Laura's face as she asked, "Who? Is the man dead?"

"Oh, he's dead, all right. Bled like the pig he was. Come on, don't bother your head with it," said Kate, putting her arm around Laura's shoulders. "They've got a nice fire going in the front room downstairs. I'm sure you could do with something to eat and drink."

"I don't think I could eat anything, thank you," Laura began, but Kate guided her firmly to the head of the stairs.

Norm and Dave looked up and greeted her warmly. She still felt strange and violated, and was glad to be led to a comfortable armchair beside the fire. Before she sat however, she looked anxiously into the cradle beside Dave. Joseph Junior looked back at her, and a huge, toothless grin lightened his pink face. Her heart full, Laura sat back and sighed deeply.

Norman Lee patted her arm and handed her a small glass."Drink this. It will soothe your nerves."

"I reckon you should send for that Joseph Martin," said Dave through swollen lips. "His place is with you and this little lad. Where is he, do you know?"

Laura shook her head, and nodded her thanks to the Doctor. "Perhaps I could ask you to enquire at the Land Agent's office in Mudgee when you return, Doctor Lee? If he doesn't know exactly, he will probably be able to send a message somewhere."

"Certainly. I'm going to leave Kate with you tonight, Dave. She can keep an eye on you both, as well as help with the baby." He got up and prepared to leave. "I'll come back out to Hargraves on Monday, after surgery. But I've no doubt I'll have to go to the Police Officer first, and help him make out a report on the dead man."

"He is dead, then," said Laura quietly. "Who actually ...?"

The three relatives glanced at each other, then Kate said, "We'll never really be certain, will we? There was such a cafuffle ..."

"Can Laura stay overnight with you,too, Dave?" interrupted the doctor. "I don't think she should be on her own over there."

After final arrangements were made and once more alone in the bedroom, in the quiet and dark, the terror and disgust about her rape returned to Laura's mind, made worse by the cruel tricks of night time imaginations. What if she hadn't been rescued? Would the vile man have killed her? Would he have killed the baby? Would Joseph have returned to a scene of violent devastation? Her breathing was ragged and she tossed in a frenzy of dismay, until the image of Joseph gradually filled her mind with a longing she no longer wanted to deny.

Once or twice she started to compose answers to the expected questions; later she wrestled with whether she was brave enough to reveal her feelings for him, and what would be his response.

Her mind in turmoil, recalled the incident outside the Sailor's Home in Sydney, on their way to Hargraves. Would he accuse her of encouraging the attack? The prospect brought tears to her eyes, and again she wept quietly into the pillow. Exhaustion brought oblivion, and she fell asleep.

She was woken early next morning by Kate, who carried a tray decorated with a strikingly yellow hibiscus flower. Kate laid the hearty breakfast across Laura's knees, and wooden rings rattled as she pulled the curtains aside. She smiled at Laura. "Before you ask, the baby has been cared for, and is sleeping in his crib out in the garden."

"Kate, I can't thank you and your uncle enough. Where would we have been without you?"

"We don't need thanks," said Kate brightly. "I was getting under Dad's feet anyway - that's why we'd come out to see Uncle Davey yesterday." Laura sipped the warm tea and nibbled toast while Kate continued. "Uncle Davey is going to let me live here with him, and I will help him with the Hargraves pub."

Laura frowned. "But Kate, what if something horrible like that happens again? You may not be so lucky."

"Lightning never strikes twice in the same spot," Kate replied flippantly. "Besides, Uncle Davey swears he won't be so naive again, and I think those Brown boys said they would always have a shotgun with them, in future." Laura looked unconvinced. "Besides, I can fill in extra time helping you with little Joseph, and in the shop. You could take an afternoon off and go with Uncle Davey into town, perhaps?" She added the last idea as though it had just come to her, and would be the clincher for her argument.

Laura needed little convincing then. She realised how lonely she'd been and suddenly, the future looked more inviting. Joseph would surely not object to Kate's help, if she assured him the safety of his son and that his enterprise would be increased with an extra hand.

"I ... we couldn't pay you anything ..." she began, and Kate laughed loudly.

"Just as long as you don't get me talking with that funny accent of yours, I'll be happy."

Laura blushed, and ate her breakfast.

Kate tended the shop on the Monday; it took a lot of hard scrubbing to fade the blood stains - when the boards were dry, she covered the remaining marks with a sack, righted goods that had become strewn around the floor, and removed the tray of plundered toffee from the window. By closing time, the Hargraves Store was shipshape again and Laura was pleased that several of the village wives had wandered in, bought items, and asked about her well-being. The sales made her fastidious book entries quite impressive.

At four o'clock Laura made afternoon tea, her friendship with Kate blossoming, when the young girl noticed the initialled sugar tongs being used. "Well, that's rotten posh if y'don't mind," Kate teased. "For all the gold that was here, I bet no-one was posh enough to have silver tongs in Hargraves."

"They're very special to me," Laura said softly. "They belonged to my mother." While they enjoyed the hot brew and little scones Laura had made, she told Kate all about growing up in Tolton, with countryside very much like the damaged picture. Her face saddened again as she looked at the torn print which she'd extracted from the broken frame, and memories seared through her.

Kate sensed her distress, and said quickly, "I'm sure Uncle Davey has spare picture frames. I'll take it home with me and he'll fix it."

Laura bravely shook off her sadness, and rose to clear away the teacups. "Thank you, Kate. We'll be all right now. You'd better go and make sure your uncle is comfortable and fed - he looks very bruised still."

"He's a tough old coot," said Kate. "But if you're sure, I know he'd like a bit of company this evening."

Laura smiled, willing herself forward from her terrible experience, and waved to her new friend as she turned at her uncle's front door. Nevertheless, the loneliness of the coming hours returned a weight to her heart, softened only by the familiar whimper for attention, that came from the back room. She was about to close and lock the shop, when a flurry of movement caught her eye.

Her hand stifled the gasp of pleasure that escaped, as she recognised the figure riding in frantic haste across the Louisa Creek bridge. The jingle of timbers and supporting links was a fanfare in her ears. Not knowing quite what to do, she stood her ground at the top of the steps and waited for Joseph Martin to dismount outside the shop. He secured his horse, strode up the steps, grasped her by the shoulders and glared into her eyes. "Laura - you are all right?"

With the suddenness of his appearance, Laura's tentative control dissolved and her face crumpled. "Oh, Jo ... Mister Martin ... Joseph!" she wailed. His arms enveloped her and she leaned heavily against him, as he led her inside and closed the door. He said nothing, but held her firmly whilst her heart-broken sobs erupted against his chest. Laura didn't care if he was about to berate her, she was not concerned with the piercing questions he was going to ask - she was aware only of his nearness, like a great impenetrable barrier between her and recent events.

When her immediate tumult died down, he guided her gently into the back room and sat her down in one of the fireside armchairs. He glanced at his son who had drifted back to sleep, then sat on the edge of the opposite chair, leaned forward and enclosed Laura's trembling hands with his own.

Within a short time, they had revealed deeply controlled feelings towards each other; there were no recriminations from Joseph, there were no accusations of neglect from Laura. Instead, there were many hours of revelation, and declaration. Layers of pride and reserve stripped away, and left only complete dependence, and commitment.

They sat by the comforting fire, hands still clasped. They spoke softly and urgently. Once Joseph stroked Laura's cheek as though trying to brush away her trauma, and they sat closely, drawing on each other's reserves and resiliency. Joseph didn't kiss her, he knew instinctively any physical advance would be repugnant to her at this moment, and Laura knew he had no intention of invading her trembling privacy.

"My God, if I had imagined for one moment ..." Joseph said for the third time.

"Hush," said Laura, firmly now. "It is enough that it happened, and more than enough that you returned as soon as you could."

"I was in Bathurst," he explained yet again. "I ... dear Laura, can you ever forgive me for ..."

"Can we forget it?" said Laura.

"I am not naive enough to believe you can wipe such an ugly thing from your mind like a chalkboard, but my course is clear. Laura, I shall remain in Hargraves with you and my son, from now on. I have achieved much in land purchase in the district, as well as Bathurst. My place now, is here with you."

Laura's heart swelled, and she made no attempt to free her hands from his. She began nervously, "I think ... Joseph, that is the most heart-warming statement I have ever heard from you."

His eyebrows drew together, and for a moment Laura was afraid that she had been too outspoken again, but her doubt was replaced by amazement when he spoke.

"A man would be a fool to brush aside his own common-sense. We have revealed our fondness for each other, Laura, and my duty prompts me to request that you become my wife and a mother to my son."

Laura was startled, then confused, then blindingly clear in her soft reply. "Thank you, Joseph, but no."

His initial silence, and the pained look in his eyes spoke volumes, until he said quietly, "I see."

"No, you don't, dear Joseph," said Laura as she knelt at his feet. "I have confessed my love for you, but your offer at such a time will only seem like pity to others."

"Damn others!" Joseph's outburst made Laura flinch, but she was not dismayed.

"I also must know in my heart that your offer of marriage is not made out of pity. I shall continue to be a mother to your son - indeed, I love him as my own now. And I'm sure Jemima would be happy in that knowledge. But you, my dear, dear, Joseph, must never feel trapped and I want to be sure this will not happen, before I become your wife."

Deep inside, Laura knew that what she'd referred to as his 'offer of marriage' was actually a 'request' that she become his wife, but she loved him too much to raise the point in argument. She didn't want to, suffice that he had declared his feelings for her - although at no time had he used the word 'love', as though this was an unmanly attitude, or a sign of weakness.

Joseph regained his speech. "Very well, Laura. My intentions were honourable, but I understand your reluctance. May I ask, however, that you reconsider my proposal, say in three months from now?"

Laura laid her head on his knees and they stayed that way for a long time. Then she said, "I think we should get some sleep, now." Joseph raised her face in his hands, looked at her quizzically, and nodded.

During the following two months, the success of the Hargraves Store increased. Customers from surrounding properties came to trust in Joseph's wisdom when it came to business ventures; farmers paid him rent to graze their cattle on some of the blocks he had acquired, in order to spell their own land. He purchased timber, and hired men to build sheds on other blocks, then rented them to weekend gold fossikers. In partnership with Dave Lee, he instigated a twice weekly wagon-run into Mudgee, that way supplying the store with fresher goods, and current newspapers and periodicals.

The villagers still recognised Laura as 'Little Joseph's Nanny', especially as Joseph Senior only ever called her 'Miss Marchant' whenever there was someone within hearing. He travelled from the shop several times, but the longest trip was an overnight stay in Mudgee, when a sudden December heatwave had exhausted the horses.

"I was worried," said Laura when he arrived at Hargraves next morning. Laura had held the shop door ajar when he came in, carrying an armful of supplies. He unloaded them onto the counter, then drew her inside the back room. "Laura, my dear, may I kiss you?"

Although he had briefly embraced her often since their declaration to each other back in November, he had retained a rigid decorum and respect for Laura's reticence for any closer physical contact. So engrossed had he been with his endeavours, earnest conversations with local farmers, long hours spent adjusting and re-adjusting shop displays, that he had failed to notice Laura's reserve being replaced with a longing that flushed her face, and brought a light to her eyes. Those eyes now shone in anticipation as she lifted her face.

He kissed her almost reverently, then held her hands. "Laura, it is Christmas next week - although one would hardly think so, in this insane heat. The boy is almost four months old now, and noticing everything. I should like us to have a traditional celebration with whatever means we can employ. What do you think?"

"I'd love that," said Laura. "I could make some trimmings from paper, and you could cut down a small tree, and …"

"Laura you are so beautiful, especially when you are excited ... you will always be a lovely English Rose." Laura moved back into his arms.

Christmas Day shone brilliantly; Dave supplied a large leg of young beef given to him in token payment by the Brown brothers, although he had protested their slate was clean after their support during the attack by the obnoxious men..

Laura cooked it carefully, and prepared other traditional English delights, such as plum pudding and mince pies, and they all gathered in Dave Lee's comfortable dining room to enjoy the meal. Dave left all the doors and windows open wide as every little breeze was needed to combat the heat of the midday sun. The food was also hot, and they all perspired from lusty renditions of Christmas Carols' Spirits were high, and liquid refreshment plentiful. Kate - who had shared her time between helping her uncle in Hargraves Arms and caring for Joseph Junior, her father, Norman Lee, Joseph and Laura, formed a merry party, but it was the pert eighteen year-old, Kate, who raised the loudest cry of approval. She had overheard a slip in his decorum, when Joseph had murmured, "Merry Christmas, Laura, my dear."

"Strewth! Why don't you two get married?" she'd cried.

"Kate" remonstrated her father and uncle in unison.

"Maybe we will," Joseph replied warmly, relaxed by the evening's conviviality.

Everyone turned to Laura, who passed her hand over the pretty coif in her hair, that Kate had wreathed for her earlier. She rose to clear the table and murmured, "Maybe."

Joseph glowed visibly, but the comment was not referred to until they had wished everybody happiness for the season, and returned to the shop. Laura set the baby's cradle in its usual position near the bed, then turned to see that Joseph was standing quietly by, with the vulnerable expression on his face that she'd seen only once before and that was when he'd returned to find that Jemima had died.

But this time, his eyes were soft and wondering, and she felt her heart melt as she moved into his embrace. Their kiss was tentative, and as their passion soared, she learned that a man's desires could indeed become her own, and she trembled at the awareness.

"Stay with me, Joseph," she whispered.

Joseph reacted with the physical ardour of a man who had made a supreme effort of celibacy, since his return to Hargraves. Laura's happiness was complete, and her shattered world was repaired.

The final week of the year drew to a close, with Joseph trying to persuade Laura to marry him. He tried using the fact that New Year's Eve was an incomparable time for them to begin a new life together. "I can imagine no other woman more desirable to become my wife. We could be married quietly in the village church - Norman and Dave Lee would be willing witnesses, I'm sure ... and young Kate would be a charming bridesmaid for you, and ..."

"Tush, Joseph," chided Laura. "You speak as though you have already organised this marriage with them."

"I'll admit I spoke with the Minister in Mudgee," he confessed. "He willingly agreed to perform the ceremony during his visit to Hargraves, at the end of January."

"You did what!" Laura held back her sharpness because she was nursing the baby, but the flecks in her eyes glittered slightly. Was he once more becoming the Joseph Martin she first met? Had her burgeoning love for the man blinded her to their lifestyle together, once she committed herself? The thought that had niggled in the back of her mind since the night they had revealed their feelings for each other, now thrust itself to the forefront, and she looked away. At no time had he professed to love her - his entire approach had centred around his desires. Her head toss was almost unnoticeable - weren't his desires her own now, too? The confusion moistened her eyes.

A small cough from the baby drew their attention immediately and Laura sat him up on her shoulder. "He has a touch of wind, I believe."

Joseph grunted, his knowledge hardly extending to the vagaries of infants. Kate came into the doorway at that moment, and called out into the empty shop. "Laura? Shop! Anyone home?"

"Come on in, Kate," Laura called back.

"I might go over and have a talk with Davey," said Joseph, a little put out that their discussion had been brought to a halt. "But please think about this Laura."

He nodded to Kate as they passed at the entrance to the back room of the shop, and Laura's troubled face as she kept her eyes on the baby, prompted Kate's question, "Something wrong?"

"I don't know, and yet ..."

"Have you two argued?"

"No, it's not that. The baby seems to have a fever, and he's been coughing a bit today."

"My father is coming tomorrow morning to spend New Year's Eve with us - let him have a look at him then."

Laura nodded, stroking the baby's hot forehead as he moved fretfully in her arms. The role thrust upon her had drawn heavily on her maternal instincts, rather than knowledge. She had helped the mother of her fellow steerage family once or twice, when one of the infants had been unwell during the voyage from England. She clearly remembered that all ailments seemed to worsen, during the small hours of the morning. "Let's hope he will be early."

Next morning, after a sleepless night for all at the Hargraves Store, Norman Lee bent to examine the baby, who was whimpering and fighting for each breath. Laura and Joseph looked on anxiously, as Doctor Lee straightened and shook his head. "I fear he has a severe chest infection, Laura. I will give you a note to take into Mudgee Pharmacy straight away, Joseph."

Joseph made immediate preparations to leave, while Laura replaced the baby's clothes and cuddled him in the shawl old Billy King's housekeeper had made so lovingly for Jemima, just four months ago. She asked nervously, "He will be all right?"

"His little lungs are very noisy," said Norman Lee. "We must reduce that fever as soon as we can, and you must keep a constant watch on him. Every hour, I want you to lay him face down on your lap and rub or pat his back gently. He may vomit phlegm, but this will help. Whatever you do, you must watch that he does not choke on rising mucus."

"He'll not leave my arms," said Laura vehemently. "I'll not close my eyes until he is out of danger."

"I'll help," said Kate quickly. "You must rest at times and keep up your own strength. You've had a trying time, too, and there is a limit to everything."

Laura smiled weakly at such a young woman's wisdom but murmured her thanks, knowing she wouldn't take her eyes from this precious baby for an instant. She owed it to Jemima, to Joseph, and to herself, because of her love for the Martin family. Incorrigibly, she thought of Aunt Marchant.

Less than a year ago, she had pitied herself under the dominant rule of her father's sister; considered herself put upon by constant demands and bickering of the old lady, and longed to get away to an existence where opportunity and possible good fortune beckoned. With the entry of Joseph Martin into her life, her world had exploded with change.

And what of Aunt Marchant? She had believed herself unable to ever be concerned with her only relative again, and here she was, in a God-forsaken village in the middle of nowhere, fighting commitment to a man she could not deny loving, and nursing another woman's child as her own. When this emergency was over, she promised herself she would write to Aunt Marchant. There would probably be no reply, but her conscience would be eased

The baby was gravely ill for three days, passing through a crises early on the fourth morning, and rewarding his father and Laura with a smile of recognition, by midday. Kate had been invaluable. She and Laura took it in turns to carry out Norman Lee's instructions, while Joseph tended the shop. Neighbours and people from outlying properties had kept up a constant stream of helpful offers, some even producing meals, in pots they placed shyly on the counter 'to keep y'going'.

Joseph made no attempt to take part in the baby's care, preferring to attend to business. He left this to Laura, as if he feared that he would do more harm than good. On the fourth evening, when Laura had laid the baby in his crib for the first time, Joseph led her to one of the fireside chairs, and sat opposite her. The midsummer heat hardly abated after dark now, and their English clothing stifled them. He no longer insisted on wearing his coat during the day and at night, they lay atop the bedclothes together; tradition, and reserve relegated to a relic of their previous lives.

"I cannot thank you enough for the care you have given my son," Joseph said quietly.

"Love needs no thanks," Laura replied. "And Jemima trusted in me."

Joseph lay silent for long moments, an inner struggle clouding his eyes. Laura sensed this but was too exhausted for a deep discussion, and feared that Joseph would renew his entreaty for her to marry him. Instead, she asked him for a cool drink and they passed the evening with short innocuous comments. Too hot to talk much, they listened to the incessant chime of cicadas, using their short life span with an urgency that grew to fever pitch, as the night wore on.

The following morning, Joseph announced that he would be going to Bathurst for a week on business. Laura felt her heart wither, as if an English snowstorm had descended without warning, and the joy that had been unfolding for almost three months had dissolved beneath its weight. She remained tight-lipped, as he packed the leather bag that had stood empty and unused in the corner for so long, and turned her face when he bent to kiss her before he left. Kate crossed the road as Laura stood at the shop doorway, and watched him ride over the Louisa Creek bridge and out of the village.

"Is he going to town?" she asked, jerking her thumb in his direction.

"Yes," answered Laura, re-entering the shop. "Kate, may I ask you to attend the counters while I write a letter?"

"Of course," said Kate, a little surprised at her friend's abrupt manner. "How is the little one, this morning?"

"Much better, thank you. I will not take long."

Laura left the girl full of curiosity, but closed the inner door behind her, checked to see the baby was still sleeping, then sat at the table to write to Aunt Marchant. Her first attempt began as a litany of things that had gone wrong, but she tore that up, deciding she was not looking for sympathy. And Aunt Marchant would be the last person to turn to, if she was. It took three pages to describe the voyage, her experiences with the Martin family, Jemima's sad demise, and the latest trauma with the baby.

She preferred not to recall her own horrific episode, preferring only to praise the friendship of people they'd met, like Bel Carter in Ballarat, and Billy King, and the midwife, Miss Hills. She described the locality of Hargraves, and the many friends she'd made. Satisfied, she drew out an envelope and addressed it. She felt cleansed by her effort and had a strange clarity now, about her feelings and relationship with Joseph Martin.

"Uncle Davey is going to Mudgee today," said Kate when Laura re-entered the shop. "He'll post it for you."

Laura thanked her, gave her a coin to cover the postage and said in her best English manner, "We'll have a cup of tea now, shall we?"

8 BABY JOSEPH

Ten days later Dave Lee brought Laura a message that he had picked up from the Mudgee Land Agent. The note, in Joseph's large handwriting, said that he had arranged for the Minister to marry them at Hargraves Church on the first day of February, and that he doubted if business would let him return until then end of January. Laura's heart sank and her blood boiled in quick succession, and she found it difficult to smile at customers

She had not mentioned their plans to marry to anybody, and perhaps it was fortunate that she could not communicate with Joseph readily. His appeal that he needed her was rapidly wearing off. She glanced at the date she'd written neatly at the top of the page in the cash book. February was a little over two weeks hence, and she thought illogically, 'Maybe I won't be ready to marry that day!'

The baby peevishly brought up his milk, and while she cleaned him up, she muttered, "Seventeen days into the New Year, and your father has gone his merry way again. And I thought ..."

She laid the clean baby down and bundled the soiled clothing to soak in a bucket. "Tush, what a fool of a woman you've been, Laura Marchant. You fled one trap and landed in another."

The shop doorbell tinkled as Kate came in with her usual call. "Shop! You there, Laura?"

"In the washhouse," Laura replied curtly.

Kate went through the shop and saw that Laura's red hands were drubbing the fibres thin. She stood with her own hands thrust deep into her apron pockets. "What's up?"

"Nothing."

"Pity 'elp the washing when there is, then."

Laura looked up sharply, with a caustic reply hovering, but at the sight of Kate's cheeky grin she merely shrugged. "Nothing I can't deal with."

"Don't like being on your own now, do you? Can't say that I blame you. What would he do if you decided to leave, or go back to England, or something?"

"There's nothing to go back to," said Laura, wringing out the last little garment. Kate followed her out to the back yard where she hung the tiny clothes on the line strung between the back fence and the outhouse. "Besides, I couldn't leave little Joseph now."

"Nor the big one," said Kate shrewdly. "But you should have something of your own - he owes you that. Does he give you any money, any slave-money?"

Laura flushed. "That's not nice."

"Well," Kate drawled. "That's what you are, y'know. You look after his kid, his business, his comfort when he's here. "

"Kate!" Laura remonstrated, riling at the truth. "I hardly think it is any business of yours ..."

"I might be a lot younger than you," said Kate hotly, "but at least I gets treated with some respect. It just isn't fair - you deserve better than a pair of silver sugar tongs to call your own. He should be paying you regular wages, he should be ..."

"I think you've said enough, Kate," interrupted Laura, her face perspiring, not only from the summer sun. "I don't want us to quarrel. You're the best friend I have in Australia."

"Yes, and best friends have the right to speak plain; Even Uncle Davey says the load's too much on you, especially after you've had one nasty ..." She saw Laura's face cross with pain. "Sorry, I didn't mean to remind you ..."

Kate fell quiet, unable to find the words to express her thoughts. Laura's anger at Joseph's note had abated with their heated conversation, and she walked past Kate back into the living quarters. "Let's have a cup of tea," she said.

They talked more while they drank, and Kate pursued her concern, albeit with less brashness. "Really, Laura, have you thought about what's going to happen to you? I mean, you can't be the Nanny Housekeeper all your life, can you? And what happens if one of these days he brings home another wife - have you ever thought about that?"

The tell-tale alarm in Laura's eyes would have given everything away, but she studied her teaspoon and said, "No."

That evening, when the shop books had been carefully entered and checked against the cash drawer, and the baby had been settled, Laura took a kitchen chair and sat just outside the washhouse door. There was no breeze to stir the stifling heat. She'd brought a glass of lemonade with her, and sipping it, looked skyward at the brilliant stars. In the background, she could hear frogs croaking their delight down at the Creek, cicadas persisting as only they can and, being a Friday night, she could hear muffled voices coming cheerily from the pub. The Hargreaves Arms opened every evening except Sunday now, thanks to the business generated by the Hargraves shop. Gusts of laughter made her feel desperately alone and she didn't try to stem the tears that blurred the stars into swimming sparks of light.

She knew Kate would be helping Dave at the pub this evening, and wiping her hand across her face, began to dwell on their earlier conversation. Kate had been right - she had nothing virtually but the silver sugar tongs. Then she mentally chided herself, counting up the ten pounds she had left, the roof over her head, and the love of the baby. And his father's love?

An impulse streaked through her, with the fortitude that had caused the old Laura Marchant to answer the newspaper advertisement she'd seen in Daisy's stable. The takings in the shop were varying above six pounds most weeks - Christmas week they had reached ten pounds. The women had come in to buy odd pieces of linen to make presents, the men had treated themselves to extra tobacco. Even the children had spent valuable pennies to buy things like a pencil, or ruler for a sibling, or a novelty toy for the new baby. Clem White had bought a spade for his gardening, and the season prompted more happy gatherings needing extra tea for the caddies.

Laura decided that, in future, when the cash box had received six pounds, the first pound after that, would be hers. The audacity, even dishonesty of her plan, made her squirm. But Kate's words were true; she worked hard for nothing, and was entitled to a small share of the income. True Joseph allowed her to live on food that was stocked, she could never suffer hunger, and she wanted for nothing in the way of household goods. She had most things any woman could expect, apart from real security. If something dreadful happened to Joseph, she would be left destitute, with just her ten pounds savings, whatever was left in the cash box, and a baby to care for. No self-respecting woman would allow that to happen, surely?

She could hardly believe the thoughts that lodged themselves so firmly in her mind, especially when the following day, there were customers galore. By ten in the morning, she counted six pounds and ten shillings, then re-counted the money, to ensure it tallied with her book entries. It was easy to avoid entering the next four and five shillings worth of sales, then a shilling's worth of flour made up the pound she now had in her apron pocket... She put the money away in a small bag she'd made for this purpose, and hid it beneath the bed.

The day ended as usual with little Joseph's bath and playtime. He was already half asleep by the time she tucked him into his cot, then she made herself a meal of potatoes and bread, with beef soup. She took out her books, and decided to read her large dictionary. If she read Jane Austen or Anthony Trollope, she knew their characters would become living people in the room with her, such was the skill of the authors, and she could not bear the thought. She opened the dictionary at random, at the letter T. Immediately, the word *'theft'* leapt out at her. *An act of stealing; the unlawful taking of another person's goods or movables with an intent to deprive him of them; larceny.*

She gave a little cry and slammed the book with such vigour that she feared she may have disturbed the baby, but contented sleep is hard to disturb in one so young, and all she could hear was the sound of her own laboured breathing.

Three days later, all thoughts of her crime was swept away by the baby. He had not been able to keep his food down and he was fretful. Laura seemed to be continually washing little clothes, and she eventually had to fold ordinary bedsheets to fit into his cradle because his own bedding became offensive with the smell of his vomit. Then he developed a cough that rattled his chest deeply. His pitiful wail shredded her senses when his condition deteriorated into a fever. Norman Lee came as soon as he was notified by Dave, and without being asked, Kate operated the shop.

In agony, Laura watched over the tiny infant struggling for breath. As much as her respect for Joseph had degenerated since his departure, she yearned for him to make an appearance. She was near exhaustion; messages had been sent to the baby's father but there was no sign of his return. For six days and nights, she sponged and massaged the tiny body that gradually lost strength. She alternately sobbed, then cursed Joseph Martin for the heart less soul he was. She vowed that, should the baby live, she would make no bones about speaking her mind, and telling Mister Joseph Martin that neither she nor his son needed him, nor wanted him.

She said as much to Kate, and found an immediate ally. She could not bring herself to discuss the situation with Dave Lee, and didn't know that he heartily agreed when Kate repeated her words to him.

Norman Lee visited regularly. On the last but one day of January, he said, "Laura, I'm afraid he's fading fast. I doubt the mite will survive until the morning. I'll stay with you."

His words seemed to be as distant as the stars, and Laura choked back tears, fighting for self control. "I mustn't let it happen," she said weakly. "I must hold on to him. His father said he'd be here by now."

The doctor, Dave, and Kate hovered nearby while Laura sat in the fireside chair, nursing, crooning and wiping the baby's fevered brow with damp cloths. Little Joseph was too weak to cough any more and the rough growl in his chest as he tried to breathe filled the small room with a sound that tore at the hearts of those watching him lose his battle. His gasps for air grew lighter and more infrequent, until a small flutter told them his short life was done, and he had followed his mother.

Laura's anguished cry as she bent over the tiny form, stilled her own lungs. She could not draw breath for moments, and when she did, her sobs surrounded her words as though she alone was responsible for his death. "Oh, Jemima, I've failed you. Oh, dear Jemima ...I am so sorry. So sorry ... so sorry ..."

The vacuum of death descended That such a tiny being could create so much of a void, amazed those seeking to ease Laura's suffering. But grief rested on her shoulders with more weight than the shale hills that surrounded Hargraves. She could not accept her loss, and the following morning brought renewed agonies when she automatically looked across to the empty crib.

There was no longer a yearning for Joseph's presence, in truth she would have been content never to see him again. She gave no thought to his own anguish when he learned about the tragedy, and had no desire to even send him the news. Grief incensed her so greatly that she spurned Davey's offer to try and contact the baby's father through the Land Agent.

"Something must have happened to him. We could try through the Police ..."

"No, Dave!" Laura almost screamed. "He would have been here long ago, if he really cared."

The baby's funeral was arranged for the first day of February - the day she should have been married to his father. Kate, who was used to brighter clothing, sat uncomfortably at Laura's table in her black blouse and skirt, studying her black shoes and stockinged legs. She had gathered a small posy of daisies from her uncle's garden, and they lay atop the tiny white wood coffin besides other floral tributes, as it rested on the kitchen table.. The oppressive sadness of the day was made worse by the Summer heat, and Laura's frightening silence.

Kate's father had made arrangements with the Minister in Mudgee to perform the burial, at the little cemetery behind Hargraves Church. When the sombre Minister arrived at noon, he shook Laura's hand. "I understood from Mister Martin that I'd be required to perform a marriage ceremony today, not a funeral."

Laura drew herself erect, her black mourning dress and pale cheeks adding to the illusion of an implacable statue. "Mister Martin is not here," she said icily. "And you may dispense with his instructions for a wedding."

Kate's startled expression at this conversation, and her impulse to question Laura, was interrupted by the arrival of the school-teacher, Clem White. Together with Dave Lee and his brother, Norm, they prepared to carry the little coffin to the church for burial. .

Less than a year had elapsed since Laura's arrival in Australia and already, at the age of twenty-two, she felt an old woman. The coffin was very light; Norm Lee and Clem White carried it in turns and Dave offered his arm to Laura. She leaned heavily on him while they followed the Minister. At the Church, they passed through the rusted iron gate that hung awkwardly over a cattle grid, installed for the sanctity and respect of the dead. They stepped carefully through the crackle-dry grasses and weeds along an almost indistinguishable path. Cicadas did not halt their hypnotic chirp, and provided a bizarre chorus behind the Minister's mumbled blessing. Before the coffin was lowered into the tiny grave in the

Church's shadow by Norman Lee, Clem White stepped across and placed his hand under Laura's elbow for extra support

'I haven't even a picture of my baby,' thought Laura, and her shoulders shook with emotion.

The Hargraves Store remained closed for seven days, during which time Laura slept fitfully, woke too easily, and lived aimlessly. The City of Bathurst, Joseph Martin Senior, her own comfortable and loved England ... even Aunt Marchant, seemed a million miles away.

At Kate's request, Dave Lee took the empty cradle over to his house, "Don't destroy it," she said firmly. She quietly removed reminders of the baby's presence from the main room and carefully put aside the little clothes that Laura had made so lovingly. Her tact was was lost on the distraught Laura, who wasted visibly to a shadow.

No longer was she the vibrant Nanny who's life had evolved around her charge. The void seemed to engulf her in darkness, as though she'd been thrust into a pit without the drive or urgency to climb out of it. She could only think of the past year as one of loss; she'd given away the life she knew, lost her independence, lost her friendship with Jemima, lost baby Joseph ... lost her direction. She didn't consider that she'd lost Joseph Martin, she'd thrust him away, his unaccountable absence at this crucial time, was unforgivable.

Doctor Lee kept a constant watch on her, ostensibly visiting his daughter and brother frequently, but his purpose was to ensure that Laura's tremendous weight of tragedy did not become destructive. His task was not easy - her spirit was bruised from a continuous battering, and her usual resilience submerged.

She wept often and long, and Norman Lee was startled at his daughter's mature observation that, in all her distress, Laura never once called out for, or referred to Joseph Martin.

"It isn't natural, Dad," said Kate, her hair bouncing with vehemence. "Anyone could see those two had a lot between them - look at last Christmas."

Her father and uncle nodded in agreement. Laura had not resisted the decision that she should stay over at Dave Lee's house, so that the doctor could help more readily. The Lee's were finishing their evening meal and discussing their tragic guest who lay upstairs, grief and lack of interest taking their toll on her attractiveness. She had been bullied into a few spoonfuls of soup by Kate, but her weight was dropping at a rate that alarmed the doctor.

Davey Lee wiped his chin and pushed his chair away from the table. "Well, this can't go on, I'll leave in the morning and ride to Mudgee, then get the coach to Bathurst. I'm going to catch up with that 'gentleman' as he has the hide to call himself, and let him know what a bastard he is."

"You're not well enough, Uncle Davey," protested Kate.

"Let me try to locate him through the police," suggested Norman Lee

"No way," Dave replied. "They'd take too long and ..."

"Well, I'm coming too," argued Kate.

"And leave Laura alone?" her father countered. "No, she needs you more, Kate."

"And she could well need you, Norm," Dave pointed out. "I'm going, and that's final!"

The next morning, Kate coaxed Laura to come downstairs. She would only eat a small piece of bread and jam, but the younger girl persevered, and eventually they sat one each side of the unlit fireplace, sipping a cup of tea. Norman Lee came into the room and took his leave, saying he had to get back to surgery in Mudgee, but that he would return the following day. After a small silence when he'd left, Laura said quietly, "I haven't seen Dave this morning."

Kate shifted uncomfortably. "He's gone to Bathurst."

Laura's reaction was swift and startled. "No! He mustn't ... I don't want him ..."

"He's got to be told, Laura," said Kate, laying her hand on Laura's arm. "The baby was his son."

"He doesn't deserve ..."

"I know, Laura. But what else can you do?"

"Pack my belongings and get straight away from here, " said Laura, her cheeks flushed. "I never want to lay eyes on The Gentleman Mister Martin again, and the quicker I get away from Hargraves, the better."

"Laura," reasoned Kate. "You're not well enough to make such decisions yet, and Uncle Davey thinks he's doing the right thing by you." She didn't add that her uncle had not gone with friendship in mind, nor that Mister Joseph Martin was due for a tongue lashing in the finest Australian manner.

"Nevertheless," said Laura firmly, rising from the table. "I'm going to leave Hargraves. Would you like to help me sort the perishable foods in the shop? Or you can manage the shop. If you want to- I don't care"

Kate hesitated, unsure of what she should do, then dabbed her mouth and rose. "I'll clear the breakfast table first, then I'll come over."

This seemed to mollify Laura. She smoothed her hair and apron and crossed the road, with a cold lump blocking her throat. Monday morning; the shop should be freshly scrubbed, tempting toffee and home-made bread in the window, ready for the village women when they came in to catch up with the weekend gossip. Instead, it seemed a cold, hollow cave, walls lined with heartless stock and dampened with her tears.

She entered, then turned sharply at the footsteps behind her. The sun streaming through the doorway blinded her momentarily, and she squinted.

"Good morning, Laura," said a familiar voice kindly. "How are you today?"

"Clem- Clem White," she stammered.

"Thought I'd duck in ... Look, I'm going to Hill End for a drive this morning, and wondered if you would like to come with me?" The teacher glanced around. "Get you out of here for a while."

"But ... of course, school holidays are still on, aren't they? I seem to have lost track." Laura shook her head and attempted a smile. "Thank you, Clem, but I had other plans for today."

"Look," Clem persisted. "It's a beautiful day today, and it would do you a pile of good ..." He looked behind as another figure approached. "You'd mind the shop, wouldn't you, Kate? We've got to try and bring those English roses back into Laura's cheeks."

"Of course," said Kate readily, delighted that Laura would start to heal. "What's the plan?"

"I'm trying to persuade Laura to come to Hill End with me. I want to do a bit of research on local gold fields for lessons next term, and..."

"Good idea," said Kate eagerly. "You could help Clem, Laura, and you've often said you'd like to see Hill End one day."

Their persuasion wore at Laura's reserve until, having established that they would return before dark, she agreed to go with the teacher. She had forgotten that Hill End was some twenty-five miles over tracks that didn't deserve to be called roads. Kate didn't remind her, knowing that Clem White would take no risks, and that accommodation was plentiful in the vibrant gold-town. What she did say was, "Don't forget to wear a hat."

Laura didn't own a brimmed hat and she had disposed of Jemima's clothes, so before climbing aboard Clem's dray, she borrowed a bush hat from the stock. She jammed it onto her head firmly, and tightened the ties under her chin, much to the delight of her Australian friends, who recognised a spark of the Laura they knew. Her love of horses brought back the roses in her cheeks as they drove over the sometimes steep and treacherous tracks, and as the recent tragedy was overtaken by new experiences and new scenery, she began to relax. Clem was an interesting companion. His knowledge of native flora and fauna provided a continuous conversation between them, and by the time they arrived at Hill End, she was eagerly taking in the sights around her.

The place was rough and dirty, with little in the way of refinement. The main street was made up of dilapidated shops and Government centres; unkempt men leaned on railings outside the many pubs, and women either stood in groups talking, lugged weighty shopping, or yelled at boisterous children.

"We'll get a couple of forms from the Claims Office too, while we're here," said Clem, dismounting outside a shop front with 'Gold Assayer' painted on its window. "We'll go in here first. He's is bound to have some interesting things I can use."

"I had no idea gold-mining involved so much," Laura said an hour later as they left to walk across the street. Clem was gathering sample claim forms and Assayer's notes for his class. "It seems the big companies have taken over the industry - and I had thought of gold-miners as individuals who gave their all to scratch in the dirt."

"Mining for gold is certainly not what it used to be fifty years ago," said Clem, "but it is still a hard life, especially for the families. You won't see many silk and brocade-dressed women and children here where the rock is pounded, only back there in the cities where the stuff is bought and sold."

The Claims Office proved just as interesting to Laura, and she willingly jotted notes for Clem, when he asked for help. "Can I have one of those?" she asked, pointing to the Claim Forms.

"Going to stake y'own claim, young lady?" laughed the Clerk.

"I doubt there will be much chance of that," Laura said brightly, "but it will be a nice souvenir."

She felt a little embarrassed when Clem led the way into one of the pubs for something to eat and drink, but her discomfit was soon eased when she realised that no-one took particular notice of them. Hill End, like Ballarat, was quite used to visitors - all they really cared about was possible claim-jumpers. After lunch, they continued with their mission at the Customs House, and a much happier Laura was totally unaware of the time passing.

"We're closing now," called the Records Clerk. "You're welcome to come back tomorrow."

Laura realised with a start that the interesting day was coming to an end, and gathered the notes she'd been writing. "Good lord, we'll have to travel back on that awful road in the dark."

"I hardly think so," said Clem seriously. "Our lives would be in danger if we tried. I'm afraid we shall have to find somewhere here to stay overnight, then finish the work in the morning, and start back for Hargraves after lunch."

The fact that they had to stay, rather than dismaying Laura, brought back the sense of lightness and well-being that had departed when Joseph Martin left for Bathurst. Laura hadn't thought to bring money with her, and her embarrassment when Clem paid for two rooms at the same pub, brought another flush to her cheeks.

"Stop worrying about the money," Clem chided when she protested. "We'll enjoy a hearty dinner, and afterwards, as the evening is extremely warm, we'll walk awhile towards the edge of the township." He stopped suddenly. "That is, if you feel you are well enough."

What she had seen and learned during the day had given Laura a wonderful respite. "I am very grateful for your kindness, Clem."

During the ample meal of roast beef and vegetables, and tasty dessert of apple pie and custard, Laura and Clem conversed easily. They discussed the day's events and Laura even laughed aloud when Clem recalled the Record Clerk's remark.

"You never know," she quipped. "I might kick over a nugget in the garden and begin a new gold rush in Hargraves." Her intention to leave the village shortly, was forgotten in the relaxation of the moment.

Clem was only too willing to respond. "I'll be the first one to come and work on your claim for you."

They finished their meal and went for a walk. It was chilly, but a bright moon silvered the banksia bushes and eucalyptus trees and they spotted one or two possums dashing up the trunks. One had a baby possum clinging to her back and they stood still to watch her. Out of reach, the mother possum turned to gaze at the intruders and the baby clambered further up her back. "Aren't their eyes huge?" whispered Laura.

Clem put his hand under her elbow. "Come along, we can't have you catching cold. Time we turned back."

On the way back, they sat awhile on a paddock fence, when after a moment's comfortable silence, Clem asked, "Laura; what will you do now?"

The question saddened Laura instantly, and she fought to quell the tears that surged before she stammered, "I - I'm not really sure. I think I shall leave Hargraves."

"No, don't do that," said Clem quickly. "Will you come and help me at the school?" Laura hung her head, and thinking she was considering his suggestion, he said, "I'm sure Dave Lee would find accommodation for you."

"Thank you, Clem," whispered Laura, looking up. "But the thought of staying in Hargraves is far too painful. This afternoon has shown me that I must get on with my life - I didn't come to Australia to fail."

"But you'd be a great success at the school, don't you see? And maybe... in time ..."

Clem's fervour made his thoughts transparent, and Laura stood quickly. Men seemed expert at telling a woman how she would benefit, while they were really thinking of how a suggestion would benefit them. She turned away, chiding herself for being unfair to Clem who, ever since she'd known him, had been a gentleman. A real, open-hearted gentleman - not one who's mood fluctuated with the wind, nor one who assumed his words would prompt immediate obedience. Thoughts of Joseph Martin caused her to shiver despite the temperature, and Clem misread the sign.

"Oh dear, Laura, I am thoughtless. I have no right to talk to you like this, and so soon after ..." He stopped, crestfallen.

Laura turned to put him at his ease. "I think we shall go back, now. I am a little tired. And thank you- I will consider your suggestion." She smiled when his face lightened, and they returned to the pub, carefully avoiding the subject of her future.

Kate was standing at her uncle's gateway when they arrived back at Hargraves, late the following afternoon. She waved madly and hurried over to the shop steps as they approached and Clem helped Laura down. She noticed Laura seemed much more relaxed than when Clem drove them out of the village, but she didn't see the friendly smile the two travellers exchanged. "I'm glad you're back," said Kate warmly. "I got quite lonely."

"Is your uncle not back yet?" Laura asked.

"It's over a hundred miles to Bathurst!" said Kate, laughing. "Ol' Uncle Davey hasn't got wings like a magpie, y'know. He'll be gone for a few days, no doubt."

Laura blushed at her thoughtlessness, and said, "Well, I could do with a cup of tea. Will you join me, Clem?"

"Well, I'm off then," said Kate with a grin.

"No! You, too," said Laura, confused.

"Sure?" Kate's cheeky grin embarrassed Clem then, but she glossed over it by adding, "I'll put the kettle on, then."

Over the next few days, Laura often fell quiet, especially when she looked into the corner where baby Joseph's cradle had stood. She no longer slept in the large double bed she and Joseph Senior had occasionally shared - it made her too angry. The small bed that had been meant for her originally was still set up behind the counter, and while she lay there with only the stars or the moon to light the room, she would gaze around at the stock, and try to decide her best course of action. Several times she had planned to close the Hargraves Store, but every day a customer would come in and praise its convenience - besides, it was not hers to close. She would probably have to wait until Dave Lee returned.

She stirred early one morning, having lain awake for hours until she finally reached a decision. On Saturday, she would close the shop and pack her belongings.

She felt decidedly at ease by lunchtime - she had used the time between customers, to gather her belongings and set them out on the large bed inside. She had already packed the navy-blue serge travelling suit she wore when she'd left England, and the English countryside print that Dave had so lovingly re-framed for her. She neatly folded and piled underwear on the bed together with the prim white blouses, and the short sleeved one with a white lace collar she'd given to Jemima. The memory drew tears again. She folded her handkerchiefs, and once more wrapped the engraved silver sugar-tongs that meant so much to her, ready to be packed safely in the bottom of her travelling bag.

She would ask Davey to drive her into Mudgee, her plan being to stay there until she could get a coach into the nearest town that had a railway station. There she would take a train back to Sydney - beyond that, she wasn't clear what would eventuate.

She left her shoes until last; the pair she wore would suffice until Saturday. When she went to line up her other two pair, however, one shoe was missing. She tutted, started to look around for it, then left the task when the shop doorbell rang.

It was Clem White. "Good afternoon, Laura. I see you have fresh bread - could I have a loaf, please?"

"Of course," said Laura, taking one from the window display. "That's threepence, thank you."

Clem handed her the coins, then regarded her seriously as he tucked the loaf under his arm. "I don't suppose ... um, have you given any more thought to ..."

Laura smiled gently. "I'm leaving Hargraves on Saturday, Clem. Yours was a very kind offer, but I fear there is nothing that could persuade me to stay, now."

The shop door was open, and the small bell tinkled as Clem deliberately shut it, and turned back to her. "Am I correct in thinking you and Joseph Martin were to be married?"

His directness startled her. "Kate ...?"

"She did mention it," he admitted. "and that you now have no intention of marrying him. Has he been in contact with you?"

"No," said Laura flatly, trying not to admit to herself how much this hurt, especially when a virtual stranger spoke of it.

Clem moved to the counter and took her hand. "Laura, would you do me the honour of becoming my wife? I have admired your courage and fortitude over these past months, and can think of no one I would rather share my life with."

"Clem," she stammered. "You're so very kind, and you do me a great honour, but ..." There was a pause while she told herself what a fool she was being; here was a kind, honest man, who was offering her the life she had hoped for when she came to Australia, and she was about to turn him down. And why? Because the image of Joseph refused to blur, and because despite all that Joseph was, and all that he had done, she could not stop loving him. And there was room in her heart for only one love. That was why she had to leave Hargraves. She had no need to say more to Clem, he was too intelligent to mistake her hesitation. She had no doubts about her answer to his proposal, but the disappointment in his face made her quiver.

Impulsively, she went on, "Perhaps you would like to have tea with me on Friday?"

"Well ..."

"I intend to ask Kate and her father, and Dave Lee ... everyone's been so very kind to me, I feel I must say thank you to everybody in some way."

Clem nodded a sad agreement, and Laura watched him walk dejectedly, towards the school residence. It occurred to her that she owed a great deal to the friends she'd made in Hargraves, and incorrigibly she wept, thinking that they would surely care for Joseph's tiny grave. If ever his father returned, she doubted he would arrange for a headstone, most likely declaring it an expensive triviality with no specific purpose.

She went back into the bedroom where the large trunk took her eye and slowly she raised its lid. She extracted the telescope Joseph had declared was more important to his son's education than 'matching china', and again the tears flowed. This time, they were tears of anger. "Tush, woman," she said, replacing the scope. "Fill your mind with other things - where's that other shoe, for instance?"

She looked along the shelf where she normally kept shoes, then began searching in unexpected places. It wasn't sitting on top of her books - which reminded her, they must be packed into her trunk, as well. Neither was it hidden under the winter blankets that had been stored to one side of the bedroom. She found it underneath the bed - alongside the small cardboard box, in which lay the money she had taken from the shop's cash box. Her hands shook as she withdrew the shoe and box, and still kneeling, she looked at them both in her lap.

Somehow. they spoke of to her failure to stand even-footed and secure in this new country, and failure of the moral ethics she had been brought up with. Grief and recent trauma was still able to fluctuate her mood and sadness quickly reverted to anger as she got to her feet, stood the offending shoe by its partner and walked into the shop to place the money back in the cash box. She quickly counted money she had left in her coin purse- yes, there was just ten pounds.

She made another decision. Glancing the clock, she saw it was time to close the shop, then through the window she saw Norman Lee clambering down from his dray.

"I've heard from Dave," he said as he mounted the steps. "You'd better come and sit down."

"I'll make a cup of tea," Laura said defensively. It was the only way she knew to prepare herself for yet another disruption.

There was no indication that Dave had delivered his 'Australian mouthful' as Kate had referred to it, only a hesitancy from the doctor, as though he didn't quite know how to begin. Finally he blurted, "Laura, There's been an accident, and Joseph's been crushed."

Laura spun from hanging the kettle over the fire, the flecks in her eyes sparking and her smooth cheeks flushed. "Don't try and soften him to me, doctor. 'Crushed' indeed - I doubt if the news of his son's death did more than sadden him for a moment, and he's probably sent a string of orders with you, as to how I should be managing his shop for him, now that I have more time."

Norman Lee reeled at her outburst. She was panting slightly, determined not to cry again.

He shook his head. "No, Laura - I mean he has been crushed under a horse and carriage."

The impact of his words sank slowly, then Laura made a small sound and clapped her hand to her mouth. Her cheeks blanched. "My God ..."

"He's badly injured," the doctor went on, "and will be permanently lame."

"But how ...? I don't understand. Why didn't he let me know?" The questions tumbled from her lips while sensations of shock, dismay, and confusion merged. She felt a desperate need to close her eyes and shut away this new trauma. She sat down abruptly, and fished in her apron for a handkerchief. She blew her nose, as though she were trying to rattle some sort of order into her brain ."You'd better start from the beginning, doctor, and tell me everything."

She sat motionless while he relayed Dave's message. On arrival at Bathurst, Dave had gone to the Land Office and learned that Joseph's business was completed by 28th January, and as far as they were aware, he'd headed back to Hargraves. They told Dave that Joseph had also bought a property in Bathurst."

"Were is he now?" demanded Laura.

"It seems Dave went out to the property - a horse stud. One of the hands told him that Joseph had asked to saddle up a horse for him to ride. He'd been excited at his purchase of the stud, and tried to jump a paddock fence when the horse stumbled and rolled on top of him."

"My God ..." Laura said in a horrified whisper.

"The doctor they fetched remembered Joseph's name, and it seems was the man who attended to the first Mrs Martin, when she had the baby."

Laura wasn't listening any more, imagining Joseph's distress, and remembering Jemima's childbirth. She focussed back to Norman Lee only when he spoke again. "The kettle's boiling."

She rose automatically and poured the steaming liquid into the pot. "Please go on, doctor. Where is he ... Joseph, now?"
"He is recovering at Billy King's house, where you stayed, I understand? The doctor considered Joseph would be better there than in the hospital, as his recovery is going to be a protracted one."

Laura passed a cup of tea to him and sat with her own. "How badly...? I mean, how long will his injuries take to ...?"

"Months, I've no doubt. Davey says he will stay there until you arrive. The next coach is on Monday - I will drive you into Mudgee."

"Thank you," said Laura quietly. "I had intended to go on Saturday, anyway."

"Go? Go where?"

Laura realised the doctor would know nothing of her plans, and explained."I had planned to get to Sydney and ... oh, I don't know what I'd have done from there, or where I would have gone. Make something of my life, I sup- pose."

Norman Lee put his cup down sadly, and reached across the table for her hand. "Laura, you can't. You've been so brave up to now - not many women would have taken so much on the chin as you have, especially for a ..." He stopped, embarrassed.

Laura shook her head, but smiled briefly. "Oh, don't worry - I don't think I can go back to England now. I well and truly made my bed when I decided to come to Australia." A small frown returned. "I wonder how Joseph took the news about his son."

The doctor looked down at his cup, and twirled the spoon several times before he laid it on the table. Then he picked up his tea ,and looked evenly at her. "Dave hasn't told him, Laura. He said he didn't have the heart to lay such news on the man when he was so weak."

Laura was startled. "He doesn't know?"

"Joseph needs you, Laura, and I really think the news about his son would be far better coming from you. I'll admit I admired Dave when he left here, determined to show Joseph what a bastard we all thought he was. But circumstances have changed. Laura, you must go to him. Kate will mind the shop for you and I'll take care of anything else. You can't just up and go to Sydney now- it wouldn't be right."

Laura stared at him - was this another man challenging her to do what he considered to be correct, rather than taking her feelings and wishes into account? She brushed the thought aside, and sighed deeply. For long moments, she sat passing her hand over her forehead, then smoothed her apron as her chin tilted slightly and she looked back at the doctor. "Seems I have very little choice."

"I'll stay across the road tonight," the doctor said. "We'll come over in the morning."

When Norman Lee had gone, she looked at her belongings neatly stacked on the bed. where once she and Joseph had made such tender love. She sat on the big trunk at the end of the bed, and pulled her travel bag on to her lap. No sooner did she map out her life, than something unexpected would pull her through another avenue. Her way was always strewn with the unknown, she seemed to have little control over events, and frustration was her biggest burden. She thought of making a meal, but wasn't the slightest bit hungry. Her head felt heavy, so she eased her things aside and lay on top of the bed cover.

It was very dark when she woke, startled to realise that she had fallen asleep. She'd dreamed vividly, images that left her feeling hot and frightened. She lay in the dark, and could see herself waiting to board the Bathurst coach in Mudgee, all the time fighting a strong temptation to flee the situation. It was so easy to visualise

Joseph, lying immobilised in Billy King's garden. Maybe he used the same room that she and Jemima had shared? She shivered when Joseph's features swam through her memory, but not from fear or ire - her heart. was aching to think of him in such pain. And knowing what dreadful news she would have to give him when she got there.

She removed her shoes and skirt, and drew back the cover. The bed was warm, and still occupied with her thoughts, her hand strayed across the sheet. How would he greet her? How would she feel after such a long time of thinking she would never see him again. Would he be joyful to see her? Or would she find it difficult to make him stop talking and planning long enough to listen to her? How on earth was she going to find the words to tell him about the baby?

Her heart cringed again at the horrible task ahead of her. "That's it, then," she said aloud. "You've decided to go to him."

A welter of mixed emotions coursed through her, but now she'd made the decision. She settled back and nuzzled into the pillow, muttering, "God help me. I can't tell why, but I do love him."

9 LAURA'S LIFE CHANGES

She roused at around six o'clock the next day. It was Thursday morning, and she rested with her eyes closed, in that small peace where reality stands aside. The Spring's early morning warmth suspended her, until the doctor's news last night inexorably wore its way beneath her eyelids, and crashed into her brain. She frowned and rubbed her face, gradually becoming aware that she was becoming decidedly uncomfortable. The inside of her mouth shrivelled, her head began to feel full, and it spun as though the world had suddenly reversed its direction.

She hauled herself into a sitting position, and with a small 'oh!', got out of bed hurriedly. She managed to reach the bucket in the washhouse, before retching until she felt her innards would knot permanently. She wiped her mouth, and trembling like a débutante, staggered back to sit on the edge of the bed. The cause of her sickness left her breathless with dismay. This could not happen ... she had quite enough to cope with ... the events since Joseph left and the baby died, had helped her to lose track of time. Rapid calculations confirmed her doubts. Any benefit she'd gained from a few hours sleep vanished, as she lay back on the pillow, physically depleted. But she would not let herself cry again; breathless moments passed and her spirit gradually returned, until she almost smiled and said, "Dear God, you've made sure I won't leave him now, haven't you?"

By the time Kate and her father arrived warily on the doorstep, Laura had re-arranged her belongings back into drawers, re-packed her travel bag with the necessities for her journey to Bathurst, and surprised them with her greeting.

"Good morning Kate, Doctor. It's all right - I've done a lot of thinking overnight, and I know I must go to Bathurst. I'd like to go only into Mudgee on Saturday, though, if that's suitable to you both. I have a little business I must attend to there, before catching the coach on Monday. Do you think you can manage for a week, Kate?" Kate nodded in amazement, dumbly looking to her father for support.

"Of course she can," he said, then frowned slightly. "You realise Joseph won't be well enough to come back with you, don't you? Even when he does ..."- he looked around thoughtfully- "I don't know how you will manage."

"I can get a lot of things sorted out by the time Joseph is well enough to travel back. We'll see about arrangements then." Laura tilted her chin. "I'll make extra bread and toffee for you this morning, Kate, so that I can have tomorrow to myself."

"Well, that's settled then," said Norman. "I'll take you into town early on Saturday morning - I'm sure we'll find you a nice room for a couple of nights. Is there anything I can do for you while we're in there ... I mean, you do still look a bit peaky and I can introduce you to the Land Agent and a couple of people I know ..."

"Thank you very much, doctor, but no. I know what has to be done." She patted her hair and beckoned to Kate. "Come on, we've work to do."

Kate lifted her eyebrows and shrugged at her father, and the doctor left as they headed for the kitchen. "Dad told me ..."

Laura didn't want to discuss the matter. "No time for chatter. Get the flour for me, there's a good girl."

The following morning's crystal colours were vibrant; a cobalt blue sky highlighted the yellow, red, and pink hibiscus bushes that stood against Dave's garden fence, and even the lowliest of village dwellings managed a row of marigolds outside the door. Clem White had encouraged the children to plant bottle-brush trees and banksias in the school ground, and even weeds blatantly threw coloured flower-heads.

Laura wandered up to the school residence and found Clem, tending a row of rose-bushes he'd nurtured along the wall of the building. He looked up as she approached and stood by the gate. "Good morning, Laura. You are leaving us tomorrow, then," he said with an edge of sadness.

"Yes -but not leaving Hargraves for good as I'd planned."

Undisguised joy lit his face. "Oh, I'm so glad. Have you reconsidered my..."

"Oh, no," said Laura quickly, unwilling to raise his hopes. She hesitated before continuing, "Joseph's been injured. I'm leaving for Bathurst on Monday's coach. I'm sorry, but I will have to cancel my invitation for tea this afternoon. I'm going to Mudgee tomorrow for a few days first. I have some business."

Clem hid his disappointment by scattering an extra handful of fertilizer around the roses with zeal. "I usually stop for a mug of tea around now - will you have one, too?"

"No, thank you, Clem. I'm going up to the cemetery."

"The baby ...?"

Laura nodded. "Joseph doesn't know..."

"Here, take some of these with you." He snipped three rosebuds and carefully removed the thorns from the stems before handing them to her. "I took a little pot up there last week, so there's something to put them in. Better take some water, too."

Laura said nothing as he disappeared into the house, and emerged with a beer bottle, now filled with clear liquid. He took the buds out of her hand and put them in. "Till you get up there."

Laura thanked him warmly, and continued up the hill towards the Church wondering how she could possibly ignore such courtesy and friendship. She turned into the grounds and wished the Church was open so that she could go in and quietly gather her thoughts, and maybe say a prayer for Joseph's recovery, but the Minister only came one Sunday a month, except for funerals.

She plodded on through the dry grass and found the grave, already with tiny grass shoots over the mound. Clem's pot, and a few wilted flowers marked the spot. The grave looked such a small and vulnerable disturbance in the stony earth near the Church's back wall, but it was protected by the shadow of the wooden building and Laura somehow felt comforted. But she dreaded the thought of it remaining unmarked, and thought how distressed Jemima would be if she knew the baby she died for, would eventually disappear without a trace. She tossed away the withered stalks and replaced them with the fresh buds she carried, her lips tightening in determination.

"Dear little Joseph," she murmured as she knelt. "I wonder if you would have grown into an ambitious and thoughtless man like your father? No, sweet one, you would have been more like your mother- your real mother." She smiled faintly, "...and maybe a little like your adopted mother, too." She knelt quietly for a moment then added, "God Bless You, little one, and God help your mothers, because your father claimed our love. But now I know there will be another little Joseph, I'll not be taken for granted, and God willing, I'll watch him grow into the manhood you were denied. He'll be strong and clever like your father, but I'll teach him to think about others first." She rose to her feet whispering, "But I'll never forget you, little one."

She felt a swelling in her throat and turned away quickly, knowing her tears must be done with, and she must be stronger than ever from now on. Her firmness of step had little to do with the slope of the land as she left, and her chin tilted with the determination that had been the mainstay of her life. Nevertheless, she was thankful Clem had gone inside by the time she passed; her emotion was not all that secure.

"You've been a while," Kate greeted her. "Dad's ridden in and brought some letters for people in the village - and there's one for you. It's been done on one of those writing machine things, I think."

Kate's curiosity increased as she watched Laura's haste to open the envelope. Laura read, gasped, then re-read the contents aloud.

Miss Marchant. Your letter arrived a week after your Aunt Mrs Emily Marchant passed away. She died after a brief but virulent illness, and as her Solicitor, I have to inform you that you are to inherit a small sum from her Estate.

"Strewth!" Kate's outburst could have been Laura's if she'd been brought up to speak that way, but there was nothing different about their looks of amazement. "Bet you've got a fortune!"

"I hardly think so," said Laura, recovering. "I understood the small allowance she lived on when my uncle died, was hardly enough. I know any money I earned was quickly added and disappeared in payment of accounts for food and clothes in Tolton."

"She might have been hiding it from you." Kate's young eyes sparkled with the prospect. "You never know, she might have been a Lady whatsername, or whatever they call them Dukes and Duchesses over there."

For the first time in weeks, Laura's laugh pealed through the little shop. Her Aunt's continuous moan about anything from the cost of hay for Daisy, to the price of a loaf of bread, or maintenance to the buggy-wheels, didn't justify Kate's romantic dream. Kate urged, "Well, go on then. How much have you got?"

Laura looked back to the letter from the pompous Solicitor, and read the next paragraph. Mrs Marchant's Estate was quickly attended to ...

"I've no doubt about that," said Laura wryly.

...the proceeds from the sale of the Tolton property being adequate to cover the funeral costs and outstanding trader accounts."

"And of course, his fee!" Laura said.

"Does he say that?" asked Kate, still agog.

"No, but one reads between the lines in legal matters."

"Well, go on then, does he say how much you'll get?"

Laura chuckled and shook her head. "You're nothing but a fortune-hunter, Kate."

"Better than scratching in the dirt for one though, isn't it?" She clapped her hands impatiently. "He'd have to tell you somewhere, doesn't he?"

"Yes," said Laura:, folding the letter. "It appears that, after Bank transfer fees from England to Sydney, the sum of one hundred and twenty pounds has been deposited in my name at the Bank of New South Wales, in Sydney."

"One hundred and twen ...that's a huge pile of money." Kate said this with awe, then quickly changed her mind. "Of course, it isn't a fortune ..."

"Kate, you're a trial," laughed Laura. "However, it will have to sit there awhile. I've a lot more on my mind. I know now, that I have to go to Joseph. He needs to know that ... well, about the baby, for instance."

Kate sobered, not realising the real import of Laura's words. "You've got to feel sorry for him, I mean, he must be in a lot of pain still, and hearing that his little son has died, well ..."

"I must make sure I have everything," said Laura quickly to change the subject. "There's never many customers on Friday afternoon, most of them go into Mudgee, so I think we'll shut up shop early. So off you go ... and don't go telling your Dad and Uncle Davey that I'm some sort of English Countess who's inherited a fortune- I'll never live it down."

"Oh, I won't," said Kate cheerily. Before going through the front door she turned and said, . "But I might string them along a bit, just for the fun of it."

Laura shook her head again as the little bell tinkled behind her young friend, and went into the kitchen. The speed of events made her squeeze her fingers across her eyelids, then she sighed walked into the bedroom and looked at the English countryside picture that lay on the chest of drawers. She hadn't hung it up again, still harbouring thoughts that once the business with Joseph was settled , she could be sure of her own mind.

Who really could say what would happen? Would Joseph be able to come back to Hargraves? How much of an invalid would he be? Would he get well enough to revert to his old wanderlust ways, and would she be left in Hargraves again, to cope with the birth of his son?

She had no doubts about it being a son. When a person is left alone, thoughts spiral madly through the mind and she sat heavily on the bed, contemplating the outcome if she kept her pregnancy to herself.   She could deal with the situation in Bathurst, she was willing to help Joseph where necessary, and eventually, she could make her way to Sydney with a little more security now.

"Tush, Laura," she said softly. "Stop deceiving yourself. You love the father of your child, and you have good friends here in Hargraves. You'd be a foolish woman to throw all that away."

Norman Lee was ready with the horse and dray outside the shop when Laura emerged, at six in the morning. She gave him her travel bag to stow behind, and patted the strong horse before letting the doctor assist her aboard. "It's a lovely morning for the journey," she said lightly. "Will we be there by midday?"

"Certainly," said the doctor, rattling the rein-signal to the horse. "You comfortable?"

"Yes, thank you."

 Kate rushed out of Dave's house, waving madly. "Don't worry, Lady Laura," she called, "everything's fine."

Laura laughed and waved back, until they rattled over the Louisa Creek Bridge. She looked down to one or two heavily booted and skimpily dressed men crouching at the water's edge. "My goodness, they are at it early."

"Yes," chuckled Norman. "Fools think they'll be first to get a payload from the alluvial dirt there - always thinking today, will be the day."

"Do they ever get any?" asked Laura

"Specks sometimes. Not worth the months and years of effort. It's a fever, and not one that I can fix, either."

There were comfortable silences between them, and they chatted occasionally, although Laura was careful to let the doctor and his horse concentrate on the more treacherous sections of the stone-littered and often steep road.

They drew up at The Greyhound, the hotel where they stayed overnight on their arrival, and Laura was grateful when Norman insisted on seeing that she was accommodated well. Having paid for a one night stay, Laura walked with the doctor to a small and littered yard, in Mudgee's backstreet.

Laura shaded her eyes trying to see signs of life, while her companion rattled on the wooden framework of the shed. "You there, Snowy? It's Doctor Norman Lee."

From the gloom a wiry man with white hair shuffled into the sunlight and squinted as his visitors. He held a mallet in his hand, and his trousers, secured with string at the knee, were covered in a whitish powder. "G'day, doctor." He nodded to Laura. "Miss."

"I know you don't like to work on a Saturday afternoon, Bill," said Norman, "but this lady wants a special job done, and you're the best bloke at this I know. "

Snowy Wilson turned to Laura and scratched his hair. "What can I do for you, Miss ...er"

"Marchant," said Laura, offering her hand. "I'm from Hargraves, too."

Snowy wiped his callused hand down his trousers, (which didn't help to clean it much,) and shook hers. "Any friend of the doc's ..."

"I'll leave you to it, then, Laura," said Norman. "I'll start straight back. Kate's going to open the pub and I'll help in Davey's absence. I don't want to leave her on her own. The Brown brothers will be there, no doubt, but .."

"Of course," smiled Laura, "and thank you very much, doctor. I can manage from here."

"Now, Miss Marchant, " said Snowy, dragging a tatty notebook from his back pocket. A piece of string holding a pencil was attached to it, and he licked the lead.. "What sort of thing would you like?"

"It's for a little baby," Laura began. "I'd like ... well I'd better ask for prices first. I haven't very much money and ..."

"How about a little stone cross?" said Snowy. "Stone's not as pricey as marble - the inscription wears off a bit quicker, of course."

"How long?"

"Depends.. . the weather over the years, the grave's position in the cemetery... I'd say something between fifty to seventy years. Marble lasts forever."

"Stone," said Laura. "Perhaps we could get it replaced with marble, later."

"Stone it is then. Inscription?"

"Joseph," Laura began softly. "Died thirtieth of January, eighteen seventy eight. Aged six months, son of Joseph and Jemima Martin." She gave the unforgettable information slowly, with her bare head bowed, as though re-living the event.

Snowy paused with his scribble, and looked at her. "I'm sorry. I thought Doctor Lee called you 'Laura' ?"

"I was the baby's nanny."

The Stonemason nodded his understanding, then looked back to his notes. "Sorry, Miss Marchant, but we're not going to get all that on a cross - you'd be better off with a slab. I could round the corners off," he added quickly at Laura's expression, "and how about some nice scroll and flowers around the edge?"

"How much will all this cost, Mister Wilson?"

Laura had already used some of her ten pounds to pay for her accommodation and meals There was still the coach fare to pay for; she would have to put some money aside for the week she would be in Bathurst, and there was her return fare.

"I dare say I could do that for five pounds for you," said Snowy Wilson kindly. "Breaks my heart when jobs like this come in for such little scraps that never had a chance to grow up."

Laura carefully counted the money into his dusty hand, a deep sense of satisfaction warming her. She didn't care if Joseph Martin objected to her action, this was for Jemima and herself.

"I should be back in Mudgee around next Friday," she said. "Is it possible to have it ready for me to take back to Hargraves?"

"Lor' Bless you, Miss," said Snowy, pocketing his book and pencil. "I'll get my boy to take it out before then, if you'll tell me where we'll find the grave. In the Churchyard, I suppose, but perhaps you could make it easier by giving me a little drawing, so I can find it easier?"

"Thank you very much," said Laura, relieved because she hadn't actually warned Doctor Lee they would have a heavy stone to take back over those roads. "I'm not good at drawing," Laura confessed. "You could call at the School Residence, and Mister Clem White would be happy to take you to the right spot."

"Sounds right," nodded Bill. "Leave it to me, then. I guarantee you'll be pleased."

'I know I will,' Laura thought as she walked back towards her hotel. '...and to the Devil with any objections from you, Joseph Martin.'

She passed by Mudgee's biggest department store, where Joseph had stopped to buy their initial requirements, when they first came to the area. She stopped to look in the window. The Hargraves shop was dwarfed by the long established Mudgee store and she wondered at the acumen of people who handled such large businesses, and decided it must be a talent she had not been blessed with. Selling a few household requirements or tools is my limit, she thought.

Moving to the next window, she spotted an array of millinery, some ingeniously decorated with feathers or blown silk roses. Others were more practical with wide brims to protect delicate skins. She'd been bullied into wearing shady hats long ago by Kate, and Clem White had insisted she wear a bush hat when they rode into Hill End.

She slept fitfully at The Greyhound hotel that night, and was up early, to have breakfast before boarding the coach to Bathurst. She still wore mourning clothes, with a wide-brimmed black hat. She kept her coppery hair drawn into a neat bun, these hot days, but her English country complexion had already suffered from sunburn, and the succession of calamities had added lines to her forehead..

Although still an extremely attractive woman, the pallor of grief had given her face translucence, and her eyes had not lost a vaguely haunted quality. But as she made her way towards the coach pick up point, she felt an unexpected contentment, because she'd determined her course, and set out on it.

Billy King met the coach when it drew into Bathurst later that day, but instead of taking her to his house and Joseph, he took her to a teashop, so that he could warn her about what to expect. Joseph's injuries had included nasty gashes to his face, and the familiar bushy beard had been removed for the Doctor to attend to them. The lower half of Joseph's body was badly crushed when the startled horse rolled over him, and this had been exacerbated when one of its hooves stomped into his groin, as it scrambled to its feet.

"You almost lost him," Billy said. "He was unconscious for nearly a week. He's a very lucky man to still be alive."

When Dave Lee had arrived and found Joseph, a few days earlier, they'd talked for a while about the couple, over a beer. "Got a hard time ahead of them, those two," Dave had remarked.

"Ay, but she's a tough one, that Miss Marchant. I'm a mite surprised that she's not Missus Martin, by this time."

"Not for want of Joseph asking her," Dave commented, settling himself at the little wooden table. "But these young women, these days ... my niece Kate, was telling me that Laura didn't like him going away all the time, and felt as though he was making use of her as a mother to his child."

"And was he?" asked Billy.

"Maybe ... at first."

"I wonder how it's going to be now that the baby ..."

Dave had shrugged. "Have to see how he takes the news first. It's a terrible thing to have to tell a man, when he's been as sick as that one."

"Mm," said Billy, handing his companion another beer. "that's why neither of us could do it." Laura's small intake of breath was audible as she stepped into the garden, and Joseph looked up from the book he was reading. She approached him, and saw him try to get his feet to embrace her, but he was too weak to do more than lift his hands to clasp hers. All the things she'd been prepared to say, flew out of her mind. She sank to her knees on the grass beside him.

"Joseph, oh my dear Joseph ..." There were no formalities between the two people in the garden - with tear-filled eyes Laura buried her face into Joseph's chest, and they remained silent, while he embraced her and stroked her hair. She struggled to remain calm, knowing instinctively that his contentment at her presence, surpassed any need for words. They stayed close for long moments, until Laura drew back and look into his face. Her fingertips tentatively traced the still raw marks down his cheek, and he flinched. "Oh, I'm sorry my dearest, I didn't mean to hurt you."

"The doctor tells me the nerves will be extremely sensitive for a long time yet," Joseph answered. "But the pain is nothing to my joy that you are here. Oh, my own Laura."

"We will soon have you feeling better," Laura soothed. Billy had told her the doctor's prognosis was that Joseph would become mobile again, but that he would probably require the aid of walking sticks. "We'll soon have you enjoying life just the same."

"I will never be the same," Joseph said bitterly. "I shall be a cripple all the rest of my life, and of no use to woman nor child."

"Tush, " chided Laura. "You've a great deal of living to do yet." Her words were meant to bolster Joseph's mood, but there was a hesitancy in her manner that made his brows knit as he released her. His chin sunk to his chest. Despite it being the middle of May, it was a cool day and he wore a brown velvet lounge jacket over a cotton shirt, which he drew closer, as if to hide the amount of weight he had lost. His appetite had returned, thanks to the diligence of Billy, but he was extremely conscious that he was no longer the well-built and imposing man Laura had known.

His pleasure at the news that Laura was coming to Bathurst had been tinged with concern for her acceptance of him, now that he was less than a man. He had already decided that he could no longer expect her to become his wife, but hung on desperately to the hope that she would not desert his son. The most he could expect, he told himself, was that Laura would stay with them, until the boy was old enough to be sent away to school.

He read her hesitancy as a rejection of the invalid he now was, and his anxiety darkened his expression. "I do not expect marriage now, Laura. I wanted you to come to Bathurst. so that I could tell you that."

Laura opened her mouth to contradict him, and he said, "Don't interrupt me, my dear. I have had long hours to consider my position, and that of my son ..."

"Joseph," Laura persisted as she rose to her feet. She laid a trembling hand on his arm, and sensed his tension when he looked at her. But she didn't realise it was because he saw, for the first time, that she was dressed in black. Her grograin skirt topped with a matching jacket, gave her an even slimmer appearance, and the lace-ruffled blouse beneath looked startlingly white against her soft throat. Her black hat had been removed, and was on the grass beside them. Laura knew the drab colours she wore emphasised the paleness of her features. Joseph's voice was tired when he spoke.

"Did you think you were coming to bury me, Laura?"

She turned away sharply, clasping her trembling hands against her temples. "Oh my God, Joseph, I wish I didn't have to tell you this."

Joseph began to breathe heavily with apprehension. The thought of Laura at his side, albeit as a free woman, had been a mainstay throughout the disaster, and he mistook her distress for revulsion at the sight of him.

"Don't tell me," he said gruffly. "I do understand."

Laura spun to look at him and said, "No you don't, Joseph. And I..." Words failed her and she knelt back beside him, taking his hands in hers.

Joseph's shoulders drooped. "A handsome woman like you could not be expected to …"

"Joseph," Laura interrupted resolutely. "Your son. Our little boy - is dead."

She saw Joseph mentally reel, and the raw nerves in his face twitched at the news. Her grip on his hands tightened, and although she tried to make her strength and courage flow between them, her heart seared for him. She could see questions stunning the mobility of Joseph's mind, but his head shook from side to side in denial.

The child was alive when he left Hargraves; he'd nursed the baby, and Laura had made him smile at his father. Why was she saying this? If it was true, why had he not been told?

"I don't understand," he managed. Tears flowed freely down Laura's cheeks, as she watched the man she loved so dearly, struggle with the terrible news. "How did it happen?"

While Laura softly told him of the event, he sat as if stone had weighted his chest, with a helplessness far worse than that of his injured legs. He listened to details of where the baby had been buried, and winced at the one note of recrimination that Laura failed to control, when she mentioned his unexplained absence. Chiding herself immediately, she continued, "My dearest, we must be strong."

"I will never be strong again," he said brokenly.

The despair that choked his voice tore at Laura's heart. She wrapped her arms around him, and laid her cheek on the top of his head. "Then I shall be, for both of us."

The load bore Joseph down, until he begged Laura to leave him alone for a while in the garden. Inside, she broke down and wept against Billy's chest when the concerned old man put his arm around her shoulder. The pressure of the past weeks, and tiredness from her long coach journey, caused a depression that seemed almost too much for her to bear.

She had fought bravely to retain her composure in front of Joseph, reasoning with herself that his injuries had already taken their toll. Now she was heavy with guilt, because she had increased that toll. "Such a burden," she kept repeating. "And I have done nothing but add to it. It will be a long time before he regains his confidence."

"Hush, Laura," soothed Billy, guiding her to a chair before he sat her down gently. "You had no choice. He had to be told at sometime. Getting all your rotten potatoes in one sack is the best way, I've always said."

Laura dabbed her eyes, a wan smile acknowledging her good friend's bush philosophy. "I know you're right, Billy, but it doesn't make the tragedy any easier to bear, for either of us." She accepted the cup of tea Billy had made for her, and while stirring sugar into the brew she added, "We'll let him be in the garden for a while, then I'll lighten his load."

Billy looked at her, but held his curiosity. He broke her small silence by asking, "Shall I take your bag to your room? No doubt you could do with a rest, too."

"Thank you, Billy, for everything you have done for Joseph."

"Seems I've been fated to help the Martins right along," said Billy diffidently. "I well remember Missus Martin ... Jemima, and how you was both like my own daughters to me. Besides, no-one would have done any different for anyone as badly hurt as he's been."

Laura leaned forward and kissed his cheek lightly, before following him up the stairs to her room. He put her bag on the bed, and said, "I'll sleep in Joseph's room - you'll remember there's two beds in there? You'll not have to worry about him. Now you rest up here, and I'll call you when the meal's ready tonight."

When he'd gone downstairs, Laura crossed to the window that overlooked the garden, and gazed down at the man she loved so dearly. He sat hunched in the chair, just as she had left him, and it was as much as she could do not to rush back to his side. She was torn between her instinct to be with him, and the stubbornness that had flashed when he dismissed her. The spirit in him was fleeting, but she clung to it as a sign that he would overcome this difficulty in his life, and even though he may think it at present, all was not lost.

Without the familiar bushy beard, and with such a lighter frame, he looked frail and boyish Maternal stimuli, already throbbing in her veins because of her pregnancy, made her fold and grip her arms tightly, in order to compose herself. Her heart ached for the mental torment he must be enduring at that very moment. Thinking she could not bear to watch him any more, she was about to turn away when Billy appeared in the garden, and crossed to him. He placed his hand on Joseph's shoulder, and said something which caused the injured man to look up to her window.

She lifted her hand hesitantly, noting the almost haunted expression, but Joseph made no indication that he had seen her. Billy shook his head, then managed to lift Joseph into a wheeled chair, before taking him inside.

Laura's shuddering sigh was the only sound in the small room, and she drew the curtains across, to ease the glare of the sunset. She lay down gratefully, imagining Joseph being laid on his bed in the room on the ground floor. She thought of Billy's words and well recalled the two beds; memories of the months she and Jemima lived there, crowded in. More raw memories of the night Jemima gave birth to little Joseph, brought renewed tears to her eyes.

She didn't realise she'd fallen asleep until Billy knocked politely. When she answered, he called through the door that their evening meal would be ready shortly, and was she up to joining them?

"Of course," said Laura. "I won't be a moment."

She refreshed her hands and face in the jug and basin on the marble washstand, and patted her hair tidily. She regarded her reflection in the oval mirror above the washstand, and stood on tiptoe, smoothing the black cloth of her skirt across her stomach. There was no indication of her pregnancy yet, but tonight she would choose her moment, to tell Joseph about their coming child.

Joseph had not slept but lay staring up at the ceiling, trying to come to terms with his losses. Not only had he lost his son, his manhood, and his self-respect, he was about the lose the woman he realised he'd loved almost from the moment he'd met her so long ago, in Lyon's Tearooms.

Memories of her feisty challenge at the treatment of Jemima aboard the Mariana, of her fortitude in support of his first wife throughout those early months, and her loyalty in looking after his son, chased each other in circles through his mind. A dismal anger surged in his heart when he thought of the danger Laura had endured, when attacked in Hargraves. This was softened almost immediately, when he remembered the happiness they'd shared over the Christmas season.

So many disparate emotions fluctuated through the afternoon, that he felt just as exhausted when Billy put his head around the door, and asked if he felt well enough to join them for dinner.

"Thank you, Billy, but no. I fear I would be sorry company, and Laura has had quite enough to bear for one day. I'll have a small piece of toast and a cup of tea in here, if I may."

Billy shrugged and withdrew, conveying Joseph's message to Laura as she came through the door behind him. "He will never recover with an attitude like that," she said spiritedly. "Leave him to me."

Billy looked on in amusement as Laura disappeared down the corridor, and he whispered, "There'll be fireworks before long, and she'll be the one lighting the crackers."

Laura opened the door of Joseph's room and stood for a moment with the hall gas light creating a halo around her face, before entering and closing the door gently behind her.

Joseph gave a weak smile. "For a moment you reminded me of twhen we were in the back yard at Hargraves and I showed you the Milky Way through my telescope. Your hair glowed that time, too."

"I remember that," said Laura, crossing to sit on his bed.

"That was a lovely evening, my dear," he went on wistfully.

"And this one will be, too," replied Laura firmly, "...when you join us. Billy has gone to great pains to cook us a meal and I think the least we could do is show our appreciation."

Laura didn't indicate that Davey had told her of his earlier refusal to join them; there was no advantage in letting him think his friends were covertly manipulating him. She sensed he was about to give her the same answer, so took his hand and brought it to her lips..

"Before we go into the dining room, Joseph, " she said softly, "I think you should understand that I have every intention of arranging our marriage during the next week, and I will not hear a jot of objection from you."

Joseph struggled to raise himself to his elbows. "I forbid you to do any such thing."

Laura laughed and pressed her hands to his shoulders, forcing him back against the pillows. "I forbid you to forbid me."

His face darkened, but only for a moment. He joined in with Laura's laughter, and Laura continued. "Joseph. I know what you must be thinking, but I have the right to be with the man I love, especially now."

Joseph sobered. "What can I offer you now? A life of pity for a cripple, an inheritance of a few worthless blocks of land and a horse stud,that I cannot even manage myself any more." He looked angry again, then added as if a final sword thrust, "I cannot even be a proper husband to you."

Laura smoothed his brow. "Are you saying that you cannot fulfil your role as a husband and father?"

"Of course that's what I'm saying," Joseph growled, turning his head to the wall. "A young and healthy woman like you, does not deserve to be shackled to a cripple like me."

Laura straightened her back. "You are not a cripple, Joseph Martin. You may never regain your former strength and aptitude, my dearest, but the doctor has assured us that you will be able to get about again."

"On sticks," Joseph almost snarled as he swivelled to face her. "An effigy of a man."

"There will be some things beyond you, but there will be many responsibilities and duties only you can undertake."

The sharpness of Laura's tone made him match her challenge with his own derision. "Such as?"

"Someone will have to oversee the hands at the stud, and I have no intention of undertaking that task."

"I shall sell Tangarra."

Laura softened. "Is that what it's called?"

"I shall sell everything. I shall give you enough money to return to England if that is your desire, and you can be free of this gargoyle I have become. So you can forget all your ideas about marriage ..." Joseph's voice had become more agitated and Laura stood hastily, to walk to the window. She looked out into the shadowy garden with its apple tree and bushes silhouetted against the moonlit sky and swallowed hard to control the quaver in her reply.

"And what is to become of our child?"

"Don't mock me, Laura. Didn't you tell me he has died?"

Laura turned and faced Joseph, noting that anger had brought a flush to his pale cheeks and reddened the scar that ran along his cheek. "That was Jemima's son, Joseph."

For a long moment, Joseph stared at Laura as though she had spoken in a foreign tongue. Then an inkling of what she could be referring to pierced his ire. "Are you trying to tell me ...?"

"Not trying, my dearest," said Laura, crossing swiftly to be at his side again. "I'm telling you that I am carrying our child, and it will be born around September."

Billy had been sitting quietly at the table, listening to the raised voices but unable to distinguish what they were saying. He shook his head and clicked his teeth several times, then said, "Stubborn man, that Joseph Martin. Sick as he is, he has the stupidity to argue with a woman who is worth more gold than has ever been found in Ballarat, Hill End, or Hargraves put together!"

Laura appeared at the kitchen door, her face beautiful and triumphant. "Billy, would you help Joseph to his wheelchair please? He has decided to join us."

Billy grinned, and Laura replied with an impish look. During dinner, he spoke cautiously at first, unable to tell how badly Joseph had been affected by the news of his son's death. After yet another silence he ventured, "Right sad about the boy, Joseph. He was a bonza little kid."

Joseph breathed deeply and said, "Thank you. I am overwhelmed to think that..."

"Any wonder," said Billy quickly, to put Joseph at ease. "You've taken a bit of a pounding in a couple of ways, and nobody in his right mind would blame you for wanting to toss everything aside."

Joseph shook his head slightly, and said, "And I would have too, but for Laura's courage."

Billy's eyes twinkled when he saw Laura was blushing gently, then he roared his approval when Joseph went on to tell him that they were to be married.

"Congratulations to both of you" said Billy. "Here, I've got a special bottle of sherry tucked away for such times. Don't go away, I'll get it." He rose from the table and went to rummage in the back of the sideboard against the wall.

"You never cease to surprise me, Billy," Joseph smiled.

"And you'll be married in the garden, of course?" asked Billy as he rejoined them at the table, red-faced from his excitement. "It's a lovely time of the year to get wed."

Joseph looked at Laura, and she smiled shyly and nodded. They had agreed they would say nothing about the coming baby, and were content to revel in their host's joy at such a forthcoming event, as a wedding in his garden.

"Now, how about you young people sit out in the lovely moonlight for a while," said Billy, scraping back his chair, "so's I can clear up? We've got a lot of plans to make."

Billy couldn't have been happier if Laura had been his own daughter. He helped her carry Joseph out of the back door and, finally content that Laura was settled on the small chair beside the invalid, he went back inside..

"He's such dear friend," said Laura softly. "Imagine him calling us 'young people'."

"I suppose to him, we are," said Joseph. "I'm not offended, are you? In fact, I'm rather pleased that he's given me the chance to talk with you."

"We have all our lives to talk," said Laura dreamily, glowing from the good quality sherry, and the outcome of the day. She leaned her head against his shoulder.

After a moment, he said, "I purchased Tangarra in an effort to convince you of my love, and ..."

Laura lifted her head sharply and scrutinised his shadowed profile

"What is it?" he asked.

"That's the first time," Laura said softly.

"First time?" Joseph was nonplussed.

"Yes. First time you've said you love me."

He regarded her upturned face, translucent in the moonlight, and it occurred to him that she had never looked so beautiful. But he was still slightly bemused. "You mean you weren't sure?"

"Pay no mind," whispered Laura happily. "Tell me about Tangarra."

Joseph described the rows of stables that housed more than a dozen high quality horses with a breeding background that was much sought after in the area. "And there's a gentle mare and trap that you can use to drive into town, when you go squandering all my hard-earned money."

"I shall call her Daisy," Laura said immediately. "And I'll have my own saddle, and maybe I can ride her around the property?"

Joseph's reply was blunt. "I'd be happier if you used the rig, my dear. One accident in the family is more than enough."

Laura didn't argue with him, but listened in rapture as he described the grand four-bedroomed home that was part of Tangarra, with its well-equipped kitchen, the dining-room large enough to entertain a dozen people, and the study-cum-library that led off the luxurious sitting room.

"Does Tangarra have a verandah?" Laura asked with girlish excitement. Her eyes had widened with his description, and she clung to his arm, as though fearing the mirage would follow the moon, and disappear before morning.

"Verandahs all around, my dear Laura," chuckled Joseph. "From the front one, you can sit and see the lovely garden and bushes that have been planted there, and from the back one, you can watch the horses being trained and exercised."

"And French windows?" she asked impishly.

"Onto the side verandah from the dining room," he answered surprisingly. "I had already decided to have a special play area built on that side, so the child can play out of the hot sun."

Laura subsided, realising he had planned this for little Joseph, but she said nothing. Not wanting to spoil the tenderness of the moment. Joseph, sensing her thoughts straight away, leaned towards her and kissed the top of her head. "How gifted I am that my plans can still come true."

"My dear," said Laura hesitantly. "It sounds a lot to cope with. Feeding and caring for the stock, as well as managing and paying the men - I assume there are employees at the stables?"

"The yard foreman and two lads," Joseph informed her. "And one of my first responsibilities will be to hire a good housekeeper."

After a short silence, Laura said, "I had not realised that you'd been so successful with your land buying projects, dearest. Are you telling me our circumstances are, well ...? " She stopped, embarrassed at the first real discussion of their financial situation. "Of course there must be help with the stables, but a housekeeper ...it all sounds very expensive. I am quite happy to manage on my own."

"I knew what I wanted to do before I came to Australia," Joseph mused, as though he hadn't heard her doubts. "In the beginning, I was misdirected and thought that success would come from the gold-field areas, but I quickly realised any land was an excellent investment, so I changed my tactics. In just over a year, I have bought and sold land, made several profitable deals and now, my dear, you have no need to worry about finances. I shall arrange an allowance for you for regular household expenses, and if you require anything else, you need only to discuss it with me."

"Oh, Joseph, " said Laura mistily. "I had no idea ... how Jemima would have loved the thought of Tangarra." Observing a flicker of discomfit in his eyes, she quickly went on, "Have you heard from her parents?"

"No," Joseph answered simply. "I notified them that she had died in childbirth, of course, and of our son. Her father had kept in touch, until I was able to return the money he'd loaned me, then nothing more. Almost as if I'd played right into his hands, by suggesting I marry Jemima."

"How sad. Should we notify them about little Joseph's death?"

"You may, if you wish," said Joseph, but with little interest. He eased himself with his elbows so that he could look at her more directly. "However, I have something more to tell you."

Laura sat back on her seat, prepared. "If you are going to discuss your visits to the ladies in various hotels.,."

Joseph was visibly shaken. Having quickly realised what a mistake he'd made over Jemima, and bearing a certain degree of guilt for transporting her so far away from her accustomed life-style, he'd considered his proper course was not to burden his first wife with his needs, after their honeymoon. By then, of course, it was too late and she was pregnant with his child. To him, it had been far better to attend to his urges by frequenting the abodes of 'friendly ladies'. He'd also tried valiantly to deny his growing appreciation of the womanhood that Jemima's companion had represented. This attitude had long since been supplanted, when he and Laura confessed their feelings to each other at the end of the last year, and her referral to those events now, startled him."My dear ..." he stammered.

"I do not wish to hear another word about the matter," said Laura firmly. "Those occasions were in another life, and …"

"You are well aware that they could never recur?" Joseph said this with a tinge of sarcasm.

Laura frowned that he should think her so inconsiderate."Joseph! I didn't mean ..."

"Say no more, my dear," he said, drawing her closer again. "We are bound to be sensitive to certain matters. But let's not spoil the evening - no, what I have to tell you will be, I hope, a pleasant surprise."

"I love surprises," breathed Laura.

"And those who provide them?"

"Of course." Laura stretched up and touched her lips to his. "Please tell me."

"In Bathurst," he began,"there is a man who acts as my Business Manager and Solicitor. His name is Andrew Thompson."

"Oh?" Laura began to think her idea of a 'pleasant surprise' differed greatly from Joseph's, but waited for him to continue. "Another purpose of coming here was to arrange a wedding present for you."

"Tangarra?" asked Laura, mystified.

"No," he answered, teasingly.

"Oh, do tell me," she pleaded.

"The Land Title to the shop at Hargraves has been transferred into the name of Laura Martin." Joseph looked smug.

She gasped, unable to grasp the full import of his words immediately. In all the visions of her future, especially at times when this had seemed extremely bleak and she'd doubted the wisdom of hoisting her life from virtual sobriety to total insecurity, she had never imagined herself as a land owner. "But dear," she stammered, "I know nothing about owning property."

"It is little enough," Joseph patted her hand. "Unfortunately, Hargraves is a doomed area. You know the gold petered out long before we arrived, and I know the populace is declining every week. The shop was ample for you to live on and care for my son, but I never anticipated we would make a fortune there."

"But, I don't understand. If we are to make our home at Tangarra, what is to happen to the shop?"

"You won't need it now," Joseph explained, not realising the clarity of his motive was only in his own mind. "Andrew Thompson arranged the sale of all the land blocks I'd bought in Hargraves and surrounding districts, and with the proceeds, I bought Tangarra. I arranged for him to retain just the one block, and for it to be transferred to your name."

"But. .. "

"For investment," persisted Joseph. "Land will always be a good investment and who knows, as Australia's population increases, and people start looking for land further afield than the cities, Hargraves may well be revived."

Laura shook her head and tried to follow his reasoning. "I don't quite know what to say, my dear, but I think it is lovely that you have done this for me. I shall be very proud to know I am an actual landowner."

She had said the word with a modicum of awe, and Joseph chuckled at her naivete, then took her face between his hands. "My dear Laura, it will only begin to repay you for the loyalty and love you have shown other members of the Martin family. And now, when we are married, you will be Mrs. Martin in every way, and I shall have the chance to be happy once more."

Laura resolutely put further doubts to one side, and by the time Billy came back out into the garden, she had managed to make Joseph forget his dreadful injuries for a while.

10 THE WEDDING, BIRTHDAY and NEW BABY

Their wedding was a pretty event. Davey Lee came back down to Bathurst a few days before and he and Billy decorated the garden, with vases of brilliant orange and pink hibiscus flowers. The beautiful display, provided by the midwife, Miss Hills, was well appreciated.

Laura met her in town one day, whilst buying herself a wedding outfit. They'd spent an hour in the little teashop on the main street, and Laura had related all the events since Jemima's death.

Miss Hills was delighted when Laura invited her to the wedding, and revelled in ordering the two old men around, quite determined that Laura and Joseph would have a ceremony to remember all their lives together.

Billy and Davey had spurned Joseph's offer of money and pooled their own to provide a commendable spread for the bride and groom and their few guests. There were nine of them sitting around the garden after the simple ceremony. Kate and her father, Norman, arrived early in the day, Clem came later, Davey Lee and Miss Hills found an immediate rapport, and lots of laughter came from the kitchen where they were preparing the meal. Billy King and the Vicar quaffed their share of the ale Davey had provided, from the Hargraves Arms, and everybody commended the delectable spread the women had prepared.

Laura was a beautiful bride in the long, pale blue dress she had chosen, with ecru lace decoration at the throat, and around the edge of its short sleeves. Kate had brushed Laura's hair into a gleaming coiffure, and the tiny froth of matching blue netting perched on top, was perfect. At Kate's insistence, Laura put a little rouge on her cheeks, and dabbed Kate's perfume behind her ears.

Carrying the posy of pink roses that Clem had brought, Laura walked shyly into the garden on Billy's arm, and stood by Joseph's side.

Joseph, his usually pale face flushed with pride, sat in his special chair with Davey's best tartan blanket over his legs, He wore the jacket of his immaculate Sunday suit, over a striped shirt, and stiff white collar. In his buttonhole, he wore one of the pink roses from Laura's posy, and it looked extremely suave against the grey stripe.

During the ceremony, Laura's hazel eyes flicked from one to another of their friends. It occurred to her that, apart from Kate and no doubt, Miss Hills, in due course, she had associated with and befriended more men in the past year or so, than she had in all her life. And she'd suddenly wished with all her heart, that the child she was carrying, would prove to be a girl. She needed female company. Joseph had enlisted Billy's help in ordering a simple, white and pink wedding cake. Laura had protested at the expense at first, but Joseph would brook no argument, and she was happy not to disrupt the euphoria of the occasion.

Her stomach hadn't swollen enough to spoil the line of her wedding dress, so her pregnancy was a secret only she and her husband shared, which seemed to add to the magic of the afternoon.

Billy's delight when Laura asked him to be a 'stand-in father' was glowing, as he stood at Laura's side, and held her flowers while the Minister conducted the ceremony. Then, he helped Davey and Miss Hills serve the small sandwiches and cakes, while still grinning like a Cheshire cat – according to Davey.

Davey and the midwife were the official witnesses, and the doctor had brought along his beloved camera. He took a photograph of the Minister and the newly-weds, then he and Billy took turns at photographing the group.

The tartan rug was the only unusual sight when the photographs were subsequently developed. They recorded a groom who sat erect with a haughty, yet proud expression, while the bride stood slightly behind the chair, her pretty bouquet in one hand and the other hand resting lovingly on his shoulder, while her Mona Lisa smile told the story.

A step to their right, the Minister's patronising smile was full of correctness, and no-one who saw the image later, would have been able to foretell subsequent events. There had been a lot of chatter and laughter by early evening, and as the Minister took his leave, Joseph began to show signs of weariness which everyone was quick to notice.

"I think you have had more than your share of excitement today, Joseph," said the doctor kindly. "You mustn't tax your strength."

Laura knelt at Joseph's side and their hands and their eyes met immediately. "The doctor is right, my love," she said.

"Righto," said Clem cheerfully, his glow coming from the bottles of wine and sherry the party had enjoyed. "Would you like to give me a hand to get him inside, Doc? Billy and Miss Hills will soon clear things away, and Laura can divvy the cake up. I'll get shot if I don't take a piece home to young pupils, y'realise?"

"You must all take some," said Laura happily.

Kate and Clem prepared to leave soon after, with such a long journey ahead of them. When he shook hands with Joseph, Clem whispered, "Fine woman, that, Joseph. I wish..." His instinct said, 'she'd married me', but he finished, "I wish you both every happiness."

Whether Joseph read more into Clem's words or not, everyone parted on the best of terms. Kate hugged Laura, and said, "Don't worry about the shop. I'll handle that until you get back."

"Might be a long time," said Laura, doubtfully.

"By the way," said Kate, smoothing on her gloves. "Did you get that money from your Aunt's estate?"

"Why no," Laura said. "I'd forgotten all about it."

"O-oh!" Kate grinned. "Lady Laura is that rich now..."

"Oh, be quiet," laughed Laura, and hugged her best friend again. "You really are a tease. Pity help the man you marry!"

Miss Hills busied herself to help Billy, then prepared to leave, first thanking Laura again, for her piece of wedding cake. "I have not spent all my life in the business without gaining insight, m'dear," she added. " When you have need of my services, I shall gladly make myself available."

Laura gasped at the midwife's insight, and flushed with embarrassment. She had been confident that no-one except Joseph was aware of her condition, and didn't know how to answer the midwife with other than a soft, "Thank you."

Billy had not heard their conversation and escorted the buxom nurse from the garden and towards the front door, still bubbling with the excitement of the day. "Wonderful afternoon, Miss Hills. She's a brave woman, the new Mrs Martin."

"She's strong," admitted Miss Hills.

"Going to have to be," said Billy seriously, and shook hands with the midwife.

Returning to the dwindling group in the garden, Billy said, "Righto, Davey. I reckon it's been a great day, but I think Joseph should rest now."

"Quite right," broke in the doctor, without waiting for Davey's reply. "Joseph's recovery is paramount, and your role will be vital from now on, Laura." He reached for his hat on the hall-stand and patted the case in which he carried his camera. "I shall have this developed in town as soon as possible - and have a copy myself, if I may?"

"Of course," said Laura happily. "Will you let me pay for copies for Billy and Davey?"

"That's all been taken care of," said Norman.

The men helped Joseph into the ground floor bedroom they'd prepared, and fussed around him like a batch of leghorn chickens. Laura busied herself clearing away the last things, like empty bottles, half-eaten sandwiches and crumbs of wedding cake, Everyone had been talking so much, even final cups of tea went cold, but no-one minded. She sighed happily in the quiet garden now, and looked to the sequinned sky, thinking she'd never seen the stars look so brilliant.

Everyone said good night to Norman Lee as he left, and Billy King said, "One for the road, Davey?" "But I'm not taking the road," replied Davey. "You said I could stay overnight with you."

"So I did, you ol' soak," said Billy, grinning. "We have to sleep in one bed, y'know?"

"If you snore, I'll kick you out and you can sleep on the floor," replied the publican, with equal amusement. "But I'll still have that one for the road."

"I'll go up and rescue Laura's belongings," said Billy. "Help yourself."

"Now that I'm Mrs. Martin," said Laura, with a smile, "I think I will join my husband."

"I should think so," said Davey. "Don't let us keep you up."

"Good night then, and thank you both so much, for all your help, and for the happiest day of my life."

The two great friends, smiled and pecked her cheek. "Good night, lovely lady."

Laura let herself into the bedroom carefully, but there was no need for caution, Joseph was wide awake.

"I heard what everybody was talking about," he said. "I had hoped someone would suggest you join me, and my heart lightened when I heard it was you who brought the matter up."

"I did not suggest," said Laura, an impish look adding to her attractiveness, as she removed the frothy blue hat and laid it carefully on the chest of drawers. "You are my husband, Joseph Martin, and I will not entertain thoughts of anyone else caring for you in future."

Billy interrupted any reply Joseph would have made, by tapping the door and calling for Laura. There was a few moments of flurry while he deposited her bag and sundry items on her bed, and retrieved his own shaving gear and spare clothes. Then he bade them a good night again, and left.

"Such a kind man", sighed Laura. we are extremely lucky, Joseph, to have such a friend."

Joseph began to draw himself up on the pillows, and she hastened to aid him. "Let me do it, Laura," he said briskly. "I do not intend to become a hopeless invalid for the rest of my life." He reached to the drawer beside him, and withdrew a soft folder. "Come and sit beside me, my dearest. Our day is not yet finished."

"Can it wait until I have changed into my nightclothes?" asked Laura, reaching behind her to unbutton her dress.

"No," came the firm answer. "Sit beside me now."

Laura smiled gently at his attempt to be firm, even though weariness was beginning to weaken his tone. She ceased her fumbling, and sat on the edge of his bed. Her hazel eyes were shining with happiness; she no longer had to deny her love for this man.

This was far removed from the wedding night and honeymoon, she had envisaged as a young girl, and in the back of her mind she knew both she and Joseph would have to wrestle with personal and private longings, that few others would be burdened with, especially at the outset of their marriage.

Joseph undid the toggle fastening on the brown leather folder and withdrew a large piece of parchment. He cleared his throat importantly, and said, "My dear, this is the Deed of Entitlement to the land at Hargraves, upon which stands the shop." He unfolded it and spread it on the covers between them. "As you will observe, the name of Mrs Laura Martin has been inserted, and I am handing you this with my deepest love and gratitude."

He swivelled the document so that she could read; at the head was the Royal Crest of Queen Victoria, and this was followed by formal terms relating to the 'Sale of Crown Lands in Our Colony of New South Wales. Then came Laura's new name handwritten in copperplate script, showing her as the owner of the 'Allotment or Parcel of Land hereinafter described.' Handwritten in the same script was a description of the land, its boundaries, and bearings, and alongside was a hand-drawn image of the land. Two small squares of grey paper were sandwiched together by a circle of red wax with an embossed seal impression.

Below· the date, various signatures appeared, including Joseph's and Andrew Thompson's, and there was a blank line. Joseph pointed to it and said, "You can take this with you into the Bank of New South Wales tomorrow, and my friend Mr Sutton, the Manager, will witness your signature.   He is well aware of my affairs and handles my accounts."

Laura gasped in awe at the imposing document and the grandeur of the moment, and could hardly tear her eyes away from it. She had never seen her name written in such an impressive manner before and the newness of seeing the word Martin after her Christian name, left her spellbound. Eventually, she whispered, "It is wonderfully generous of you, my love, and I shall always treasure this."

"It is a small gift," said Joseph, "to a woman who has committed herself to such a life as we will have together. There is so much more I should have been able to …"

Laura leaned forward and touched his lips with her fingers.

"I have your love, dearest, and we have our child. We are still very gifted, and I will not be so patient ever again, if I hear you castigating yourself, for a stroke of fate that cannot be undone. We must live only for the future: and for that of our child."

"Kiss me: Laura," he said thickly, and the Land Deed crackled between them as she moved into his arms ..

Three weeks flew by, and the day was sultry and overcast. The newly-weds sat in Billy's kitchen, talking quietly over plans. Billy had opened all the windows and doors, but the hot breeze did nothing to lighten the atmosphere, and Laura continually wiped the perspiration that trickled between her breasts, under her open blouse. Joseph, unable to get up, was uncomfortable against his cushions and Billy had pulled his shirt out over his trousers. Davey defied all convention, apologised to Laura and Joseph, and removed his shirt altogether.

"Strewth, it'll be hot in Hargraves today," he observed, quaffing beer Billy had produced from his cupboard. Kate will be glad it's Sunday and she's not in that shop of yours."

"You'll be going back now: Davey?" asked Billy.

"Looks like it," Davey answered: his eyes twinkling as he nodded towards Laura and Joseph. "The Brown boys will be running up more than I can handle, if I leave it too much longer. Kate's had Clem White helping her run the pub after shop hours, I know, but he's no match for his cousins once they get going - con the horns off a bull, those two could, given half the chance."

They all laughed at Davey's rueful comment. Bill Brown and his brother had hearts of gold, even though they had never been men whose lives revolved around the lucrative metal. Their amiable nature could charm the most hardened villager, but everyone knew who to call when in need of an extra hand.

Laura dabbed her lips with her napkin, and grew serious. "I'll have to go back myself, shortly. I never imagined I would be moving to Bathurst permanently when I left there, but there's no way we can keep the shop going now. Kate has been a marvellous friend, but I shouldn't presume on that friendship for much longer."

"Quite right, my dear," said Joseph, "but I beg you to hasten back at the earliest moment. We have so much to arrange about Tangarra - the doctor insists I stay here for a few months at least and …"

"Well, that's it, then," Davey chimed in. "We can't leave old Billy here to cope on his own, so how about you take the coach to Mudgee on Tuesday, Laura, and I'll stay here till you come back? That way you won't be so worried about Joseph."

"Here ... not so much of the 'old', Davey Lee," quipped. Billy. "You've got years on me."

"Two." Davey emptied his glass and wiggled his eyebrows at their host. "And that means I deserve another beer."

Laura was quick to see the sense in the arrangement he'd suggested, but loathe to leave Joseph, when their marriage was but a few weeks old. She sat holding his hand while all three men talked and joked, and thought to herself that although great changes were to be made in her life now, some things would remain the same. The past months at Hargraves had instilled in her the need for self-sufficiency; whether it had been the amount of bread to be baked for sale or the replenishment of stock, she'd learned to make and take decisions.

The prospect of Tangarra and all it involved was daunting, but she knew that without her strength of purpose, Joseph would not be able to cope, and there was no question in her mind that all previous events and plans for her future, must now be put aside. Her future was with Joseph, their child, and Tangarra, and she glowed from the realisation. "Laura," Joseph said quietly, not wanting to interrupt the friendly banter between Davey and Billy. "Could I ask you, my dear, to make sure you bring my telescope when you come back?"

Laura patted his hand and chuckled, "We are to start anew, my love, and I shall bring everything I can back with me. But I will not allow you to spend too many evenings gazing into that contraption, or I shall become jealous."

Joseph touched her nose with his fingertip. "As if I would." His happiness clouded momentarily as he continued, "You will have to tolerate much more than an ordinary wife, my Laura, but I promise that I will do my utmost to make our marriage a happy and prosperous one."

"Just stay in love with me," Laura replied. "I can cope with everything else."

Her words had a stronger confidence than she felt inside, but love and an overpowering joy kept buoying her determination. She realised Joseph would need a vast amount of support when he recovered enough to attempt walking, and that most of his courage would be drawn from her. She would also have to learn so many things very quickly - how to cope with everyday running of the household for example, and she had every intention of at least understanding Joseph's business interests and activities. All this, and coping with a newborn child as well. She quashed the fleeting worries.

Davey had contacted his brother, Norman, and informed him that Laura would be arriving on the coach that arrived in Mudgee on Tuesday. The doctor was at the coaching station waiting for her and remarked on her looking so well, despite the tiring journey. He helped her board the dray and while the brown horse plodded faithfully to Hargraves, she described what had happened over the previous couple of weeks since the wedding. .

"I am so pleased for you, my dear," Norman Lee said, guiding the horse along a narrow part of the track that wound between gum trees and scrub. The wheels grinding along the gravel seemed comforting, after the noise of the busy Bathurst streets; she quickly spotted scurrying lizards and pointed to the pink and grey cloud that rose into the air as galahs screeched an objection to the disturbance.

"I will miss these sights, I'm sure, Doctor. But I will not miss the loneliness. I'll miss Kate, too, and will always love her for all she's done for me. I hope she won't be too despondent when I tell her the news."

"I wouldn't worry," Norman Lee chuckled. "Seems she's getting a soft spot for that teacher, Clem White. And he's made all the right moves, too."

"Clem?" asked Laura, half surprised at the sensation that coursed through her, adding quickly, "he'd make her a good husband."

They arrived at the shop just as Kate was closing the door for the day, and she flew down the steps to greet Laura. Flinging her arms around her she said, "Oh, I'm so pleased to see you, Laura. And I've got so much to tell you, and …"

"I think we'd better let Laura ... Mrs Martin settle down first, Kate."

The three of them went inside the shop and by the time Laura had refreshed herself, Doctor Lee and his daughter had set out a meal that they all enjoyed, while telling each other their news.

"I'll close the place down, of course," said Laura, sipping her tea later.

She'd taken out the Land Title which she'd carefully packed in her bag, after it had been signed and witnessed on the Monday. She had rejected to deposit the Deed in a Bank Safety box, and brought with her, unwilling to let it out of her custody. However, she'd known instinctively that its present worth was minimal, the property was unsaleable. Hargraves was considered a dying village and the impressive parchment represented a sentimental value only to her.

"Oh, and by the way, Kate," said Laura. "I checked on that money from Aunt Marchant's will. I had to visit the Bank Manager for Joseph, and took the chance to discuss it with him."

"What's it worth now? A thousand pounds?"

The doctor looked mystified, but could soon tell it was a joke, from Kate and Laura's laughter. "Oh, Kate," Laura gasped. "You're incorrigible!"

"Are you being rude?" said Kate, and they laughed again.

"Of course not," said Laura. "It means you're an incurable tease!"

Kate suddenly looked sad. "I'm going to miss you so much, Laura. You've made a big difference in my life, apart from all these posh words you've been teaching me."

Laura hastened to reassure her. "I'll always been in your debt, Kate. So please, never be afraid to call on me. Anyway, I think Clem White would be happy to have you as another pupil."

Norman decided to join in the fun and said, "I think Clem has other ideas for Kate."

"Dad!" said Kate, and Laura warmed at the sight of her friend's blush.

"You don't owe me nothing," said Kate, brightening. "But I will have a few pots and things from the shop. I'm going to start a glory box."

Laura said, "I want to finish as quickly as I can. Will you come and help me tomorrow, please Kate?"

"Sure. Come on, Dad. You'd better stay over at Uncle Davey's house with me tonight. I'm not having you drive that rickety old cart back to Mudgee in the dark."

Alone in the bedroom later, Laura lay in the dark and remembered all that had happened while she lived under this roof. Her inexperience had turned quickly into efficiency as she learned about retailing the goods Joseph had stocked the shop with; the dreadful attack by those ruffians; her first sale - a darning needle to Clem White's housekeeper.

She let her eyes close drowsily, but the image of Clem swam beneath her lids and she was unaccountably relieved to know that he was away from Hargraves temporarily. In Sydney, Kate had said, on a special teacher's course, as it was school holidays again.

Laura remembered the day he had taken her with him to Hill End; he'd looked so tall and erect beside her in the dray and his deep brown eyes had seemed velvety whenever he turned them towards her. She thought of that journey with pleasure; the long and sometimes dangerous track made by a stream of miners and their families, especially when they began to desert Hargraves for the more lucrative fields the other side of the mountain range, that divided the two areas.

She remembered hanging onto the bush hat she 'borrowed' from the shop stock while the cart jostled precariously over the gibbered track, and laughing spontaneously for the first time when he recounted tales of the bush. She flushed in the darkness of the little bedroom, remembering Clem's declaration of his love for her later, and his eventual proposal.

At the time, she hadn't been sure why she refused his offer, but now she could admit to the consuming love she'd always had for Joseph. She also knew that nothing would please her more, than learning that Clem and Kate were to become a couple.

Joseph was the great, and intense sensation that filled her heart now. And yet, it was not to be the fulfilling life she'd dreamed about, as a young girl. Joseph's future would be fraught with weakness, pain and frustration; hers was to be one that would call on her inner strength, fortitude, and the ability if not the necessity of foregoing her own needs and urges, in order to succour her invalid husband and unborn child. But it was a future that did not frighten her, so sure was she that her love would help her.

She turned on her side, lifted on her elbow, and pummelled the pillow, before she lay down again, her tired body aching for sleep. But the walls seemed impregnated with memories that were determined to keep sleep at bay; these included memories of the evening she and Joseph had opened their hearts to each other. And the baby - poor little innocent, who had suffered with Jemima's weakness, and become such a large part of her life. She fancied she could still sense the tiny body breathing steadily in the corner of the room, and in the silence that was broken only by the sounds of creatures that scuttled or chirruped or croaked in the night, her nerves began to tense, as though waiting for the tiny wail she was once accustomed to. She forced herself to relax and eventually drifted into welcome sleep, making a decision to visit the baby's grave before she left Hargraves.

The following day seemed to end before there was time to sort everything out. Most things she gave to Kate; Joseph had assured her they would afford new furnishings and household equipment for Tangarra, and there was no point in transporting anything other than their personal belongings. She packed these in Joseph's large trunk. His books and telescope were not to be left behind, of course, and she was certain she'd find a place to hang her beloved print of the English countryside. While she packed her own few books alongside Joseph's, she noticed a thick one he owned, and her eyebrows raised in surprise at its title. *Beeton's Book of Household Management by Mrs Isabella Beeton*

She opened the book and found herself caught up with the wealth of information between its covers, and decided she would ask Joseph if she may have this book handy to her in the kitchen, at Tangarra. Thoughts of setting up in the wonderful house Joseph had described, lent vigour to her efforts and she revelled in telling Kate about their future in Bathurst.

"Joseph has arranged for a couple to act as Caretakers while he recuperates during the next few months, and it seems he has every confidence in the men in the stables to keep things going for him. Apparently, the foreman will come into Bathurst every week and give him a report."

"How far away is Tangarra from Bathurst, then?" Kate asked, wiping perspiration from her face, after they lugged the big trunk into a spot near the front door, ready to be loaded on the cart into Mudgee.

"Oh, about five miles out of town, I understand," said Laura, sitting heavily on the trunk for a spell. "Mister King has offered to drive us both out there one afternoon, just for me to see the place."

"That's nice of him," said Kate, with just a tinge of disgruntlement because she wouldn't be able to see Tangarra. "I don't suppose we will ever see you again, then?"

Laura sensed her young friend's attempt at pragmatism and rose quickly to embrace her. "How about we make a pact, Kate? I can see you as a bride too, in the very near future. What say you and your husband honeymoon at Tangarra when the time comes? I'm sure Joseph would be happy to see you, and we could have a wonderful time again, like we all did last Christmas. Does that sound a proposition to attract you?"

The glow that lit Kate's face was answer enough, and with renewed spirit, they returned to their task of emptying the shop of its stock and furnishings. Both women were exhausted and dishevelled as evening closed in. Regarding her grubby hands and elbows Kate said, "What a mess we're in. I'm going to have an early night, and so should you. We'll soon have it all sorted."

"You're right," said Laura, looking at her own state. She attempted to smooth her tousled hair and wiped her hands down her soiled apron. "Thank you, Kate. I could never have managed without your help." She kissed Kate lightly, and watched her trail wearily over to Davey Lee's house before, locking the door behind her. Laura was grateful in a way, to be alone to relax. Kate's girlish prattle about events, Clem White in particular, were enjoyable but tiring, and halfway through the day, Laura felt the baby quicken. She wanted to be alone with her secret, and lay expectantly on the bed that would soon be carted over to Davey's shed for storage.

Kate's 'glory box' was to be a big one, which was convenient, especially as Clem White's teacher salary was minimal. Laura lay on her back, her hands lightly stroking her stomach, wishing and hoping that her child would announce its presence again. But new life grows at its own pace, and she fell asleep waiting.

A few days later, she was almost ready for her move to Bathurst, and her new life with Joseph. Norman Lee had driven her into Mudgee the day before, and she had visited both Land Agents in town, listing her property for sale but neither of them were very enthusiastic. With advice from the doctor, she set the sale price on the land and shop, allowing extra for the selling Agent's fee, but was daunted by the reception her listing received.

"I doubt if you'll sell anything out there, these days, Mrs. Martin," said one. He was a corpulent, cigar-puffing chauvinist, who'd held a lifelong opinion that women had no business involving themselves in Real Estate. "But leave it with me, and I'll see what I can do." Immediately Laura had left his office, he tossed the details she'd given him into a large tray on his desk. The yellowed antiquity of the tray's contents gave the impression that, once consigned to this holding area, no document was ever referred to again.

Whilst waiting to rendezvous with Norman Lee for the journey back to Hargraves, she wandered into Mudgee's large department store, and realised she'd never taken the time to investigate its stock closely. She'd known the store offered a great array of goods, remembering the initial load Joseph put on their dray when they first arrived, but had never considered the diversity of stock offered. Walking slowly between the counters of haberdashery, appliances, clothing, even requisites for the garden enthusiast, she couldn't help comparing it with the meagre stock they'd offered in the Hargraves shop. But Joseph's priorities had been correct; there was no chance of them selling the range of millinery she saw before her now, nor the variety of sweetmeats, ornaments, mirrors, even perfumed stationery.

As she moved into another section of the store, she came upon a range of uniforms, obviously purchased by the financially secure for their staff. There was a wax model wearing a housemaid's black dress topped with a primly starched apron and a frill of white lace edged linen for a cap. Evidently, all cooks were buxom she decided, regarding the range of aprons that were lined up with military precision, and immediately recalled Joseph's insistence that they should hire staff for Tangarra.

She assumed there would be experienced people available to employ in Bathurst, and surprised herself by thinking she would enjoy training someone unskilled. After all, she had quickly read Mrs Beeton's instructions on the Duties of a Housemaid, and the Duties of a Laundry Maid, and was sure there were other interesting chapters she'd not seen as yet, in the hefty volume she'd found among Joseph's belongings.

The euphoria of her changed life wrapped her in a mantle of security, as she casually moved further along the wooden floor, and at the far end of the Staff Uniforms section, she smiled to see a deep claret dress that had a small white collar, and a sign which read: "Perfect for the family Governess."

She'd never worn anything so designated; when a Governess in England. She had worn a grey worsted dress, that she'd had to continually darn at the elbows from· leaning on the desk whilst pointing out details to her pupil. What a long time ago that seemed to be, and how her life had changed. She had no yearnings to return to England, though. Her mind was fixed firmly on the future and a dedication to make Joseph's life as comfortable and happy as she could.

It occurred to her, as she neared the front entrance again, that Joseph had given her a wedding present and she had given him nothing She retraced her steps to the counter that displayed "The Gentleman", and stood looking at the plethora of gift-boxed items. There was a magnificent shaving brush and cup, but she decided against that in case he mistakenly thought she would prefer him to remain clean-shaven. She loved him, with or without his bushy beard. A pleasant-faced assistant suddenly appeared, and after a short conversation with her, suggested that "Sir may be pleased with this cravat pin, madam? It is a very good quality and shows impeccable taste."

Laura turned the small black box several ways, allowing the sunlight that shone through a nearby window to spark the gold coloured pin, shaped like an Arthurian sword. She stood admiring the tiger-eye stone atop the hilt, but hesitated. "It's price?"

"Two pounds, madam, and a beautiful piece. Guaranteed to give pride to any man who wears it."

Joseph had insisted that Laura have money in her purse before she left him, but she brought out the small coin-holder she'd hugged to herself, since leaving Tolton. She carefully counted out the money, and waited while the assistant wrapped the box, with its pin carefully in special paper he retrieved from beneath the counter. She had shyly presented Joseph with two handkerchiefs at the Christmas party they'd had, at the same time as she'd given one each to Davey and Norman Lee. But this was to be the first present of real value to her dear Joseph, and her heart warmed at the thought of surprising him.

She had supper with Kate and her father that evening when they got back, and mentioned that during her stay, she intended visiting the little churchyard and the baby's grave, so that she could give Joseph a first hand description of the headstone that was in place now.

"Oh, you'll be so happy with it, Laura," enthused Kate. "Snowy Wilson made a very good job of it."

"Will you visit little Joseph's grave now and then, for us, Kate? We would be so pleased to know he hadn't been neglected. One of these days, I might enquire if I couldn't arrange for his little coffin to be transferred to his mother's grave in Bathurst."

"Of course," said Kate quickly. "But you needn't worry. Clem has made a point of going there every week for you. He's a good man, that, and only a few days before you came back, he let slip how he missed you from behind the shop counter."

"Oh, stop exaggerating, you minx," said Laura, colouring. "That is very kind of him. Please, next time you see him, tell him how much I ... Joseph and I, appreciate his thoughtfulness."

The following day was to be her last at Hargraves. She walked slowly up the hill to the church, then climbed the rise to the graveyard. The baby's grave was resplendent with the headstone, just as she'd envisaged it would be, and her eyes misted over as she knelt and touched the mauve daisies, and coral nasturtiums, that were the sign that Clem White had not forgotten to visit the baby's grave before he left for Sydney.

"Bless you, Clem," she breathed.

One of her final tasks before she locked the door to the now empty shop the following morning, was the result of an instinct that came upon her the night before. The bed from the shop had been hauled across to Davey's shed and she'd slept in Davey's house, or rather tossed and turned, partly from the excitement at soon being with Joseph again, and partly from sadness at finally leaving Hargraves. She'd assured Kate that she would visit her again one day, but knew it was an empty promise, as her life would be fully occupied from now on with her husband's well-being, their coming child, and Tangarra.

She'd felt a little guilty because she hadn't revealed her pregnancy to Kate, and been eternally grateful that her bout of nausea had not returned. She'd experienced uncomfortable mornings but said nothing, preferring to recall the old wives tale that heartburn indicated the new baby would be born with a mass of hair on its head.

She rose at five that last morning, crossed the road with the Land Title clutched in her hand and quietly entered the shop. It seemed lonely, and her footsteps rang hollow on the wooden floor as she proceeded into the kitchen area. There, where she had carefully raked and cleaned the ashes from the fireplace, she leaned forward; with the document rolled in brown paper and bound with a piece of string she jammed it out of sight into a niche in the chimney.

A refreshing coolness made the journey back to Bathurst tolerable, and as the coach drew to a stop with a clatter of hooves and a rattle of horse-brasses, Laura spotted Billy King waiting on the other side of the road. He had a rather large cart, and a hugely muscled horse pawing between its shafts. She alighted and waved, and Billy hustled the horse alongside the luggage compartment of the Cobb & Co coach, saying "Welcome back, Laura. Joseph said you'd have a large trunk, so I borrowed this from Sam the Blacksmith, in the main street"

The noise and chatter were too much for a self-respecting horse who was eager to get on with his work, and he jostled impatiently between the shafts, while two brawny men heaved the trunk aboard Billy's cart.

"How are we going to get it off?" asked Laura.

"Oh, don't you worry about that," Billy said, helping her aboard. "Old Sam is coming later to pick up his horse and cart, and between him and old Davey, we'll have no trouble."

Laura patted his hand to indicate she was ready for them to move, and smiled at the familiarity that had obviously grown between her two friends. "Joseph? He is well?"

"He was quiet while you were away, but as soon as we mentioned you over a meal, he seemed glad to join in with our conversation, even taking it over, at times."

Laura smiled knowingly, as Billy guided the dray towards the end of town, where his house had become a haven for the Martin family. "Did he shave?"

"No," said Billy, surprised by Laura's question. "I think he's trying to grow that beard back again."

"The quicker we can get him back to normal, the better," she said firmly. "I want to get him on his feet at the soonest possible moment."

Billy rocked gently with the sway set up by the horse, and looked at her sideways. "The Doctor did explain to you ...?"

"Oh yes," Laura answered. "But I will teach Joseph to accept his walking sticks as normal, in due time. Our child will see his father standing on his own two feet." She covered her mouth suddenly, and uttered a small 'oh'.

Billy quickly reigned in the horse, who tossed his head and snorted, glad of respite from the heavy load. "What is it, Laura. You're not ill?"

Laura swallowed hard and said, "I hadn't meant to tell you this way."

"Tell me what?" Billy looked confused for a moment, then realisation lit his face with surprise. "You mean ... you trying to tell me ...?"

"Our baby will arrive in September. But please, Billy, don't let Joseph know I've told you. Let him tell you himself."

'Well I'll be ..." said Billy, slapping his leg. "Does ol' Davey know? "

"No. But I'll tell him as soon as I get the chance – before dinner tonight, at least."

"I think I've got another special bottle in the cupboard," chuckled Billy as he flipped the reins. "Things is sure happening fast - makes life interesting, doesn't it?"

Laura lapsed into her thoughts for the rest of the journey back to the house. Perhaps she had been wrong not to tell Kate her news, but somehow she had not wanted her - or anyone in Hargraves - to know the circumstances while she was there. Davey would obviously spread the news when he returned, but she wouldn't have to explain herself.

Joseph and Davey greeted her, with an enthusiasm that could have been reserved for a relative who had been missing for many years, and Laura revelled in the attention. The large trunk was carried into Billy's living room, where it vied with the cedar table for the centre of attention. Having divested herself of her travelling suit, and donned a much lighter pink dress, Laura rejoined the men in the kitchen, thirsting for the cup of tea Billy had promised. Davey asked questions about the welfare of Kate and whether his pub was being looked after, and kept looking quizzically at Billy, who moved around with a smug look on his face.

"What's up with you, you ol' bugger?" said Davey. "You look like you lost a sixpence and found a gold nugget!"

"I can look how I want to, can't I?" countered Billy. "I'm just pleased to see Laura back with us."

He started whistling tunelessly, and Laura squeezed Joseph's hand. "Excuse me, my dear, will you come with me a moment, please?"

Laura pushed her mystified husband's chair into their room, and he watched while she fished in the bottom of her travel bag. "I have brought you my wedding present," she said, handing him the small package and kissing his prickly chin.

He unwrapped it carefully and looked at the golden cravat pin, before shaking his head. "How can I live up to this ... this love you give me, Laura? I do not deserve you."

"Nonsense," said Laura briskly. "Maybe in a year's time, when I have nagged and cajoled you onto your feet again, you may well regret those words, Joseph Martin." She leaned forward and embraced him and for a moment, though she dare not lift her head to look, she could have sworn she felt emotion catch in his throat.

The rest of the day flew as she chatted to them all about her visit to Hargraves, and having arranged with Joseph that he should announce about their coming child at dinner, her one regret was that she'd been unable to gain Davey's individual attention first. When Joseph had spoken, Davey's silence worried her at first, until he turned to Billy and said, "You knew about this, didn't you, you old fraud? And you didn't say a word to me."

"Only because Laura wanted to tell you herself," Billy remonstrated, "but you've been yakking so much all afternoon, she couldn't get a word in sideways."

Both men were grinning widely throughout their banter, and it stopped only when Davey said, "Well, let's have yer, then. I'm sure you can find another bottle in that cupboard of yours."

Long after that evening had faded into Laura's mental album, she kept reminding herself what a wonderful 'family' she had acquired, with not one, but two stand-in fathers. Billy King and Davey Lee were the father figure she'd never had, Joseph and their child had become her purpose, and her future looked bright, with the excitement of a new beginning.

Next day, she walked the mile into Bathurst's main street of shops, for exercise she told them all. When she had gone, Joseph revealed to Billy and Davey that the twelfth of May was to be her twenty-third birthday.

"We'll have a party for her," enthused Billy, always ready for an excuse to bring out his good china, and immediately went to his cupboard to check his supply of wine. Between Laura's arrival, the wedding, and now the birthday, his bottles were diminished.

When he said as much to Davey, the answer was, "Well, you've saved them long enough, you ol' skinflint. Don't worry, I'll supply you with more – the least I can do."

"No you won't," said Billy vehemently. "We'll go halves."

Joseph was resting in the garden, and Davey joined him to read the newspaper. Compared to Hargraves, there was much activity in Bathurst and he revelled in the stories of social gatherings, the various sports activities such as cricket, and harness racing, that took place at the Show-ground, and pondered whether he should try and sell his house and pub in Hargraves, and move to the City. But he'd dismissed the idea, telling himself that at the age of eighty-one, he was too set in his ways He added to his conviction by reading aloud the latest story of larrikins, that were making a nuisance of themselves each evening, in Bathurst's main street.

"Don't know what the world's coming to," he said, but Joseph wasn't listening.

"Davey," said Joseph thoughtfully. "I want to give Laura a very special birthday present. Will you help me?"

"'Course," came the prompt reply. "What would you like for her?"

When Joseph revealed his idea, Davey whistled. "Are you sure?"

"Quite sure." Joseph's lips tightened a little, making the scar on his face stand out amongst his fledgling beard, but his grey eyes were flint-like with determination. The past weeks with Laura at his side had brought back a lot of the Joseph Martin personality that she'd known when they first met, and she'd magnanimously bowed to his wishes, in an effort to help him regain his normality.

A chorus of kookaburras woke Laura on her birthday. She stretched contentedly in her bed, before turning to Joseph's to see if he was awake.

"Good morning, my love" he said as their eyes met. "And a very happy birthday."

Laura slipped from between the covers, crossed the room and kissed his forehead. "Thank you, my dear. I know it will be a happy one because we are together now. Are you ready?"

Joseph smiled and tossed his cover aside, and Laura sat on his bed, before rolling up the legs of the long-johns he wore. Slowly, she massaged the wasted calf muscles and gently pummelled his thighs. After ten minutes of this she gripped each ankle in turn, and pushed so that his knees folded, then pulled his legs straight again. She'd devised this morning ritual the day after their wedding; at first Joseph complained that she was wasting her time and energy but he began to look forward to the exercise, acknowledging the fact that despite the damage to the nerves in the lower half of his body, he was by no means paralysed, and both Laura and the doctor were adamant that he would one day regain a modicum of mobility.

"I swear your legs feel stronger to me," encouraged Laura. "We'll have you on your feet by the time our baby arrives, you'll see."

At breakfast later, Billy said officiously, "Now, you're not having your presents until this afternoon, Mrs Martin. Me'n Davey's got it all planned, so you two just enjoy yourselves, and leave it all to us." Laura had been reading to Joseph in the garden for a while after lunch, then when he dozed she went back into their room to bathe herself and change. She took her time, smoothing oil of lavender into her arms and hands, and puffing a light talcum powder over her body, whilst thinking of her recent shopping trip. She'd been unable to resist a pair of plump cushions covered with green brocade and edged with a thick gold velvet cord, that fitted the picture she had of their living room at Tangarra. When purchasing several items for the baby, she'd remembered the times with Jemima, when they wandered these same stores, excited plans brightening their chatter.

Before she left town, she walked to the cemetery and visited Jemima's grave. Already weeds were rampant around the cement border, and as she pulled a few aside, she vowed that when they were settled in Tangarra, she would persuade Joseph that Jemima's baby should be re-interred from Hargraves, to be with his mother.

Laura took her time with a careful toilette, knowing that Davey and Billy would ensure Joseph sat quietly in the garden, and they would summon her the moment she was needed. When eventually dressed in her undergarments, she brushed her hair until it shone like burnished copper. She twisted it carefully into a pile on the top of her head, and secured it with a a tortoiseshell comb that was edged with mock pearls.   During the shopping foray she'd also bought herself a beautiful maternity dress. At first, she'd hesitated because there wasn't long to go now. "Hardly justified," she'd muttered at her reflection in the fitting room's mirror. "But go on, spoil yourself, for once."

Looking into the bedroom mirror now, she smiled, because the white lace collar on the lemon chiffon bodice, gave a brilliance to her hair that seemed to banish any vestige of the trials she'd undergone since arriving in Australia. The full skirt of a deeper gold taffeta sat snugly over her hips, the swell of her stomach just noticeable and she thought she'd never owned such a beautiful item of clothing before.

Davey had said they would have a special high tea in the garden at four, so like a Queen making a grand entrance at a Diplomatic Embassy function, Laura sailed through the garden door with a radiance that seemed to light the entire area. Then her hand flew to her mouth, as with her hazel eyes sparking a mixture of confusion and alarm, she saw the men were on their feet to greet her.

All three of them.

In each hand, Joseph was gripping walking canes that belonged to Billy; the tip of each support was set in an almost imperceptible depression in the grass, and the two older men stood tentatively close to their invalid, ready to thrust a hand beneath his armpits, should he lose his balance. But Joseph's determination made this unnecessary, and Laura hardly dared to move, in case he wavered.

"Happy birthday, my dear," Joseph said softly.

Laura glanced at the excited smiles either side of him, and knew immediately this greeting had been a planned, hard won victory for them all. She felt her heart would burst as she glided across the grass, put a cool hand each side of Joseph's face and kissed him fully on the lips. She wanted to embrace him, to feel his arms circle her back, but knew this was impossible - instead she kissed Billy and Davey in turn, and her throat felt too restricted to speak for a moment. Then she found her voice, and said, "Thank you, Joseph. I couldn't have wished for a grander birthday gift."

"Yes, well you'd better sit down now- both of you," said an emotional Billy. "Me'n Davey here's got everything ready."

Laura took the canes out of Joseph's hands while the men lowered him back into his chair, then she moved to arrange the light blanket over his knees. "Let's do without that, this afternoon," he said. "Let's pretend this is the first day of real recovery for me."

"Let's not pretend at all," Laura said gently, kissing him again. "This really happened and we'll go on from there."

Billy and Davey walked into the house to produce the grand afternoon tea they'd prepared, Davey blowing his nose loudly.

"Davey is going back to Hargraves in a few days," said Joseph. "I shall miss him greatly."

"We both shall," said Laura. The news was not unexpected, but saddened her just the same. She settled on the low stool beside Joseph, then inclined her head towards the house. "They helped you to your feet, didn't they?"

"Every day you were away," said Joseph, "they took turns at massaging my legs as you have done, and I actually took two steps yesterday, but they wouldn't risk my trying to walk towards you, in case I fell. Which I think I may have, you looked so beautiful when you appeared. I wanted to, my God, how I wanted to hasten to you and take you in my arms."

"You will soon, my love," whispered Laura, her eyes shining with emotion. "You will."

The following Tuesday found her emotions torn a different way; Davey had booked passage on the Cobb & Co coach returning to Mudgee, and she couldn't find the words to express her love for the old man as he shook hands with Joseph, and hugged her, before leaving the house. Billy was to walk to the coaching station with him for company, and as the two figures grew smaller before they turned the corner into town, Davey turned and waved.

Laura felt choked and gripped Joseph's hand; she had pushed his chair to the door to farewell Davey, and his eyes were sad at the inevitable departure. "He must come to stay with us awhile at Tangarra, when we are settled," he murmured. Laura could only nod.

Between being monitored by the doctor, Billy's paternal concern and Laura's constant care, Joseph's mobility improved over time, although he grew tired very easily from the effort to propel himself. He limped badly, and some days needed to lean heavily on the canes, and would easily have lost his confidence had it not been for the tremendous moral support he was given. Once only, in a fit of depression, he had bemoaned his impotency to Laura, and she had brushed this aside, remarking that the growing baby would have made her spurn any intimacy anyway, and that she attached far more importance to their love, than their lovemaking.

11 TANGARRA

Although the temperature rose as May moved into July, several evenings had been spent with Billy around the large fire he insisted on lighting, in the lounge room. "Can't have anything going wrong at this stage," he'd said firmly, when Laura remonstrated that they would be warm enough in their room.

Laura had occupied herself by learning all she could about Tangarra; the Manager and his wife called every week to give Joseph a report on situations that arose, and she listened carefully to every instruction he gave them.

Tom Weekes and his wife, Betty, had been living in the house in order to maintain it. While the men discussed the horses, their training and plans for entering various harness races the following year, Laura kept one ear open to them while she chatted to Betty. She absorbed every detail she could about her future home.

"You should come out and have a look," said Betty kindly. "At least you'd have an idea of what to expect."

"Well, I don't know," Laura hesitated, not wanting to go there without Joseph, at least for her first visit. "The baby is due in a little over five weeks ..."

"Why don't we?" chimed in Joseph, who had overheard Betty's remark. "If you feel you can make the journey, we could trot out there one afternoon. It's only five miles out of town." With the aid of the blacksmith's cart that Billy occasionally borrowed, they had made several trips into Bathurst, and Joseph had become strong enough to help a little when they moved him. "I'm sure if I can manage a mile into the shops, I can manage the distance to Tangarra, as long as you can, my dear."

Laura struggled with her concern for her husband and their baby, and it vied with her longing to see Tangarra. They had agreed they would stay with Billy until the baby was born, as it was much more convenient for the midwife. They would both feel more confident, knowing medical assistance was close at hand in the case of emergencies.

She looked for a long moment at Joseph's expectant face; his beard had fully grown again to completely cover his scar and his grey eyes were bright with enthusiasm, as she had known him before the accident. Her pregnancy had been comfortable and trouble-free, so that she had no qualms about her own ability to take the journey, and the prospect of Joseph being with her when she first saw Tangarra, was temptation enough.

"Very well," she said softly to Betty, "we'll come out tomorrow."

"Great," chipped in Tom Weekes. "We'll have a nice meat pie and veggies ready for you, and you can take your time getting to know the place."

"Tom," chided his wife. "I doubt if Missus Martin will want to tuck into a big meal like that. Don't worry," she added, "I'll see you don't go hungry - the men can have a slice of beef or a pie if they want to. We'll have scrambled eggs, or something light like that."

"Oh please," remonstrated Laura, "You mustn't go to a lot of trouble."

"Nonsense," chortled Betty Weekes. "It will give me an excuse to pretty the place up. Tom's not one much for flowers and things, but I like them around the house. Do you?"

"Yes, I do," breathed Laura. "Are there flowers in the garden?"

"God Bless you," answered the buxom country woman. "The place is full of them."

Laura was so excited, she hardly slept that night.

They had to go through town next day, to reach the southern outskirts and the Tangarra property. They passed a rather important looking edifice next to the Bank, and Joseph pointed out that the offices belonged to Andrew Thompson, his Solicitor and Business Manager.

"Billy, I wonder if I could prevail on you to call on him tomorrow morning, and ask him to come and see me Friday, after lunch, please?"

"Certainly," Billy answered, flicking the reins . "I have to come in for supplies anyway."

"I would like you to meet him, my dear," Joseph continued to Laura, as they neared the end of the main street. "If you are to understand and help me handle the business, there is no time like the present for you to learn the intricacies."

Laura sensed a twinge of the former Joseph again, but smiled at the thought that she would be on a much more equal footing with him now and 'the intricacies' that he referred to held no fears for her. She had rather surprised herself by the speed with which she had come to understand the men when they discussed stocks and shares and dealings in horses that Joseph had been overseeing from his sickbed.

Approximately five miles beyond town, Billy, who had been driving with the utmost consideration for the condition of his two passengers, turned the cart into a red dirt drive. The entrance to Tangarra was a huge wrought iron archway, that had the name of the property wound into the span overhead. Stone walls led from the entrance for about a hundred yards, then petered out to a vast expanse of rolling paddocks.

One of the most striking memories Laura had of their journey from Melbourne during those first weeks in Australia, was the country's seemingly limitless horizons, and here they were, swaying gently with the motion of the cart, travelling through a tract of land that was not only endless with no more than clumps of trees visible, but the land was theirs. The thought made her speechless.

About a mile further along the pathway, she began to see greener paddocks that were in large squares laced together with white painted fences, and in each square was two, sometimes three magnificent horses. She gasped with the sheer beauty of the animals, and Joseph smiled at her enthusiasm. All at once the pathway curved between a tall canopy of dense evergreens that lent a charm to the drive. The sudden shade reminded Laura of picnics in the glades of England's Epping Forest, where she and Aunt Marchant had spent their holiday one year.

With euphoria flushing her cheeks, she clasped Joseph's arm and he squeezed her hand in his. They emerged from the cool tunnel and, as though they had entered a different world, Laura saw her future home.

Tangarra was as resplendent as any of the grand homes she had known at Tolton. She turned again quickly to Joseph but no words came - she was almost fearful of this being a dream that would dissolve into a sordid reality, if she dared wake.

Billy halted the carriage alongside the three wide steps that reached up from the driveway to the front entrance; the cedar door had coloured glass inserts in a fan shape above it, and to either side, ran a verandah that stretched along the entire length of the building. Small paned windows set each side of the imposing front door seemed to smile a welcome to her.

Above the verandah, the sun gleamed from the white painted walls of the upper storey, and it seemed incongruous that there should be smoke spiralling gently from two of the chimneys. It was a great effort for Laura to look away for the moment it took Billy to help her down from the cart, and as her feet set on Tangarra for the first time she breathed, "Oh, Joseph, it's beautiful."

The front door was suddenly opened by a beaming Betty Weekes. "Tom's here to help with Mister Martin," she said, as her husband appeared behind her. "Come on in, Missus Martin. Strewth, hark at me inviting you in to your own home." She moved down two steps and took Laura's arm to assist her, as there was no handrail. "Y'gets to feel a bit clumsy towards the end, don't you? Been there often enough myself, so I know, although my kids are all long grown up and left us."

"Thank you, Betty," said Laura, a little breathless after the effort. Then she turned to Joseph as the men helped him onto the verandah. "I think my husband should sit down."

"I think you both should," said Billy paternally then he gazed across the scene in front of them. In the immediate foreground were shrubs that were a riot of pink, red, coral and white hibiscus flowers. Beyond them was a small orchard of lemon, mulberry and orange trees and beyond, was a vista of rolling hills that were already bright green from recent rains that had broken yet another drought.

"Have a rest," said Betty leading them to white wicker chairs that stood beside a similar table on the verandah, already laid with glasses and a plate of small biscuits. "I'll just check on lunch."

"Laura will probably want to see inside the house, Mrs. Weekes," said Joseph. "Take her with you - I have already seen it. I'll be quite content with Billy here, just looking at the view.

"I'll take you to the stables after," Tom said to him. "The women can have a good natter."

"I can wait till after lunch," said Laura, realising that Betty would be hard pressed to show her around the house and keep an eye on lunch at the same time. Besides, she loved the excitement of anticipation - as a child she had often been chastised for balancing the last strawberry on her diminishing mound of ice cream, savouring the last mouthful. To Aunt Marchant, it was 'playing with her food.'

Billy, Tom and Joseph chatted on general subjects and Laura was happy to sit back with the glass Betty had filled with cool lemonade, and contemplate her good fortune. Aunt Marchant, had she lived, would have been delighted with her fortuitous marriage, and if this had been England, would have ensconced herself as part of the household within weeks. Laura sipped her drink and smiled enigmatically. Destiny had a most unexpected approach to most lives. Her eyes clouded momentarily, realising that Tangarra was exactly the wonderful home Jemima had been expecting and again, she considered herself blessed.

The lunch Betty laid on the verandah table was as she'd promised, hearty for the men, and light for the women. Gazing across the orchard as she ate, Laura considered she would never tire of such magnificent scenery and mentally promised herself that she would spend at least half an hour a day out here, if only to soak up the tremendous calm that seemed to pervade Tangarra.

She was not naive enough to forget that there would be times of tribulation, especially as Joseph seemed daily to pick up the threads of his old personality - maybe not quite so domineering now that she was his wife. All was right with her world, and she absorbed the atmosphere like parched flowers do rain.

"Off you go then, dear," said Joseph as soon as lunch was finished. "I shall be with Tom - Billy, you'll come with us?"

"Pleased to," said Billy, who had already been told he was welcome to move into Tangarra with them, if he wished. However, he'd declined, saying he would gladly be a regular visitor, but his home was in Bathurst proper and he was too old to change his ways now. He assisted Joseph to his feet and with Tom's help, the three of them made their way down the steps and around to the back of the house.

"That's got them busy," said Betty with a wink. "Now, in you come, Missus Martin."

"Please call me Laura. I'm very proud to be Joseph's wife, but all my friends call me Laura."

"Ooh, I couldn't," said Betty crestfallen. "Me'n Tom will work for you, and make sure all goes right for you, but we knows our place."

Laura thought this was a quaint attitude to find in Australia - already she become used to the almost classless familiarity she met, and Betty's attitude surprised her. She changed the subject. "Where will you both live when Joseph and I move in?"

"We have a little cottage about a mile the other side of the stables, and I looks after the men. My Tom, the foreman Albert, and the young lads, Kenny and David," answered Betty, obviously relieved. "We're very comfortable there, and I can be handy for you if you wants me.

"I'm sorry," said Laura, a little confused. "I thought Joseph had hired you as housekeeper."

"I'm too old for that now," chuckled Betty. "You'll likely get a much more able woman for that from Bathurst. There's plenty looking for a good job."

"Are they trained?"

"You'll likely have to do that yourself, Missus Martin. Most of the good women available are looking for work because their husbands have failed at the mines, or can't take to farming, so they take to the beer,. She handed Laura a tray of empty glasses and piled the lunch plates on to another. "Come on, we'll go into the kitchen first."

Laura's surprise at Betty's revelation was overtaken by curiosity as she followed her into the house; the hallway they stepped into had a polished cedar floor. With pleasure, Laura noticed that the sun striking through the fanlight created a golden pattern on the boards. The hallway was devoid of any artefact, but led to an imposing staircase. Either side of the hall way the doors were closed but they moved forward to an entrance beneath the staircase that opened into the kitchen.

A low ember fire glowed in the fireplace at one end, and the scrubbed wooden table with two chairs, looked out of place. Food stuffs and a few pots and pans stood on a shelf against one wall and a bench that contained a sink ran under the uncurtained window that overlooked the area behind the house. Apart from that, the kitchen was bare.

Laura felt there was something amiss, but said nothing, her attention taken by the sight of Joseph, Tom, and Billy outside, making their way through a gate in a walled area, which she guessed was the stable-yard. Behind that, she could see some of the fenced paddocks they'd observed as they drove in, and revelled in the fact that some of the handsome stock could be seen from, the kitchen window.

Betty stacked the dishes in the sink. "We'll leave these - you'll want to see the rest of the house."

The study-cum library that opened off the large lounge room had some empty bookshelves lining the walls; the lounge room itself, the dining room, the reception room off the other side of the hallway were spacious, had ornate ceilings and cornices but were like the four bedrooms and bathroom upstairs - empty. Betty was so busy showing her around that she failed to notice Laura's increasing dismay.

Descending the bare staircase again, Laura found her voice. "Betty... I er. .. I hadn't expected the house to be unfurnished."

"Tom said that's how Mister Martin bought it at such a reasonable price. The previous owners took all their things with them, and he presumed you would be putting all your own stuff in." Betty showed some bemusement. "Didn't Mister Martin tell you?

"He's been very ill," Laura stuttered. "No doubt he thought he'd mentioned it."

Tom and Billy were helping Joseph to mount the dray when the women reappeared on the verandah. "You've had enough excitement for today," Billy called. "We had to hang on to this husband of yours to stop him trying to see everything at once."

Joseph looked pale but happy and Laura didn't have the heart to do anything else but join in the friendly farewell banter. However, she determined to discuss the situation with him, as soon as they were alone in their room later that evening. Joseph and Billy kept asking her what she thought of Tangarra on the way home, and neither of them seemed to notice the dulling of her previous excitement.

Later that evening, none of them were particularly hungry after the sumptuous lunch Betty had provided so they nibbled on cold lamb sandwiches, then retired early. Laura was glad to rest from the weight she was carrying now, and laid back with a sigh of relief after she had helped Joseph undress, and settled him in his bed. Thoughts about Tangarra tumbled in her head and she found it difficult to sort her doubts from her enthusiasm.

The days were short at this time of the year, and she loved to lay back and look at the twinkling velvet that was the night sky. Tonight however, she had many other things on her mind and that was no recipe for a restful sleep.

"Joseph," she said, smiling at the mumbled response that told her he was sleepy. "I loved Tangarra, the moment I saw it."

"I'm glad," was the spare reply.

"I hadn't expected to find it empty." There was no response, so she took courage and continued, "Can we afford to furnish all the rooms properly?"

Laura had already made the acquaintance of William Sutton, the Bank Manager, and over the past few months she had become used to making withdrawals, according to Joseph's instructions. His allowance to her had been more than generous so that, for the first time in her life, she had been free to browse, shop, and purchase whatever took her fancy. However, she had no idea of the extent of Joseph's finances, and refused to make the fact known at the Bank. Such a confession seemed to her to be an accusation of her husband, and this was sacrilege.

It did appear though, that her purchase of the two brocade cushions was inopportune, considering there was no furniture for them to decorate, and several other items she'd bought to store in the large trunk, had suddenly lost their importance in her scheme of things. She had to know just what was going to happen. Would they be living in an imposing shell, furnishing it over a period of weeks, months, years maybe?

"Joseph? I asked …"

"I did hear, my dear," he rumbled. "I thought that, as soon as you are well enough after the baby arrives, we would go into Graveby's large furniture store together, and you can choose whatever furnishings you want."

"What a wonderful prospect," Laura murmured in the dark. But in his inimitable manner, he hadn't made it clear as to the amount of expenditure they could afford. Deviously she added, "We shall have to furnish the bedrooms first, of course, then the kitchen ..."

"We'll equip the whole house at once," he said suddenly. "Then we can get down to business. Now, I'm rather tired so good night, my dear."

The euphoria that had floated her earlier in the day returned, and it was a long time before she could allow sleep to dull her brain.

The following morning, Joseph awoke fresh and eager but Laura felt as though she had been awake all night. She knew that wasn't so, because vivid pictures of people clambering up and down stairs, all calling at once and asking her where she would like varying boxes and cupboards placed, had pounded through her dreams and left an exhaustion that weighted her eyes. She was thankful that the baby's activity had eased of late. "Preparing itself for the coming birth," Miss Hills had said during her last visit.

Laura raised herself to her elbow as sunlight filled the room and looked over to Joseph. "Would you mind if I don't massage your legs this morning, dear?" she asked. "I'm afraid I was too excited to sleep very well, and ..."

"That's perfectly all right," said Joseph kindly. "Time will be a little scarce this morning anyway. I have some papers to put in order before Andrew comes."

"Oh dear," said Laura, setting her feet hurriedly to the floor. "I had forgotten Mr Thompson's appointment. I shall help you, if I may. It will be good for me to understand what you are to discuss with him, before he arrives."

Joseph looked pleased with her eagerness, but waved his hand towards her. "There is plenty of time, my dear. Don't rush. You must take extra care of yourself and our child at this late stage. You are feeling well, I trust, and know what to do when the time arrives?"

Laura chuckled at his concern. "Women have been giving birth for thousands and thousands of years, my love. I don't think my labour will be very much different." She tried to sound as reassuring as she could, but memories made her say a small prayer that her coming travail would be infinitely easier than Jemima's had been.

She assisted Joseph with his daily ablutions then selected the clothes they would wear for the day. For herself, she chose the navy blue dress she had made to minimise her bulk; it had a starched white Puritan collar and she felt confident that it gave her an air of efficiency with which she intended to impress Joseph's solicitor. To back the impression, she spent the morning listening carefully as Joseph explained the various documents he kept in a large wooden box ,and her satisfaction was complete when he asked her opinion on several items he wished to discuss, during the afternoon's meeting with Andrew Thompson.

Bathurst's richest business manager was prompt; Joseph Martin was his most valued client and one worth cultivating, so all others were set aside when the command was received. Since the accident, instructions from Joseph Martin had been delivered by hand but this was the first time he'd been asked to attend his client personally. However, the extent of the man's wealth had increased phenomenally - he had the gift of knowing just when to buy or sell, and Thompson had ridden on the crest of his success.

The wily man always walked or sat, with a rigid spine, having convinced himself very early in his life that this would recompense for his lack of stature. He now stood with the same rigidity before the unlit hearth in Billy's lounge room, awaiting his client's entrance. He was not prepared for his client's wife to be with him.

"Missus Martin," he oiled when Joseph introduced Laura.

She felt an immediate distaste for the limpness of his hand shake, but gave no sign. "Mister Thompson, I'm pleased to meet you."

Laura helped Joseph, then sat beside him on Billy's ancient sofa, indicating the armchair opposite to Andrew Thompson. He perched on its edge as though nervous that his black business suit would pick up dust, and occupied the next five minutes in desultory chatter about the weather, the local population now exceeding four thousand, and that he'd learned the train journey from the heart of Sydney to Bathurst, now took only six hours. Laura listened politely, but wondered if men always spent so long discussing subjects other than the reason for their meeting? It appeared to be a dreadful waste of time if they did.

It then occurred to her that their un-likable visitor was waiting for her to leave, and that Joseph had not indicated she was to be party to their business discussions. She decided to squash Andrew Thompson's expectations and reached to the table for the portfolio of papers Joseph had placed there.

"Joseph, dear, I'm sure we are using up Mister Thompson's valuable time - do you need these?"

"Quite right," said Joseph accepting the folder, completely oblivious to Laura's motives. He opened it and as Laura leaned towards him, she sensed Thompson's pained expression that she should be scrutinising documents he considered privy to himself and his client. "Now, Andrew,, Laura and I have decided to sell these two properties in Orange - we have a lot of expenditure shortly to furnish Tangarra, and the proceeds will replenish the coffers."

Andrew Thompson looked aghast. The notion that Laura could have had any influence over his client's decision was almost unthinkable- until now, he'd been adept at supervising the extensive Martin Investments folio. Between Joseph's trust in his capabilities, and his ability to swindle respectable sums from the various business deals, he'd been able to live comfortably and at the same time, gamble on horses. Now there was another factor in the set up, and that disturbing entity was a woman. Joseph Martin's wife no less, with every legal claim to the Martin holdings. Thompson paled, and for a moment his spine seemed not to support him.

"Mister Martin ... er, this does not strike me as being a good idea, sir."

"Why ever not?" said Laura, determined not to be cut out of the conversation.

Thompson's sideways glance at her was a flash of frustration, and Laura found it difficult to keep her features composed. Her instinctive dislike of the man had entrenched itself during the interview, and she felt almost evil in her determination to keep him mentally off-balance. Joseph seemed too engrossed in the rest of the folio to have noticed the mental challenge between his wife and his business manager, but looked up sharply at the icy tone in Andrew Thompson's reply.

"Because, Madam," - he began haughtily, then hesitated at Joseph's reaction and changed his manner. "Well, dear lady, the market for properties such as these, is rather depressed and ... but we could not expect you to understand."

Laura bristled at his patronising tone and sat erect. She asked, "Has the property market in Orange slumped suddenly. Mister Thompson? Why, only a few days ago the Western Plains newspaper was extolling the buoyancy of the market in Bathurst, Orange, Dubbo and even Wellington."

Thompson flushed angrily at Laura's knowledge, and his ire increased when Joseph patted his wife's hand, and said, "Bravo. my dear. You have been extremely vigilant. I'm proud of you."

"Very well," said Thompson gruffly, his rigidity returning. "I shall try to ..."

"You will sell them," Joseph interrupted. "Thank you for your advice, Andrew, but as I'm sure you will agree, the final decision rests with us."

Thompson could not argue, and Laura gave a loud sigh of relief when she closed the front door behind him. She hoped fervently that he would not be a regular visitor, here nor at Tangarra, because she did not want her golden dreams of the future tarnished by having to deal with such an impossible man. She would bow to Joseph's experience of course, and believed that he would have made many enquiries before choosing Thompson as his business manager - however, there was no rule in her mind that stipulated she must like the man.

She brushed the incident aside during the next few weeks, preferring to concentrate on her own plans for furnishing Tangarra. There would be carpets and curtains to choose, tasteful sofas and chairs to select for the lounge, and reception room. She'd always longed for a dining table and chairs that would seat at least twenty guests. The kitchen would be fitted with the finest copper pans and enamel dishes.

Her loved books of Jane Austen, Anthony Trollope, and so many other good authors, would sit in the library bookcase, alongside Pitt's encyclopedic dictionary, Roget's Thesaurus and the other books she had acquired slowly during her life in Australia. Mrs Beeton's Cookery Book, she decided, would be more suitably kept in the kitchen.

Joseph should set out his books himself on the shelves in the library, she decided. And he must have a desk. Maybe she would have one made especially for him, leather-topped and gold-tooled, and have it set in the centre of the room, so that he could have ample access to them on walking canes, or in his invalid chair.

Then there was the nursery to consider. An amused Joseph watched as she drew up endless lists, and he patiently listened to her endless talk. "You know, Laura, you could be a child-bride rather than a twenty-two year old mother-to-be."

Laura laughed easily. "I feel like a child-bride – I think the twenty-two year old mother-to-be will soon come to the fore."

"Best take it easy, lass," said Billy with a grin one evening. "You'll have no energy to birth that baby of yours if you're not careful."

"I feel as strong as an ox," Laura bantered. "In fact, I could clean this house from top to bottom, the way I'm feeling today."

"Oh yes?" said Billy knowingly. "You know what Miss Hills said."

What Miss Hills had foretold was a tremendous burst of energy just hours before a mother went into labour, and again Laura proved her right. Contractions began in an almost fleeting wave across the small of her back around five o'clock on the second evening of September.

Billy hastened to summon the midwife as the contractions increased, and Joseph held Laura's hand until she arrived. The efficient Miss Hills promptly banished the men to the kitchen, having already given instructions for water to be boiled, and cheerfully managed Laura through her labour.

By ten o'clock the following morning. Laura felt she had made her maximum effort and with heart-thumping she strained against the seemingly immovable object that wedged in her groin. She lay on her back fighting for another hour, her hands gripped onto the iron bed-rails behind her, the pillow beneath her damp hair stained with perspiration, until, with a sensation akin to pure hatred, she ejected her baby girl. The hatred was immediately overtaken by a flood of mother-love as she heard her baby cry, and her painful gasps subsided into tears of pure joy, as Miss Hills cut the umbilical cord. "Good girl, good girl."

The midwife attended to immediate necessities. then stuck her head out of the bedroom door and yelled, "It's a girl. You can come in shortly."

In the kitchen, Billy pumped Joseph's hand and his face was wreathed in smiles. Neither of them had slept through the night, although Billy had dozed by the fire, spasmodically rousing to poke it into life. Joseph had tried to concentrate on a book but couldn't help glancing towards the door, when urgent sounds filtered down the corridor.

The mid-morning sunlight on September 3rd, did not have scintillating shafts of Summer, but the new life that had begun under their roof was being welcomed with a gentle brilliance.

"It's all over, son," said Billy, " and I'll bet you're feeling a a right clever clogs?"

Joseph's expression was a mixture of relief and embarrassment at Billy's enthusiasm, but he couldn't disguise his pride. He willingly accepted the celebratory glass when Billy pressed it into his hand, and took a sip. "I rather think that Laura should be called the clever one," he observed happily. then his face clouded. "I do hope she is all right."

"I shouldn't worry," said Billy, "Miss Hills wouldn't let anything happen to Laura or the baby, and she would have called the doctor quick if something had gone wrong. Have no fear, Joseph m'boy, all's well."

Joseph was grateful to rely on the old man's judgement, but waited with growing nervousness until the nurse appeared at the door and said. "You can go in, now, Mister Martin. She's a beautiful baby, and they are both extremely well. Wish all births were as straightforward as that one. I could do with a cup of tea, Billy."

Joseph didn't hear her last remarks, he had already begun limping towards the bedroom, his canes beating an impatient tattoo on the boards. He tapped quietly on the door with one of them then let himself in; the sun filtered weakly though the lace curtains and the ambience in the room was one of hallowed wonder as Laura, pale but radiant, gazed at him, then down to their daughter in her arms.

Joseph kissed Laura's forehead gently, then sat on the edge of the bed and looked at the unbelievably small bundle. Jemima's death had been the main memory, not the soft vulnerability of his son, who had been several days old when he first saw him. So he felt that this baby, his and Laura's baby, was the first time he had been party to the miracle that is childbirth.

"Hello, Lydia," he whispered, his voice hoarse with emotion. "You are nearly as beautiful as your mother."

"You remembered," smiled Laura.

"We agreed, " Joseph smiled back. "If it was a son, we'd name him Joseph. A girl was to be named after your mother."

"Are you disappointed?"

"In no way. This is to be our only baby. Laura. and I thank God we were given her before it was too late. My son is a sad memory to us both, but our daughter shall have everything a father can bestow on her, and I know our pride will know no bounds as she grows into a beautiful replica of you, my dearest love."

Laura's heart was full with so much love, she could not stop the tears escaping her eyes and she bent over the baby trying not to let Joseph see, but he did.

"What is it, my love," he asked with concern.

"Nothing," she said illogically. "It's just that I'm so happy."

"And exhausted, no doubt," said Joseph. "I'll leave you now to rest."

"No," she replied, brushing a tear-drop from the baby's forehead. "Please, I'm sure Billy would like to see our daughter. too."

Billy was hovering outside the door and came in eagerly when Joseph called - quietly, for fear of alarming the baby. With an air of reverence Billy leaned towards the new arrival and unobserved, tucked something into the folds of the shawl, while Laura held her face up to receive his kiss.

"You didn't say her name," he admonished Joseph.

"Lydia." Laura said the name softly, as though hearing it for the first time. "Isn't she beautiful, Billy?"

"She's your daughter, isn't she?" said Billy, intimating the baby's appearance was a foregone conclusion. "Anyway, my best congratulations to you both. I'll send a message up to Davey directly. He'll be like a cattle-dog that's just been given his first bone."

"Righto," said Miss Hills, appearing busily. "Off you go. The lass needs some sleep now".

"Thank you, Billy. And I know Kate will be so thrilled, too," said Laura, then added a little wearily, "I think I shall sleep, now."

"Of course, my dear," said Joseph. "We have all our lives together to enjoy our baby daughter."

The door closed behind her visitors and Laura's content seemed unassailable. She had a husband that loved and indulged her, a baby daughter she could adore, friends and acquaintances she could rely on and a wonderful home to look forward to. Days before, Joseph had informed her that Andrew Thompson had sold the Orange properties. Even her distaste for their obnoxious business manager seemed insignificant, in the light of her happiness. She drifted into blissful sleep, completely unaware of the tragedy that would eventually destroy her present world.

12 ANOTHER CHALLENGE

Lydia's fifth birthday was approaching, and Laura was justly proud of their little daughter. Her prettiness drew constant remarks, as did her pretty pout. Joseph had never recovered from his dreadful accident and Laura struggled daily to cope with everyone's oscillating spirits. 'Nevertheless,' she often reminded herself, 'you haven't enough fingers to count your blessings.' They included Tangarra, their lovely home which, over the years, Laura had transformed into a mansion.

Little patent shoes pattered along the hallway, and Laura scooped up the child in a motherly hug. "Who's nearly five, then?"

"Me!"

Laura kissed 's soft cheek as she carried her into the library, where Joseph sat at his desk, poring over figures.

"Daddy," said Laura. "Our angel is nearly five years old."

"An' I want a pony."

Ever mindful of his own dreadful accident, Joseph had been adamant when Laura suggested this, as Lydia's birthday present.

"Certainly not," Joseph had retorted. "The child's far too small."

Lydia bounced in Laura's arms and her voice rang out loudly. "Wanna pony, wanna pony!"

"Hush," said Laura sharply. "Your father is very busy, right now. Wait and see what the birthday fairy brings."

The child buried her head in Laura's shoulder - she did not like being chastised.

"Joseph, my dear, I should like to ask Tom if he will drive me into Bathurst, this afternoon. There are a few things that I need, and Betty will look after Lydia."

Soon after taking up residence in Tangarra, Laura and Betty had come to an agreement, making it unnecessary for another housekeeper to be hired. The homely couple had retained their cottage on Tangarra, and it was like a second home for Lydia.

"Be home by five, then," Joseph answered, without looking up. "I would like to go to bed early, tonight."

Laura smiled tolerantly. "Yes, dear." She set on her feet. "Give your father a kiss, Lydia dear. We're going to see Aunty Betty this afternoon."

The child did as she was told, and Joseph ruffled her hair. "My little girl, eh?" He adored his daughter, and rarely refused her anything. He look up at Laura and said, "I'd like you to visit Andrew Thompson while you are in Bathurst. There are some urgent matters I wish to discuss, so I'd like him to visit me."

Laura nodded and picked up her daughter again. She loathed this particular task that Joseph asked of her, but consoled herself that they were to have an early night. This occurred less frequently, of late, but she never objected to Joseph's needs.

Joseph and Tom were thoroughly engrossed in harness-racing by this time, and Tangarra was becoming well-known as a Champion horse stud. Bathurst Harness Races would never be the same without at least two Tangarra entries and the trophies Joseph had won with his favourite, Laura's Gold, stood proudly on the mantelpiece in the library.

At noon, having left the little girl in the capable hands of Betty Weekes, Laura chatted brightly to Tom about their latest win, and the new harness rig they'd bought recently. They owned a comfortable carriage now, and Tom was always proud to drive it into Bathurst, for his friends to see.

"I suspect that Joseph lost confidence a little bit, when he tried to drive the rig himself," remarked Tom.

"Sadly, yes. But it gives me heart to see him try these things. I just wish he'd have enough confidence to allow Lydia on a horse. She loves them so, and I can't think how to persuade him."

"With your permission, Laura, I'd like to suggest to him that Lydia could eventually become a top harness driver for us. Do you think that might persuade him?"

"You are certainly welcome to try," said Laura, "But I won't mention this to Lydia, it might falsely build her hopes."

"I understand," Tom said. "We'll see how things go, by her birthday."

Laura smiled. "Thank you, anyway Tom. Here we are at the "Grande Department Store". Wonder what they can tempt me with today?"

Tom chuckled, and pulled up outside Mudgee Department store, where she had become well known. He helped her to the footpath, saying, "I will wait for you at half past four, outside the Solicitor's office..

"Thank you, Tom. I should have everything done, by that time."

Tom grinned. "I'll go and have a beer with my mates, then,"

Laura jogged his elbow, jokingly. "Make sure it is only one, then."

"Yes, Ma'am," Tom grinned cheekily as he got back on board and headed for the Bathurst Hotel. "Enjoy your afternoon."

With two huge floor fans stirring the hot air, the inside of the Department Store was tolerably comfortable, compared to out in the street. Drought, this time, had lasted a few years, and the heat whenever she visited Hargraves, to see her old friends, had been almost unbearable.

She always went into the building that was the shop, to 'check around my property" as she put it. The floor boards had split open, cupboard doors had warped and spiders had evidently enjoyed the peace and quiet, considering the number of cobwebs hanging from the ceiling. She hadn't forgotten to check her 'hoard' in the chimney before leaving, and smiled at the comfort it gave her.

"Laura! Lovely surprise, and so nice to see you."

Laura looked up from the table linen she was examining, and held out her arms to hug Kate, who now carried her own little girl on her hip.

"My dear Kate," Laura said, before tickling the baby's chin. "And hasn't Charlotte grown?"

"Kids do usually," said Kate, cheekily."And how is Lydia? She'll be five soon, won't she? My, how the time flies." She said this in an old spinster's querulous voice, and they both burst out laughing.

"Come and have a cup of tea with me, Kate,"

"Oh, yes, they have a posh tearoom here now, don't they? Am I allowed a cream bun?" Kate had gained a comfortable weight, which she called her 'happiness'.

"Of course you are," Laura laughed, and they headed for the discreet tearoom at the back of the store. "I won't let on to Clem."

Having asked about old Dave and people in the village, Laura said, "And Clem? Is he still teaching?"

"Oh, yes," said Kate, brightly. "And he helps Uncle Davey with the pub nowadays. The old man is weakening, but he keeps going with Clem's help. The village would be lost without him."

"Who?" joked Laura. "Uncle Davey, or Clem?"

"Both of them, really," said Kate, and again they laughed.

They were enjoying the afternoon of friendship when Tom suddenly dashed into the tearoom, his eyes wide. "Mrs Martin!"

Laura looked up in surprise. "Tom, whatever's happened?" she asked.

"The business Manager, Thompson. Just shot himself in the head! I'll get the carriage."

Laura reeled at his words, and watched speechless as he dashed outside again.

Kate looked with concern at Laura. "Does that mean you have to go?"

"Oh yes," said Laura hastily. "Joseph will want to know immediately. He is, er, was the man handling all our business."

"Strewth!" said Kate. "You'd better get going then. I'm heading for home anyway, so I'll let them all know in Hargraves."

The journey home was much faster and more stressful, with thoughts and conjectures dominating their conversation. Laura frantically wondered how Joseph would handle this shocking news, and voiced her thoughts. Tom said he and Betty had been worried about Joseph's apparent deterioration of late, anyway. "But, we're here for you."

"Thank you for your concern," said Laura. "Yes, he has been working far too much on those account books of his. Some days, he hardly leaves his desk. When we had that special desk made to accommodate his wheelchair, I didn't expect him to use it so much. As a matter of fact, Tom, he was progressing so well when we moved into Tangarra, I didn't expect him to be using the wheelchair at all, by now. But..."

Her words trailed off and her face saddened even more. "I don't think Lydia has ever seen her father on two feet."

"Oh, I am sorry, Laura. We both are, but if we can do anything at all to help, no matter how little, please let us."

Laura's smile was weak, but showed her gratitude. "I wonder why on earth that man killed himself? I must confess I never really liked him, but hate to think of the pressures that must have driven him to do that. Was he married, I wonder?"

"No," answered Tom. "But I understand he went overseas on holiday very often - who knows, he may have had a wife, family, or lady-friend at least, in some foreign country."

They had reached Tangarra, and Tom drew up alongside the verandah steps. "Would you like me to come in with you, Laura?"

"No, thank you, Tom," said Laura, mounting the veranda. "Please tell Betty I will be along shortly to fetch Lydia."

"Don't you worry about the little girl," Tom nodded. "She'll be fine with us. Take your time, and worry about Joseph, instead."

Laura walked straight into the library, not stopping to remove her coat and hat. "Joseph, oh, Joseph..."

He looked up, startled. "What is it? ...is she hurt?"

"No, she is fine. It's Andrew."

"Andrew?" The surprise on his face was quickly replaced by horror, when Laura told him the news. "Good God! The man must have been crazed."

"I have no idea what it is all about, Joseph. We came back as quickly as we could - of course, I didn't get to deliver your message to him." Laura was lost for words, unable to tell from Joseph's expression, just how she should help, or handle the situation.

"Tell Tom, I want him to drive me into town, now."

"But, Joseph..."

"Now, Laura," said Joseph, quietly, but firmly.

Tom came bustling into the library. "Hang on, Joseph. It is far too late in the day to be going into Bathurst, and you won't get any answers, until the Police Chief has done all he has to."

Joseph opened his mouth to protest, but thought better of it. "Tomorrow morning then, eight o'clock sharp!"

Relieved, Tom nodded to Laura as she held open the door for him, and whispered,. "Keep an eye on him tonight."

"I will," affirmed Laura and closed the door quietly behind him. She crossed to Joseph's side and placed her arm around his shoulders. "Can I get you anything, dear? Cup of tea? Or, perhaps a whisky?" Laura acknowledged the seriousness of the situation by suggesting liquor, this early in the evening.

He closed his eyes and put his head against her. "Yes, please, m'love. I don't know how long it will take to sort out his business," Joseph said, "but I do know it will be complicated. I shall go and see the Bank Manager tomorrow to see if he has anything to add to the matter."

Laura poured and took the glass to him, then sipped the wine she'd set out for herself. "What's the problem, dear?"

"That of money, my dear. Andrew has been slow in transferring money to my account, of late. I need to know what the procedure is to claim all he owes me."

Unaccountably, a chill rippled across Laura's shoulders. "I didn't know you were having trouble, my dear?"

"I had no need to concern you," answered Joseph, as if it would have been beyond Laura's understanding.

She riled a little, then brushed the feeling aside. "May I come with you tomorrow?"

Joseph hesitated, then nodded miserably. "I think that would be wise, then you could handle some of the correspondence that will no doubt, become necessary."

"I will go and ask Betty if she could look after Lydia for me, for a few days."

Joseph looked up as if to object, but just nodded.

The following day, Tom drove Laura and Joseph into town, and set them down at the Bank. "I'll come back in an hour and I'll wait here, if you aren't finished."

Laura raised a smile - she knew where Tom would spend that hour, but didn't begrudge him the chance to talk with his friends at the Hotel.

Joseph used the wheelchair mostly at Tangarra, and because they tired him so quickly, only used the heavy crutches in town. Luckily there were no steps into the bank, and the Manager, William Sutton, was there to greet them. He steered them into his office, settled his portly frame into his desk chair, and from his filing tray, picked up a large folder.

"I've checked right through, Joseph, and can confirm that no payment has been made into your account for over six weeks, by

Thompson. But, after your last withdrawal, I must warn you that your balance is in overdraft, for three hundred pounds.."

"My last withdrawal was to pay for the new racing harness," said Joseph, puzzled. "May I see an up-to-date statement, please?"

"Certainly," said the Manager, handing over the top page of the file. "Regular withdrawals by Mr Thompson, have been made out to various horse studs, and a firm called "Jayprops."

"Jayprops? Never heard of them." Joseph's terse reply sent shivers along Laura's spine, and she looked questioningly at her husband. She had severe misgivings about today's outcome, and her fears were becoming real.

"How has this happened?" she asked the Bank Manager

William Sutton shook his head. "I can only assume, Mrs Martin, that Andrew Thompson, somehow, had control of Mr. Martin's cheque book."

Laura turned to Joseph. "Could that be, dear?" She tried to control the quaver in her voice. "Did that man have one of your cheque books?"

"Since I had the accident, he's been running the financial affairs for me and I just hadn't got back to doing it myself, again."

"Could he do that?" Laura asked Sutton.

"If Joseph gave him Power of Attorney," was the answer, and again Laura turned to her husband.

"Did you?"

"Yes. Dammit, woman, he'd been handling things for me, ever since we came to Australia. He was my Property Manager, as well as Solicitor"

"Joseph!" Laura's voice was sharp with horror at Joseph's outburst, as much as the situation. Her earlier trepidation turned to cold fear, as possible consequences crashed through her mind. Without stopping to think, she continued, "How could you allow this to happen? Why didn't you give the Power of Attorney to me?""

He did not reply, but remained slumped in his chair with his head leaning against his crutches.

Laura spun to face William Sutton again. "What can be done?"

"I'm afraid Mr. Martin will have to declare bankruptcy, Mrs Martin."

"He'll declare nothing of the sort," retorted Laura. "Surely there must be some legal way to get back the money from this criminal's Estate?"

"I doubt it, Mrs Martin. And even if it were a possibility, any settlement could take many years. And your account with the Bank..."

Shaking visibly, Laura placed her hand on Joseph's arm "What is to be done, my dear?"

Joseph roused and looked at her with haunted eyes. "We have to sell Tangarra."

"No!" Tears formed in Laura's eyes. "There must be another way. What about the rest of your properties?" Another thought flashed through her mind. "Of course, Jayprops. Joseph's Properties. The man has been embezzling your money for years!"

"Please don't state the obvious," said Joseph, petulantly. "The only thing left is to sell Tangarra, and move back to the shop in Hargraves."

"I could arrange a mortgage against the shop, if you wish, sir," Sutton cut in. Joseph was no longer the bank's most valued customer, besides the Mayor, but he still deserved respect.

"How would I be able to repay that," replied Joseph, a tinge of sarcasm in his voice. "Anyway,
the property is not mine to mortgage."

William Sutton looked puzzled.

Laura drew herself up and said bravely, "It is mine, Mr Sutton, and I have no intention of raising a mortgage. Our lives are going to be very difficult for a while, but we shall manage. Hopefully you can keep an eye on the proceedings of the suicide inquiry, and let us know of developments immediately?"

Sutton nodded, admiration for Laura's stoicism lighting his face. "Please feel free to come to me, Mrs Martin, if you think I can help "

Laura felt a little embarrassed that he should have addressed his last remark to her, rather than them both. Joseph obviously was beyond caring, as he struggled to regain his feet, then put out his hand.

"Thank you, William. I'll get that overdraft paid as soon as I can - probably with the sale of the furniture."

"There's no pressure," said Sutton, and shepherded them to the front door. "I know an honest man, when I see one."

Tom arrived just then and took in the situation quickly. There was no need for questions, their faces told the sordid story. William Sutton watched sadly, as the loyal houseman assisted Joseph back into the carriage and Laura made sure her husband was comfortable.

"Don't worry about your little girl," Tom said, flicking the reins on the horse's rump. "She'll be fine with us, until this is sorted out."

"You realise we won't be able to employ you and Betty any more?" Laura tried hard to adjust to the situation. "We'll have to let you both go."

"We'll stay here to look after the place," said Tom. "If there's to be new owners of Tangarra, hopefully we can be employed by them." Tom was aiming to be pragmatic, but there was a deep sadness in his voice.

When they got home, Laura guided Joseph into the library, and he sat in his wheelchair, completely demoralised. She made him comfortable, then went back into the hall to remove her coat and hat. She glanced in the mirror, and noticed the darkness under her eyes. "Come on, girl, you can do it." she whispered, and straightened her dress, before re-entering the library.

"You can safely leave the house and furniture sale to me," she began, "and take heart. I have a surprise for you, in Hargraves."

"As long as it isn't another child", was the dour reply.

Laura bit her lip at his words, but refrained from revealing her surprise. She wasn't quite sure how to turn the lump of gold she'd found, and hidden in the shop chimney, into money, but knew Clem would help her. They wouldn't be destitute.

13 JOSEPH

Laura slept fitfully that night. It seemed never-ending; she was very conscious of Lydia's absence, Joseph's restlessness, and her own vulnerability. This was not the life she had left England for, but there was no turning back now.

Joseph seemed reluctant to rise next morning, and it suited her to let him lie in. While she attended to the usual morning chores, Betty Weekes arrived. "Morning, Laura," she said, donning her floral wrap-around apron. . "Dreadful news about that solicitor man, isn't it? Anything you'd like done, before I get to the tub?"

"No, thank you," Laura answered, hesitated, then said, "Yes, there is. Where is Lydia right now?"

"Right behind you," Betty grinned. "Never keeps still, does she?"

Laura turned as her daughter threw herself into her arms. "Mother, I had jelly at Aunty Betty's! And pineapple, too." Laura hugged her little girl, and felt comforted by the normality of their love for each other. "Can I stay with Aunty Betty and Uncle Tom again, please?"

"Of course you can," Laura said. "Now, how about you go and wake father? We've a lot to talk about, and there's a lot to do."

When the child had skipped away, Laura said, "Betty, I'm sorry to burden you, but could you look after Lydia for a few days, please? No doubt Tom has told you of our predicament, and I'll have a lot of sorting to do, before we return to Hargraves. I haven't told Lydia yet."

"Has she been there before?"

"No," said Laura. "I can only hope she will adjust to the harshness, after the luxury of Tangarra. I know I will miss the trees and..."

"Time enough for tears," said Betty, as pragmatic as her husband.

Betty cleared the breakfast table while Laura browsed through the letters that had arrived.. Most were addressed to Joseph, and had official looking markings, so she put them aside for him. One was addressed to her, in Kate's familiar writing - bold, large, and written with care. She described life of late in Hargraves, since the terrible flood that happened just after Christmas.

"At first, the rain was welcome because it broke the drought, and we certainly had enough of that. However, when it kept on and on, we knew what to expect. The main street was awash very quickly because there's no drainage here. Louisa Creek flooded, enough to mount the steps to your shop, but I don't think it got in. Unfortunately, it kept rising, until Clem had to close the school. The children didn't mind that, of course, but the damage weighed heavily on everybody's shoulders. Seems I've done nothing but clean muddy floors and desks. Oh dear, I could certainly enjoy a good holiday, right now.

"A couple of folks here in Hargraves were dealing with that crackpot man, and you should have heard the fuss when news of his suicide spread. Hope everything's alright for you and Joseph."

Betty returned to clean out the fireplace, and Laura told her of Kate's letter. She also told of Kate's help when Joseph's baby son was taken, and Betty clicked her teeth in sympathy.

"Do you think she would like to come to Tangarra for a holiday?" she asked casually.

"Oh, I'm sure she would," said Laura. Her enthusiasm soon dissolved when she stopped to think of that latest events. "But perhaps we'd better get this business about Mr Martin's Solicitor sorted out, first. I'm sure he would have no objection, and Kate won't have another chance to..."

Her face saddened when she thought about Martin's decision to sell Tangarra, in order to try and stay solvent. "I know Lydia would love to see Kate, but I'm more worried about her ability to cope with moving away from Tangarra. It's been the only home she's known."

Betty stood and wiped her hands down her apron. "Don't you go worrying about that, my dear. Little ones get used to new surroundings very quickly, and she's an intelligent child. Look...!"

Laura spun to follow Betty's finger - she was pointing to Lydia clasping Tom around his neck, while he helped her up to the back of Snowy, a docile pony born on the property.

"Oh, my lord," Laura exclaimed. "We mustn't let her father see that. She knows she's not permitted to... she is a naughty girl, at times."

Too many things were happening at once, for Laura's liking. She rushed through the door, and ran to the stable yard. "Lydia! You're such a naughty... get her down off Snowy straight away, Tom. Joseph has forbidden..."

Lydia started to cry loudly, and Tom lifted her back to the ground. "I'm so sorry, Laura. I had no idea that..."

"That's very naughty," Laura stooped to admonish her daughter. "You know your father..."   "He probably will, in time," said Tom. "We'll have to think of a way that Lydia can gain her confidence. Learning at a young age is always better and she so loves horses."

"I know," Laura sighed. "She's like me, and I hate denying her."

Tom patted Laura's arm. "I'll talk to him later". Lydia cried, as he led Snowy away.

"Hush now, angel," said Laura, feeling guilty for her outburst towards the child. "Let's wait and see what the fairies bring for your birthday, soon."

Lydia was mollified, but sniffled on their way back into the house. Betty was on her way to the wash-house when Laura got back in. "Is Joseph up, yet?" she asked. "We have to go back into Bathurst, shortly. Oh!..." A thought struck her, "I forgot to ask Tom to take us in."

Laura could feel her nerves tightening..

"Don't worry so," chided Betty. "You go and see to everything, and I'll go to the stables to tell Tom."

"Thank you, Betty," said Laura, relaxing a little. "I'll go and settle Lydia, then see to Joseph - he's probably up right now, anyway, and will want to know what the fuss was."

Laura found her daughter in the library, predictably reading a picture book about ponies. She was surprised that Joseph was not there, too.

"Was Father awake when you went into him?"

Lydia didn't look up. "He wouldn't talk to me. Probably cross because I was getting on the horse." She look up with eyes full of tears. "Why can't I have a horse, Mummy?"

Laura turned on her heel and went quickly into their bedroom. "Joseph, my dear... Joseph?"

He didn't move.

"Joseph?..." Laura felt as icy as he did, when she put out her hand to stroke his face. "Joseph...no! No!"

She screamed out, "Lydia. Go and fetch Uncle Tom."

Bewildered, Lydia ran to the front door and bumped into Betty, who had heard Laura's scream. "What's wrong?"

"I dunno, Aunty Betty. Perhaps she wants to tell Uncle Tom off again."

Betty called out to Tom over her shoulder. "Come here, quickly, Tom."

She reached the bedroom door and with a glance, could tell what was wrong. Laura's head was buried in Joseph's counterpane, and her shoulder heaved with staggering passion.

Betty crossed quickly and clasped Laura to her bosom. "Oh, my God, whatever's happened? He's dead, isn't he?"

Laura's anguished cries chilled Betty's bones, and when Tom appeared at the bedroom door, his wife said, "Fetch Doctor Sobden , quick!"

Tom disappeared without a word, and immediately, Lydia appeared in the doorway. "Mother! What's the matter? Aunty Betty..." The child threw herself onto her mother's form and started sobbing, without understanding why, or what had happened. Betty, with tears streaming down her face, grasped them both and led them out of the bedroom..

She took them both into the front room, and Laura clasped her daughter to her as they sat down. "Oh, my baby, my baby."

"Mummy, why are you crying?" Lydia sobbed. "I don't like it when you cry."

"Hush now, pet," said Betty, mopping her face, then child's wet and flushed cheeks.. "Your mother's very sad, because..." She couldn't bring herself to say the words.

Laura moaned. "Joseph, oh, Joseph. You can't leave me."

At the sound of her father's name, Lydia said, "What's the matter with Father?"

The question pierced Laura's grief, and again, she clasped the little girl to her. "Oh, my angel," she sobbed. "Your dear father's gone to heaven."

Innocence prevailed. "Why?"

Laura's own face was deathly pale as she struggled to compose an answer for the child, and she looked desperately to Betty.

"Come on, pet," Betty said, as she picked up the confused girl. "I'll take you home and tell you all about Heaven, while we're having hot milk and a biscuit. How do you like that?"

Lydia's eyes brightened. She put her arms around Betty's neck, and said, "Yes, please!"

Laura's expression changed momentarily from grief to gratitude, especially as Tom came back at that moment. "The doctor's on his way. I'll make you a cup of tea, Mrs Martin."

By the time Doctor Sobden arrived, Tom had turned Joseph onto his back, and respectfully placed pennies on his eyelids, before arranging the bed sheet up to his chin. The doctor gave Joseph's body a quick examination, then made notes in his book. "Looks like a massive heart attack. ."

"That doesn't surprise me," said Tom. "Not after all he's been through, and then yesterday..."

He went on to explain his opinion as to the possible cause of Joseph's death, and Doctor Sobden nodded wisely. "Ghastly affliction, money. I've seen such a lot of men who succumb to the quest for money."

The two men moved back into the front room. Laura had drunk her tea, and was quietly sobbing into her handkerchief. She attempted to stand as they appeared and the doctor waved her back.

"Please stay seated, Mrs Martin. My sincere condolences - you have obviously suffered a very nasty shock." Laura nodded and tried to answer, but she dissolved into tears again. "I will give you a salve which will hopefully, help to settle your nerves."

He placed his bag on the table and took out a small bottle of laudanum, and as he prepared a small dose, he said, "What about Lydia. Where is she?"

Tom retrieved Laura's teacup to return to the kitchen, and said, "My wife has her. Poor little mite, I don't think she really knows what's happened."

"Mm. Can your wife look after the child for a few days? Mrs Martin will need the rest."

"Of course," said Tom.

Laura felt cold and lifeless as the potion took over. Normally, she would object strongly to being discussed, as though she were not there. Right now, she felt unable to raise even a modicum of emotion, and sat motionless.

Several days later, when obligatory notices had been posted and the funeral planned, Laura and Tom followed Joseph's coffin to the church, where Jemima had been buried. The cemetery was crowded with friends and acquaintances from Hargraves, as well as the many business associates Joseph had developed since emigrating to Australia.

Laura, hidden behind a thick veil, saw nothing but Joseph's coffin being lowered from the funeral hearse, to the side of his grave. She watched, with a great stillness, as his coffin was lowered, and she appeared not to hear anything intoned by the vicar. As mourners left, some offered her their condolences. Others, like Billy King, Kate, Clem and Dave Lee, embraced her, before Tom led her back to the carriage.

"My God, that girl has suffered such a lot since she came to Australia," Clem said quietly to Kate and Dave. "I don't know how she copes."

"She will, for Lydia's little daughter's sake," murmured Kate. "She's a survivor."

Laura glanced backwards at Joseph's grave, and wondered how she would arrange for little Joseph's remains to join his parents. Beyond that, all she wanted was to return to Tangarra, and be quiet.

Weeks of mourning saw her wasted to a shadow, with no enthusiasm for life. Betty brought Lydia back to her mother in time for her birthday on the third day of September, and they all did what they could, not to spoil the day. After a special tea of scones and jelly and birthday cake with five candles, Lydia opened the pink package given to her from Betty and Tom. Inside was a pink satin pillow that Betty had lovingly made and embroidered with the initials, LM.

Laura gave the birthday girl a small package, saying, "I think you are grown up enough to have this special brooch that Uncle Billy put into your shawl, the day you were born."

Lydia opened the blue velvet box and revealed a gold circle that had leaves and white pearls like mistletoe, and a glowing sapphire in its centre.

Laura wished Billy could have been there to see his god-daughter's face as she looked at the beautiful gift, that he had given to his wife on their wedding day. "It's what they call a precious antique brooch," said Laura, "so you must take great care of it."

"It's lovely," breathed the little girl, nodding. "I'd keep it in the music box he gave me for Christmas."

The memory of last Christmas, and Joseph, and Lydia's joy brought tears again to Laura, and Betty took over clearing away the birthday paper and dishes. "Come on, young lady. You've had a very exciting day, and you have school in the morning."

Slowly, the little girl's vivacity began to break through Laura's grief, and they were sitting down for supper one day, when Lydia said, "Aunty Betty says Father went to Heaven, because the angels needed him up there."

Laura nodded sadly.

"But, Mummy," the little voice quavered, "we need him down here, too, don't we?"

Laura hugged her daughter, and tearfully explained why they must manage without him, in future.

"Don't worry, Mummy," said Lydia innocently. "I won't go to Heaven. I'll stay and look after you."

Laura smiled for the first time, at the child's wisdom.

Billy stayed with her at Tangarra for a while, helping her to sort out Joseph's belongings and donate them to the church. Some things, like the cravat pin she had given him as her wedding present, and his telescope, she put aside. She emptied the large trunk's contents onto the bed, and found treasures evidently placed there by Jemima. Some linen and manchester was still wrapped as wedding gifts, and there was an ornate, blue and gold vase. It was a family heirloom, and Laura determined to contact Jemima's family, with a view to returning it to them. She'd found the address of Jemima's parents- they lived in the Cotswolds, in England..

In a small bundle, Laura found her silver tongs, and she decided she'd keep them. as an heirloom for Lydia. "That's as long as I don't have to pawn them," she said ruefully.

"That will be good," said Billy. "The child will be able to use them as a talking point, when entertaining. A lot of my things have little stories behind them, and guests love that."

Laura hugged him and said, "Trust you to think ahead, Billy. Where would I have been without you, solid as a rock!"

14 LIFE CHANGES AGAIN

The heartbreak of packing up Tangarra's contents, disposing of what she could, and trying to explain to Lydia what was happening, stressed Laura immensely. She remained the thin and wan woman she had become, after Joseph's death.

Her appetite had all but vanished, and her face was that of a fifty year old. "I've even got grey hairs on my head," she wailed to Betty.

"You really should eat more," scolded the motherly woman. "You mustn't let yourself go like this." They were clearing out the large cupboard where bed-linen and blankets were kept.

"But there's so much to do," said Laura, frowning. "And I still can't accept the fact that we will be back in Hargraves in two weeks time."

"Neither can I," Betty moaned. "If the new owners don't want me and Tom, and we have to move out of the cottage, I don't know what we shall do. Move into Bathurst, I suppose, and try to find work there." She didn't sound too confident about the prospect.

"Oh, I'm sure they will," encouraged Laura. "You have my highest recommendation, and they couldn't find anyone more suitable, I'm sure."

"We'll see." Betty shrugged, then bent to look closer at something in the bottom of the cupboard. "What's this, then?" She drew out a dark green box, and removed its lid.

"Oh," Laura exclaimed. "I'd forgotten about that. Its the Chess Set Joseph bought me for my birthday, one year. I was taught to play the game while on board the ship coming to Australia.

Lovely family- settled in Melbourne, I believe. That was the only thing I was able to teach Joseph. We had some fun with it - Lydia was only a baby, of course."

"Never understood the game myself," said Betty. "Do you want to keep it?"

Laura hesitated, then nodded. "I can teach Lydia, when she is a little older. Well, I think that's cleared everything out. I've put aside what I want to take with me, and Tom is going to take the rest to the Salvation Army depot."

"They'll think all their Christmases have come at once," said Betty glumly. "Seems such a shame you have to give all this up."

"Please don't start, Betty."

Betty blew her nose hard. "I'm sorry, Mrs Martin. I can't help it."

A knock at the front door saved the situation, and Betty hurried to answer it while Laura carried the box of linen into the hallway. It was Laurence Simpson, the Solicitor that Billy King had referred Laura to. "Very reliable," Billy had said, "He's the one I use."

Laura shook his hand, then led him into the library. "Would you care for a cup of tea, Mr. Simpson?"

"Thank you, Mrs Martin, but no. I've called to let you know that payment for Tangarra has been cleared, and the monies dispersed among the creditors."

"And Joseph's legacies?"

"All safe and secure, Mrs. Martin. As instructed by you, half of Lydia's money has been invested in very secure bonds, and you will receive a quarterly report as to their progress."

"And the rest?"

"In a Trust Account which she cannot access until the age of twenty one. All documents, including your Will and Testament, have been deposited in a Safety Box at the Bank of New South Wales, in Sydney."

"That's a relief," sighed Laura. "I trust you have allocated money to cover your fees?"

"All that's been attended to. You will receive a written report and account as soon as the matter is completed. If you have any further wishes, please do not hesitate to contact me, Mr Martin."

"There is one more thing, Mr. Simpson. I deposited a small amount in the Bank of NSW in Bathurst some years ago. It was from my English Aunt's Will, and I think Mr. Sutton invested it for me, as an inheritance for my daughter, Lydia."

"Would you like me to follow it up for you, Mrs. Martin?"

"If you would, please. I don't want to disturb it, just reassure myself that it is there for Lydia."

"Of course. I'll let you know as soon as I have checked up on it. It is held in your name, I presume?"

Laura nodded. "Thank you, Mr Simpson." They got to their feet and shook hands. The Solicitor bowed slightly as he left the front door. Tom had brought his carriage and handed him the reins, as he climbed aboard. He settled himself, and doffed his hat. "A pleasure to deal with you, Mrs Martin."

"We've received a letter," said Tom, after he'd gone. He handed it to Laura. "We've been retained by the new Owners, Mr and Mrs Bowen."

"Oh, I'm so pleased." Laura scanned the letter. "It's somehow very comforting to know you and Betty will still be here, because I would like to visit you, sometimes - if you have no objection."

"You're poking fun at me," Tom chided. "You know we'd object if you didn't, and I'm sure Betty would welcome Lydia like her own child."

Laura smiled wanly, and felt a shudder of apprehension. All she had left now, was Lydia, the land and shop at Hargraves that had a value of fifteen to twenty pounds, a few precious belongings, and the lump of gold, hidden in the shop chimney.

Tom and Betty accompanied Laura and Lydia to Hargraves. Following Laura's directions, they drove through Bathurst, onto Mudgee, and turned left at the Church, for the journey into Hargraves village.

When they arrived, she sat staring at the Hargraves Shop, scenes of her previous life there, flashing through her mind. The baby Joseph, the father, Joseph, his frequent absences leaving her to care for the baby and the shop. Would her regular customers of that time, come back?

Tom lifted Lydia onto the verandah, then turned to give his wife a hand. "Mrs Martin?"

"I can manage," she answered, finding courage in that statement. She looked the shop window, and frowned. "The window's very clean," she remarked to Betty. "Have you been out here, before me?"

"Bless you, no," chortled Betty. "we wouldn't have known how to get here."

Laura swivelled in the seat to look across to Dave Lee's house. It seemed empty, until she noticed Kate and her daughter Charlotte, waving from a window. She waved back, and alighted. By this time, Betty, Tom and Lydia had gone into the shop, and she could hear Lydia daughter squealing with delight, as she trotted around on the bare floorboards.

Floorboards that had been scrubbed, and cupboard doors that closed easily, and no cobwebs.

"Mummy! Come and see!"

"In a moment, dear. We have a visitors." Laura stepped into the road and Kate rushed over, with Charlotte at her heels.

"Welcome home, Laura!" Kate hugged her, then held her friend at arm's length. "Stone the crows, but you've lost so much weight. You look half-starved. What have you been doing? Or, not doing, is more like. I've got a large hot pot ready and waiting for you. We'll soon fatten you up." She hugged Laura again, then turned to her little girl and said, "Say hello to Mrs. Martin, Charlotte."

"Hello, Mrs. Martin, where's Lydia?"

With a surprised look, Laura answered,"Why, in the shop." Before anything else was said, the little girl skipped up the steps and Kate laughed at the look on Laura's face. "I've talked so much about you, she needs no introduction. I'm so happy she will have Lydia as a friend."

The louder squeals coming from the shop, was proof of Kate's words.

Betty's voice rose above the noise. "Now settled down, you two. Why don't you go out into the garden to play?"

1   The noise diminished, and Lydia asked, "How's Clem?"

"Oh, still putting all his time into the school," Kate answered. "Having a lot of trouble with the old building falling down." Again she laughed at Laura's expression. "Well, almost, that is."

Without question, Laura replied, "You must come in and tell me all about it. Seems to me someone has been very busy making sure this old place doesn't fall down!"

"Oh, you can thank Clem for that."

" And you cleaned the windows, didn't you?"

Grinning, Kate tucked Laura's arm in hers and together they walked arm in arm up onto the verandah. Kate stood aside to let Laura through the front door. Coming in from the brilliant sunlight, Laura couldn't see much, at first. Her eyes adjusted, and she saw Lydia and Charlotte were jumping up and down, in front of the fire. Her instinct was to pull the little girl away from the flames, saying, " I thought you were told to go out into the garden to play?" She propelled both girls towards the back door, and added, "I must get a wire guard, as soon as I can."

"I've got a spare one," said Kate. "I'll go and bring it right over."

She disappeared through the door, and Laura looked up as Betty and Tom came into the shop, from the bedroom. "What a welcome," said Betty. "That was Kate, I gather?"

"Yes," said Laura. "She's grown a lot since I first met her. She's a lovely girl. It was Kate that cleaned the windows and..."

Laura turned back to the fire, and horror shadowed her face. Her jaw dropped, and she looked desperately to Tom. Unable to stop herself, she said, "My Deeds!"

"Mr Simpson probably has those, all safe and sound," Tom answered benignly, not registering Laura's look of dismay."We've made the bed up ready for you, and there was a cot already in there. That will suit Lydia for a while."

"Oh, no!" Laura shouted, and knelt by the fireplace, trying to look up the chimney.

"Mrs Martin!" yelled Betty. "What are you doing, woman?"

Tom strode over to wrestle Laura to her feet. "Whatever's going on? Don't you feel well? Come and sit down, please."

Lydia backed away, and stood against the wall with her thumb in her mouth, and her blue eyes wide. Then watched her mother cry in anguish again as she was led to a chair. The child's eyes brimmed with tears. "Mummy... what's amatter?"

Betty and Tom looked at each other, completely mystified.

At that moment, carrying the metal fire-guard, Kate reappeared. "Oh, Lord," she said, dumping the guard in front of the fire. "Laura..."

"Talk to us, Mrs Martin. Whatever's wrong?" Betty was distraught.

"Everything," sobbed Laura. Then she took a deep breath, and turned to Kate. "Did you light the fire?"

"Well...yes, but...." Kate was uncomfortable, and looked at Tom and Betty.

Betty interrupted. "Kate was very kind." She said this, as if to reprimand Laura for lack of appreciation.

"Oh, it's not that I am ungrateful," said Laura, dabbing her eyes. "It's just that..."

Kate fished in her apron. "Are you worried about these?"

Confounding Tom and Betty even further, Laura rose and wrapped her arms around Kate.

"I was going to wait until we were on our own," said Kate, bashfully. "I thought, as you had hidden them, you wouldn't want anyone else to know about them."

"Hidden what?" demanded Betty.

"The Deeds for this land and shop," Laura explained, taking the packet from Kate. "Joseph arranged for them to be transferred to me as sole owner, and I hid them up the chimney. Of course, when I saw the fire was lit, I presumed they had burned away."

"Oh, well that's all right, then," said a much relieved Tom. "If it is alright with you, Mrs Martin, I will go across and say 'hello' to Dave Lee.

"Oh, Mr Weekes," said Kate. "You can't. Uncle Davey passed away in his sleep, a few days ago."

"Oh no!" Laura blanched, and put her arms around Kate. "What happened?"

"It was his time," said Kate, practically. "He died at the Hargraves pub, so I guess he was happy. The funeral is next Wednesday. But first, we must get you settled."

Laura's mind was spinning and she gave a little cry. She went even paler, and sat back heavily in her chair. Laura screamed and ran to her mother. "Mummy! Please don't die!"

Betty grabbed the child and said, "Hush, my angel. Hush, now. Everything's alright. I promise you, it's all right." She shunted Lydia back outside to play with her new friend.

Laura pulled herself together, and addressed her friends. "I'm so sorry to have caused a fuss. I just feel everything has piled on top of me, and I've lost control."

"You worry too much," said Kate. "I'll go and get that meal I made for us all. You get the dishes out.. Do you mind if I leave

Charlotte to play with Lydia? Seems like they're good mates, already."

Tom patted Kate's arm. "Don't you worry about us, either, young lady. Now we know Mrs. Martin is in safe hands, we must start back - it's a long journey and Mr. and Mrs. Bowen are moving in tomorrow early, so we should be there."

Lydia had crept back in, and went over to Betty to hug around her knees. "I come with you, Aunty Betty?"

"No, angel," Betty answered, picking the little girl up. "But we'll come and see you, soon."

Laura took her daughter from Betty, and cuddled her. "I can't thank you two enough, for everything you have done for us."

"No need for thanks," said Tom, gruffly. "You get yourself settled, and I hope we see you a lot better, next time."

Everyone said their farewells, with a few tears. "Now, no more crying," Tom said. "You show them what you are made of, Mrs. Martin."

Laura, Lydia and Kate, waved to their visitors until they disappeared over the Louisa Creek bridge, then Kate went across the road to retrieve the meal. When she came back, she handed a small, linen-wrapped package to Laura, and said, "I haven't looked, but I'd say you have something pretty valuable in there. To hide it in the chimney, an' all."

Laura thanked her profusely, then put the package on the table beside her, and they proceeded to eat their meal. She immediately started to feel better and they talked enthusiastically, exchanging their news. The steaming pot of lamb and vegetables was redolent with rosemary and thyme, and Laura tucked in as though she hadn't eaten for days. The girls only wanted the gravy "without the lumpy bits".

Beginning to relax, Laura described recent events at Tangarra and went on to explain about the package.

"Gold?" asked Kate, incredulously. "You mean, real gold? Not fool's gold?"

Laura laughed at Kate's expression - eyes wide and staring, and eyebrows as high as they could go. "You are the only one, besides me, who knows about it."

"But, what are you going to do with it? Wouldn't it have been valuable enough to save Tangarra for you? Why didn't you tell

Joseph, or the Bank Manager - or anyone, for that matter? What were you thinking of, Laura?"

"Kate, my dear friend, enough questions. Suffice to say that I'll never know why I kept such a secret, in the face of all that's happened. Perhaps I was scared, perhaps I wanted a chance to think what to do - and I certainly haven't had the time to do that, lately."

"And now?"

"When I have settled down, and the shop is running properly, I might think about asking Clem for help. He would know where I start to have the nugget valued."

"Good choice," said Kate, approvingly. "Could I have a look at it, please?"

Laura glanced at her daughter, and both women giggled because Lydia was nodding off to sleep, with a spoon dangling out of her mouth and she was leaning on Charlotte who was asleep already..

"Bless her," whispered Kate. "Let's put them to bed first."

After the children were comfortably in bed, Laura unwrapped the package, and they both gazed at the gold in silence. The nugget weighed about thirty ounces, and reddish brown soil rested in the various crevices. The bright glint of pure gold held their attention for minutes.

Laura carefully wrapped it again. "Promise you won't tell anyone about it?"

Kate nodded in silence. Then she said, "Why not? You might start another gold rush, like the Kerr's Hundredweight did in 1851"

"The huge lumps of gold the doctor's aborigine worker sat on every lunchtime?."

Kate laughed out loud."That was the legend. Don't know about sitting on them, but one lump was broken in two, and by the time they'd dug them out, they weighed over a hundredweight, altogether."

"Close to Hargraves, was it?"

"Yes, Doctor Kerr's land backs on to Uncle Davey's house, well, our house now. Although the nuggets were a fair distance away. What a fuss that caused. and the Hill End Gold rush began. All the villages around were full of thousands of gold-diggers. The Court House was built here, Police Headquarters transferred from

Avisford to here, and about seventy slab and bark houses appeared. Uncle Davey told me that Hargraves town was gazetted in 1859."

It was Laura's turn to be surprised. "Good Lord," she said. "It's hard to believe - the village is almost dead, these days."

"When the gold petered out in Hill End, all the fossikers moved on, looking for better gold fields in Victoria, even America. But there are still traces of gold locally. That's why you'll still be able to sell panning equipment."

"I always wondered why Joseph insisted on stocking those things. I suppose I shall have to again, now you've told me that."

"I'm surprised Joseph hadn't told you," said Kate.

"He told me very little during the time we were here. In fact, I very rarely saw him, and then he only spoke about his latest business ventures in Bathurst, or Sydney. Now, tell me about your Uncle Davey - he seemed so healthy last time he came to Bathurst, to Joseph's funeral."

"He was over eighty, you know," Kate began "and in his own words, had 'lived a life of colour and fun.'"

"Still..." Laura searched for the right words. "He was such a good friend to us."

"He was, to many people," said Kate. "He left the house to me and Clem, and even a bit of money for Charlotte. Wanted to give her a good start, he said"

"And what's happened about the pub?"

"Uncle Davey couldn't manhandle the kegs of beer, or do the maintenance any more, and the authorities threatened to pull it down. So Clem bought it. He's all for preserving history, and wouldn't hear of the pub being closed again."

"Sounds like the school building is enough for Clem to cope with. How does he cope with the two?"

"Oh, I run the pub for him three days a week. He's gone to Bathurst overnight, to sort out some builders to do jobs for him. He'll be over to see you when he comes back, no doubt."

Laura considered this for a while, then yawned. "I'm sorry, Kate, it's just that I suddenly feel very tired."

"Of course you are," said Kate wisely. "Come on, off to bed with you. I'll take Charlotte to her own bed, then come back in the morning to help you. Don't forget, you will be expected to make that toffee of yours again."

Laura chuckled and stood up. She picked up the Deeds and gold nugget, and put them in her carpet bag, before heading for the bedroom.

"You put those somewhere safe," advised Kate, as she wrapped Charlotte with a blanket and headed for home."

"I will," Laura said. "Thank you so much, Kate. Good night."

The next morning, Laura dressed in her 'shop' clothes. Full black linen skirt, a white cotton blouse with the long sleeves rolled to her elbows, and a brooch Joseph had given her for their fourth anniversary. She knew that traditionally, this was the silk anniversary, so had chosen this silver oval, with green silk in the centre which was embroidered with wine coloured silk. LM

She loved the brooch, more so, because it would become Lydia's, someday. Her little girl was still blissfully asleep, so Laura went into the shop and started to prepare for opening. She had bought some wholesale goods in Bathurst before she left, and arranged them carefully in the window.

Sweets at the front, where the children going past towards the school, would be able to see what they could buy with the pocket money they received each week.

"I must speak to Clem about Lydia going to school soon," she muttered. 'And the gold' she thought.

Kate arrived, fresh and bubbly. "It is wonderful to have you back in the shop, Laura. I spoke with several women in the village when I knew you were coming, and they all said they would be glad to have the shop open again - somewhere to have a chat. The men have the pub."

Laura smiled at Kate's enthusiasm. "That makes me feel good. Where's Charlotte, this morning?"

"I've left her sleeping. She was tuckered out after all the excitement. Now, let's have a cup of tea before we start."

Laura grinned at her friend. "You sound like an English woman, saying that!"

"See? Picking up your bad habits, now." Kate pulled a face, then added, "You sound like an Aussie woman, too! Saying 'tuckered out."

15 THE FIRE

Three years passed; Lydia was nearly eight years old and Kate hadn't stopped teasing Laura, now that she was thirty and 'an old woman'. A great deal of hard work had turned the shop into a thriving business, and Laura was assured of a regular income as a result. She still owned the Land Deeds for the shop, and although severely tempted to sell the lump of gold at times, her tenacity had won through.

Clem's wooden school was Hargraves' main goal, as it was now very unsuitable for the growing population. It was draughty and cold in the winter, and the summer heat often obliged Clem to close the school and send the pupils home.

One particularly hot afternoon in January, Laura was hanging bedsheets out at the back of the shop, and expecting Lydia to be sent home from the school at any moment. She had to wash bedding more frequently in this temperature, because of perspiration. She repeated words she'd never imagined in England - "I'll be glad when it gets cooler."

She bent to pick up another pillowcase from the basket, and noticed the smoke, when she straightened. Almost immediately, she noticed the familiar smell of wood-smoke and groaned. "Not again!" Mudgee and District were prone to bush fires, because of the concentrations of eucalyptus trees in the surrounding areas. Banksia bushes and bracken was tinder-dry because of the latest drought, and at the slightest provocation, would burst into vicious flame.

She heard a voices in the main street, yelling hysterically. The last bush fire had raced passed the village, but several back street houses had burnt to the ground. The singed and injured wildlife added to the heartbreak and it took more than a year to recover. The banksias, that had to burn before they procreated, showed green shoots some six months later, but the blackened trees and branches looked like bomb devastation.

Luckily, this time, the red and orange flames and crackling timber fire skirted the school, the Hargraves Inn, the shop and house opposite, but it managed to gut the disused church halfway up the hill. Laura was devastated, because she couldn't get to little Joseph's grave behind the church, but knew the headstone would survive the fire.

'My very first job when this is over,' she promised herself. 'I can afford to have his coffin and headstone moved to Bathurst now, and he can be with his mother and father.' This was a fleeting thought, because the prevailing situation was so serious. Everyone suffered with the choking smoke, and searing heat, and when the wind increased, there had to be a strict patrol to ensure the hot and glowing embers from the bush, didn't land on roofs.

When Lydia came home from school, Laura quickly took her over to Kate's where the two girls were wrapped in wet blankets, and sat in the heavy bath, with firm instructions not to get out until someone came for them. Laura, Kate and Clem, the Brown brothers joined the rest of the villagers in forming a chain-gang for the buckets of water being hauled from the Louisa Creek. It had reduced its water flow because of the drought, but there was still enough to fill the continual chain of buckets as water was transported up the hill to the church. Everyone soaked their own house roof and walls first, so the church building was the last to be drenched. But it was too late, and as they all stood back and watched the roof cave in. A couple of trees exploded and collapsed in the graveyard, and there was general sadness to accompany the exhaustion.

'My very first job when this is over,' she promised herself. 'I can afford to have his coffin and headstone moved to Bathurst now, and he can be with his mother and father.' This was a fleeting thought, because the prevailing situation was so serious.

Everyone suffered with the choking smoke, and searing heat, and when the wind increased, there had to be a strict patrol to ensure the hot and glowing embers from the bush, didn't land on roofs. Blackened and sweating bodies continued to flail the fire with soaked sacking, because the wind kept driving the flames towards the main village.

Laura had never known anything to explode with such frightening noise as when embers settled on the gum trees and set them alight. When the wind abated, and the fire swept on south, towards Hill End, both men and women heaved a great sigh of relief and gathered with the children, in the Hargraves Arms. They were so hot and thirsty, they drank the pub dry of beer, spirits, and soft drinks. Laura brought all her stock of soft drink in tins to the pub, and she helped Kate tend to some of the burned hands and cheeks of the fire-fighters.

The children were herded into a corner, and Clem began calming them with stories of animals who survived these fires, and how they must search the area when it cools down, for wounded koalas, wallabies, rabbits, birds and even snakes.

"Don't try to handle them, especially the snakes," Clem warned the children. "Just make sure you don't search alone and when you find something, one of your party should come back here to fetch a grown-up."

Lydia and Charlotte found a possum with its eyes badly blistered, and its paws burned. After treatment, came the inevitable question. "Can we keep him, Mummy? We'll look after him, honest."

Laura and Kate made eye-signs to each other, knowing full well that, in a short time, they would have to look after the 'pet'.

"No," said Kate firmly. "They belong with their own family in the bush, and that's where they should go after we've helped them."

"Aww!" said the little girls, but mothers knew best.

Typically, torrential rain started to fill Louisa Creek a few days later. Laura rewashed the bed linen, soiled black and smoky by the fire, and cleaned the soiled stock in the shop. The school had re-opened and pupils spent the first days cleaning desks and windows, before Clem started by thanking them all for their work, and efforts with the animals. They had begun a quiet afternoon, writing stories about their experiences during the fire, when the rain began.

Lydia and Charlotte waited for him to lock the school door when the lessons ended, and he took them to Kate who supervised them until the shop closed. Clem then took some of Kate's home-made soup over to Laura, and they sat at the table in the corner of the shop.

After talking awhile, Laura said, "I've decided to go to Sydney to live, Clem."

He choked on his spoon, and looked in disbelief. "Why?"

"There's nothing here for Lydia," she said.

"What about all your friends here? What about the shop? Kate will be so upset, and Charlotte will be devastated without Lydia to play with."

"I know, but I have to think of Lydia's future. You and Kate will always be my best friends, and I'm so happy for you both. You have your whole life planned, now."

Clem had finished his soup, and pushed the dish aside. "Yes, we are happy, but I'd be happier if you found someone you could love, too."

"I've only ever loved one man, and that's Lydia's father."

"Oh, I know that," said Clem, his eyes twinkling again. "I tried hard enough to persuade you to marry me."

"I know," sighed Laura. "But Destiny has a strange way of working."

Clem sat back. "You have done wonders to develop this shop. What did you do about that nugget you showed me?"

"Nothing," Laura confessed. "I still have it tucked away for a rainy day."

They looked at each other, looked outside to the continuing downpour, and burst out laughing.

"Well, you've certainly got your rainy day," said Clem "It will be a big move for you, Laura. Do you feel up to it?"

Laura nodded. "Considering how things were when I came back to Hargraves, I have improved both financially and in my health."

"You certainly glow, now, compared to then."

Laura grinned. "Are you still trying to seduce me, Mr White?"

"I can't deny a concern for you, Laura, but Kate is the one for me. She's bright, intelligent, and loves children, as you do. "

Laura rose to clear the soup dishes. "You can't help being happy, you two! But I have to think of our future. I told Kate of my decision this morning."

""She didn't say anything when I took the girls home."

"I asked her not to. I wanted to tell you myself."

I suppose she cried," said Clem, as he got to his feet to greet Lydia. "Hello, young lady. You tired of our house, already?" Growing into a beautiful girl, she gave him a cheeky smile, and dumped a book on the table in front of him. "Hullo, what have we here?"

"Will you help me with my homework, please, Mr. White?"

"Lydia," her mother admonished. "I'd say Mr White has had quite enough of school today."

Clem patted Lydia's hand. "I do have some homework of my own to do, so maybe another time?"

"I'll be in Sydney, in Teacher's College by then," said Lydia, trying to sound mature.

"You've got a long way to go yet, madam," Laura laughed. "Sorry, Clem. She's getting a bit above herself, these days."

Clem prepared to leave, saying "Thank you for the soup, Laura."

"Don't thank me, thank your wife." She helped him into his raincoat, and he kissed her lightly on the cheek.

"We'll miss you. Don't forget to ask me if you want any help with your move."

"I will. Thank you." Laura watched him close the shop door, and thought of what her life could have been.

Lydia picked up on his parting comment immediately. "Why will Mr. White miss you, Mummy?" Slight panic showed in her voice as she went on, "Are you going to leave me?"

Laura hugged her and stroked the fair hair she knew so well. "Of course not, angel. Now, do your homework while I make tea and close the shop. Then we'll have a talk."

"About what?" An eight-year old is permanently active with questions.

"You'll see," said Laura, kissing her little girl's forehead. "Now, off you go."

Lydia looked strangely at her mother, but did as she was told.

Laura busied herself with the necessary end-of-day routine, and mentally organised her announcement to Lydia, about their coming move to Sydney. She was confident about her plans, knowing Lydia would benefit from her world broadening. She finished her chores, and looked around the shop. 'I'll get an agent to sell the business, and that should finance us well, at least until I can get work,' she thought. 'Oh, Joseph, please help me make the right choices.'

When the evening meal was finished, and dishes cleared away, Laura sat with her daughter at the table, to explain her plans. At first, Lydia was horrified. The thought of leaving her friends, her school, the life she took for granted, was hard to accept. But with Laura's patience and explanation, she could understand her mother's aims. And yes, she did want to be a teacher – or a doctor.

Clem and Kate arranged a farewell and birthday party at the pub, for Laura and Lydia. People came into Hargraves from the neighbouring villages, and as far afield as Mudgee and Bathurst. The number of wishes for good luck she had, made her feel even more confident about her move. The mother of one of Lydia's school-friends even gave her an address in Sydney, where she could stay. "She's my sister, and runs a boarding house."

Lydia's ninth birthday passed by, and the shop was still unsold. Laura discussed the situation with the estate agent who was handling the sale.

"What do you think I should do?" she asked.

"Have you considered leasing the business?" was the answer, and Laura confessed she hadn't. Two weeks into November, the agent introduced her to Mr. Geoffrey Drake. He was a happy young man, around twenty-five years old, and eager to take over.

Laura invited him to have a meal with them, so that she could explain how she ran the business, and was pleasantly surprised at his aptitude.

"Have you handled something like this previously, Mr. Drake," she asked, piling lamb and vegetables on his plate.

"Please - call me Geoff," he returned, as he opened a bottle of wine he had brought with him. "Do I detect an English accent, there?"

"Why, yes," Laura laughed. "Seems you have one, too? How long have you been in Australia?" Then she noticed that Lydia was gazing at him rapturously, and said, "Lydia, you know it is rude to stare."

They sat down, and Geoff smiled at the girl. "Lydia - well, that's a pretty name."

"Yes," Lydia straightened in her chair, and lifted her chin. "I was named after my Grandmother, you know. I never met her, because she had died before I was born, but mother has often spoken about her." She reached forward and picked up the tongs in the sugar bowl. "See? These belonged to her, and she had the same initials as me. LM - only she was Lydia Marchant. The tongs will be mine, one day."

"Eat your food, Lydia," said Laura sternly. "Mr. Drake doesn't want to know all our history." She turned to Geoff, and went on, "Lydia is an only child, and they tend to grow up much faster."

Geoff had a strange look on his face, and Laura became uncomfortable. She lifted her glass to take a sip of wine, and tried to divert his attention. "How long did you say you'd been in Australia?"

His answer made her drop her cutlery noisily on the plate. "I emigrated with my parents nearly twelve years ago. We arrived on the SS Mariana, in 1861."

"Geoffrey! Mr. and Mrs. Drake's son. Your father taught me to play chess during the voyage."

"I thought I recognised you," said Geoff. "Your name threw me - you were Miss Marchant, then. Well, I'll be..."

Laura leaned across the table and shook his hand, warmly. "I can hardly believe it - to think you should be the one to take over my shop! And your parents - how are they?"

Lydia was fascinated by the revelation, there was so much excited conversation, their food started to go cold. "Mother has taught me to play chess," she said. "Perhaps we could have a challenge after dinner?"

Geoff tucked into his food, saying, "Well, let's not waste this lovely meal. But I'll not play chess, because I was too conceited to learn. Your mother was a lot wiser." He grinned across to Laura. "What a coincidence, eh? Unfortunately, my mother only lived for the first year in this country, but my father and I have kept going. He lives in Sydney, and I visit him every week. Wait till I tell him who I've bumped into. He will be delighted."

"Oh, I am sorry to hear about your mother," Laura said. "Was she ill for very long?"

"No, thankfully. She had a heart problem, and died in her sleep. Was a big blow to me and father, but we've lived through it."

"We're going to live in Sydney," Lydia piped up. "Perhaps we can go and see him, Mother?"

"Whoa, matey," said Laura, imitating Dave Lee. "Geoff's father may prefer not to see us. Twelve years is a long time."

"Of course he will," scoffed Geoff. "He often talks about the young woman who was companion to Mrs. Martin. Her husband was a bit of an ogre, wasn't he?"

Laura's face clouded, and she said, "I think it is time for you to go to bed, Lydia. You have school tomorrow, and Mr. White will not be happy if you miss out."

"Oh, Mother!"

Laura patted her hand, and smiled. "Geoff is going to stay in Hargraves this weekend, so you'll see him again. Now, off you go, and say 'good night' politely."

Lydia looked as though she wanted to pout, but attending school was not a chore to her, so she shook hands with Geoff gravely, and kissed her mother's cheek. "Can't wait to tell them our news, at school."

She skipped into the bedroom, and closed the door, and Geoff and Laura could hear her humming away to herself.

"Bright young girl, that," smiled Geoff.

"Yes, I'm very proud of her. I'll pour us a cup of tea, then we can sit by the fire, and I'll tell you about the Martins."

By the time Laura had briefly described events since she arrived in Australia, she could hardly believe it herself. She didn't burden Geoff with her feelings when these events happened, but described the journey to Hargraves from Melbourne, including their stay at Bathurst, where the first Mrs. Martin died. She didn't mention the rape when she came to Hargraves, either. But Geoff was an astute young man, and shook his head.

"Strewth! You've had a bad time of it, Laura. We had more luck. At least, until Mum died. But Dad was determined to make a life for me here, so he sent me back to England and Cambridge University. I was there for three years, and came back to Australia, as soon as I'd qualified."

Laura's eyes twinkled. "Strewth? That doesn't sound like a University vocabulary."

Geoff laughed back and said, "Dad made sure I would not be labelled a 'toffee-nose', and we enjoyed our visits to the local pub when we could. Surprising what you can learn at a pub."

"We have the Hargraves Arms, and I know what you mean. It's owned by the school headmaster now, Mr Clem White. You are sure to meet him as soon as you take over the shop. He has always been a loyal friend to me."

"Sounds great to me, Laura. Can't wait to meet people here."

"You'll have plenty of time. You said you were staying in Mudgee for the week, I think?" She glanced at the big wooden clock on the mantelpiece over the fire. "It's getting late. Are you sure you will be all right - it's a dark road to Mudgee."

"I learned how to get around without street lights, before going to Cambridge," Geoff laughed. "I'll be fine. You have our address, in Sydney, don't you?

Laura nodded, and when he got up on the buck-board, he said, "You wait until I tell Dad the news. You must come and meet him again, Laura. I know he would be delighted to learn about you."

"I'll try, as soon as we settle in Sydney."

And now, it was time for the big move to the city. On the last day in Hargraves, Laura waited for Clem and Kate to pick them up, and she gazed around the familiar rooms.

"I'm going to miss Charlotte," Lydia said. They were almost like sisters now. "But Uncle Clem said she will probably go to Teacher's College a couple of years after me, so we'll be together again." Laura didn't seem to hear what was being said. "What are you thinking of, Mummy?"

"Nothing, dearest. On the other hand, everything" Right then, her eyes rested on the chimney, where she had hidden her treasures. "So long ago..."

Lydia interrupted her reverie. "Uncle Clem's here!"

Clem, Kate and Charlotte took them to Bathurst Railway Station, and the tearful girls hugged each other. Kate leaned on Clem's shoulder as they waved when the train started off, and Laura couldn't stop tears filling her eyes, as they watched their dear friends disappear. She dabbed her face and took her seat, glad the rest of the carriage was empty.

Lydia was nervous about this first time on a train, and looked out of the window in fascination, as the scenery sped by. "When will we get to Sydney, Mummy?"

"In a few hours, dear. Look, I've brought a book for you."

That was enough to occupy the girl, as she loved reading. Laura smiled at her concentration, then gazed out of the window, realising that her own nerves were fluttering.

When they arrived at Grand Central Station in Sydney, she hired a carriage that took them and their luggage, out to the address in she'd been given. It was in a suburb called Stanmore.

Arriving at the door of Mrs Emma Doyle's home in Cambridge Street, they were greeted warmly.

"Welcome, Mrs Martin. Please come in - I hope the train journey was comfortable?"

A homely woman, around fifty years of age, Mrs Doyle led them into her front room, and the driver carried in their luggage. Laura paid and thanked him while Emma leaned over and touched Lydia's cheek. "Such a pretty little girl, and what's your name, then?"

"Lydia", answered Laura, because her daughter had suddenly lost her tongue. "I think she's a little tired and overwhelmed."

"Lots of strangers," nodded Emma. "Let's settle you both into your room, and then we'll have tea. I have scones and strawberry jam and cream - how do you like that, then, Lydia?"

Lydia nodded eagerly, and the two women laughed as Emma led them upstairs. Their room overlooked the street and in the distance, they could see the taller buildings of the City. Emma left them to unpack, and it wasn't long before Lydia was tucking into the promised scones, and chattering in her usual manner.

They settled surprisingly well. As if by design, there was an excellent school for Lydia, at the City end of Cambridge Street. Within the month, new friends arrived to do their homework with Lydia, and Emma Doyle proved to be a walking encyclopedia. She confessed to Laura that helping the girls had opened up her life for her, and she revelled in their questions. Within six months, Lydia had developed her schooling skills immensely.

Laura found herself employed in a department store, in George Street and quickly adapted to travelling every day by tram, into the City. She made several friends there, including Janet, who was another sales-lady. She also learned how impermanent City friendships can be, when Janet left to have a baby. The floor manager, Mr. Lincoln, was always extremely fair, and joined in with the after-hours farewell party for Janet, where the mother-to-be was showered with baby gifts. Laura had kept some of the tiny items she'd made for little Joseph, and Lydia, so gift-wrapped them and added her card to congratulate Janet.

Conversation over the evening meal, which Emma Doyle always had ready for them, was bright with stories from the city and school. Saturday mornings were shopping days, and Sundays were occupied with hobbies like chess, knitting for Emma, and word games that they all loved.

Emma Doyle became Laura's closest friend and they enjoyed each other's company.. "You've never felt inclined to remarry?" she asked Laura one day. They were knitting in the summer sunshine, in the garden which was well stocked with flowers and vegetables.

"No," answered Laura quietly.

"I know how you feel," said Emma."I could never replace Mr Doyle. He was a wonderful man."

Laura said nothing, She hadn't discussed Joseph with anyone else other than Kate. And Lydia, when she inquired about her father.

"He was a good man," Laura answered quietly. which seemed to satisfy Emma's curiosity.

"Coping with your job?"

Emma's query wasn't idle chatter, Laura knew. On several mornings, she had remarked on her pallor, and Laura always brushed it aside as 'city living.'

"Yes, quite well, thank you, Emma. It took me a little while to find my way around - it is such a large store."

"And it will get bigger," her landlady nodded wisely. "A Welshman started that, you know, in eighteen-thirty-something. Done well for himself, he has."

"Well, he's certainly done me well," Laura smiled. She set her knitting aside. "They're already talking about promoting me to the china department, because of my English accent."

"That's nice. Yes, it still is very noticeable. How long have you been in Australia now?"

Laura paused. "Nearly twelve years."

"I guess it will rub off one day" Mrs. Doyle chuckled, winding up her own knitting. "Getting a bit hot out here. Let's go in and have a lemonade."

Laura wasn't too sure she wanted her English accent to 'rub off', but she answered "That would be perfect, Emma. Thank you."

While they sipped at the cool drink in the sun-room, Emma asked, "Young Lydia's birthday, soon, isn't it? How old will she be then?"

"Yes, on the third of September. She'll be ten years old this year. My how the time flies."

"She must have a nice party," declared the kindly landlady. "How about you leave that to me? Keeping up at David Jones is enough for you to cope with."

Laura knew she'd been very tired some days, on returning from the store. She worked five days a week, and was always grateful to relax at the weekends. She was paid a little extra at stocktaking time, because her ability to organise her department had saved time and money for her employers.

Clem, Kate and Charlotte had promised to come to Sydney for Lydia's birthday and Mrs. Doyle had kindly given them accommodation for a few days. They had employees of their own, by this time, "so we'll be able to escape more often now," said Kate.

"What about Charlotte's schooling?" Laura asked.

"Daddy makes me do homework, even when we're away," said the girl, grumpily.

"Don't pretend," scolded Kate. "You know you love every minute of it."

Charlotte grinned sheepishly. She and Lydia were enjoying themselves while sitting at the table, comparing their very similar marks for school tests..

"I'm very proud of my daughter," said Laura She reduced to a whisper and leaned forward."I was secretly getting a little worried about her precociousness, but since she's been schooling down here, she has matured a great deal."

Clem leaned forward in the same conspiratorial way, but with a grin on his face. "Are you telling me my school wasn't good enough for her?"

"Oh, Clem!" laughed Laura, and Kate joined in the fun.

"What are you all laughing at?" asked Lydia from across the room.

"Stop eavesdropping," Kate replied to her. Then she hugged her good friend, and said, "Me, too! Our girls are going a long way."

Emma was a good as her word, and Lydia's tenth birthday party was a great success. She had two of her school-friends in for the party, as well as Charlotte, her friend from Hargraves. and their squeals of joy at the Princess items Lydia was given, echoed into the kitchen, where Laura was lighting candles.

"Charlotte misses Lydia," said Kate, holding the door open so that Laura could carry the cake through. "But I'm happy to see your decision to leave Hargraves seems to have been the right one."

The White family prepared to return to Hargraves the next day, and there was a lot of hugging and kissing, especially with the two young girls. "We couldn't come to your birthday last month," Lydia said to Charlotte, "my mother had to work."

"You will come down and stay with us again, I hope?" said Laura.

"Of course," said Clem, pecking her cheek.

Emma and Lydia revelled in preparing the house with Christmas decorations at the beginning of December, and Laura permitted her daughter to join in with the street singing of Christmas Carols. Young people grouped around the Salvation Army band, and "*Away In A Manger*" had never sounded so lovely. Christmas Eve on a hot starry night, still seemed a little wrong to Laura, but she enjoyed the festivities and coloured lights. New Year's Eve came, and the year passed into 1899 with the usual celebrations.

Laura had been promoted to Head of the Kitchen and Chinaware Department at David Jones early that year, and it was July, when she was struck down. She hadn't felt well for weeks, but didn't say anything. Until the morning she fainted, while wrapping a set of kitchen knives for a customer.

The customer screamed, and another counter assistant rushed to cradle Laura's head. Mr. Lincoln immediately sent out for a doctor, but Laura regained consciousness within moments.

"Oh, I'm so sorry, Mr. Lincoln. I don't know what happened."

"Stay still, Laura. A doctor is on his way. Do you have any pain?"

"I feel so hot," Laura confessed.

Word flashed around the store departments, and by the time Mr. Lincoln rescued a wheelchair from their Medical Appliances area and taken to the front door, practically all the David Jones staff were there, to watch Laura being taken to the Sydney Infirmary.

A message was relayed to Emma Doyle, advising her of the situation, but also requesting that she not visit Laura, until the evening, to allow investigations to be carried out. Laura drifted in and out of consciousness, trying to make out what was happening.

A distinguished man in his late forties, came into the ward. "Good afternoon, Mrs. Martin. My name is Doctor Metcalf." Laura nodded, too dizzy to speak. "We have to run some tests on you."

"Oh, no!" Laura managed.

"Now, don't panic, Mrs. Martin. It may take few days to establish what is happening here."

Laura sank onto the pillow, and tears coursed down her cheeks. "But, I have a little girl, and a job..."

"Is there someone to care for your daughter?"

"Yes, but..."

"That's all right, then," Doctor Metcalf said. He looked through Laura's medical file that was alongside her bed, and nodded. "We will let your employers know what's happening, and I'm sure you won't lose your job."

A ward sister approached Laura's bed. "Doctor Metcalf, sir? We have another emergency for you, in the Outpatients Department."

"Very well," came the answer. "I'll come right along." He turned back to Laura. "You rest, Mrs. Martin, and let us do all the worrying."

Through blurry eyes, Laura watched him go, and suddenly felt extremely vulnerable again. A young probationer nurse came along, put a cool hand on Laura's hot forehead, and said, "I'll get you a cup of tea, Mrs. Martin."

By the time the nurse returned, Laura was feeling distinctly unwell, and had started to breathe heavily. The nurse placed her tea noisily on the bedside cabinet, and went out quickly.

Within minutes, Doctor Metcalf strode in, took one look at Laura, and ordered, "Quarantine!"

She was barely aware of what happened to her from then on, as the fever took over and she was in a semi-conscious state. Her bed was quickly wheeled into a nearby ward, with no other patients, and Doctor Metcalf spoke to the nursing Sister who had appeared.

"Mercurochrome, please, Sister. And I want a continual watch on Mrs. Martin, until the fever breaks."

"Very well, Doctor Metcalf." The Sister disappeared to arrange the intensive care.

Two days passed; her face and body was smothered by an angry red rash, and the fever didn't seem to improve. Whichever nurse was on duty with her, spent most of her time changing the wet bedclothes, or mopping Laura's face with cool flannels. Several times, Laura said, "Joseph!", but she remained unconscious.

On the third day, her condition weakened even more, and the Ward Sister sent a message to Doctor Metcalf. He arrived and examined Laura, then straightened. "I'm not happy about her condition. Her fever must break tonight, Sister, or I'm afraid she won't live till the morning."

Meanwhile, the atmosphere in Cambridge Street, Stanmore, was one of despondency and fear. When Emma Doyle received word of the trauma, her first instinct was to take the train into Sydney, and visit Laura.

The department manager, Mr. Lincoln, had brought the news. "There's no point, Mrs. Doyle," the distressed man said. "Laura is in quarantine, and no-one but the medical staff are allowed near her."

When he visited Stanmore a few days later, his news was even worse. "She is not responding to treatment, I'm afraid, and still unconscious. I spoke with the doctor in charge today - a Doctor Metcalf. He said it was Scarlet Fever, and an extremely bad case of it. Apparently, there is an epidemic building and we are advised not to visit Laura, until the fever breaks."

"I want to see my mother!" Lydia said loudly, having overheard Mr. Lincoln's conversation.

"Hush," said Mrs. Doyle, drawing the child close to her. "Your mother would be so upset if she thought she'd passed it on to you. Most of the time, people get over this Scarlet Fever, but it sounds like your mother has been affected very badly by it."

Lydia began to cry. "Is she going to die?"

"This Doctor Metcalf is doing all he can," broke in Mr. Lincoln, upset by the girl's distress. "I'm sure she will get well, soon."

"Of course she will,," said the landlady, stroking Lydia's head, which was buried into her bosom. "Your mother is a fighter, and it will take a lot of germs to knock her down."

"When can we see her?" Lydia asked tearfully.

"Soon, pet, soon." Emma Doyle wasn't quite sure how to handle the situation, but she knew Lydia's mind must be kept positive. "Thank you for coming, Mr. Lincoln."

"I live within walking distance to the hospital," said Mr. Lincoln. "I'll pop in there every day, and keep you up to date."

"You are so kind, Mr. Lincoln," said Emma. ""We'll look forward to your next visit."

In the hired carriage on the way back to Sydney Central, Mr. Lincoln hoped his next visit would be with good news. He could not face having to relay news that Laura had died. He'd become quite fond of the brave young mother in the past few months.

16 PHILIP LINCOLN

Behind the closed ward door, the low light over Laura's bed head illuminated her desperately pale and sweaty face. Painfully thin, her arms lay without life, on the lightweight blanket. The Night Nurse rose from her chair when Laura moaned softly. It was ten minutes past three in the morning, and Laura began turning her head from side to side.

The nurse was well aware that this was a dangerous time - for some unknown reason, patients with their life at risk, succumbed to their illness around this turn of the clock She wrung out a cold flannel and gently laid it on Laura's forehead.

"Come on, Mrs. Martin. Fight it, fight it."

The girl's voice seemed to penetrate, and Laura's eyes fluttered open. Her lips moved and her tongue licked the dryness. She closed her eyes again, and the nurse bent over her with a glass of water. She didn't have the strength to drink, so the nurse dipped the facecloth into the glass.

"Are you with us, Mrs. Martin?" She lifted Laura's head gently and placed the wet cloth against Laura's mouth. Laura gave a small cough as the liquid dribbled into her throat, then moaned again.

At that moment, Robert Metcalf walked into the room and crossed quickly to the bed. "How is she?"

"I think the fever has broken, doctor," the nurse answered.

"Thank God for that," he said. "She will be very weak, but will probably drift off into a natural sleep for a few hours, now. Send for me if anything else happens. I'm going for a few hours myself, and I'll come back to check on her in the morning."

"Very well, Doctor Metcalf. I'll keep a close watch on her."

Next day, when Mr. Lincoln relayed the good news to Mrs. Doyle and Lydia, all three cried in relief.

"I knew she would fight it," said Mrs. Doyle, wiping her eyes. Then she wiped Lydia's tears away. "You see? You have a remarkable woman for your mother. We must take special care of her when she gets back home."

"Can't we go and see her now, Mrs. Doyle?"

"We'll let her have a good rest today, and she will probably be able to talk to you, this evening."

"I will come and pick you both up at four o'clock," said Mr. Lincoln, having blown his nose hard. "And I will wait to bring you home, afterwards."

"That is so kind of you, Mr. Lincoln," said Emma. "You must let me pay you something for our fares."

"Nonsense, you leave the money business to me."

"You must live in a big house, Mr. Lincoln." Lydia was remembering Tangarra. "We had a carriage like that, once."

"Bless you," said the kind man. "It's not my carriage. I just hire it when I need it."

Emma Doyle looked shocked. "But that must cost you a fortune. Please, let me assist with the costs."

"I won't hear of it," said Mr. Lincoln. "I am very fond of Laura, and consider it my privilege to help her family."

Emma recognised a warmth in his voice, and smiled. "I'm sure Laura will be happy to learn of it."

That evening, when Mrs. Doyle led Lydia into the isolation ward, they gasped to see the healthy and virile young woman they knew, lying pale and listless against a stack of pillows. She appeared to be sleeping, but sensed their presence and turning her head, she slowly opened her eyes.   Lydia was clearly disturbed by her mother's pallor, and drew back.

Laura whispered, "Hello, my angel."

Nervously, Lydia whispered back. "Are you going to die, Mummy?"

"Of course not," said Emma Doyle busily. "Now, give your mother a little kiss."

Lydia approached carefully, then began to cry against her mother's chest. "I thought you were going to go to heaven, to be with father."

Laura stroked her daughter's hair. "Sweet child, we have a lot more to do before that happens,"

Emma fought hard to control her emotions, then wiped her eyes. "What has the doctor said, my dear?"

Robert Metcalf entered the room at that moment, and Laura was grateful. She felt too worn out to talk much, and her main concern was Lydia who was still crying. "Hush, angel, hush. All will be well, soon."

"Can you come home, now?"

"No, my pet," said Laura wearily, but with greater control. "Doctor Metcalf says I must rest a lot."

"That's right," cut in the doctor. He shook hands with Emma Doyle. "You must be her landlady?" Emma nodded, and whispered, "Thank you, Doctor Metcalf, for looking after her."

Then he addressed Lydia. Nervous sobs still racked her young body, but she'd stopped the tears. "Your mother has been extremely ill, young lady. We will keep her in here until she regains strength, but you must be very good, and help her, when she comes home."

Lydia nodded seriously, as though the Good Lord himself had spoken.

When they visited a week later, Mr Lincoln came into the ward with them. Laura had improved noticeably and shared a new ward with several other ladies. Doctor Metcalf arrived and drew the curtains around Laura's bed. He shook hands with her visitors, and tilted Lydia's head.

"Your mother is doing well."

"Can she come home, now?"

Laura smiled at the doctor, and said, "I must go home, soon, or who knows what mischief these two will get up to."

Mrs. Doyle and Lydia exchanged impish grins, and the doctor said, "You behave yourselves, ladies I don't want to see Laura in here again." He patted Laura's feet under the blanket. "She's been a star patient for me."

"Your job is still waiting for you, Laura," Mr. Lincoln cut in. "How long before she will be able to come back to David Jones, doctor?" His question had a faint edge, and gave the impression that, once she got home, Laura was his concern, not that of the doctor's.

"Early days, yet."

Instinctively, Laura looked at her landlady. "I will not be able to earn money for a while, Emma. So I'll not have enough coming in for our rent."

"Don't you worry about that," Emma said. "You just get yourself better, and do what the doctor says."

The two men shook hands again, while Lydia gave her mother a hug, and Emma lightly kissed her cheek. "You're looking a bit tired again, my dear.. Rest up now. Come along, Lydia, your mother needs some peace and quiet."

Alone again, after tearful farewells, Laura laid back, grateful for Mrs. Doyle's generosity. Geoffrey Drake's money for the lease of Hargraves Store, was still very reliable, but it wasn't enough to pay the rent and living in Stanmore. The balance would have to be paid eventually, despite her landlady's reassurances.

Then she thought about her gold, still packed away in the big trunk, at the foot of her bed at home. Perhaps now was the time to sell it? Indeed, there seemed no other way. "This surely is my rainy day, Clem," she whispered.

Her dinner arrived a little later, and while she ate, she did a lot of thinking. She trusted Clem White, and knew that next to Kate, and his daughter Charlotte, she was a highly regarded figure in his life. Since Joseph's sudden death, few men had been important to her, although she had been pleasantly surprised at the reception she had from Geoff's father, when they visited him.

James Drake lived in Rose Bay, an exclusive part of Sydney. Through Geoff, and their many visits to Rose Bay, she'd learned that James had done extremely well as an Australian businessman. His business acumen, which he had obviously instilled in his son, had established him firmly in the new country, and unlike many others who had emigrated to the new country and made their fortune, it had not gone to his head, and he'd retained his fresh and positive outlook. The estate where he had built his house was very close to Rose Bay Lodge on Sydney Harbour. Lydia loved their visits, as James Drake had allocated a docile pony and a stableman, to teach her the joys of horse-riding.

Laura was so proud of her daughter's 'natural seat' as James called it, and often thought sadly of Joseph's ban on horse-riding. He would have seen the glow of delight on his daughter's face, had he lived.

James and Laura had exchanged visits a few times during the year, and he was always very concerned that his son didn't let her down. Laura continually reassured him. "I couldn't have wished for a more pleasant, or capable leaseholder. Geoff has been extremely successful, and you should be very proud of him."

"Oh, I am, I am," James averred.

The ward lights were extinguished at nine o'clock promptly, but Laura didn't sleep very well. She had too much on her mind, and although the night nurses tried, they couldn't quieten the clang of bedpans in the sluice room, and the consistent calls for "Nurse!"

Around three in the morning, a patient caused a disturbance in the corridor outside the ward.

"Leave me alone!" a querulous voice shouted.

"Now, come along, Mrs. Smith. Back to bed."

"But I've got to do my shopping," the voice objected. "All the bargains will be gone if I don't go early."

"Well, the shops aren't open at this time, Mrs. Smith, so you may as well rest in bed for a while."

Breakfast arrived at seven next morning, and one of the nurses explained to Laura, that the fuss had been caused by an old lady, "who, unfortunately, has lost her mind. She is in here for a while, to give her family a rest from looking after her."

Laura wasn't hungry, but she swallowed her tea while thinking how lucky she was really, to have had a complaint that could be helped. She was sitting up in a much more confident mood when Robert Metcalf visited later.

"How are we feeling? I won't be in to see you tomorrow. I have an important operation to perform." His eyes twinkled and Laura appreciated his bedside manner. "So... I must make sure my scalpel is nice and clean."

Despite her tiredness, Laura had to smile. "I like your sense of humour, Doctor Metcalf."

She was discharged from hospital a few days later, and again, Mr. Lincoln hired the carriage to transport her. Travelling West along the Parramatta Road, towards Stanmore, she snuggled into the warm blanket provided by her landlady, and observed the shops and buildings that had developed since she'd come to Sydney. The strangeness of incarceration for weeks, then release from the Infirmary, made her look around with increased pleasure, and she compared this ride to the one behind Daisy, in Tolton. Then, the wagon ride to Ballarat with her dear friend, Jemima, filled her mind and memories flooded her, until Mr. Lincoln spoke.

"Are you quite comfortable, Laura?" He felt he had earned the right to use her first name, especially after hearing Doctor Metcalf doing the same.

"Yes, thank you, Mr. Lincoln. It is so good to be out in the fresh air again, without the smell of carbolic soap and ether."

"Why don't you call me Philip?"

Laura glanced quickly at him, but his face was turned stoically ahead. His profile, with an aquiline nose, and a rim of dark hair beneath his baldness, struck her as noble, and she cleared her throat. "Because you were not introduced to me as any other than, Mr. Lincoln."

"That was some time ago, so I would be very happy now, if you called me by my first name."

His request was so formal, Laura hesitated, remembering how Joseph very often spoke with similar command. Philip's voice, however, did not have the hard edge to it, and her reaction was slower. She smiled, and nodded.

They arrived at Stanmore just as Lydia came home from school, and there was such excitement. "Mummy, oh, Mummy, I've missed you so much," prattled Lydia, as she flung herself onto Laura.

"Welcome home, Laura," Emma Doyle smiled. "I'll bet quids on you being ready for a nice hot cup of tea!"

"Lovely, " Laura said. "I'll need that to set me on my feet."

"Now, don't you go trying to rush at things, Laura," Philip Lincoln cut in. For some reason, the look of concern on his face made Laura feel bashful. "Remember what Doctor Metcalf said. You have to take it easy and slow for a few days, then you'll start feeling better."

"I feel better already," Laura laughed. "But, thank you for your concern, Philip. You can rest assured that I will return to work at the first possible minute. In fact, if you have any light work I can do at home here, for a few weeks, I'd be glad to take it on."

Philip Lincoln gathered his gloves, and sagely, said "Aah!"

Laura picked up on it in an instant, and looked at him keenly. "There is something wrong, Philip?"

"No, no," he replied quickly. "I will go now, to let you rest from the excitement of being home. May I call on you again, in a few days? Just to check on your progress?"

"You, and everyone at David Jones, have been so kind," Laura said. "I really hadn't expected a card from anyone, particularly Mr. Jones. Please thank them all for their wonderful thoughts and prayers."

Philip tipped his hat, and shook her hand. Then he turned and shook Mrs. Doyle's hand, and with an imperceptible bow, he said "I look forward to meeting you all again, soon." With a serious expression, Lydia held out her hand and said, "Me too, Mr. Lincoln." There were smiles all around with the girl's attempt at maturity, and Mrs. Doyle showed him to the door.

Immediately he'd gone, Emma Doyle took on the role of nursemaid, and tucked a blanket around Laura's knees. "My goodness, woman, you have lost so much weight. But we'll soon have that fixed. We're having Lancashire Hotpot and Dumplings for dinner, and I want you to eat every morsel on your plate."

"Ooh, I love that," said Lydia, beaming. "Can I have seconds, please?"

"Firsts first", said Emma, tipping the girl's nose. "And that includes the carrots! Come along now, help me peel the vegetables." They both disappeared into the kitchen, and left Laura alone with her thoughts.

'Catching up on the outstanding rent is not going to be easy,' she told herself. 'You'll just have to get extra money, somehow.' With heavy heart, she decided that her gold nugget would have to be sold. She had planned to keep it, and make it part of Lydia's inheritance, but could not have foreseen the recent events.

"As soon as I can travel, I will visit Hargraves and Clem White." Having made that decision, she drifted off into sleep, and dreamed that Joseph, Doctor Metcalf, Mister Lincoln and Clem White were standing around her, and holding out their hands. She awoke with a start, and began wondering about her dream, when she spotted a bundle of unopened letters on the nearby table. She leaned over and took them up, idly flipping through - those from the Mudgee Council were easy to distinguish, and several recognisable envelopes from Lydia's school, she set aside.

One, however, was handwritten and came from Hargraves. It was written by Geoff Drake, and listed some points of maintenance required on the Hargraves Store.

"I have asked Mrs. White to look after the store for me, to allow me a visit to my father, shortly. I am well aware how ill you have been, lately, Laura, but I would really like to visit you, while I'm in Sydney. My father has said he would like to see you again, also, and I'm writing to ask if April 10th would be a suitable date for you?"

Laura glanced quickly at a small book she kept in her handbag. The date on the letter was April 2$^{nd.}$. Too late perhaps, to send him a reply. She would write a letter to Mr. James Drake. saying she looked forward to both of them visiting her and she would explain to Geoff then, why she had written to his father, instead of him, and hoped he would understand.

Delicious smells were wafting in from the kitchen, and Laura rose from her chair, to set the cutlery out on the table.

Lydia bounced into the room. "I'll do that, Mama. Mrs. Doyle said to tell you that dinner will not be long."

Laura smiled, and sat back down. "We are having a visit from Mr. Drake and Geoffrey soon."

"Hooray!" Lydia shouted. "I like Geoff."

"And his father, I should hope?"

"Of course, Mama."

"Why do you suddenly call me 'Mama'?" asked Laura.

"Because my best friend in school, calls her mother that, and I like it."

The fact that she hadn't spoken about this to Laura, gave her in insight to her developing child. A flash of Joseph shone through Lydia's attitude, and Laura quietly hoped her daughter would benefit from this.

17 THE ELUSIVE HAPPINESS

The day before the visitors were due, Laura rose early to help Emma with the preparations, and Lydia trotted off to school for the last day of term. About eleven in the morning, Laura answered a ring on the doorbell, and found Philip Lincoln standing there. "Philip, what a nice surprise.".

"Laura, may I speak with you privately, please?"

"Of course," said Laura, wiping the flour from her hands. "I'll be back in a minute, Emma," she called, and led the visitor into the garden. "What's the mystery, Phil? Should I sit down?"

Laura said this flippantly, but staying on his feet, Philip Lincoln looked decidedly uneasy. "I'm afraid I have some bad news for you, Laura... Mrs. Martin."

Laura braced herself, then her heart plummeted when he spoke. "It has been decided to cease your employment with David Jones Department Store, as of the end of this month. The Management have acknowledged that, during the coming Christmas period, you will hardly be strong enough to stand on your feet all day, and it would be advantageous for us to train another assistant for this."

"But, I thought my position was safe, Ph... Mr. Lincoln."

"I'm afraid not, Mrs. Martin. I did try to avoid this happening, but we didn't appreciate how long you would be ill for. I'm so sorry."

He stated the facts without emotion, and this hurt Laura more than his news. "I don't know what to say," she replied. She didn't know how to address him either, as he obviously had ducked behind the curtain of formality.

"The salary you're entitled to will be drawn up, as of that date, and sent to you by Special Courier. I'm very sorry to bring you this news, but it was my duty." He prepared to go back into the kitchen, and doffed his hat as he replaced it. "I'll bid farewell to Mrs. Doyle on the way through, and see myself out."

Once again, men were taking control of her life, and Laura thought bitterly, about the last few minutes. She re-entered the kitchen slowly, and said, "I've lost my job, it seems."

"Oh no!" exploded Emma. "Is that what he came for? I thought he'd plucked up enough courage to ask you to dinner, or something."

"Hardly," said Laura. "He couldn't even bring himself to say my name, let alone ask me to share a few Brussels sprouts with him!"

Emma couldn't help bursting out with laughter, and Laura grinned sheepishly when she said, "The story of my life!" She felt a little sad at this, but more so because she had allowed herself to think Philip Lincoln could become an important part of her life, but obviously she had misjudged him.

She was glad that Lydia wasn't there to hear him dismiss her, and decided to find another job before she said anything that would upset, and therefore hinder, her daughter's school work. Lydia had no idea of their financial position and Laura said a prayer, that the good Lord would help her.

She and Emma sat with a cool drink in the garden, later in the afternoon. "I won't be able to catch up on the rent now," said Laura. "I'm so sorry, Emma. But Lydia and I will make arrangements as soon as we can, and I assure you part of those arrangements will be to repay you."

Emma nodded wisely. "But don't forget, there's no incidence of pressure here. Pay me what you can, and when you can. I'm not going anywhere."

Laura leaned over and took her hand. "You are so kind, Emma. We really are so very lucky."

Lydia's excitement when James Drake walked in with his son, brought a smile to everyone's face. "Come and see our garden," Lydia said, taking Geoff by the hand. "Mummy helped me plant some flowers and herbs, and they've all grown." She made the last statement, wide-eyed, and Geoff dutifully followed her outside.

James Drake pecked Laura's cheek, and handed her a bunch of fragrant sweet peas. "From my own garden," he said. "Now you'll have to let me win at chess."

Laura laughed, and pushed her nose into the blooms. "Aah!," she sighed. "One of my favourite flowers. Thank you, James. That's really sweet of you."

Emma and James burst out laughing at the pun, and Emma asked, "Everyone for a cup of tea?"

"Yes, please," said James, with much enthusiasm. "I'm worn out listening to Geoff going on about the Hargraves Store. You know, that's the best thing that's ever happened to him, Laura?"

"I'm so pleased," said Laura.

They settled themselves at the kitchen table, and James said, "I'm so pleased to find you looking as fit as an eighteen-year old, m'girl. Really had me worried there, for a while."

Laura chuckled at his frankness, and teased, "Oh, I must apologise, sir. But I didn't fall ill on purpose, y'know!"

"And I see you've got your spirit back, too," chortled James.

Laura realised she was thoroughly enjoying the banter with James Drake, and turned a happy face to Geoff and Lydia, as they came through the garden door. "Hello, what have you two been up to?"

"I might ask the same," bantered Geoff.

"Mama, you're blushing."

"That's enough, you two," James intervened. Then he added, "Laura, Geoff and I have a proposition for you."

"What does that mean?" asked Lydia.

"Be quiet, Lydia," said Laura quickly. James Drake's statement had suddenly brought her into the moment. "What sort of proposition?"

Just then, Emma appeared, pushing a low trolley that was loaded with cups and saucers, and all things nice for afternoon tea. "Tea for four at five o'clock. There's lemonade for you, Lydia,".

There followed much small talk, rattling of china, and mumbles of delight over the home3-made shortbread, then Lydia challenged Geoff to a game of cricket, out in the garden, as Emma rolled the trolley out again.

Laura sat back in her chair and said, "Now, about that proposition, James."

"Finally," he replied, good-naturedly. Suddenly serious, he leaned forward and put his elbow on his knee. "Laura, I would like to buy the Hargraves Store from you, and I promise you the price I offer, will be fair."

Laura sat up and took a deep breath. She hadn't expected this, and took a moment to consider her answer. To sell the shop would certainly give her a sum of money enough to repay Emma, and handle part of Lydia's education. On the other hand, she wouldn't receive a regular income from the shop, and she would be unable to pay Emma anything, unless she found another job. Which could take some months. The complexities of letting go her main asset, put a frown to her forehead. "I presume you and Geoff have discussed this?"

Not prepared for this hesitation from Laura, James' eyebrows drew a little closer, and he said, "No. I wanted to get everything finalised, and give it to him as a Christmas present."

"I see," said Laura, quietly.

"As a matter of fact, that's why I came down to see you." James appeared to be grabbing straws from a haystack he hadn't expected to run into.

"Well, I dared to hope you had come down especially to see me," said Laura, still struggling for a suitable answer to his proposal. But her eyes twinkled.

"Well, I did," said the embarrassed James, "What I mean is..."

"James, I'm sorry," said Laura, "I shouldn't tease. The truth is, I am not sure which way to decide. I would be very happy for Geoff to have the shop, but right now, it is my only income, and having lost my job, I must protect it."

"Hmm, I understand," said James, leaning over and placing his hand over hers.. "But you will at least, consider my proposal?"

At that moment, Geoff and Lydia came in from the garden, and both Laura and James jumped back guiltily.

"Hello," said Geoff. "What's been going on here, then?"

Caught unawares, James blurted, "Nothing. I've just made Laura a proposition."

Geoff's eyebrows shot up. "What?"

Laura leapt in to clear the confusion, and said, "Your father wants me to sell the shop."

"What?" said Geoff again. He stared at his father. "What for?"

"For you," said Laura.

"For your Christmas gift," cut in James.

"Father, you've never discussed this before. What if I don't agree?"

James's eyebrows drew a little closer, and he said, "Geoff, I've heard you prattle on enough times, about what you would like to do to that shop. So, I thought it would be the ideal Christmas gift for you. I'd hoped you would be happy with that?"

Geoff swallowed hard, and looked appealingly at Laura. "I can assure you, Mrs. Martin, this is entirely my father's idea."

"Do you not want the shop, then?"

"Oh, I can't think of anything I'd like more, but it was your home, Mrs. Martin. Yours and Lydia's - I couldn't bear it if you thought it was a connived proposition."

"Mummy," said Lydia, forgetting her maturity for a moment. "Would that mean we can't go back to Hargraves again?"

"Of course not," said James with a cheerful voice. "You can come back to Hargraves at any time. Because I'm going to buy the house opposite as an investment, and you can and stay any time."

Laura cut in. "Do you mean Dave Lee's house, where Clem and Kate White live now?"

"Yes," came the answer. "Kate's expecting twins, and the house will be to small for them, so Clem is buying the big house next door to the school. Didn't you know that? Of course, you must have missed out on a lot while you were in hospital."

"Why no, I had not heard." Laura's voice became frail again, as though this news was a little too much to take in at once. "Please, James. Would you give me time to think about this?"

Emma Doyle, who had overheard the babble of fast conversation as she came in, sat on a chair by the window. "Laura, I think you've had enough excitement for one day. You're still a little weak, you know."

James Drake was crestfallen. His enthusiasm had disappeared and he said, "I'm so sorry, Laura. I didn't think straight. I should have left everything until after Christmas."

Wise as ever, Emma said, "Lydia's finished school for this term. And it's her birthday on the 3rd September. What about you and

Geoff spending that weekend with us, James? I have plenty of spare room – and Laura will be much stronger then,"

Lydia, not quite understanding what all the fuss was, clapped her hands, and said, "Ooh, yes. Please do." She turned to Geoff. "Then I can beat you again at cricket!"

His humour returned, James Drake slapped his knee. "Darned good idea, Mrs. Doyle! We'll go shopping that morning, Geoff, m'lad. We can get a few presents, and I can't think of a better way to spend a weekend."

"Whoopee!" Lydia shouted. "Will I be able to come with you, Mr. Drake?"

"Lydia!"

"I'll be all right, Mama. Mr Drake and Geoff will look after me, and I can get some presents for you and Mrs. Doyle."

"Yes, we'll take care of her," said Geoff, picking Lydia up and twirling her around. He kissed her as she lowered her, and Lydia's eyes glowed. He'd become her hero..

Laura was completely overwhelmed, and merely nodded.

Lydia chattered like a galah bird during the following two hours, until James and his son finally ended their visit. When the day was gone, a tired Laura said, "I feel as though I'm living a dream. Is this really happening?"

"You poor little thing," crooned Emma, as though Laura was her daughter. "Everything's happening so quickly, isn't it? But don't upset yourself, I'll make sure you're not rushed into things".

"Thank you, Emma."

Lydia's birthday weekend arrived, and Laura greeted their visitors happily on the Friday evening. "The birthday girl is so excited," she said to James. "Anyone would think this is her first birthday celebration."

"Well, she's only had ten, and half of those she wouldn't remember," James smiled. .

"Glad to see you again," said Emma, taking James' coat. Geoff had already hung his, and followed Lydia to see her birthday cards.

"We"re having some good old fish and chips," said Emma. "Won't be long."

James and Laura settled by the table, for a "quick game of chess, before dinner." James sorted the black and white pieces and Laura busied herself, pouring each of them a glass of sherry.
"Well, do you have an answer for me?" asked James.

"Yes, I do," Laura answered. There was a long silence, and James concentrated on the chess board.

"I've decided ..." Geoff and Lydia came into the room, and Laura looked hopelessly at James.

"Geoff, how about you and Lydia take our things to our bedroom, and unpack them.?" James winked at Laura, and waited until the youngsters had disappeared.

Laura folded her hands thoughtfully, then answered, "I'm sorry, James, but I can't."

James looked mortified. "But, why ever not?"

Laura hesitated. "Because I need the income from the shop to see Lydia through school," she admitted. "Maybe in six or eight years time? If you are still interested, that is."

James' face was a mixture of frustration and dismay. "You would be the most independent woman I know, Laura Martin." His face clouded as he continued, "Geoff is going to be so disappointed."

"I'm very sorry," whispered Laura, head bowed. "I hate refusing your offer, and I hope you will both understand why. Lydia is my sole responsibility and she must come first. I must think of her."

James sat silently, playing with the white queen chess piece. He looked up and studied Laura's pained expression. "And what about you, Laura Martin? After all you've been through, I think you deserve some consideration, too."

"Maybe," said Laura. "When Lydia's graduated."

"That could be another eight years away. You'll have forgotten how to think about yourself!"

Laura smiled. "I'll only be forty two. Time enough to enjoy myself."

"Maybe that will be too late, for me."

James hadn't looked away from the chess piece he held, and Laura mystified, studied his profile. He was older than her certainly, but he was strong enough for her to think he had more than eight years left. "What do you mean, James. Is there something you are not disclosing?"

James put the game piece down deliberately, and looked at her square on. "I mean, Mrs. Martin, too late for me to ask you to be my wife."

Laura's eyes widened, and she put her hand to her mouth as if to stop a reply.

"I'm sorry," said James, "I hadn't intended to throw that remark at you like this. I'm very good at saying things I can't take back, but I couldn't take the thought of you being a martyr while I wait in the wings." He got to his feet quickly, and smacked his forehead. "There! I've done it again., that sounds selfish of me."

Laura joined him the other side of the table, and put her hand on his arm. "James, please don't be hard on yourself. I really am quite fond of you, because you have done so much for Lydia. Teaching her how to ride horses, playing chess with her, and I do admire the way you've raised your son alone. And I am very flattered by your proposal."

"But your answer is no," said James.

"I must admit you have caught me by surprise," Laura said. "Now I am totally unsure of myself, and unsure of what to do. And I'd hate to think your proposal had anything to do with procuring the shop for Geoff."

As soon as the words were spoken, Laura knew she'd taken her turn at saying the wrong thing, and she was extremely grateful that Emma called from the kitchen. "Will you lay the table for us, please, Laura? The fish and chips are almost ready to serve."

"Yes, certainly!" Laura called, moving to the cutlery draw. "James," she continued, "Would you like to call Geoff and Lydia, please. They should have finished by now."

James' expression changed from surprise to a frown. "Yes."

Laura noted his curt reply, and felt the pressure lift as he disappeared through the door, calling for the youngsters. Emma noticed a strain between Laura and James while they ate their meal, but the mood was kept light with Lydia's excitement about her birthday party next day. Geoff spent his time teasing her, saying eleven-year olds are too big for toys and dolls now, so she will have to put up with hats, scarves and gloves for presents.

"That was excellent, Emma," said James, patting his stomach. "I'm sure there's a man out there that would love to have you for his wife."

"Oh, go on with you," said Emma, blushing.

One look at Laura's face told him that was something else he shouldn't have said, and he covered it with, "Well, I'm off for an early night. I'm sure this birthday girl will run us ragged around the shops tomorrow morning."

"Me too," said Geoff. "She's worn me out already."

Emma and Laura laughed politely, and Laura added, "You, too, Lydia. You'll be up early tomorrow morning, I expect."

Lydia was only too willing to obey, and when all three had said goodnight, and disappeared, Emma and Laura cleared away the meal. While drying the dishes for Emma, Laura was very quiet, and Emma regarded her over her shoulder.

"Something wrong, Laura?"

"Emma, I am faced with a big decision. I have to catch up with the rent, after all these weeks in the Infirmary. No doubt a big sum, by now."

"Now I told you not to concern yourself about that," answered Emma, firmly.

"But I must," Laura insisted. "And I can take one of two actions."

"Oh?"

"Either I sell the shop to James Drake, or I sell my piece of gold."

"What gold?"

"Oh, I'm sorry, Emma. You didn't know about that. I've only ever told Kate and Clem, and a dear man in Ballarat, called Billy King. He was like a father to me."

"Did he give it to you?"

"No. I found it near a little boy's grave, many years ago." Laura proceeded to tell Emma the whole story, and by the time she had finished, they were sitting quietly in the dining room.

"My goodness, Laura, I had no idea of what you must have gone through. It's no wonder that Scarlet Fever pulled you down so much. It's a wonder you didn't give in to it."

"I know," Laura sighed. "I have been so lucky, and always hung on to the thought that Joseph was still looking after me. But now, I'm well aware that he is not here to make decisions for me, and I feel so vulnerable."

"What's been said to make you as sad as this, Laura? Has that man been pressuring you to sell the shop again?" Emma was on the defensive immediately.

"Not really," Laura said. "It's my own fault for being so indecisive. I'm so afraid of making the wrong move."

"Well, I can't decide for you, as you know. But if you ask me, you'd be far better off not to do anything, or decide on anything, until you are a lot stronger. I'll barge in on James if he tries to hassle you again..."

"Oh, Emma," said Laura, unable to suppress a giggle. "He's not being an ogre. And I think he is quite nervous of the whole situation."

"And so he should be," declared Emma. "I'll keep an eye on him. Now, you look quite tired and pale again – I think you had better go to bed, too. I'll lock up and go to bed soon."

"Yes, Mum," joked Laura. "But you are right. I'll think clearer in the morning."

"That's if young Lydia allows any of us to think, tomorrow."

They kissed each other goodnight, and Laura was soon in bed, staring out of the window. She wondered if Daisy, the little pony at Aunt Marchant's, was still alive, and remembered how his brown rump jogged along in front of her. She remembered boarding the Mariana, and poor little Jemima. And her baby Joseph. 'Dear child' she thought. 'Didn't have the chance to grow up.' Then she recalled her fight to get a headstone for him and her subsequent marriage to his father, Joseph.

"Oh my dear, Joseph," she whispered. "What would you have me do about the store? I'm not strong enough to face up to being in debt again, and that's the only place I can go back to, if anything should go wrong down here. Maybe I should sell my piece of gold, and pay Emma?" Her mind was tired of indecision, and she drifted into a restless sleep.

The next morning was a chaos of Lydia opening birthday cards that Laura had kept back as they arrived in the post. Kate and Clem's was the first, and Lydia shrieked with delight when she opened one, specially made for her by Charlotte. Billy King never forgot to send her a card, and Miss Hills always enclosed a little note for her. A few of her school-friends had sent cards, and of course, there was one from Emma, James and Geoff, and 'Mama'.

"I'm so lucky," Lydia crooned. "So many friends, and people that love me."

Straight after breakfast, James and Geoff kept their word and took Lydia shopping. Meanwhile, Laura and Emma made ready for the afternoon party, which five of Lydia's school-friends were attending.

"Oh, dear, I've only got four party hats," wailed Emma.

"Don't worry," said Laura. "I'll make Lydia a special birthday hat." Which she did, and was very pleased with its reception later on. The shoppers arrived home, with a lovely leather school-bag bought by the Drakes for Lydia, and a small bottle of perfume each for Emma and Laura. In no time, it seemed, after some hilarious party games, everyone was tired out and back in their beds.

Laura lay thinking how grateful she was that James hadn't raised any pertinent questions, and yet
wary of the following morning, before the men left for Rose Bay. Geoff was due to return to Hargraves early Monday morning, and was spending the night with his Dad. Laura wondered if they would discuss the question of the shop, before he left.

"I hope you'll both come and spend the Christmas holiday with us," said Emma, as James and Geoff prepared to leave. "I'll have a good excuse to put up my tree and decorations."

"Why, thank you, Emma," said James. "We might just do that. I'll send you a letter to confirm, closer to Christmas."

Laura found herself very happy because he hadn't refused the invitation, and cheerfully made plans with Emma. She also decided not to try and find work until after the holiday, so spent the ensuing months helping Emma produce mince pies, puddings, and shortbread.

Christmas Day arrived, and Emma's house in Cambridge Street was aglow with red and green Christmas lights, a beautifully decorated Christmas Tree, and bunches of glossy-leafed holly with red berries. James Drake and his son arrived on Christmas Eve, and there was laughter as Lydia hung up a decorated stocking for each of them, over the fireplace in the living room.. "You know, I still can't get used to Christmas Day being in the middle of summer in this country" said James, "although I am grateful that there's no snow."

"You should come to Hargraves in the winter," said Geoff. "Then you'll see snow, and plenty of it. Isn't that true, Laura? Snow, to me, belongs on Christmas cards."

Next day began early, with Lydia racing around handing out presents, and opening her presents under the Christmas tree. Almost unnoticed, Emma bundled up the discarded wrapping paper, then set about making a light breakfast for them all. Lydia was beside herself with excitement, and declared, "This is the best Christmas I've ever had." Laura smiled at the daughter she idolised, knowing that at this age, everything was "the best I've ever had."

Dinner that evening was unforgettable; the succulent turkey provided by James Drake, lamb and peas, all the usual trimmings and Emma's delicious Christmas pudding, ubiquitously alight with brandy. The prattle of an excited eleven-year old was tolerated, and the humour of James Drake kept everyone laughing.. Laura felt so privileged to be alive, and when Emma suggested they have a sing-song around her ancient piano, she felt impelled to join in. They sang carols, Christmas songs, and popular songs like "*I'll take you home again, Kathleen.*"

Finally exhausted, Lydia went to bed, and the grown-ups sat chatting over a lovely hot chocolate drink and Dundee cake. It was near midnight when Emma and Geoffrey retired to their rooms.

"I'll help you wash up," said James.

"Gentlemen don't do things like that," scoffed Laura, gathering the chocolate mugs and biscuit plates.

"Well, this gentleman does," answered James.

Laura prepared herself for the inevitable, and for a moment, they washed and wiped the dishes in silence. Then James started humming the tune of Silent Night, and Laura joined in. James folded the tea towel as Laura emptied the sink, and he waited while she wiped her hands.

"Laura," he said quietly. "Have you decided about my offer? I promise I will never ask you again, neither do I want to keep Geoffrey in suspense. Please say you will."

Laura was disturbingly aware of his proximity, and her breathing increased. "Say 'I will' to what? Selling the shop, or marrying you?"

He placed his hand on her shoulder, and tilted her chin with the other. "Laura, please don't try to avoid the issue. I need to know if you will sell Hargraves Store to me, and of course I want to marry you." Laura took a deep breath and answered, "Yes, and no."

James smacked his head and turned away in frustration. When he turned back to chastise her, he was confounded to see that she had a beautiful smile on her face.

"I mean 'yes', I will marry you, and 'no', I will not sell the shop to you."

James ignored her answer about the shop; he gathered her into his arms, and pushed his face into her hair. "Oh, Laura. You have given me the best Christmas present any man could ask for. I promise you will never regret your decision." He held her at arms length, and studied her beaming face. "You are sure, aren't you? And you will come and live with me, in Rose Bay?'"

"Yes."

He embraced her again, and he led her to sit on the sofa on the other side of the room. "I am so happy, Laura," he began, "but what made you decide against selling the shop?"

"I realised I can't sell it, because I want to give it to Geoff."

"Oh, no. That would not be fair to you, after all the work you've put into it."

"The shop was my only asset with which to educate Lydia."

"You need not worry about that any more. Lydia will be as my own child, and I am going to take on the responsibility of her education. Besides, I'm looking forward to her riding lessons – she will go a long way, that girl."

Laura leaned forward and kissed him.

The next day outstripped the euphoria of Christmas, when James and Laura announced their intentions. Plans were made and re-made, and ended when Laura decided to accompany Geoff back to Hargraves, to finalise the handover.

"Can I come, too?" asked Lydia.

"She can stay here with me," volunteered Emma.

"Or come home with me," said James, ruffling her hair.

At her age, Lydia was becoming very conscious of her looks, and objected. "Aw! Mr. Drake", she grizzled.

Laura laughed, and said, "I think you can call him Uncle James, from now on. Who do you want to stay with? I'll only be away for a few days."

Lydia pouted, and said, "I want to come with you."

Emma, as always, came to the rescue. "How about you stay with me, and I can make you a lovely bridesmaid's dress for the wedding?"

That settled the question, and the following day, James left for Rose Bay, while Laura and Geoff made their way back to Hargraves.

When Kate and Clem heard her news, they were ecstatic for her. Laura spent a few days with them, and the handover was effected. William Sutton added his hearty congratulations, when Laura visited him, and the Deeds were handed over to Geoff. Only her gold, was left.

During dinner that last night, Clem talked about his school, of course, and how the elements had degraded the building. The council didn't see fit to erect a new school, it seemed, declaring the pupils should be transferred to Mudgee, or Hill End.

Laura handed her gold nugget to the Headmaster, with a big smile. "This is a 'rainy day' if ever I've seen one, Clem. You need it more than me, now. Get the men in the village to help you rebuild the school, and I shall be very happy."

*****

Relevent Data

Distance from Melbourne – Sydney (Inland route):
Approx 717 miles

Distance from Sydney – Bathhurst (Inland route):
Approx 120 miles

Distance from Bathurst to Mudgee (Inland route):
Approx 180 miles

Distance from Mudgee to Hargraves (Inland route):
Approx 45 miles.

Made in the USA
Charleston, SC
28 September 2013